PENGUIN ENGLISH LIBRARY

The Way of All Flesh

Samuel Butler (1835–1902) was an author, literary critic, philosopher, painter and translator of Homer. After a disagreement about his career with his father, a clergyman who had been pressured into joining the Church by his own father, Butler left England to become a sheep farmer in New Zealand. The letters he wrote home to his father formed the basis of his utopian satire *Erewhon*. *The Way of All Flesh*, a semi-autobiographical exploration of Victorian family life, was published posthumously in 1903.

D1146596

9112000098604

The Way of All Flesh

BY SAMUEL BUTLER

...

PENGUIN ENGLISH
LIBRARY

PENGUIN BOOKS

Published by the Penguin Group
Penguin Books Ltd, 80 Strand, London WC2R ORL, England
Penguin Group (USA) Inc., 375 Hudson Street, New York, New York 10014, USA
Penguin Group (Canada), 90 Eglinton Avenue East, Suite 700, Toronto, Ontario, Canada M4P 2Y3
(a division of Pearson Penguin Canada Inc.)
Penguin Ireland, 25 St Stephen's Green, Dublin 2, Ireland
(a division of Penguin Books Ltd)
Penguin Group (Australia), 250 Camberwell Road, Camberwell, Victoria 3124, Australia
(a division of Pearson Australia Group Pty Ltd)
Penguin Books India Pvt Ltd, 11 Community Centre,
Panchsheel Park, New Delhi – 110 017, India
Penguin Group (NZ), 67 Apollo Drive, Rosedale, Auckland 0632, New Zealand
(a division of Pearson New Zealand Ltd)
Penguin Books (South Africa) (Pty) Ltd, Block D, Rosebank Office Park,
181 Jan Smuts Avenue, Parktown North, Gauteng 2193, South Africa

Penguin Books Ltd, Registered Offices: 80 Strand, London WC2R ORL, England

www.penguin.com

First published 1903
Published in Penguin Classics edited by James Cochrane 1986
This edition first published in the Penguin English Library 2012

001

Front cover illustration: Matt D...

Inside front cover: Samuel Butler by Al... ...tler
Collection of the Chapin lil...

'A Victorian Son' from Collected Es...
permission of Peters, Fraser & Dur...
on behalf of the est...

Set in 11/13 pt...
Typeset by Jouve (...
Printed in England by...

ISBN: 978-0-141-19915-3

www.greenpenguin.co.uk

ALWAYS LEARNING   **PEARSON**

Contents

The Way of all Flesh

By

Samuel Butler

Author of " Erewhon "

"We know that all things work together for good to them
that love God."—Rom. viii. 28

London
Grant Richards
1903

Chapter One

When I was a small boy at the beginning of the century I remember an old man who wore knee-breeches and worsted stockings, and who used to hobble about the street of our village with the help of a stick. He must have been getting on for eighty in the year 1807, earlier than which date I suppose I can hardly remember him, for I was born in 1802. A few white locks hung about his ears, his shoulders were bent and his knees feeble, but he was still hale, and was much respected in our little world of Paleham. His name was Pontifex.

His wife was said to be his master; I have been told she brought him a little money, but it cannot have been much. She was a tall, square-shouldered person (I have heard my father call her a Gothic woman) who had insisted on being married to Mr Pontifex when he was young and too good-natured to say nay to any woman who wooed him. The pair had lived not unhappily together, for Mr Pontifex's temper was easy and he soon learned to bow before his wife's more stormy moods.

Mr Pontifex was a carpenter by trade; he was also at one time parish clerk; when I remember him, however, he had so far risen in life as to be no longer compelled to work with his own hands. In his earlier days he had taught himself to draw. I do not say he drew well, but it was surprising he should draw as well as he did. My father, who took the living of Paleham about the year 1797, became possessed of a good many of old Mr Pontifex's drawings, which were always of local subjects, and so unaffectedly painstaking that they might have passed for the work of some good early master. I remember them as hanging up framed and glazed in the study at the Rectory, and tinted, as all else in the room was

1

tinted, with the green reflected from the fringe of ivy leaves that grew around the windows. I wonder how they will actually cease and come to an end as drawings, and in what new phases of being they will then enter.

Not content with being an artist, Mr Pontifex must needs also be a musician. He built the organ in the church with his own hands, and made a smaller one which he kept in his own house. He could play as much as he could draw, not very well according to professional standards, but much better than could have been expected. I myself showed a taste for music at an early age, and old Mr Pontifex on finding it out, as he soon did, became partial to me in consequence.

It may be thought that with so many irons in the fire he could hardly be a very thriving man, but this was not the case. His father had been a day labourer, and he had himself begun life with no other capital than his good sense and good constitution; now, however, there was a goodly show of timber about his yard, and a look of solid comfort over his whole establishment. Towards the close of the eighteenth century and not long before my father came to Paleham, he had taken a farm of about ninety acres, thus making a considerable rise in life. Along with the farm there went an old-fashioned but comfortable house with a charming garden and an orchard. The carpenter's business was now carried on in one of the outhouses that had once been part of some conventual buildings, the remains of which could be seen in what was called the Abbey Close. The house itself, embosomed in honeysuckles and creeping roses, was an ornament to the whole village, nor were its internal arrangements less exemplary than its outside was ornamental. Report said that Mrs Pontifex starched the sheets for her best bed, and I can well believe it.

How well do I remember her parlour half-filled with the organ which her husband had built, and scented with a withered apple or two from the *pyrus japonica* that grew outside the house; the picture of the prize ox over the chimney-piece, which Mr Pontifex himself had painted; the transparency of the man coming to show light to a coach upon a snowy night, also by Mr Pontifex; the little old man and little old woman who told the weather; the china shepherd and shepherdess; the jars of feathery flowering grasses with a peacock's feather or two among them to set them off, and the china bowls full of dead rose leaves dried with bay salt. All has long since vanished and become a memory, faded but still fragrant to myself.

Nay, but her kitchen – and the glimpses into a cavernous cellar beyond it, wherefrom came gleams from the pale surfaces of milk cans, or it may be of the arms and face of a milkmaid skimming the cream; or again her storeroom, where among other treasures she kept the famous lipsalve which was one of her especial glories, and of which she would present a shape yearly to those whom she delighted to honour. She wrote out the recipe for this and gave it to my mother a year or two before she died, but we could never make it as she did. When we were children she used sometimes to send her respects to my mother, and ask leave for us to come and take tea with her. Right well she used to ply us. As for her temper, we never met such a delightful old lady in our lives; whatever Mr Pontifex may have had to put up with, we had no cause for complaint, and then Mr Pontifex would play to us upon the organ, and we would stand round him open-mouthed and think him the most wonderfully clever man that ever was born, except, of course, our papa.

Mrs Pontifex had no sense of humour, at least I can call to mind no signs of this, but her husband had plenty of fun in him, though few would have guessed it from his appearance. I remember my father once sent me down to his workshop to get some glue, and I happened to come when old Pontifex was in the act of scolding his boy. He had got the lad – a pudding-headed fellow – by the ear and was saying, 'What? Lost again – smothered o' wit.' (I believe it was the boy who was himself supposed to be a wandering soul, and who was thus addressed as lost.) 'Now, look here, my lad,' he continued, 'some boys are born stupid, and thou art one of them; some achieve stupidity – that's thee again, Jim – thou wast both born stupid and hast greatly increased thy birthright – and some' (and here came a climax during which the boy's head and ear were swayed from side to side) 'have stupidity thrust upon them, which, if it please the Lord, shall not be thy case, my lad, for I will thrust stupidity from thee, though I have to box thine ears in doing so,' but I did not see that the old man really did box Jim's ears, or do more than pretend to frighten him, for the two understood one another perfectly well. Another time I remember hearing him call the village rat-catcher by saying, 'Come hither, thou three-days-and-three-nights, thou,' alluding, as I afterwards learned, to the rat-catcher's periods of intoxication; but I will tell no more of such trifles. My father's face would always brighten when old Pontifex's name was mentioned. 'I tell you, Edward,' he would say to me, 'old Pontifex was not only an able man, but he was one of the very ablest men that ever I knew.'

This was more than I as a young man was prepared to stand. 'My dear father,' I answered, 'what did he do? He could draw a little, but could he to save his life have got a picture into the Royal Academy exhibition? He built two organs and could play the Minuet in *Samson* on one and the March in *Scipio* on the other; he was a good carpenter and a bit of a wag; he was a good old fellow enough, but why make him out so much abler than he was?'

'My boy,' returned my father, 'you must not judge by the work, but by the work in connection with the surroundings. Could Giotto or Filippo Lippi, think you, have got a picture into the Exhibition? Would a single one of those frescoes we went to see when we were at Padua have the remotest chance of being hung, if it were sent in for exhibition now? Why, the Academy people would be so outraged that they would not even write to poor Giotto to tell him to come and take his fresco away. Phew!' continued he, waxing warm, 'if old Pontifex had had Cromwell's chances he would have done all that Cromwell did, and have done it better; if he had had Giotto's chances he would have done all that Giotto did, and done it no worse; as it was, he was a village carpenter, and I will undertake to say he never scamped a job in the whole course of his life.'

'But,' said I, 'we cannot judge people with so many "ifs." If old Pontifex had lived in Giotto's time he might have been another Giotto, but he did not live in Giotto's time.'

'I tell you, Edward,' said my father with some severity, 'we must judge men not so much by what they do, as by what they make us feel that they have it in them to do. If a man has done enough either in painting, music or the affairs of life, to make me feel that I might trust him in an emergency he has done enough. It is not by what a man has actually put upon his canvas, nor yet by the acts which he has set down, so to speak, upon the canvas of his life that I will judge him, but by what he makes me feel that he felt and aimed at. If he has made me feel that he felt those things to be lovable which I hold lovable myself I ask no more; his grammar may have been imperfect, but still I have understood him; he and I are *en rapport*; and I say again, Edward, that old Pontifex was not only an able man, but one of the very ablest men I ever knew.'

Against this there was no more to be said, and my sisters eyed me to silence. Somehow or other my sisters always did eye me to silence when I differed from my father.

'Talk of his successful son,' snorted my father, whom I had fairly roused. 'He is not fit to black his father's boots. He has his thousands of pounds a year, while his father had perhaps three thousand shillings a year towards the end of his life. He *is* a successful man; but his father, hobbling about Paleham Street in his grey worsted stockings, broad-brimmed hat and brown swallow-tailed coat was worth a hundred of George Pontifexes, for all his carriages and horses and the airs he gives himself.

'But yet,' he added, 'George Pontifex is no fool either.' And this brings us to the second generation of the Pontifex family with whom we need concern ourselves.

Chapter Two

Old Mr Pontifex had married in the year 1750, but for fifteen years his wife bore no children. At the end of that time Mrs Pontifex astonished the whole village by showing unmistakable signs of a disposition to present her husband with an heir or heiress. Hers had long ago been considered a hopeless case, and when on consulting the doctor concerning the meaning of certain symptoms she was informed of their significance, she became very angry and abused the doctor roundly for talking nonsense. She refused to put so much as a piece of thread into a needle in anticipation of her confinement and would have been absolutely unprepared, if her neighbours had not been better judges of her condition than she was, and got things ready without telling her anything about it. Perhaps she feared Nemesis, though assuredly she knew not who or what Nemesis was; perhaps she feared the doctor had made a mistake and she should be laughed at; from whatever cause, however, her refusal to recognise the obvious arose, she certainly refused to recognise it, until one snowy night in January the doctor was sent for with all urgent speed across the rough country roads. When he arrived he found two patients, not one, in need of his assistance, for a boy had been born who was in due time christened George, in honour of his then reigning majesty.

To the best of my belief George Pontifex got the greater part of his nature from this obstinate old lady, his mother – a mother who though she loved no one else in the world except her husband (and him only after a fashion) was most tenderly attached to the unexpected child of her old age; nevertheless, she showed it little.

The boy grew up into a sturdy bright-eyed little fellow, with plenty of intelligence, and perhaps a trifle too great readiness at book learning. Being kindly treated at home, he was as fond of his father and mother as it was in his nature to be of anyone, but he was fond of no one else. He had a good healthy sense of *meum*, and as little of *tuum* as he could help. Brought up much in the open air in one of the best situated and healthiest villages in England, his little limbs had fair play, and in those days children's brains were not overtasked as they now are; perhaps it was for this very reason that the boy showed an avidity to learn. At seven or eight years old he could read, write and sum better than any other boy of his age in the village. My father was not yet rector of Paleham, and did not remember George Pontifex's childhood, but I have heard neighbours tell him that the boy was looked upon as unusually quick and forward. His father and mother were naturally proud of their offspring, and his mother was determined that he should one day become one of the kings and councillors of the earth.

It is one thing, however, to resolve that one's son shall win some of life's larger prizes, and another to square matters with fortune in this respect. George Pontifex might have been brought up as a carpenter and succeeded in no other way than as succeeding his father as one of the minor magnates of Paleham, and yet have been a more truly successful man than he actually was – for I take it there is not much more solid success in this world than what fell to the lot of old Mr and Mrs Pontifex; it happened, however, that about the year 1780, when George was a boy of fifteen, a sister of Mrs Pontifex's, who had married a Mr Fairlie, came to pay a few days' visit at Paleham. Mr Fairlie was a publisher, chiefly of religious works, and had an establishment in Paternoster Row; he had risen in life, and his wife had risen with him. No very close relations had been maintained between the sisters for some years, and I forget exactly how it came about that Mr and Mrs Fairlie were guests in the quiet but exceedingly comfortable house of their sister and brother-in-law; but for some reason or other the visit was paid, and little George soon succeeded in making his way into his uncle and aunt's good graces. A quick, intelligent boy with a good address, a sound constitution, and coming of respectable parents, has a potential value which a practised business man who has need of many subordinates is little likely to overlook. Before his visit was over Mr Fairlie proposed to the lad's father and mother that he should put him into his own business, at the same time promising that if the boy did well he should not want someone to bring him forward. Mrs Pontifex had her son's interest too much at heart to refuse such an offer, so the matter was soon arranged, and about a fortnight after the Fairlies had left, George was sent up by coach to London, where he was met by his uncle and aunt, with whom it was arranged that he should live.

This was George's great start in life. He now wore more fashionable clothes than he had yet been accustomed to, and any little rusticity of gait or pronunciation which he had brought from Paleham was so quickly and completely lost that it was ere long impossible to detect that he had not been born and bred among people of what is commonly called education. The boy paid great attention to his work, and more than justified the favourable opinion which Mr Fairlie had formed concerning him. Sometimes Mr Fairlie would send him down to Paleham for a few days' holiday, and ere long his parents perceived that he had acquired an air and manner of talking different from any that he had taken with him from Paleham. They were proud of him, and soon fell into their proper places, resigning all appearance of parental control, for which indeed there was no kind of necessity. In return, George was always kindly to them, and to the end of his life retained a more affectionate feeling towards his father and mother than I imagine him ever to have felt again for man, woman, or child.

George's visits to Paleham were never long, for the distance from London was under fifty miles and there was a direct coach, so that the journey was easy; there was not time, therefore, for the novelty to wear off either on the part of the young man or of his parents. George liked the fresh country air and green fields after the darkness to which he had been so long accustomed in Paternoster Row, which then, as now, was a narrow gloomy lane rather than a street. Independently of the pleasure of seeing the familiar faces of the farmers and villagers, he liked also being seen and being congratulated on growing up such a fine-looking and fortunate young fellow, for he was not the youth to hide his light under a bushel. His uncle had had him taught Latin and Greek of an evening; he had taken kindly to these languages and had rapidly and easily mastered what many boys take years to acquire. I suppose his knowledge gave him a self-confidence which made itself felt whether he intended it or not; at any rate, he soon began to pose as a judge of literature, and from this to being a judge of art, architecture, music and everything else, the path was easy. Like his father, he knew the value of money, but he was at once more ostentatious and less liberal than his father; while yet a boy he was a thorough little man of the world, and did well rather upon principles which he had tested by personal experiment, and recognised as principles, than from those profounder convictions which in his father were so instinctive that he could give no account concerning them.

His father, as I have said, wondered at him and let him alone. His son had fairly distanced him, and in an inarticulate way the father knew it perfectly well. After a few years he took to wearing his best clothes whenever his son came to stay with him, nor would he discard them for his ordinary ones till the young man had returned to London. I believe old Mr Pontifex, along with his pride and affection, felt also a certain fear of his son, as though of something which he could not thoroughly understand, and whose ways, notwithstanding outward agreement, were nevertheless not as his ways. Mrs Pontifex felt nothing of this; to her George was pure and absolute perfection, and she saw, or thought she saw, with pleasure, that he resembled her and her family in feature as well as in disposition rather than her husband and his.

When George was about twenty-five years old his uncle took him into partnership on very liberal terms. He had little cause to regret this step. The young man infused fresh vigour into a concern that was already vigorous, and by the time he was thirty found himself in the receipt of not less than £1,500 a year as his share of the profits. Two years later he married a lady about seven years younger than himself, who brought him a handsome dowry. She died in 1805, when her youngest child Alethea was born, and her husband did not marry again.

Chapter Three

In the early years of the century five little children and a couple of nurses began to make periodical visits to Paleham. It is needless to say they were a rising generation of Pontifexes, towards whom the old couple, their grandparents, were as tenderly deferential as they would have been to the children of the Lord Lieutenant of the County. Their names were Eliza, Maria, John, Theobald (who like myself was born in 1802), and Alethea. Mr Pontifex always put the prefix 'master' or 'miss' before the names of his grandchildren, except in the case of Alethea, who was his favourite. To have resisted his grandchildren would have been as impossible for him as to have resisted his wife; even old Mrs Pontifex yielded before her son's children, and gave them all manner of licence which she would never have allowed even to my sisters and myself, who stood next in her regard. Two regulations only they must attend to; they must wipe their shoes well on coming into the house, and they must not overfeed Mr Pontifex's organ with wind, nor take the pipes out.

By us at the Rectory there was no time so much looked forward to as the annual visit of the little Pontifexes to Paleham. We came in for some of the prevailing licence; we went to tea with Mrs Pontifex to meet her grandchildren, and then our young friends were asked to the Rectory to have tea with us, and we had what we considered great times. I fell desperately in love with Alethea, indeed we all fell in love with each other, plurality and exchange whether of wives or husbands being openly and unblushingly advocated in the very presence of our nurses. We were very merry, but it is so long ago that I have forgotten nearly everything save that we *were* very merry. Almost the only thing that remains with me as a permanent impression was the fact that Theobald one day beat his nurse and teased her, and when she said she should go away cried out, 'You shan't go away – I'll keep you on purpose to torment you.'

One winter's morning, however, in the year 1811, we heard the church bell tolling while we were dressing in the back nursery and were told it was for old Mrs Pontifex. Our manservant John told us and added with grim levity that they were ringing the bell to come and take her away. She had had a fit of paralysis which had carried her off quite suddenly. It was very shocking, the more so because our nurse assured us that if God chose we might all have fits of paralysis ourselves that very day and be taken straight off to the Day of Judgment. The Day of Judgment indeed, according to the opinion of those who were most likely to know, would not under any circumstances be delayed more than a few years longer, and then the whole world would be burned, and we ourselves be consigned to an eternity of torture, unless we mended our ways more than we at present seemed at all likely to do. All this was so alarming that we fell to screaming and made such a hullabaloo that the nurse was obliged for her own peace of mind to reassure us. Then we wept, but more composedly, as we remembered that there would be no more tea and cakes for us now at old Mrs Pontifex's.

On the day of the funeral, however, we had a great excitement; old Mr Pontifex sent round a penny loaf to every inhabitant of the village according to a custom still not uncommon at the beginning of the century; the loaf was called a dole. We had never heard of this custom before; besides, though we had often heard of penny loaves, we had never before seen one; moreover, they were presents to us as inhabitants of the village, and we were treated as grown-up people, for our father and mother and the servants had each one loaf sent them, but only one. We had never yet suspected that we were inhabitants at all; finally, the little loaves were new, and we were passionately fond of new bread, which we were seldom or never allowed to have, as it was supposed not to be good for us. Our affection, therefore, for our old friend had to stand against the combined attacks of archaeological interest, the rights of citizenship and property, the pleasantness to the eye and goodness for food of the little loaves themselves, and the sense of importance which was given us by our having been intimate with someone who had actually died. It seemed upon further inquiry that there was little reason to anticipate an early death for anyone of ourselves, and this being so, we rather liked the idea of someone else's being put away into the churchyard; we passed, therefore, in a short time from extreme depression to a no less extreme exultation; a new heaven and a new earth had been revealed to us in our perception of the possibility of benefiting by the death of our friends, and I fear that for some time we took an interest in the health of everyone in the village whose position rendered a repetition of the dole in the least likely.

Those were the days in which all great things seemed far off, and we were astonished to find that Napoleon Buonaparte was an actually living person. We had thought such a great man could only have lived a very long time ago, and here he was after all almost as it were at our own doors. This lent colour to the view that the Day of Judgment might indeed be nearer than we had thought, but nurse said that was all right now, and she knew. In those days the snow lay longer and drifted deeper in the lanes than it does now, and the milk was sometimes brought in frozen in winter, and we were taken down into the back kitchen to see it. I suppose there are rectories up and down the country now where the milk comes in frozen sometimes in winter, and the children go down to wonder at it, but I never see any frozen milk in London, so I suppose the winters are warmer than they used to be.

About one year after his wife's death Mr Pontifex also was gathered to his fathers. My father saw him the day before he died.

The old man had a theory about sunsets, and had had two steps built up against a wall in the kitchen garden on which he used to stand and watch the sun go down whenever it was clear. My father came on him in the afternoon, just as the sun was setting, and saw him with his arms resting on the top of the wall looking towards the sun over a field through which there was a path on which my father was. My father heard him say 'Goodbye, sun; good-bye, sun,' as the sun sank, and saw by his tone and manner that he was feeling very feeble. Before the next sunset he was gone.

There was no dole. Some of his grandchildren were brought to the funeral and we remonstrated with them, but did not take much by doing so. John Pontifex, who was a year older than I was, sneered at penny loaves, and intimated that if I wanted one it must be because my papa and mamma could not afford to buy me one, whereon I believe we did something like fighting, and I rather think John Pontifex got the worst of it, but it may have been the other way. I remember my sister's nurse, for I was just outgrowing nurses myself, reported the matter to higher quarters, and we were all of us put to some ignominy, but we had been thoroughly awakened from our dream, and it was long enough before we could hear the words 'penny loaf' mentioned without our ears tingling with shame. If there had been a dozen doles afterwards we should not have deigned to touch one of them.

George Pontifex put up a monument to his parents, a plain slab in Paleham church, inscribed with the following epitaph: –

SACRED TO THE MEMORY

OF

JOHN PONTIFEX

WHO WAS BORN AUGUST 16TH, 1727, AND DIED

FEBRUARY 8, 1812, IN HIS 85TH YEAR,

AND OF

Chapter Three

RUTH PONTIFEX, HIS WIFE,
WHO WAS BORN OCTOBER 13, 1727, AND DIED
JANUARY 10, 1811, IN HER 84TH YEAR.
THEY WERE UNOSTENTATIOUS BUT EXEMPLARY
IN THE DISCHARGE OF THEIR
RELIGIOUS, MORAL, AND SOCIAL DUTIES.
THIS MONUMENT WAS PLACED
BY THEIR ONLY SON.

Chapter Four

In a year or two more came Waterloo and the European peace. Then Mr George Pontifex went abroad more than once. I remember seeing at Battersby in after years the diary which he kept on the first of these occasions. It was a characteristic document. I felt as I read it that the author before starting had made up his mind to admire only what he thought it would be creditable in him to admire, to look at nature and art only through the spectacles that had been handed down to him by generation after generation of prigs and impostors. The first glimpse of Mont Blanc threw Mr Pontifex into a conventional ecstasy. 'My feelings I cannot express. I gasped, yet hardly dared to breathe, as I viewed for the first time the monarch of the mountains. I seemed to fancy the genius seated on his stupendous throne far above his aspiring brethren and in his solitary might defying the universe. I was so overcome by my feelings that I was almost bereft of my faculties, and I would not for worlds have spoken after my first exclamation till I found some relief in a gush of tears. With pain I tore myself from contemplating for the first time "at distance dimly seen" (though I felt as if I had sent my soul and eyes after it), this sublime spectacle.' After a nearer view of the Alps from above Geneva he walked nine out of the twelve miles of the descent: 'My mind and heart were too full to sit still, and I found some relief by exhausting my feelings through exercise.' In the course of time he reached Chamonix and went on a Sunday to the Montanvert to see the Mer de Glace. There he wrote the following verses for the visitors' book, which he considered, so he says, 'suitable to the day and scene': –

Lord, while these wonders of thy hand I see,
My soul in holy reverence bends to thee.
These awful solitudes, this dread repose,
Yon pyramid sublime of spotless snows,
These spiry pinnacles, those smiling plains,
This sea where one eternal winter reigns,
These are thy works, and while on them I gaze
I hear a silent tongue that speaks thy praise.

Some poets always begin to get groggy about the knees after running for seven or eight lines. Mr Pontifex's last couplet gave him a lot of trouble, and nearly every word has been erased and rewritten once at least. In the visitors' book at the Montanvert, however, he must have been obliged to commit himself definitely to one reading or another. Taking the verses all round, I should say that Mr Pontifex was right in considering them suitable to the day; I don't like being too hard even on the Mer de Glace, so will give no opinion as to whether they are suitable to the scene also.

Mr Pontifex went on to the Great St Bernard and there he wrote some more verses, this time I am afraid in Latin. He also took good care to be properly impressed by the Hospice and its situation. 'The whole of this most extraordinary journey seemed like a dream, its conclusion especially, in gentlemanly society, with every comfort and accommodation amidst the rudest rocks and in the region of perpetual snow. The thought that I was sleeping in a convent and occupied the bed of no less a person than Napoleon, that I was in the highest inhabited spot in the old world and in a place celebrated in every part of it, kept me awake some time.' As a contrast to this, I may quote here an extract from a letter written to me last year by his grandson Ernest, of whom the reader will hear more presently. The passage runs: 'I went up to the Great St Bernard and saw the dogs.' In due course Mr Pontifex found his way to Italy, where the pictures and other works of art – those at least which were fashionable at that time – threw him into genteel paroxysms of admiration. Of the Uffizi Gallery at Florence he writes: 'I have spent three hours this morning in the gallery and I have made up my mind that if of all the treasures I have seen in Italy I were to choose one room it would be the Tribune of this Gallery. It contains the Venus de' Medici, the Explorator, the Pancratist, the Dancing Faun and a fine Apollo. These more than outweigh the Laocoon and the Belvedere Apollo at Rome. It contains, besides, the St John of Raphael and many other *chefs-d'œuvre* of the greatest masters in the world.' It is interesting to compare Mr Pontifex's effusions with the rhapsodies of critics in our own times. Not long ago a much esteemed writer informed the world that he felt 'disposed to cry out with delight' before a figure by Michelangelo. I wonder whether he would feel disposed to cry out before a real Michelangelo, if the critics had decided that it was not genuine, or before a reputed Michelangelo which was really by someone else. But I suppose that a prig with more money than brains was much the same sixty or seventy years ago as he is now.

Look at Mendelssohn again about this same Tribune on which Mr Pontifex felt so safe in staking his reputation as a man of taste and culture. He feels no less safe and writes, 'I then went to the Tribune. This room is so delightfully small you can traverse it in fifteen paces, yet it contains a world of art. I again sought out my favourite arm-chair which stands under the statue of the "Slave whetting his knife" (L'Arrotino), and taking possession of it I enjoyed myself for a couple of hours; for here at one glance I had the "Madonna del Cardellino," Pope Julius II., a female portrait by Raphael, and above it a lovely Holy Family by Perugino; and so close to me that I could have touched it with my hand the Venus de' Medici; beyond, that of Titian. . . . The space between is occupied by other pictures of Raphael's, a portrait by Titian, a Domenichino, etc., etc., all of these within the circumference of a small semi-circle no larger than one of your own rooms. This is a spot where a man feels his own insignificance and may well learn to be humble.' The Tribune is a slippery place for people like Mendelssohn to study humility in. They generally take two steps away from it for one they take towards it. I wonder how many chalks Mendelssohn gave himself for having sat two hours on that chair. I wonder how often he looked at his watch to see if his two hours were up. I wonder how often he told himself that he was quite as big a gun, if the truth were known, as any of the men whose works he saw before him, how often he wondered whether any of the visitors were recognising him and admiring him for sitting such a long time in the same chair, and how often he was vexed at seeing them pass him by and take no notice of him. But perhaps if the truth were known his two hours was not quite two hours.

Returning to Mr Pontifex, whether he liked what he believed to be the masterpieces of Greek and Italian art or no he brought back some copies by Italian artists, which I have no doubt he satisfied himself would bear the strictest examination with the originals. Two of these copies fell to Theobald's share on the division of his father's furniture, and I have often seen them at Battersby on my visits to Theobald and his wife. The one was a Madonna by Sassoferrato with a blue hood over her head which threw it half into shadow. The other was a Magdalen by Carlo Dolci with a very fine head of hair and a marble vase in her hands. When I was a young man I used to think these pictures were beautiful, but with each successive visit to Battersby I got to dislike them more and more and to see 'George Pontifex' written all over both of them. In the end I ventured after a tentative fashion to blow on them a little but Theobald and his wife were up in arms at once. They did not like their father and father-in-law, but there could be no question about his power and general ability, nor about his having been a man of consummate taste both in literature and art – indeed the diary he kept during his foreign tour was enough to prove this. With one more short extract I will leave this diary and proceed with my story. During his stay in Florence Mr Pontifex wrote: 'I have just seen the Grand Duke and his family pass by in two carriages and six, but little more notice is taken of them than if I, who am utterly unknown here, were to pass by.' I don't think that he half believed in his being utterly unknown in Florence or anywhere else!

Chapter Five

Fortune, we are told, is a blind and fickle foster-mother, who showers her gifts at random upon her nurslings. But we do her a grave injustice if we believe such an accusation. Trace a man's career from his cradle to his grave and mark how Fortune has treated him. You will find that when he is once dead she can for the most part be vindicated from the charge of any but very superficial fickleness. Her blindness is the merest fable; she can espy her favourites long before they are born. We are as days and have had our parents for our yesterdays, but through all the fair weather of a clear parental sky the eye of Fortune can discern the coming storm, and she laughs as she places her favourites it may be in a London alley or those whom she is resolved to ruin in kings' palaces. Seldom does she relent towards those whom she has suckled unkindly and seldom does she completely fail a favoured nursling.

Was George Pontifex one of Fortune's favoured nurslings or not? On the whole I should say that he was not, for he did not consider himself so; he was too religious to consider Fortune a deity at all; he took whatever she gave and never thanked her, being firmly convinced that whatever he got to his own advantage was of his own getting. And so it was, after Fortune had made him able to get it.

'Nos te, nos facimus, Fortuna, deam,' exclaimed the poet. 'It is we who make thee, Fortune, a goddess'; and so it is, after Fortune has made us able to make her. The poet says nothing as to the making of the 'nos.' Perhaps some men are independent of antecedents and surroundings and have an initial force within themselves which is in no way due to causation; but this is supposed to be a difficult question and it may be as well to avoid it. Let it suffice that George Pontifex did not consider himself fortunate, and he who does not consider himself fortunate is unfortunate.

True, he was rich, universally respected and of an excellent natural constitution. If he had eaten and drunk less he would never have known a day's indisposition. Perhaps his main strength lay in the fact that though his capacity was a little above the average, it was not too much so. It is on this rock that so many clever people split. The successful man will see just so much more than his neighbours as they will be able to see too when it is shown them, but not enough to puzzle them. It is far safer to know too little than too much. People will condemn the one, though they will resent being called upon to exert themselves to follow the other.

The best example of Mr Pontifex's good sense in matters connected with his business which I can think of at this moment is the revolution which he effected in the style of advertising works published by the firm. When he first became a partner one of the firm's advertisements ran thus: –

'Books proper to be given away at this Season. –

'The Pious Country Parishioner, being directions how a Christian may manage every day in the course of his whole life with safety and success; how to spend the Sabbath Day; what books of the Holy Scripture ought to be read first; the whole method of education; collects for the most important virtues that adorn the soul; a discourse on the Lord's Supper; rules to set the soul right in sickness; so that in this treatise are contained all the rules requisite for salvation. The 8th edition with additions. Price 10d.

⁎ 'An allowance will be made to those who give them away.'

Before he had been many years a partner the advertisement stood as follows: –

'The Pious Country Parishioner. A complete manual of Christian Devotion. Price 10d.

'A reduction will be made to purchasers for gratuitous distribution.'

What a stride is made in the foregoing towards the modern standard, and what intelligence is involved in the perception of the unseemliness of the old style, when others did not perceive it!

Where then was the weak place in George Pontifex's armour? I suppose in the fact that he had risen too rapidly. It would almost seem as if a transmitted education of some generations is necessary for the due enjoyment of great wealth. Adversity, if a man is set down to it by degrees, is more supportable with equanimity by most people than any great prosperity arrived at in a single lifetime. Nevertheless a certain kind of good fortune generally attends self-made men to the last. It is their children of the first, or first and second, generation who are in greater danger, for the race can no more repeat its most successful performances suddenly and without its ebbings and flowings of success than the individual can do so, and the more brilliant the success in any one generation, the greater as a general rule the subsequent exhaustion until time has been allowed for recovery. Hence it often happens that the grandson of a successful man will be more successful than the son – the spirit that actuated the grandfather having lain fallow in the son and being refreshed by repose so as to be ready for fresh exertion in the grandson. A very successful man, moreover, has something of the hybrid in him; he is a new animal, arising from the coming together of many unfamiliar elements and it is well known that the reproduction of abnormal growths, whether animal or vegetable, is irregular and not to be depended upon, even when they are not absolutely sterile.

And certainly Mr Pontifex's success was exceedingly rapid. Only a few years after he had become a partner his uncle and aunt both died within a few months of one another. It was then found that they had made him their heir. He was thus not only sole partner in the business but found himself with a fortune of some £30,000 into the bargain, and this was a large sum in those days. Money came pouring in upon him, and the faster it came the fonder he became of it, though, as he frequently said, he valued it not for its own sake, but only as a means of providing for his dear children.

Yet when a man is very fond of his money it is not easy for him at all times to be very fond of his children also. The two are like God and Mammon. Lord Macaulay has a passage in which he contrasts the pleasures which a man may derive from books with the inconveniences to which he may be put by his acquaintances. 'Plato,' he says, 'is never sullen. Cervantes is never petulant. Demosthenes never comes unseasonably. Dante never stays too long. No difference of political opinion can alienate Cicero. No heresy can excite the horror of Bossuet.' I dare say I might differ from Lord Macaulay in my estimate of some of the writers he has named, but there can be no disputing his main proposition, namely, that we need have no more trouble from any of them than we have a mind to, whereas our friends are not always so easily disposed of. George Pontifex felt this as regards his children and his money. His money was never naughty; his money never made noise or litter, and did not spill things on the tablecloth at meal times, or leave the door open when it went out. His dividends did not quarrel among themselves, nor was he under any uneasiness lest his mortgages should become extravagant on reaching manhood and run him up debts which sooner or later he should have to pay. There were tendencies in John which made him very uneasy, and Theobald, his second son, was idle and at times far from truthful. His children might, perhaps, have answered, had they known what was in their father's mind, that he did not knock his money about as he not infrequently knocked his children. He never dealt hastily or pettishly with his money, and that was perhaps why he and it got on so well together.

It must be remembered that at the beginning of the nineteenth century the relations between parents and children were still far from satisfactory. The violent type of father, as described by Fielding, Richardson, Smollett and Sheridan, is now hardly more likely to find a place in literature than the original advertisement of Messrs. Fairlie & Pontifex's 'Pious Country Parishioner,' but the type was much too persistent not to have been drawn from nature closely. The parents in Miss Austen's novels are less like savage wild beasts than those of her predecessors, but she evidently looks upon them with suspicion, and an uneasy feeling that *le père de famille est capable de tout* makes itself sufficiently apparent throughout the greater part of her writings. In the Elizabethan time the relations between parents and children seem on the whole to have been more kindly. The fathers and the sons are for the most part friends in Shakespeare, nor does the evil appear to have reached its full abomination till a long course of Puritanism had familiarised men's minds with Jewish ideals as those which we should endeavour to reproduce in our everyday life. What precedents did not Abraham, Jephthah and Jonadab the son of Rechab offer? How easy was it to quote and follow them in an age when few reasonable men or women doubted that every syllable of the Old Testament was taken down *verbatim* from the mouth of God. Moreover, Puritanism restricted natural pleasures; it substituted the Jeremiad for the Paean, and it forgot that the poor abuses of all times want countenance.

Mr Pontifex may have been a little sterner with his children than some of his neighbours, but not much. He thrashed his boys two or three times a week and some weeks a good deal oftener, but in those days fathers were always thrashing their boys. It is easy to have juster views when everyone else has them, but fortunately or unfortunately results have nothing whatever to do with the moral guilt or blamelessness of him who brings them about; they depend solely upon the thing done, whatever it may happen to be. The moral guilt or blamelessness in like manner has nothing to do with the result; it turns upon the question whether a sufficient number of reasonable people placed as the actor was placed would have done as the actor has done. At that time it was universally admitted that to spare the rod was to spoil the child, and St Paul had placed disobedience to parents in very ugly company. If his children did anything which Mr Pontifex disliked they were clearly disobedient to their father. In this case there was obviously only one course for a sensible man to take. It consisted in checking the first signs of self-will while his children were too young to offer serious resistance. If their wills were 'well broken' in childhood, to use an expression then much in vogue, they would acquire habits of obedience which they would not venture to break through till they were over twenty-one years old. Then they might please themselves; he should know how to protect himself; till then he and his money were more at their mercy than he liked.

How little do we know our thoughts – our reflex actions indeed, yes; but our reflex reflections! Man, forsooth, prides himself on his consciousness! We boast that we differ from the winds and waves and falling stones and plants, which grow they know not why, and from the wandering creatures which go up and down after their prey, as we are pleased to say without the help of reason. We know so well what we are doing ourselves and why we do it, do we not? I fancy that there is some truth in the view which is being put forward nowadays, that it is our less conscious thoughts and our less conscious actions which mainly mould our lives and the lives of those who spring from us.

Chapter Six

Mr Pontifex was not the man to trouble himself much about his motives. People were not so introspective then as we are now; they lived more according to a rule of thumb. Dr Arnold had not yet sown that crop of earnest thinkers which we are now harvesting, and men did not see why they should not have their own way if no evil consequences to themselves seemed likely to follow upon their doing so. Then as now, however, they sometimes let themselves in for more evil consequences than they had bargained for.

Like other rich men at the beginning of this century he ate and drank a good deal more than was enough to keep him in health. Even his excellent constitution was not proof against a prolonged course of overfeeding and what we should now consider overdrinking. His liver would not unfrequently get out of order, and he would come down to breakfast looking yellow about the eyes. Then the young people knew that they had better look out. It is not as a general rule the eating of sour grapes that causes the children's teeth to be set on edge. Well-to-do parents seldom eat many sour grapes; the danger to the children lies in the parents eating too many sweet ones.

I grant that at first sight it seems very unjust, that the parents should have the fun and the children be punished for it, but young people should remember that for many years they were part and parcel of their parents and therefore had a good deal of the fun in the person of their parents. If they have forgotten the fun now, that is no more than people do who have a headache after having been tipsy overnight. The man with the headache does not pretend to be a different person from the man who got drunk, and claim that it is his self of the preceding night and not his self of this morning who should be punished; no more should offspring complain of the headache which it has earned when in the person of its parents, for the continuation of identity, though not so immediately apparent, is just as real in one case as in the other. What is really hard is when the parents have the fun after the children have been born, and the children are punished for this.

On these, his black days, he would take very gloomy views of things and say to himself that in spite of all his goodness to them his children did not love him. But who can love any man whose liver is out of order? How base, he would exclaim to himself, was such ingratitude! How especially hard upon himself, who had been such a model son, and always honoured and obeyed his parents though they had not spent one hundredth part of the money upon him which he had lavished upon his own children. 'It is always the same story,' he would say to himself, 'the more young people have the more they want, and the less thanks one gets; I have made a great mistake; I have been far too lenient with my children; never mind, I have done my duty by them, and more; if they fail in theirs to me it is a matter between God and them. I, at any rate, am guiltless. Why, I might have married again and become the father of a second and perhaps more affectionate family, etc., etc.' He pitied himself for the expensive education which he was giving his children; he did not see that the education cost the children far more than it cost him, inasmuch as it cost them the power of earning their living easily rather than helped them towards it, and ensured their being at the mercy of their father for years after they had come to an age when they should be independent. A public school education cuts off a boy's retreat; he can no longer become a labourer or a mechanic, and these are the only people whose tenure of independence is not precarious – with the exception of course of those who are born inheritors of money or who are placed young in some safe and deep groove. Mr Pontifex saw nothing of this; all he saw was that he was spending much more money upon his children than the law would have compelled him to do, and what more could you have? Might he not have apprenticed both his sons to greengrocers? Might he not even yet do so to-morrow morning if he were so minded? The possibility of this course being adopted was a favourite topic with him when he was out of temper; true, he never did apprentice either of his sons to greengrocers, but his boys comparing notes together had sometimes come to the conclusion that they wished he would.

At other times when not quite well he would have them in for the fun of shaking his will at them. He would in his imagination cut them all out one after another and leave his money to found almshouses, till at last he was obliged to put them back, so that he might have the pleasure of cutting them out again the next time he was in a passion.

Of course if young people allow their conduct to be in any way influenced by regard to the wills of living persons they are doing very wrong and must expect to be sufferers in the end, nevertheless the powers of will-dangling and will-shaking are so liable to abuse and are continually made so great an engine of torture that I would pass a law, if I could, to incapacitate any man from making a will for three months from the date of each offence in either of the above respects and let the bench of magistrates or judge, before whom he has been convicted, dispose of his property as they shall think right and reasonable if he dies during the time that his will-making power is suspended.

Mr Pontifex would have the boys into the dining-room. 'My dear John, my dear Theobald,' he would say, 'look at me. I began life with nothing but the clothes with which my father and mother sent me up to London. My father gave me ten shillings and my mother five for pocket money and I thought them munificent. I never asked my father for a shilling in the whole course of my life, nor took aught from him beyond the small sum he used to allow me monthly till I was in receipt of a salary. I made my own way and I shall expect my sons to do the same. Pray don't take it into your heads that I am going to wear my life out making money that my sons may spend it for me. If you want money you must make it for yourselves as I did, for I give you my word I will not leave a penny to either of you unless you show that you deserve it. Young people seem nowadays to expect all kinds of luxuries and indulgences which were never heard of when I was a boy. Why, my father was a common carpenter, and here you are both of you at public schools, costing me ever so many hundreds a year, while I at your age was plodding away behind a desk in my Uncle Fairlie's counting house. What should I not have done if I had had one half of your advantages? You should become dukes or found new empires in undiscovered countries, and even then I doubt whether you would have done proportionately so much as I have done. No, no, I shall see you through school and college and then, if you please, you will make your own way in the world.'

In this manner he would work himself up into such a state of virtuous indignation that he would sometimes thrash the boys then and there upon some pretext invented at the moment.

And yet, as children went, the young Pontifexes were fortunate; there would be ten families of young people worse off for one better; they ate and drank good wholesome food, slept in comfortable beds, had the best doctors to attend them when they were ill and the best education that could be had for money. The want of fresh air does not seem much to affect the happiness of children in a London alley: the greater part of them sing and play as though they were on a moor in Scotland. So the absence of a genial mental atmosphere is not commonly recognised by children who have never known it. Young people have a marvellous faculty of either dying or adapting themselves to circumstances. Even if they are unhappy – very unhappy – it is astonishing how easily they can be prevented from finding it out, or at any rate from attributing it to any other cause than their own sinfulness.

To parents who wish to lead a quiet life I would say: Tell your children that they are very naughty – much naughtier than most children. Point to the young people of some acquaintances as models of perfection and impress your own children with a deep sense of their own inferiority. You carry so many more guns than they do that they cannot fight you. This is called moral influence, and it will enable you to bounce them as much as you please. They think you know and they will not have yet caught you lying often enough to suspect that you are not the unworldly and scrupulously truthful person which you represent yourself to be; nor yet will they know how great a coward you are, nor how soon you will run away, if they fight you with persistency and judgment. You keep the dice and throw them both for your children and yourself. Load them then, for you can easily manage to stop your children from examining them. Tell them how singularly indulgent you are; insist on the incalculable benefit you conferred upon them, firstly in bringing them into the world at all, but more particularly in bringing them into it as your own children rather than anyone else's. Say that you have their highest interests at stake whenever you are out of temper and wish to make yourself unpleasant by way of balm to your soul. Harp much upon these highest interests. Feed them spiritually upon such brimstone and treacle as the late Bishop of Winchester's Sunday stories. You hold all the trump cards, or if you do not you can filch them; if you play them with anything like judgment you will find yourselves heads of happy, united, God-fearing families, even as did my old friend Mr Pontifex. True, your children will probably find out all about it some day, but not until too late to be of much service to them or inconvenience to yourself.

Some satirists have complained of life inasmuch as all the pleasures belong to the forepart of it and we must see them dwindle till we are left, it may be, with the miseries of a decrepit old age.

To me it seems that youth is like spring, an over-praised season – delightful if it happens to be a favoured one, but in practice very rarely favoured and more remarkable, as a general rule, for biting east winds than genial breezes. Autumn is the mellower season, and what we lose in flowers we more than gain in fruits. Fontenelle at the age of ninety, being asked what was the happiest time of his life, said he did not know that he had ever been much happier than he then was, but that perhaps his best years had been those when he was between fifty-five and seventy-five, and Dr Johnson placed the pleasures of old age far higher than those of youth. True, in old age we live under the shadow of Death, which, like a sword of Damocles, may descend at any moment, but we have so long found life to be an affair of being rather frightened than hurt that we have become like the people who live under Vesuvius, and chance it without much misgiving.

Chapter Seven

A few words may suffice for the greater number of the young people to whom I have been alluding in the foregoing chapter. Eliza and Maria, the two elder girls, were neither exactly pretty nor exactly plain, and were in all respects model young ladies, but Alethea was exceedingly pretty and of a lively, affectionate disposition, which was in sharp contrast with those of her brothers and sisters. There was a trace of her grandfather, not only in her face, but in her love of fun, of which her father had none, though not without a certain boisterous and rather coarse quasi-humour which passed for wit with many.

John grew up to be a good-looking, gentlemanly fellow, with features a trifle too regular and finely chiselled. He dressed himself so nicely, had such good address, and stuck so steadily to his books that he became a favourite with his masters; he had, however, an instinct for diplomacy, and was less popular with the boys. His father, in spite of the lectures he would at times read him, was in a way proud of him as he grew older; he saw in him, moreover, one who would probably develop into a good man of business, and in whose hands the prospects of his house would not be likely to decline. John knew how to humour his father, and was at a comparatively early age admitted to as much of his confidence as it was in his nature to bestow on anyone.

His brother Theobald was no match for him, knew it, and accepted his fate. He was not so good-looking as his brother, nor was his address so good; as a child he had been violently passionate; now, however, he was reserved and shy, and, I should say, indolent in mind and body. He was less tidy than John, less well able to assert himself, and less skilful in humouring the caprices of his father. I do not think he could have loved anyone heartily, but there was no one in his family circle who did not repress, rather than invite his affection, with the exception of his sister Alethea, and she was too quick and lively for his somewhat morose temper. He was always the scapegoat, and I have sometimes thought he had two fathers to contend against – his father and his brother John; a third and fourth also might almost be added in his sisters Eliza and Maria. Perhaps if he had felt his bondage very acutely he would not have put up with it, but he was constitutionally timid, and the strong hand of his father knitted him into the closest outward harmony with his brothers and sisters.

The boys were of use to their father in one respect. I mean that he played them off against each other. He kept them but poorly supplied with pocket money, and to Theobald would urge that the claims of his elder brother were naturally paramount, while he insisted to John upon the fact that he had a numerous family, and would affirm solemnly that his expenses were so heavy that at his death there would be very little to divide. He did not care whether they compared notes or no, provided they did not do so in his presence. Theobald did not complain even behind his father's back. I knew him as intimately as anyone was likely to know him as a child, at school, and again at Cambridge, but he very rarely mentioned his father's name even while his father was alive, and never once in my hearing afterwards. At school he was not actively disliked as his brother was, but he was too dull and deficient in animal spirits to be popular.

Before he was well out of his frocks it was settled that he was to be a clergyman. It was seemly that Mr Pontifex, the well-known publisher of religious books, should devote at least one of his sons to the Church; this might tend to bring business, or at any rate to keep it in the firm; besides, Mr Pontifex had more or less interest with bishops and Church dignitaries and might hope that some preferment would be offered to his son through his influence. The boy's future destiny was kept well before his eyes from his earliest childhood and was treated as a matter which he had already virtually settled by his acquiescence. Nevertheless a certain show of freedom was allowed him. Mr Pontifex would say it was only right to give the boy his option, and was much too equitable to grudge his son whatever benefit he could derive from this. He had the greatest horror, he would exclaim, of driving any young man into a profession which he did not like. Far be it from him to put pressure upon a son of his as regards any profession and much less when so sacred a calling as the ministry was concerned. He would talk in this way when there were visitors in the house and when his son was in the room. He spoke so wisely and so well that his listening guests considered him a paragon of right-mindedness. He spoke, too, with such emphasis and his rosy gills and bald head looked so benevolent that it was difficult not to be carried away by his discourse. I believe two or three heads of families in the neighbourhood gave their sons absolute liberty of choice in the matter of their professions – and am not sure that they had not afterwards considerable cause to regret having done so. The visitors, seeing Theobald look shy and wholly unmoved by the exhibition of so much consideration for his wishes, would remark to themselves that the boy seemed hardly likely to be equal to his father and would set him down as an unenthusiastic youth, who ought to have more life in him and be more sensible of his advantages than he appeared to be.

No one believed in the righteousness of the whole transaction more firmly than the boy himself; a sense of being ill at ease kept him silent, but it was too profound and too much without break for him to become fully alive to it, and come to an understanding with himself. He feared the dark scowl which would come over his father's face upon the slightest opposition. His father's violent threats, or coarse sneers, would not have been taken *au sérieux* by a stronger boy, but Theobald was not a strong boy, and rightly or wrongly, gave his father credit for being quite ready to carry his threats into execution. Opposition had never got him anything he wanted yet, nor indeed had yielding, for the matter of that, unless he happened to want exactly what his father wanted for him. If he had ever entertained thoughts of resistance, he had none now, and the power to oppose was so completely lost for want of exercise that hardly did the wish remain; there was nothing left save dull acquiescence as of an ass crouched between two burdens. He may have had an ill-defined sense of ideals that were not his actuals; he might occasionally dream of himself as a soldier or a sailor far away in foreign lands, or even as a farmer's boy upon the wolds, but there was not enough in him for there to be any chance of his turning his dreams into realities, and he drifted on with his stream, which was a slow, and, I am afraid, a muddy one.

I think the Church catechism has a good deal to do with the unhappy relations which commonly even now exist between parents and children. That work was written too exclusively from the parental point of view; the person who composed it did not get a few children to come in and help him; he was clearly not young himself, nor should I say it was the work of one who liked children – in spite of the words 'my good child' which, if I remember rightly, are once put into the mouth of the catechist and, after all, carry a harsh sound with them. The general impression it leaves upon the mind of the young is that their wickedness at birth was but very imperfectly wiped out at baptism, and that the mere fact of being young at all has something with it that savours more or less distinctly of the nature of sin.

If a new edition of the work is ever required I should like to introduce a few words insisting on the duty of seeking all reasonable pleasure and avoiding all pain that can be honourably avoided. I should like to see children taught that they should not say they like things which they do not like, merely because certain other people say they like them, and how foolish it is to say they believe this or that when they understand nothing about it.

If it be urged that these additions would make the catechism too long I would curtail the remarks upon our duty towards our neighbour and upon the sacraments. In the place of the paragraph beginning 'I desire my Lord God our Heavenly Father' I would – but perhaps I had better return to Theobald, and leave the recasting of the catechism to abler hands.

Chapter Eight

Mr Pontifex had set his heart on his son's becoming a fellow of a college before he became a clergyman. This would provide for him at once and would ensure his getting a living if none of his father's ecclesiastical friends gave him one. The boy had done just well enough at school to render this possible, so he was sent to one of the smaller colleges at Cambridge and was at once set to read with the best private tutors that could be found. A system of examination had been adopted a year or so before Theobald took his degree which had improved his chances of a fellowship, for whatever ability he had was classical rather than mathematical, and this system gave more encouragement to classical studies than had been given hitherto.

Theobald had the sense to see that he had a chance of independence if he worked hard, and he liked the notion of becoming a fellow. He therefore applied himself, and in the end took a degree which made his getting a fellowship in all probability a mere question of time. For a while Mr Pontifex senior was really pleased, and told his son he would present him with the works of any standard writer whom he might select. The young man chose the works of Bacon, and Bacon accordingly made his appearance in ten nicely bound volumes. A little inspection, however, showed that the copy was a second-hand one.

Now that he had taken his degree the next thing to look forward to was ordination – about which Theobald had thought little hitherto beyond acquiescing in it as something that would come as a matter of course some day. Now, however, it had actually come and was asserting itself as a thing which should be only a few months off, and this rather frightened him inasmuch as there would be no way out of it when he was once in it. He did not like the near view of ordination as well as the distant one, and even made some feeble efforts to escape, as may be perceived by the following correspondence which his son Ernest found among his father's papers written on gilt-edged paper, in faded ink and tied neatly round with a piece of tape, but without any note or comment. I have altered nothing. The letters are as follows:

'My Dear Father, – I do not like opening up a question which has been considered settled, but as the time approaches I begin to be very doubtful how far I am fitted to be a clergyman. Not, I am thankful to say, that I have the faintest doubts about the Church of England, and I could subscribe cordially to every one of the thirty-nine articles which do indeed appear to me to be the *ne plus ultra* of human wisdom, and Paley, too, leaves no loop-hole for an opponent; but I am sure I should be running counter to your wishes if I were to conceal from you that I do not feel the inward call to be a minister of the gospel that I shall have to say I have felt when the Bishop ordains me. I try to get this feeling, I pray for it earnestly, and sometimes half think that I have got it, but in a little time it wears off, and though I have no absolute repugnance to being a clergyman and trust that if I am one I shall endeavour to live to the Glory of God and to advance His interests upon earth, yet I feel that something more than this is wanted before I am fully justified in going into the Church. I am aware that I have been a great expense to you in spite of my scholarships, but you have ever taught me that I should obey my conscience, and my conscience tells me I should do wrong if I became a clergyman. God may yet give me the spirit for which I assure you I have been and am continually praying, but. He may not, and in that case would it not be better for me to try and look out for something else? I know that neither you nor John wish me to go into your business, nor do I understand anything about money matters, but is there nothing

else that I can do? I do not like to ask you to maintain me while I
go in for medicine or the bar; but when I get my fellowship,
which should not be long first, I will endeavour to cost you
nothing further, and I might make a little money by writing or
taking pupils. I trust you will not think this letter improper;
nothing is further from my wish than to cause you any uneasiness. I hope you will make allowance for my present feelings
which, indeed, spring from nothing but from that respect for my
conscience which no one has so often instilled into me as
yourself. Pray let me have a few lines shortly. I hope your cold is
better. With love to Eliza and Maria, I am, your affectionate son,

'Theobald Pontifex.'

'Dear Theobald, – I can enter into your feelings and have no wish
to quarrel with your expression of them. It is quite right and
natural that you should feel as you do except as regards one
passage, the impropriety of which you will yourself doubtless feel
upon reflection, and to which I will not further allude than to say
that it has wounded me. You should not have said "in spite of my
scholarships." It was only proper that if you could do anything to
assist me in bearing the heavy burden of your education, the
money should be, as it was, made over to myself. Every line in your
letter convinces me that you are under the influence of a morbid
sensitiveness which is one of the devil's favourite devices for luring
people to their destruction. I have, as you say, been at great expense
with your education. Nothing has been spared by me to give you
the advantages which, as an English gentleman, I was anxious to
afford my son, but I am not prepared to see that expense thrown
away and to have to begin again from the beginning, merely
because you have taken some foolish scruples into your head,
which you should resist as no less unjust to yourself than to me.

'Don't give way to that restless desire for change which is the
bane of so many persons of both sexes at the present day.

'Of course you needn't be ordained: nobody will compel you;

you are perfectly free; you are twenty-three years of age, and should know your own mind; but why not have known it sooner, instead of never so much as breathing a hint of opposition until I have had all the expense of sending you to the University, which I should never have done unless I had believed you to have made up your mind about taking orders? I have letters from you in which you express the most perfect willingness to be ordained, and your brother and sisters will bear me out in saying that no pressure of any sort has been put upon you. You mistake your own mind, and are suffering from a nervous timidity which may be very natural but may not the less be pregnant with serious consequences to yourself. I am not at all well, and the anxiety occasioned by your letter is naturally preying upon me. May God guide you to a better judgment. – Your affectionate father,

'G. Pontifex.'

On receipt of this letter Theobald plucked up his spirits. 'My father,' he said to himself, 'tells me I need not be ordained if I do not like. I do not like, and therefore I will not be ordained. But what was the meaning of the words "pregnant with serious consequences to yourself"? Did there lurk a threat under these words – though it was impossible to lay hold of it or of them? Were they not intended to produce all the effect of a threat without being actually threatening?'

Theobald knew his father well enough to be little likely to misapprehend his meaning, but having ventured so far on the path of opposition, and being really anxious to get out of being ordained if he could, he determined to venture farther. He accordingly wrote the following:

'My Dear Father, – You tell me – and I heartily thank you – that no one will compel me to be ordained. I knew you could not press ordination upon me if my conscience was seriously opposed to it; I have therefore resolved on giving up the idea, and believe that if you will continue to allow me what you do at present, until I get my fellowship, which should not be long, I will then cease putting you to further expense. I will make up my mind as soon as possible what profession I will adopt, and will let you know at once, – Your affectionate son,

'Theobald Pontifex.'

The remaining letter, written by return of post, must now be given. It has the merit of brevity.

'Dear Theobald, – I have received yours. I am at a loss to conceive its motive, but am very clear as to its effect. You shall not receive a single sixpence from me till you come to your senses. Should you persist in your folly and wickedness, I am happy to remember that I have got other children whose conduct I can depend upon to be a source of credit and happiness to me. – Your affectionate but troubled father,

'G. Pontifex.'

I do not know the immediate sequel to the foregoing correspondence, but it all came perfectly right in the end. Either Theobald's heart failed him, or he interpreted the outward shove which his father gave him as the inward call for which I have no doubt he prayed with great earnestness – for he was a firm believer in the efficacy of prayer. And so am I under certain circumstances. Tennyson has said that more things are wrought by prayer than this world dreams of, but he has wisely refrained from saying whether they are good things or bad things. It might perhaps be as well if the world were to dream of, or even become wide awake to, some of the things that are being wrought by prayer. But the question is avowedly difficult. In the end Theobald got his fellowship by a stroke of luck very soon after taking his degree, and was ordained in the autumn of the same year, 1825.

Chapter Nine

Mr Allaby was rector of Crampsford, a village a few miles from Cambridge. He, too, had taken a good degree, had got a fellowship, and in the course of time had accepted a college living of about £400 a year and a house. His private income did not exceed £200 a year. On resigning his fellowship he married a woman a good deal younger than himself who bore him eleven children, nine of whom – two sons and seven daughters – were living. The two eldest daughters had married fairly well, but at the time of which I am now writing there were still five unmarried, of ages varying between thirty and twenty-two – and the sons were neither of them yet off their father's hands. It was plain that if anything were to happen to Mr Allaby the family would be left poorly off, and this made both Mr and Mrs Allaby as unhappy as it ought to have made them.

Reader, did you ever have an income at best none too large, which died with you all except £200 a year? Did you ever at the same time have two sons who must be started in life somehow, and five daughters still unmarried for whom you would only be too thankful to find husbands – if you knew how to find them? If morality is that which, on the whole, brings a man peace in his declining years – if, that is to say, it is not an utter swindle, can you under these circumstances flatter yourself that you have led a moral life?

And this, even though your wife has been so good a woman that you have not grown tired of her, and has not fallen into such ill-health as lowers your own health in sympathy; and though your family has grown up vigorous, amiable, and blessed with common sense. I know many old men and women who are reputed moral, but who are living with partners whom they have long ceased to love, or who have ugly disagreeable maiden daughters for whom they have never been able to find husbands – daughters whom they loathe and by whom they are loathed in secret, or sons whose folly or extravagance is a perpetual wear and worry to them. Is it moral for a man to have brought such things upon himself? Someone should do for morals what that old Pecksniff Bacon has obtained the credit of having done for science.

But to return to Mr and Mrs Allaby. Mrs Allaby talked about having married two of her daughters as though it had been the easiest thing in the world. She talked in this way because she heard other mothers do so, but in her heart of hearts she did not know how she had done it, nor indeed if it had been her doing at all. First there had been a young man in connection with whom she had tried to practise certain manoeuvres which she had rehearsed in imagination over and over again, but which she found impossible to apply in practice. Then there had been weeks of a *wurra wurra* of hopes and fears and little strategems which as often as not proved injudicious, and then somehow or other in the end, there lay the young man bound and with an arrow through his heart at her daughter's feet. It seemed to her to be all a fluke which she could have little or no hope of repeating. She had indeed repeated it once, and might perhaps with good luck repeat it yet once again – but five times over! It was awful: why, she would rather have three confinements than go through the wear and tear of marrying a single daughter.

Nevertheless it had got to be done, and poor Mrs Allaby never looked at a young man without an eye to his being a future son-in-law. Papas and mammas sometimes ask young men whether their intentions are honourable towards their daughters. I think young men might occasionally ask papas and mammas whether their intentions are honourable before they accept invitations to houses where there are still unmarried daughters.

'I can't afford a curate, my dear,' said Mr Allaby to his wife when the pair were discussing what was next to be done. 'It will be better to get some young man to come and help me for a time upon a Sunday. A guinea a Sunday will do this, and we can chop and change till we get someone who suits.' So it was settled that Mr Allaby's health was not so strong as it had been, and that he stood in need of help in the performance of his Sunday duty.

Mrs Allaby had a great friend – a certain Mrs Cowey, wife of the celebrated Professor Cowey. She was what was called a truly spiritually minded woman, a trifle portly, with an incipient beard, and an extensive connection among undergraduates, more especially among those who were inclined to take part in the great evangelical movement which was then at its height. She gave evening parties once a fortnight at which prayer was part of the entertainment. She was not only spiritually minded, but, as enthusiastic Mrs Allaby used to exclaim, she was a thorough woman of the world at the same time and had such a fund of strong masculine good sense. She, too, had daughters, but, as she used to say to Mrs Allaby, she had been less fortunate than Mrs Allaby herself, for one by one they had married and left her so that her old age would have been desolate indeed if her Professor had not been spared to her.

Mrs Cowey, of course, knew the run of all the bachelor clergy in the University, and was the very person to assist Mrs Allaby in finding an eligible assistant for her husband, so this last named lady drove over one morning in the November of 1825, by arrangement, to take an early dinner with Mrs Cowey and spend the afternoon. After dinner the two ladies retired together, and the business of the day began. How they fenced, how they saw through one another, with what loyalty they pretended not to see through one another, with what gentle dalliance they prolonged the conversation discussing the spiritual fitness of this or that deacon, and the other pros and cons connected with him after his spiritual fitness had been disposed of, all this must be left to the imagination of the reader. Mrs Cowey had been so accustomed to scheming on her own account that she would scheme for anyone rather than not scheme at all. Many mothers turned to her in their hour of need and, provided they were spiritually minded, Mrs Cowey never failed to do her best for them; if the marriage of a young Bachelor of Art was not made in Heaven, it was probably made, or at any rate attempted, in Mrs Cowey's drawing-room. On the present occasion all the deacons of the University in whom there lurked any spark of promise were exhaustively discussed, and the upshot was that our friend Theobald was declared by Mrs Cowey to be about the best thing she could do that afternoon.

'I don't know that he's a particularly fascinating young man, my dear,' said Mrs Cowey, 'and he's only a second son, but then he's got his fellowship, and even the second son of such a man as Mr Pontifex the publisher should have something very comfortable.'

'Why, yes, my dear,' rejoined Mrs Allaby complacently, 'that's what one rather feels.'

Chapter Ten

The interview, like all other good things, had to come to an end; the days were short, and Mrs Allaby had a six-miles' drive to Crampsford. When she was muffled up and had taken her seat, Mr Allaby's *factotum*, James, could perceive no change in her appearance, and little knew what a series of delightful visions he was driving home along with his mistress.

Professor Cowey had published works through Theobald's father, and Theobald had on this account been taken in tow by Mrs Cowey from the beginning of his University career. She had had her eye upon him for some time past, and almost as much felt it her duty to get him off her list of young men for whom wives had to be provided, as poor Mrs Allaby did to try and get a husband for one of her daughters. She now wrote and asked him to come and see her, in terms that awakened his curiosity. When he came she broached the subject of Mr Allaby's failing health, and after the smoothing away of such difficulties as were only Mrs Cowey's due, considering the interest she had taken, it was allowed to come to pass that Theobald should go to Crampsford for six successive Sundays and take the half of Mr Allaby's duty at half a guinea a Sunday, for Mrs Cowey cut down the usual stipend mercilessly, and Theobald was not strong enough to resist.

Ignorant of the plots which were being prepared for his peace of mind and with no idea beyond that of earning his three guineas, and perhaps of astonishing the inhabitants of Crampsford by his academic learning, Theobald walked over to the Rectory one Sunday morning early in December – a few weeks only after he had been ordained. He had taken a great deal of pains with his sermon, which was on the subject of geology – then coming to the fore as a theological bugbear. He showed that so far as geology was worth anything at all – and he was too liberal entirely to pooh-pooh it – it confirmed the absolutely historical character of the Mosaic account of the Creation as given in Genesis. Any phenomena which at first sight appeared to make against this view were only partial phenomena and broke down upon investigation. Nothing could be in more excellent taste, and when Theobald adjourned to the rectory, where he was to dine between the services, Mr Allaby complimented him warmly upon his *début*, while the ladies of the family could hardly find words with which to express their admiration.

Theobald knew nothing about women. The only women he had been thrown in contact with were his sisters, two of whom were always correcting him, and a few school friends whom these had got their father to ask to Elmhurst. These young ladies had either been so shy that they and Theobald had never amalgamated, or they had been supposed to be clever and had said smart things to him. He did not say smart things himself and did not want other people to say them. Besides, they talked about music – and he hated music – or pictures – and he hated pictures – or books – and except the classics he hated books. And then sometimes he was wanted to dance with them, and he did not know how to dance, and did not want to know.

At Mrs Cowey's parties again he had seen some young ladies and had been introduced to them. He had tried to make himself agreeable, but was always left with the impression that he had not been successful. The young ladies of Mrs Cowey's set were by no means the most attractive that might have been found in the University, and Theobald may be excused for not losing his heart to the greater number of them, while if for a minute or two he was thrown in with one of the prettier and more agreeable girls he was almost immediately cut out by someone less bashful than himself, and sneaked off, feeling as far as the fair sex was concerned, like the impotent man at the pool of Bethesda.

What a really nice girl might have done with him I cannot tell, but fate had thrown none such in his way except his youngest sister, Alethea, whom he might perhaps have liked if she had not been his sister. The result of his experience was that women had never done him any good and he was not accustomed to associate them with any pleasure; if there was a part of Hamlet in connection with them it had been so completely cut out in the edition of the play in which he was required to act that he had come to disbelieve in its existence. As for kissing, he had never kissed a woman in his life except his sister – and my own sisters when we were all small children together. Over and above these kisses, he had until quite lately been required to imprint a solemn flabby kiss night and morning upon his father's cheek, and this, to the best of my belief, was the extent of Theobald's knowledge in the matter of kissing, at the time of which I am now writing. The result of the foregoing was that he had come to dislike women, as mysterious beings whose ways were not as his ways, nor their thoughts as his thoughts.

With these antecedents Theobald naturally felt rather bashful on finding himself the admired of five strange young ladies. I remember when I was a boy myself I was once asked to take tea at a girls school where one of my sisters was boarding. I was then about twelve years old. Everything went off well during teatime, for the Lady Principal of the establishment was present. But there came a time when she went away and I was left alone with the girls. The moment the mistress's back was turned the head girl, who was about my own age, came up, pointed her finger at me, made a face and said solemnly 'A na-a-sty bo-o-oy!' All the girls followed in rotation making the same gesture and the same reproach upon my being a boy. It gave me a great scare. I believe I cried, and I know it was a long time before I could again face a girl without a strong desire to run away.

Theobald felt at first much as I had myself done at the girls' school, but the Miss Allabys did not tell him he was a nasty bo-o-oy. Their papa and mamma were so cordial and they themselves lifted him so deftly over conversational stiles that before dinner was over Theobald thought the family to be a really very charming one, and felt as though he were being appreciated in a way to which he had not hitherto been accustomed.

With dinner his shyness wore off. He was by no means plain, his academic prestige was very fair. There was nothing about him to lay hold of as unconventional or ridiculous; the impression he created upon the young ladies was quite as favourable as that which they had created upon himself; for they knew not much more about men than he about women.

As soon as he was gone, the harmony of the establishment was broken by a storm which arose upon the question which of them it should be who should become Mrs Pontifex. 'My dears,' said their father, when he saw that they did not seem likely to settle the matter among themselves, 'wait till to-morrow, and then play at cards for him.' Having said which he retired to his study, where he took a nightly glass of whisky and a pipe of tobacco.

Chapter Eleven

The next morning saw Theobald in his rooms coaching a pupil, and the Miss Allabys in the eldest Miss Allaby's bedroom playing at cards with Theobald for the stakes.

The winner was Christina, the second unmarried daughter, then just twenty-seven years old and therefore four years older than Theobald. The younger sisters complained that it was throwing a husband away to let Christina try and catch him, for she was so much older that she had no chance; but Christina showed fight in a way not usual with her, for she was by nature yielding and good tempered. Her mother thought it better to back her up, so the two dangerous ones were packed off then and there on visits to friends some way off, and those alone allowed to remain at home whose loyalty could be depended upon. The brothers did not even suspect what was going on and believed their father's getting assistance was because he really wanted it.

The sisters who remained at home kept their words and gave Christina all the help they could, for over and above their sense of fair play they reflected that the sooner Theobald was landed, the sooner another deacon might be sent for who might be won by themselves. So quickly was all managed that the two unreliable sisters were actually out of the house before Theobald's next visit – which was on the Sunday following his first.

This time Theobald felt quite at home in the house of his new friends – for so Mrs Allaby insisted that he should call them. She took, she said, such a motherly interest in young men, especially in clergymen. Theobald believed every word she said, as he had believed his father and all his elders from his youth up. Christina sat next him at dinner and played her cards no less judiciously than she had played them in her sister's bedroom. She smiled (and her smile was one of her strong points) whenever he spoke to her; she went through all her little artlessnesses and set forth all her little wares in what she believed to be their most taking aspect. Who can blame her? Theobald was not the ideal she had dreamed of when reading Byron upstairs with her sisters, but he was an actual within the bounds of possibility, and, after all, not a bad actual as actuals went. What else could she do? Run away? She dared not. Marry beneath her and be considered a disgrace to her family? She dared not. Remain at home and become an old maid and be laughed at? Not if she could help it. She did the only thing that could reasonably be expected. She was drowning; Theobald might be only a straw, but she could catch at him, and catch at him she accordingly did.

If the course of true love never runs smooth, the course of true match-making sometimes does so. The only ground for complaint in the present case was that it was rather slow. Theobald fell into the part assigned to him more easily than Mrs Cowey and Mrs Allaby had dared to hope. He was softened by Christina's winning manners: he admired the high moral tone of everything she said; her sweetness towards her sisters and her father and mother, her readiness to undertake any small burden which no one else seemed willing to undertake, her sprightly manners, all were fascinating to one who, though unused to woman's society, was still a human being. He was flattered by her unobtrusive but obviously sincere admiration for himself; she seemed to see him in a more favourable light, and to understand him better than anyone outside of this charming family had ever done. Instead of snubbing him as his father, brother and sisters did, she drew him out, listened attentively to all he chose to say, and evidently wanted him to say still more. He told a college friend that he knew he was in love now; he really was, for he liked Miss Allaby's society much better than that of his sisters.

Over and above the recommendations already enumerated,

she had another in the possession of what was supposed to be a very beautiful contralto voice. Her voice was certainly contralto, for she could not reach higher than D in the treble; its only defect was that it did not go correspondingly low in the bass: in those days, however, a contralto voice was understood to include even a soprano if the soprano could not reach soprano notes, and it was not necessary that it should have the quality which we now assign to contralto. What her voice wanted in range and power was made up in the feeling with which she sang. She had transposed 'Angels ever bright and fair' into a lower key, so as to make it suit her voice, thus proving, as her mamma said, that she had a thorough knowledge of the laws of harmony; not only did she do this, but at every pause added an embellishment of arpeggios from one end to the other of the keyboard, on a principle which her governess had taught her; she thus added life and interest to an air which everyone – so she said – must feel to be rather heavy in the form in which Handel left it. As for her governess, she indeed had been a rarely accomplished musician: she was a pupil of the famous Dr Clarke of Cambridge, and used to play the overture to *Atalanta*, arranged by Mazzinghi. Nevertheless, it was some time before Theobald could bring his courage to the sticking point of actually proposing. He made it quite clear that he believed himself to be much smitten, but month after month went by, during which there was still so much hope in Theobald that Mr Allaby dared not discover that he was able to do his duty for himself, and was getting impatient at the number of half-guineas he was disbursing – and yet there was no proposal. Christina's mother assured him that she was the best daughter in the whole world, and would be a priceless treasure to the man who married her. Theobald echoed Mrs Allaby's sentiments with warmth, but still, though he visited the Rectory two or three times a week, besides coming over on Sundays – he did not propose. 'She is heart-whole yet, dear Mr Pontifex,' said Mrs Allaby, one day, 'at least I believe she is. It is not for want of admirers –

oh! no – she has had her full share of these, but she is too, too difficult to please. I think, however, she would fall before a *great and good* man.' And she looked hard at Theobald, who blushed; but the days went by and still he did not propose.

Another time Theobald actually took Mrs Cowey into his confidence, and the reader may guess what account of Christina he got from her. Mrs Cowey tried the jealousy manoeuvre and hinted at a possible rival. Theobald was, or pretended to be, very much alarmed; a little rudimentary pang of jealousy shot across his bosom and he began to believe with pride that he was not only in love, but desperately in love or he would never feel so jealous. Nevertheless, day after day still went by and he did not propose.

The Allabys behaved with great judgment. They humoured him till his retreat was practically cut off, though he still flattered himself that it was open. One day about six months after Theobald had become an almost daily visitor at the Rectory the conversation happened to turn upon long engagements. 'I don't like long engagements, Mr Allaby, do you?' said Theobald imprudently. 'No,' said Mr Allaby in a pointed tone, 'nor long courtships,' and he gave Theobald a look which he could not pretend to misunderstand. He went back to Cambridge as fast as he could go, and in dread of the conversation with Mr Allaby which he felt to be impending, composed the following letter which he despatched that same afternoon by a private messenger to Crampsford. The letter was as follows:

'Dearest Miss Christina, – I do not know whether you have guessed the feelings that I have long entertained for you – feelings which I have concealed as much as I could through fear of drawing you into an engagement which, if you enter into it, must be prolonged for a considerable time, but, however this may be, it is out of my power to conceal them longer; I love you, ardently, devotedly, and send these few lines asking you to be my wife, because I dare not trust my tongue to give adequate expression to the magnitude of my affection for you.

'I cannot pretend to offer you a heart which has never known either love or disappointment. I have loved already, and my heart was years in recovering from the grief I felt at seeing her become another's. That, however, is over, and having seen yourself I rejoice over a disappointment which I thought at one time would have been fatal to me. It has left me a less ardent lover than I should perhaps otherwise have been, but it has increased tenfold my power of appreciating your many charms and my desire that you should become my wife. Please let me have a few lines of answer by the bearer to let me know whether or not my suit is accepted. If you accept me I will at once come and talk the matter over with Mr and Mrs Allaby, whom I shall hope one day to be allowed to call father and mother.

'I ought to warn you that in the event of your consenting to be my wife it may be years before our union can be consummated, for I cannot marry till a college living is offered me. If, therefore, you see fit to reject me, I shall be grieved rather than surprised. – Ever most devotedly yours,

'Theobald Pontifex.'

And this was all that his public school and University education had been able to do for Theobald! Nevertheless, for his own part, he thought his letter rather a good one, and congratulated himself in particular upon his cleverness in inventing the story of a previous attachment, behind which he intended to shelter himself if Christina should complain of any lack of fervour in his behaviour to her.

I need not give Christina's answer, which, of course, was to accept. Much as Theobald feared old Mr Allaby, I do not think he would have wrought up his courage to the point of actually proposing but for the fact of the engagement being necessarily a long one, during which a dozen things might turn up to break it

off. However much he may have disapproved of long engagements for other people, I doubt whether he had any particular
objection to them in his own case. A pair of lovers are like sunset
and sunrise: there are such things every day but we very seldom
see them. Theobald posed as the most ardent lover imaginable,
but, to use the vulgarism for the moment in fashion, it was all
'side.' Christina was in love, as indeed she had been twenty times
already. But then Christina was impressionable and could not
even hear the name 'Missolonghi' mentioned without bursting
into tears. When Theobald accidentally left his sermon case
behind him one Sunday, she slept with it in her bosom and was
forlorn when she had to disgorge it on the following Sunday; but
I do not think Theobald ever took so much as an old toothbrush
of Christina's to bed with him. Why, I knew a young man once
who got hold of his mistress's skates and slept with them for a
fortnight and cried when he had to give them up.

Chapter Twelve

Theobald's engagement was all very well as far as it went, but there was an old gentleman with a bald head and rosy cheeks in a counting-house in Paternoster Row who must sooner or later be told of what his son had in view, and Theobald's heart fluttered when he asked himself what view this old gentleman was likely to take of the situation. The murder, however, had to come out, and Theobald and his intended, perhaps imprudently, resolved on making a clean breast of it at once. He wrote what he and Christina, who helped him to draft the letter, thought to be everything that was filial, and expressed himself as anxious to be married with the least possible delay. He could not help saying this, as Christina was at his shoulder, and he knew it was safe, for his father might be trusted not to help him. He wound up by asking his father to use any influence that might be at his command to help him to get a living, inasmuch as it might be years before a college living fell vacant, and he saw no other chance of being able to marry, for neither he nor his intended had any money except Theobald's fellowship, which would, of course, lapse on his taking a wife.

Any step of Theobald's was sure to be objectionable in his father's eyes, but that at three-and-twenty he should want to marry a penniless girl who was four years older than himself, afforded a golden opportunity which the old gentleman – for so I may now call him, as he was at least sixty – embraced with characteristic eagerness.

'The ineffable folly,' he wrote, on receiving his son's letter, 'of your fancied passion for Miss Allaby fills me with the gravest apprehensions. Making every allowance for a lover's blindness, I still have no doubt that the lady herself is a well-conducted and amiable young person, who would not disgrace our family, but were she ten times more desirable as a daughter-in-law than I can allow myself to hope, your joint poverty is an insuperable objection to your marriage. I have four other children besides yourself, and my expenses do not permit me to save money. This year they have been especially heavy, indeed I have had to purchase two not inconsiderable pieces of land which happened to come into the market and were necessary to complete a property which I have long wanted to round off in this way. I gave you an education regardless of expense, which has put you in possession of a comfortable income, at an age when many young men are dependent. I have thus started you fairly in life, and may claim that you should cease to be a drag upon me further. Long engagements are proverbially unsatisfactory, and in the present case the prospect seems interminable. What interest, pray, do you suppose I have that I could get a living for you? Can I go up and down the country begging people to provide for my son because he has taken it into his head to want to get married without sufficient means?

'I do not wish to write unkindly, nothing can be farther from my real feelings towards you, but there is often more kindness in plain speaking than in any amount of soft words which can end in no substantial performance, Of course, I bear in mind that you are of age, and can therefore please yourself, but if you choose to claim the strict letter of the law, and act without consideration for your father's feelings, you must not be surprised if you one day find that I have claimed a like liberty for myself. – Believe me, your affectionate father,

'G. Pontifex.'

I found this letter along with those already given and a few more which I need not give, but throughout which the same tone prevails, and in all of which there is the more or less obvious shake of the will near the end of the letter. Remembering Theobald's general dumbness concerning his father for the many years I knew him after his father's death, there was an eloquence in the preservation of the letters and in their endorsement 'Letters from my father,' which seemed to have with it some faint odour of health and nature.

Theobald did not show his father's letter to Christina, nor, indeed, I believe, to anyone. He was by nature secretive, and had been repressed too much and too early to be capable of railing or blowing off steam where his father was concerned. His sense of wrong was still inarticulate, felt as a dull dead weight ever present day by day, and if he woke at night-time still continually present, but he hardly knew what it was. I was about the closest friend he had, and I saw but little of him, for I could not get on with him for long together. He said I had no reverence; whereas I thought that I had plenty of reverence for what deserved to be revered, but that the gods which he deemed golden were in reality made of baser metal. He never, as I have said, complained of his father to me, and his only other friends were, like himself, staid and prim, of evangelical tendencies, and deeply imbued with a sense of the sinfulness of any act of insubordination to parents – good young men, in fact – and one cannot blow off steam to a good young man.

When Christina was informed by her lover of his father's opposition, and of the time which must probably elapse before they could be married, she offered – with how much sincerity I know not – to set him free from his engagement, but Theobald declined to be released – 'not at least,' as he said, 'at present.' Christina and Mrs Allaby knew they could manage him, and on this not very satisfactory footing the engagement was continued.

His engagement and his refusal to be released at once raised Theobald in his own good opinion. Dull as he was, he had no small share of quiet self-approbation. He admired himself for his University distinction, for the purity of his life (I said of him once that if he had only a better temper he would be as innocent as a new-laid egg) and for his unimpeachable integrity in money matters. He did not despair of advancement in the Church when he had once got a living, and of course it was within the bounds of possibility that he might one day become a Bishop, and Christina said she felt convinced that this would ultimately be the case.

As was natural for the daughter and intended wife of a clergyman, Christina's thoughts ran much upon religion, and she was resolved that even though an exalted position in this world were denied to her and Theobald, their virtues should be fully appreciated in the next. Her religious opinions coincided absolutely with Theobald's own, and many a conversation did she have with him about the glory of God, and the completeness with which they would devote themselves to it, as soon as Theobald had got his living and they were married. So certain was she of the great results which would then ensue that she wondered at times at the blindness shown by Providence towards its own truest interests in not killing off the rectors who stood between Theobald and his living a little faster.

In those days people believed with a simple downrightness which I do not observe among educated men and women now. It had never so much as crossed Theobald's mind to doubt the literal accuracy of any syllable in the Bible. He had never seen any book in which this was disputed, nor met with anyone who doubted it. True, there was just a little scare about geology, but there was nothing in it. If it was said that God made the world in six days, why He did make it in six days, neither in more nor less; if it was said that He put Adam to sleep, took out one of his ribs and made a woman of it, why, it was so as a matter of course. He, Adam, went to sleep as it might be himself, Theobald Pontifex, in a garden, as it might be the garden at Crampsford Rectory during the summer months when it was so pretty, only that it was larger, and had some tame wild animals in it. Then God came up to him, as it might be Mr Allaby or his father, dexterously took out one of his ribs without waking him, and miraculously healed the wound so that no trace of the operation remained. Finally, God had taken the rib perhaps into the greenhouse, and had turned it into just such another young woman as Christina. That was how it was done; there was neither difficulty nor shadow of difficulty about the matter. Could not God do anything He liked, and had He not in His own inspired Book told us that He had done this?

This was the average attitude of fairly educated young men and women towards the Mosaic cosmogony fifty, forty, or even twenty years ago. The combating of infidelity, therefore, offered little scope for enterprising young clergymen, nor had the Church awakened to the activity which she has since displayed among the poor in our large towns. These were then left almost without an effort at resistance or co-operation to the labours of those who had succeeded Wesley. Missionary work indeed in heathen countries was being carried on with some energy, but Theobald did not feel any call to be a missionary. Christina suggested this to him more than once, and assured him of the unspeakable happiness it would be to her to be the wife of a missionary, and to share his dangers; she and Theobald might even be martyred; of course they would be martyred simultaneously, and martyrdom many years hence as regarded from the arbour in the Rectory garden was not painful, it would ensure them a glorious future in the next world, and at any rate posthumous renown in this – even if they were not miraculously restored to life again – and such things had happened ere now in the case of martyrs. Theobald, however, had not been kindled by Christina's enthusiasm, so she fell back upon the Church of Rome – an enemy more dangerous, if possible, than paganism itself. A combat with Romanism might even yet win for her and Theobald the crown of martyrdom. True, the Church of Rome was tolerably quiet just then, but it was the calm before the storm, of this she was assured, with a conviction deeper than she could have attained by any argument founded upon mere reason.

'We, dearest Theobald,' she exclaimed, 'will be ever faithful. We will stand firm and support one another even in the hour of death itself. God in His mercy may spare us from being burnt alive. He may or may not do so. Oh, Lord' (and she turned her eyes prayerfully to Heaven), 'spare my Theobald, or grant that he may be beheaded.'

'My dearest,' said Theobald gravely, 'do not let us agitate ourselves unduly. If the hour of trial comes we shall be best prepared to meet it by having led a quiet unobtrusive life of self-denial and devotion to God's glory. Such a life let us pray God that it may please Him to enable us to pray that we may lead.'

'Dearest Theobald,' exclaimed Christina, drying the tears that had gathered in her eyes, 'you are always, always right. Let us be self-denying, pure, upright, truthful in word and deed.' She clasped her hands and looked up to Heaven as she spoke.

'Dearest,' rejoined her lover, 'we have ever hitherto endeavoured to be all of these things; we have not been worldly people; let us watch and pray that we may so continue to the end.'

The moon had risen and the arbour was getting damp, so they adjourned further aspirations for a more convenient season. At other times Christina pictured herself and Theobald as braving the scorn of almost every human being in the achievement of some mighty task which should redound to the honour of her Redeemer. She could face anything for this. But always towards the end of her vision there came a little coronation scene high up in the golden regions of the Heavens, and a diadem was set upon her head by the Son of Man Himself, amid a host of angels and archangels who looked on with envy and admiration – and here even Theobald himself was out of it. If there could be such a thing as the Mammon of Righteousness Christina would have assuredly made friends with it. Her papa and mamma were very estimable people and would in the course of time receive Heavenly Mansions in which they would be exceedingly comfortable; so doubtless would her sisters; so perhaps even might her brothers; but for herself she felt that a higher destiny was preparing, which it was her duty never to lose sight of. The first step towards it would be her marriage with Theobald. In spite, however, of these flights of religious romanticism, Christina was a good-tempered, kindly-natured girl enough, who, if she had married a sensible layman – we will say a hotel-keeper – would have developed into a good landlady and been deservedly popular with her guests.

Such was Theobald's engaged life. Many a little present passed between the pair, and many a small surprise did they prepare pleasantly for one another. They never quarrelled, and neither of them ever flirted with anyone else. Mrs Allaby and his future sisters-in-law idolised Theobald in spite of its being impossible to get another deacon to come and be played for as long as Theobald was able to help Mr Allaby, which now of course he did gratis and for nothing; two of the sisters, however, did manage to find husbands before Christina was actually married, and on each occasion Theobald played the part of decoy elephant. In the end only two out of the seven daughters remained single.

After three or four years, old Mr Pontifex became accustomed to his son's engagement and looked upon it as among the things which had now a prescriptive right to toleration. In the spring of 1831, more than five years after Theobald had first walked over to Crampsford, one of the best livings in the gift of the College unexpectedly fell vacant, and was for various reasons declined by the two fellows senior to Theobald, who might each have been expected to take it. The living was then offered to and of course accepted by Theobald, being in value not less than £500 a year with a suitable house and garden. Old Mr Pontifex then came down more handsomely than was expected and settled £10,000 on his son and daughter-in-law for life with remainder to such of their issue as they might appoint. In the month of July, 1831, Theobald and Christina became man and wife.

Chapter Thirteen

A due number of old shoes had been thrown at the carriage in which the happy pair departed from the Rectory, and it had turned the corner at the bottom of the village. It could then be seen for two or three hundred yards creeping past a fir coppice, and after this was lost to view.

'John,' said Mr Allaby to his man-servant, 'shut the gate;' and he went indoors with a sigh of relief which seemed to say: 'I have done it, and I am alive.' This was the reaction after a burst of enthusiastic merriment during which the old gentleman had run twenty yards after the carriage to fling a slipper at it – which he had duly flung.

But what were the feelings of Theobald and Christina when the village was passed and they were rolling quietly by the fir plantation? It is at this point that even the stoutest heart must fail, unless it beat in the breast of one who is over head and ears in love. If a young man is in a small boat on a choppy sea, along with his affianced bride and both are seasick, and if the sick swain can forget his own anguish in the happiness of holding the fair one's head when she is at her worst – then he is in love, and his heart will be in no danger of ailing him as he passes his fir plantation. Other people, and unfortunately by far the greater number of those who get married must be classed among the 'other people,' will inevitably go through a quarter or half an hour of greater or less badness as the case may be. Taking numbers into account, I should think more mental suffering had been undergone in the streets leading from St George's, Hanover Square, than in the condemned cells of Newgate. There is no time at which what the Italians call *la figlia della Morte* lays her cold hand upon a man more awfully than during the first half hour that he is alone with a woman whom he has married but never genuinely loved.

Death's daughter did not spare Theobald. He had behaved very well hitherto. When Christina had offered to let him go, he had stuck to his post with a magnanimity on which he had plumed himself ever since. From that time forward he had said to himself: 'I, at any rate, am the very soul of honour; I am not,' etc., etc. True, at the moment of magnanimity the actual cash payment, so to speak, was still distant; when his father gave formal consent to his marriage things began to look more serious; when the college living had fallen vacant and been accepted they looked more serious still; but when Christina actually named the day, then Theobald's heart fainted within him.

The engagement had gone on so long that he had got into a groove, and the prospect of change was disconcerting. Christina and he had got on, he thought to himself, very nicely for a great number of years; why – why – why should they not continue to go on as they were doing now for the rest of their lives? But there was no more chance of escape for him than for the sheep which is being driven to the butcher's back premises, and like the sheep he felt that there was nothing to be gained by resistance, so he made none. He behaved, in fact, with decency, and was declared on all hands to be one of the happiest men imaginable.

Now, however, to change the metaphor, the drop had actually fallen, and the poor wretch was hanging in mid-air along with the creature of his affections. This creature was now thirty-three years old, and looked it: she had been weeping, and her eyes and nose were reddish; if 'I have done it and I am alive,' was written on Mr Allaby's face after he had thrown the shoe, 'I have done it, and I do not see how I can possibly live much longer,' was upon the face of Theobald as he was being driven along by the fir plantation. This, however, was not apparent at the Rectory. All that could be seen there was the bobbing up and down of the postilion's head, which just overtopped the hedge by the roadside as he rose in his stirrups, and the black and yellow body of the carriage.

For some time the pair said nothing: what they must have felt during their first half-hour, the reader must guess, for it is beyond my power to tell him; at the end of that time, however, Theobald had rummaged up a conclusion from some odd corner of his soul to the effect that now he and Christina were married the sooner they fell into their future mutual relations the better. If people who are in a difficulty will only do the first little reasonable thing which they can clearly recognise as reasonable, they will always find the next step more easy both to see and take. What, then, thought Theobald, was here at this moment the first and most obvious matter to be considered, and what would be an equitable view of his and Christina's relative positions in respect to it? Clearly their first dinner was their first joint entry into the duties and pleasures of married life. No less clearly it was Christina's duty to order it, and his own to eat and pay for it.

The arguments leading to this conclusion, and the conclusion itself, flashed upon Theobald about three and a half miles after he had left Crampsford on the road to Newmarket. He had breakfasted early, but his usual appetite had failed him. They had left the vicarage at noon without staying for the wedding breakfast. Theobald liked an early dinner; it dawned upon him that he was beginning to be hungry; from this to the conclusion stated in the preceding paragraph the steps had been easy. After a few minutes' further reflection he broached the matter to his bride, and thus the ice was broken.

Mrs Theobald was not prepared for so sudden an assumption of importance. Her nerves, never of the strongest, had been strung to their highest tension by the event of the morning. She wanted to escape observation; she was conscious of looking a little older than she quite liked to look as a bride who had been married that morning; she feared the landlady, the chambermaid, the waiter – everybody and everything; her heart beat so fast that she could hardly speak, much less go through the ordeal of ordering dinner in a strange hotel with a strange landlady. She begged and prayed to be let off. If Theobald would only order dinner this once, she would order it any day and every day in the future.

But the inexorable Theobald was not to be put off with such absurd excuses. He was master now. Had not Christina less than two hours ago promised solemnly to honour and obey him, and was she turning restive over such a trifle as this? The loving smile departed from his face, and was succeeded by a scowl which that old Turk, his father, might have envied. 'Stuff and nonsense, my dearest Christina,' he exclaimed mildly, and stamped his foot upon the floor of the carriage. 'It is a wife's duty to order her husband's dinner; you are my wife, and I shall expect you to order mine.' For Theobald was nothing if he was not logical.

The bride began to cry, and said he was unkind; whereon he said nothing, but revolved unutterable things in his heart. Was this, then, the end of his six years of unflagging devotion? Was it for this that when Christina had offered to let him off, he had stuck to his engagement? Was this the outcome of her talks about duty and spiritual mindedness – that now upon the very day of her marriage she should fail to see that the first step in obedience to God lay in obedience to himself? He would drive back to Crampsford; he would complain to Mr and Mrs Allaby; he didn't mean to have married Christina; he hadn't married her; it was all a hideous dream; he would – But a voice kept ringing in his ears which said: 'You can't, can't, can't.'

'Can't I?' screamed the unhappy creature to himself.

'No,' said the remorseless voice, 'You can't. You are a married man.'

He rolled back in his corner of the carriage and for the first time felt how iniquitous were the marriage laws of England. But he would buy Milton's prose works and read his pamphlet on divorce. He might perhaps be able to get them at Newmarket.

So the bride sat crying in one corner of the carriage; and the bridegroom sulked in the other, and he feared her as only a bridegroom can fear.

Presently, however, a feeble voice was heard from the bride's corner saying: 'Dearest Theobald – dearest Theobald, forgive me; I have been very, very wrong. Please do not be angry with me. I will order the – the –' but the word 'dinner' was checked by rising sobs.

When Theobald heard these words a load began to be lifted from his heart, but he only looked towards her, and that not too pleasantly.

'Please tell me,' continued the voice, 'what you think you would like, and I will tell the landlady when we get to Newmar –' but another burst of sobs checked the completion of the word. The load on Theobald's heart grew lighter and lighter. Was it possible that she might not be going to henpeck him after all? Besides, had she not diverted his attention from herself to his approaching dinner?

He swallowed down more of his apprehensions and said, but still gloomily, 'I think we might have a roast fowl with bread sauce, new potatoes and green peas, and then we will see if they could let us have a cherry tart and some cream.'

After a few minutes more he drew her towards him, kissed away her tears, and assured her that he knew she would be a good wife to him.

'Dearest Theobald,' she exclaimed in answer, 'you are an angel.'

Theobald believed her, and in ten minutes more the happy couple alighted at the inn at Newmarket.

Bravely did Christina go through her arduous task. Eagerly did she beseech the landlady, in secret, not to keep her Theobald waiting longer than was absolutely necessary.

'If you have any soup ready, you know, Mrs Barber, it might save ten minutes, for we might have it while the fowl was browning.'

See how necessity had nerved her! But in truth she had a splitting headache, and would have given anything to have been alone.

The dinner was a success. A pint of sherry had warmed Theobald's heart, and he began to hope that, after all, matters might still go well with him. He had conquered in the first battle, and this gives great prestige. How easy it had been too! Why had he never treated his sisters in this way? He would do so next time he saw them; he might in time be able to stand up to his brother John, or even his father. Thus do we build castles in air when flushed with wine and conquest.

The end of the honeymoon saw Mrs Theobald the most devotedly obsequious wife in all England. According to the old saying, Theobald had killed the cat at the beginning. It had been a very little cat, a mere kitten in fact, or he might have been afraid to face it, but such as it had been he had challenged it to mortal combat, and had held up its dripping head defiantly before his wife's face. The rest had been easy.

Strange that one whom I have described hitherto as so timid and easily put upon should prove such a Tartar all of a sudden on the day of his marriage. Perhaps I have passed over his years of courtship too rapidly. During these he had become a tutor of his college, and had at last been Junior Dean. I never yet knew a man whose sense of his own importance did not become adequately developed after he had held a resident fellowship for five or six years. True – immediately on arriving within a ten-mile radius of his father's house, an enchantment fell upon him, so that his knees waxed weak, his greatness departed, and he again felt himself like an overgrown baby under a perpetual cloud; but then he was not often at Elmhurst, and as soon as he left it the spell was taken off again; once more he became the fellow and tutor of his college, the Junior Dean, the betrothed of Christina, the idol of the Allaby womankind. From all which it may be gathered that if Christina had been a Barbary hen, and had ruffled her feathers in any show of resistance, Theobald would not have ventured to swagger with her, but she was not a Barbary hen, she was only a common hen, and that too with rather a smaller share of personal bravery than hens generally have.

Chapter Fourteen

Battersby-on-the-Hill was the name of the village of which Theobald was now Rector. It contained 400 or 500 inhabitants, scattered over a rather large area, and consisting entirely of farmers and agricultural labourers. The Rectory was commodious, and placed on the brow of a hill which gave it a delightful prospect. There was a fair sprinkling of neighbours within visiting range, but with one or two exceptions they were the clergymen and clergymen's families of the surrounding villages.

By these the Pontifexes were welcomed as great acquisitions to the neighbourhood. Mr Pontifex, they said, was so clever; he had been senior classic and senior wrangler; a perfect genius, in fact, and yet with so much sound practical common sense as well. As son of such a distinguished man as the great Mr Pontifex the publisher he would come into a large property by and by. Was there not an elder brother? Yes, but there would be so much that Theobald would probably get something very considerable. Of course they would give dinner parties. And Mrs Pontifex, what a charming woman she was; she was certainly not exactly pretty, perhaps, but then she had such a sweet smile and her manner was so bright and winning. She was so devoted, too, to her husband and her husband to her; they really did come up to one's ideas of what lovers used to be in days of old; it was rare to meet with such a pair in these degenerate times; it was quite beautiful, etc., etc. Such were the comments of the neighbours on the new arrivals.

As for Theobald's own parishioners, the farmers were civil and the labourers and their wives obsequious. There was a little dissent, the legacy of a careless predecessor, but as Mrs Theobald said proudly: 'I think Theobald may be trusted to deal with *that*.' The church was then an interesting specimen of late Norman, with some early English additions. It was what in these days would be called in a very bad state of repair, but forty or fifty years ago few churches were in good repair. If there is one feature more characteristic of the present generation than another it is that it has been a great restorer of churches.

Horace preached church restoration in his ode:

> Delicta majorum immeritus lues,
> Romane, donec templa refeceris
> Aedesque labentes deorum et
> Foeda nigro simulacra fumo.*

Nothing went right with Rome for long together after the Augustan age, but whether it was because she did restore the temples or because she did not restore them I know not. They certainly went all wrong after Constantine's time and yet Rome is still a city of some importance.

I may say here that before Theobald had been many years at Battersby he found scope for useful work in the rebuilding of Battersby church, which he carried out at considerable cost, towards which he subscribed liberally himself. He was his own architect, and this saved expense; but architecture was not very well understood about the year 1834, when Theobald commenced operations, and the result is not as satisfactory as it would have been if he had waited a few years longer.

Every man's work, whether it be literature or music or pictures or architecture or anything else, is always a portrait of himself, and the more he tries to conceal himself the more clearly

* 'Though guiltless, Roman, you will pay for your fathers' sins, until you repair the decaying temples and shrines of the gods, and their smoke-blackened images' (*Odes* III.6).

will his character appear in spite of him. I may very likely be condemning myself, all the time that I am writing this book, for I know that whether I like it or no I am portraying myself more surely than I am portraying any of the characters whom I set before the reader. I am sorry that it is so, but I cannot help it – after which sop to Nemesis I will say that Battersby church in its amended form has always struck me as a better portrait of Theobald than any sculptor or painter short of a great master would be able to produce.

I remember staying with Theobald some six or seven months after he was married, and while the old church was still standing. I went to church, and felt as Naaman must have felt on certain occasions when he had to accompany his master on his return after having been cured of his leprosy. I have carried away a more vivid recollection of this and of the people, than of Theobald's sermon. Even now I can see the men in blue smock frocks reaching to their heels, and more than one old woman in a scarlet cloak; the row of stolid, dull, vacant plough-boys, ungainly in build, uncomely in face, lifeless, apathetic, a race a good deal more like the pre-revolution French peasant as described by Carlyle than is pleasant to reflect upon – a race now supplanted by a smarter, comelier and more hopeful generation, which has discovered that it too has a right to as much happiness as it can get, and with clearer ideas about the best means of getting it.

They shamble in one after another, with steaming breath, for it is winter, and loud clattering of hobnailed boots; they beat the snow from off them as they enter, and through the opened door I catch a momentary glimpse of a dreary leaden sky and snow-clad tombstones. Somehow or other I find the strain which Handel has wedded to the words 'There the ploughman near at hand,' has got into my head and there is no getting it out again. How marvellously old Handel understood these people!

They bob to Theobald as they passed the reading desk ('The people hereabouts are truly respectful,' whispered Christina to me, ('they know their betters.') and take their seats in a long row against the wall. The choir clamber up into the gallery with their instruments – a violoncello, a clarinet, and a trombone. I see them and soon I hear them, for there is a hymn before the service, a wild strain, a remnant, if I mistake not, of some pre-Reformation litany. I have heard what I believe was its remote musical progenitor in the church SS Giovanni e Paolo at Venice not five years since; and again I have heard it far away in mid-Atlantic upon a grey sea-Sabbath in June, when neither winds nor waves are stirring, so that the emigrants gather on deck, and their plaintive psalm goes forth upon the silver haze of the sky, and on the wilderness of a sea that has sighed till it can sigh no longer. Or it may be heard at some Methodist Camp Meeting upon a Welsh hillside, but in the churches it is gone for ever. If I were a musician I would take it as the subject for the *adagio* in a Wesleyan symphony.

Gone now are the clarinet, the violoncello and the trombone, wild minstrelsy as of the doleful creatures in Ezekiel, discordant, but infinitely pathetic. Gone is that scarebabe stentor, that bellowing bull of Bashan, the village blacksmith, gone is the melodious carpenter, gone the brawny shepherd with the red hair, who roared more lustily than all, until they came to the words, 'Shepherds with your flocks abiding,' when modesty covered him with confusion, and compelled him to be silent, as though his own health were being drunk. They were doomed and had a presentiment of evil, even when I first saw them, but they had still a little lease of choir life remaining, and they roared out:

wick- ed hands have pierced and nailed him, pierced and nailed him to a tree

but no description can give a proper idea of the effect. When I was last in Battersby church there was a harmonium played by a sweet-looking girl with a choir of school children around her, and they chanted the canticles to the most correct of chants, and they sang Hymns Ancient and Modern; the high pews were gone, nay, the very gallery in which the old choir had sung was removed as an accursed thing which might remind the people of the high places, and Theobald was old, and Christina was lying under the yew trees in the churchyard.

But in the evening later on I saw three very old men come chuckling out of a dissenting chapel, and surely enough they were my old friends, the blacksmith, the carpenter and the shepherd. There was a look of content upon their faces which made me feel certain they had been singing; not doubtless with the old glory of the violoncello, the clarinet and the trombone, but still songs of Sion and no new-fangled papistry.

Chapter Fifteen

The hymn had engaged my attention; when it was over I had time to take stock of the congregation. They were chiefly farmers – fat, very well-to-do folk, who had come some of them with their wives and children from outlying farms two and three miles away; haters of popery and of anything which any one might choose to say was popish; good, sensible fellows who detested theory of any kind, whose ideal was the maintenance of the *status quo* with perhaps a loving reminiscence of old war times, and a sense of wrong that the weather was not more completely under their control, who desired higher prices and cheaper wages, but otherwise were most contented when things were changing least; tolerators, if not lovers, of all that was familiar, haters of all that was unfamiliar; they would have been equally horrified at hearing the Christian religion doubted, and at seeing it practised.

'What can there be in common between Theobald and his parishioners?' said Christina to me, in the course of the evening, when her husband was for a few moments absent. 'Of course one must not complain, but I assure you it grieves me to see a man of Theobald's ability thrown away upon such a place as this. If we had only been at Gaysbury, where there are the A's, the B's, the C's, and Lord D's place, as you know, quite close, I should not then have felt that we were living in such a desert; but I suppose it is for the best,' she added more cheerfully; 'and then of course the Bishop will come to us whenever he is in the neighbourhood, and if we were at Gaysbury he might have gone to Lord D's.'

Perhaps I have now said enough to indicate the kind of place in which Theobald's lines were cast, and the sort of woman he had married. As for his own habits, I see him trudging through muddy lanes and over long sweeps of plover-haunted pastures to visit a dying cottager's wife. He takes her meat and wine from his own table, and that not a little only but liberally. According to his lights also, he administers what he is pleased to call spiritual consolation.

'I am afraid I'm going to Hell, Sir,' says the sick woman with a whine. 'Oh, Sir, save me, save me, don't let me go there. I couldn't stand it, Sir, I should die with fear, the very thought of it drives me into a cold sweat all over.'

'Mrs Thompson,' says Theobald gravely, 'you must have faith in the precious blood of your Redeemer; it is He alone who can save you.'

'But are you sure, Sir,' says she, looking wistfully at him, 'that He will forgive me – for I've not been a very good woman, indeed I haven't – and if God would only say "Yes" outright with his mouth when I ask whether my sins are forgiven me –'

'But they *are* forgiven you, Mrs Thompson,' says Theobald with some sternness, for the same ground has been gone over a good many times already, and he has borne the unhappy woman's misgivings now for a full quarter of an hour. Then he puts a stop to the conversation by repeating prayers taken from the 'Visitation of the Sick,' and overawes the poor wretch from expressing further anxiety as to her condition.

'Can't you tell me, Sir,' she exclaims piteously, as she sees that he is preparing to go away, 'can't you tell me that there is no Day of Judgment, and that there is no such place as Hell? I can do without the Heaven, Sir, but I cannot do with the Hell.' Theobald is much shocked.

'Mrs Thompson,' he rejoins impressively, 'let me implore you to suffer no doubt concerning these two cornerstones of our religion to cross your mind at a moment like the present. If there is one thing more certain than another it is that we shall all appear before the Judgment Seat of Christ, and that the wicked will be consumed in a lake of everlasting fire. Doubt this, Mrs Thompson, and you are lost.'

The poor woman buries her fevered head in the coverlet in a paroxysm of fear which at last finds relief in tears.

'Mrs Thompson,' says Theobald, with his hand on the door, 'compose yourself, be calm; you must please to take my word for it that at the Day of Judgment your sins will be all washed white in the blood of the Lamb, Mrs Thompson. Yea,' he exclaims frantically, 'though they be as scarlet, yet shall they be as white as wool,' and he makes off as fast as he can from the fetid atmosphere of the cottage to the pure air outside. Oh, how thankful he is when the interview is over!

He returns home, conscious that he has done his duty, and administered the comforts of religion to a dying sinner. His admiring wife awaits him at the Rectory, and assures him that never yet was a clergyman so devoted to the welfare of his flock. He believes her; he has a natural tendency to believe everything that is told him, and who should know the facts of the case better than his wife? Poor fellow! He has done his best, but what does a fish's best come to when the fish is out of water? He has left meat and wine – that he can do; he will call again and will leave more meat and wine; day after day he trudges over the same plover-haunted fields; and listens at the end of his walk to the same agony of forebodings, which day after day he silences, but does not remove, till at last a merciful weakness renders the sufferer careless of her future, and Theobald is satisfied that her mind is now peacefully at rest in Jesus.

Chapter Sixteen

He does not like this branch of his profession – indeed he hates it – but will not admit it to himself. The habit of not admitting things to himself has become a confirmed one with him. Nevertheless there haunts him an ill defined sense that life would be pleasanter if there were no sick sinners, or if they would at any rate face an eternity of torture with more indifference. He does not feel that he is in his element. The farmers look as if they were in their element. They are full-bodied, healthy and contented; but between him and them there is a great gulf fixed. A hard and drawn look begins to settle about the corners of his mouth, so that even if he were not in a black coat and white tie a child might know him for a parson.

He knows that he is doing his duty. Every day convinces him of this more firmly; but then there is not much duty for him to do. He is sadly in want of occupation. He has no taste for any of those field sports which were not considered unbecoming for a clergyman forty years ago. He does not ride, nor shoot, nor fish, nor course, nor play cricket. Study, to do him justice, he had never really liked, and what inducement was there for him to study at Battersby? He reads neither old books nor new ones. He does not interest himself in art or science or politics, but he sets his back up with some promptness if any of them show any development unfamiliar to himself. True, he writes his own sermons, but even his wife considers that his *forte* lies rather in the example of his life (which is one long act of self-devotion) than in his utterances from the pulpit. After breakfast he retires to his study; he cuts little bits out of the Bible and gums them with exquisite neatness by the side of other little bits; this he calls making a Harmony of the Old and New Testaments. Alongside the extracts he copies in the very perfection of handwriting extracts from Mede (the only man, according to Theobold, who really understood the Book of Revelation), Patrick, and other old divines. He works steadily at this for half an hour every morning during many years and the result is doubtless valuable. After some years have gone by he hears his children their lessons, and the daily oft-repeated screams that issue from the study during the lesson hours tell their own horrible story over the house. He has also taken to collecting a *hortus siccus,* and through the interest of his father was once mentioned in the Saturday Magazine as having been the first to find a plant, whose name I have forgotten, in the neighbourhood of Battersby. This number of the Saturday Magazine has been bound in red morocco, and is kept upon the drawing-room table. He potters about his garden; if he hears a hen cackling he runs and tells Christina, and straightway goes hunting for the egg.

When the two Miss Allabys came, as they sometimes did, to stay with Christina, they said the life led by their sister and brother-in-law was an idyll. Happy indeed was Christina in her choice, for that she had had a choice was a fiction which soon took root among them – and happy Theobald in his Christina. Somehow or other Christina was always a little shy of cards when her sisters were staying with her, though at other times she enjoyed a game of cribbage or a rubber of whist heartily enough, but her sisters knew they would never be asked to Battersby again if they were to refer to that little matter, and on the whole it was worth their while to be asked to Battersby. If Theobald's temper was rather irritable he did not vent it upon them.

By nature reserved, if he could have found someone to cook his dinner for him, he would rather have lived in a desert island than not. In his heart of hearts he held with Pope that 'the greatest nuisance to mankind is man' or words to that effect – only that women, with the exception perhaps of Christina, were worse. Yet for all this when visitors called he put a better face on it than anyone who was behind the scenes would have expected.

He was quick too at introducing the names of any literary celebrities whom he had met at his father's house, and soon established an all-round reputation which satisfied even Christina herself.

Who so *integer vitae scelerisque purus,* it was asked, as Mr Pontifex of Battersby? Who so fit to be consulted if any difficulty about parish management should arise? Who such a happy mixture of the sincere uninquiring Christian and of the man of the world? For so people actually called him. They said he was such an admirable man of business. Certainly if he had said he would pay a sum of money at a certain time, the money would be forthcoming on the appointed day, and this is saying a good deal for any man. His constitutional timidity rendered him incapable of an attempt to overreach when there was the remotest chance of opposition or publicity, and his correct bearing and somewhat stern expression were a great protection to him against being overreached. He never talked of money, and invariably changed the subject whenever money was introduced. His expression of unutterable horror at all kinds of meanness was a sufficient guarantee that he was not mean himself. Besides he had no business transactions save of the most ordinary butcher's book and baker's book description. His tastes – if he had any – were, as we have seen, simple; he had £900 a year and a house; the neighbourhood was cheap, and for some time he had no children to be a drag upon him. Who was not to be envied, and if envied why then respected, if Theobald was not enviable?

Yet I imagine that Christina was on the whole happier than her husband. She had not to go and visit sick parishioners, and the management of her house and the keeping of her accounts afforded as much occupation as she desired. Her principal duty was, as she well said, to her husband – to love him, honour him, and keep him in a good temper. To do her justice she fulfilled this duty to the uttermost of her power. It would have been better perhaps if she had not so frequently assured her husband that he was the best and wisest of mankind, for no one in his little world ever dreamed of telling him anything else, and it was not long before he ceased to have any doubt upon the matter. As for his temper, which had become very violent at times, she took care to humour it on the slightest sign of an approaching outbreak. She had early found that this was much the easiest plan. The thunder was seldom for herself. Long before her marriage even she had studied his little ways, and knew how to add fuel to the fire as long as the fire seemed to want it, and then to damp it judiciously down, making as little smoke as possible.

In money matters she was scrupulousness itself. Theobald made her a quarterly allowance for her dress, pocket money and little charities and presents. In these last items she was liberal in proportion to her income; indeed she dressed with great economy and gave away whatever was over in presents or charity. Oh, what a comfort it was to Theobald to reflect that he had a wife on whom he could rely never to cost him a sixpence of unauthorised expenditure! Letting alone her absolute submission, the perfect coincidence of her opinion with his own upon every subject and her constant assurances to him that he was right in everything which he took it into his head to say or do, what a tower of strength to him was her exactness in money matters! As years went by he became as fond of his wife as it was in his nature to be of any living thing, and applauded himself for having stuck to his engagement – a piece of virtue of which he was now reaping the reward. Even when Christina did outrun her quarterly stipend by some thirty shillings or a couple of pounds, it was always made perfectly clear to Theobald how the deficiency had arisen – there had been an unusually costly evening dress bought which was to last a long time, or somebody's unexpected wedding had necessitated a more handsome present than the quarter's balance would quite allow: the excess of expenditure was always repaid in the following quarter or quarters even though it were only ten shillings at a time.

I believe, however, that after they had been married some twenty years, Christina had somewhat fallen from her original perfection as regards money. She had got gradually in arrear during many successive quarters, till she had contracted a chronic loan, a sort of domestic national debt, amounting to between seven and eight pounds. Theobald at length felt that a remonstrance had become imperative, and took advantage of his silver wedding day to inform Christina that her indebtedness was cancelled, and at the same time to beg that she would endeavour henceforth to equalise her expenditure and her income. She burst into tears of love and gratitude, assured him that he was the best and most generous of men, and never during the remainder of her married life was she a single shilling behind hand.

Christina hated change of all sorts no less cordially than her husband. She and Theobald had nearly everything in this world that they could wish for; why, then, should people desire to introduce all sorts of changes of which no one could foresee the end? Religion, she was deeply convinced, had long since attained its final development, nor could it enter into the heart of reasonable man to conceive any faith more perfect than was inculcated by the Church of England. She could imagine no position more honourable than that of a clergyman's wife unless indeed it were a bishop's. Considering his father's influence it was not at all impossible that Theobald might be a bishop some day – and then – then would occur to her that one little flaw in the practice of the Church of England – a flaw not indeed in its doctrine, but in its policy, which she believed on the whole to be a mistaken one in this respect. I mean the fact that a bishop's wife does not take the rank of her husband.

This had been the doing of Elizabeth, who had been a bad woman, of exceeding doubtful moral character, and at heart a Papist to the last. Perhaps people ought to have been above mere considerations of worldly dignity, but the world was as it was, and such things carried weight with them, whether they ought to do so or no. Her influence as plain Mrs Pontifex, wife, we will say, of the Bishop of Winchester, would no doubt be considerable. Such a character as hers could not fail to carry weight if she were ever in a sufficiently conspicuous sphere for its influence to be widely felt; but as Lady Winchester – or the Bishopess – which would sound quite nicely – who could doubt that her power for good would be enhanced? And it would be all the nicer because if she had a daughter the daughter would not be a Bishopess unless indeed she were to marry a Bishop too, which would not be likely.

These were her thoughts upon her good days; at other times she would, to do her justice, have doubts whether she was in all respects as spiritually minded as she ought to be. She must press on, press on, till every enemy to her salvation was surmounted and Satan himself lay buried under her feet. It occurred to her on one of these occasions that she might steal a march over some of her contemporaries if she were to leave off eating black puddings, of which whenever they had killed a pig she had hitherto partaken freely; and if she were also careful that no fowls were served at her table which had had their necks wrung, but only such as had had their throats cut and been allowed to bleed. St Paul and the Church of Jerusalem had insisted upon it as necessary that even Gentile converts should abstain from things strangled and from blood, and they had joined this prohibition with that of a vice about the abominable nature of which there could be no question; it would be well therefore to abstain in future and see whether any noteworthy spiritual result ensued. She did abstain, and was certain that from the day of her resolve she had felt stronger, purer at heart, and in all respects more spiritually minded than she had ever felt hitherto. Theobald did not lay so much stress on this as she did, but as she settled what he should have at dinner she could take care that he got no strangled fowls; as for black puddings, happily, he had seen them made when he was a boy, and had never got over his aversion for them. She wished the matter were one of more general observance than it was; this was just a case in which as Lady Winchester she might have been able to do what as plain Mrs Pontifex it was hopeless even to attempt.

And thus this worthy couple jogged on from month to month and from year to year. The reader, if he has passed middle life and has a clerical connection, will probably remember scores and scores of rectors and rectors' wives who differed in no material respect from Theobald and Christina. Speaking from a recollection and experience extending over nearly eight years from the time when I was myself a child in the nursery of a vicarage, I should say I had drawn the better rather than the worse side of the life of an English country parson of some fifty years ago. I admit, however, that there are no such people to be found nowadays. A more united or, on the whole, happier, couple could not have been found in England. One grief only overshadowed the early years of their married life. I mean the fact that no living children were born to them.

Chapter Seventeen

In the course of time this sorrow was removed. At the beginning of the fifth year of her married life Christina was safely delivered of a boy. This was on the sixth of September, 1835.

Word was immediately sent to old Mr Pontifex, who received the news with real pleasure. His son John's wife had borne daughters only, and he was seriously uneasy lest there should be a failure in the male line of his descendants. The good news, therefore, was doubly welcome, and caused as much delight at Elmhurst as dismay at Woburn Square, where the John Pontifexes were then living.

Here, indeed, this freak of fortune was felt to be all the more cruel on account of the impossibility of resenting it openly; but the delighted grandfather cared nothing for what the John Pontifexes might feel or not feel; he had wanted a grandson and he had got a grandson, and this should be enough for everybody; and, now that Mrs Theobald had taken to good ways, she might bring him more grandsons, which would be desirable, for he should not feel safe with fewer than three.

He rang the bell for the butler.

'Gelstrap,' he said solemnly, 'I want to go down into the cellar.'

Then Gelstrap preceded him with a candle, and he went into the inner vault where he kept his choicest wines.

He passed many bins: there was 1803 Port, 1792 Imperial Tokay, 1800 Claret, 1812 Sherry, these and many others were passed, but it was not for them that the head of the Pontifex family had gone down into his inner cellar. A bin, which had appeared empty until the full light of the candle had been brought to bear upon it, was now found to contain a single pint bottle. This was the object of Mr Pontifex's search.

Gelstrap had often pondered over this bottle. It had been placed there by Mr Pontifex himself about a dozen years previously, on his return from a visit to his friend the celebrated traveller, Dr Jones – but there was no tablet above the bin which might give a clue to the nature of its contents. On more than one occasion when his master had gone out and left his keys accidentally behind him, as he sometimes did, Gelstrap had submitted the bottle to all the tests he could venture upon, but it was so carefully sealed that wisdom remained quite shut out from that entrance at which he would have welcomed her most gladly – and indeed from all other entrances, for he could make out nothing at all.

And now the mystery was to be solved. But alas! it seemed as though the last chance of securing even a sip of the contents was to be removed for ever, for Mr Pontifex took the bottle into his own hands and held it up to the light after carefully examining the seal. He smiled and left the bin with the bottle in his hands.

Then came a catastrophe. He stumbled over an empty hamper; there was the sound of a fall – a smash of broken glass, and in an instant the cellar floor was covered with the liquid that had been preserved so carefully for so many years.

With his usual presence of mind Mr Pontifex gasped out a month's warning to Gelstrap. Then he got up, and stamped as Theobald had done when Christina had wanted not to order his dinner.

'It's water from the Jordan,' he exclaimed furiously, 'which I have been saving for the baptism of my eldest grandson. Damn you, Gelstrap, how dare you be so infernally careless as to leave that hamper littering about the cellar?'

I wonder the water of the sacred stream did not stand upright as an heap upon the cellar floor and rebuke him. Gelstrap told the other servants afterwards that his master's language had made his backbone curdle.

The moment, however, that he heard the word 'water,' he saw

his way again, and flew to the pantry. Before his master had well noted his absence he returned with a little sponge and basin, and began sopping up the waters of the Jordan as though they had been a common slop.

'I'll filter it, Sir,' said Gelstrap meekly. 'It'll come quite clean.'

Mr Pontifex saw hope in this suggestion, which was shortly carried out by the help of a piece of blotting paper and a funnel, under his own eyes. Eventually it was found that half a pint was saved, and this was held to be sufficient.

Then he made preparations for a visit to Battersby. He ordered goodly hampers of the choicest eatables, he selected a goodly hamper of choice drinkables. I say choice and not choicest, for although in his first exaltation he had selected some of his very best wine, yet on reflection he had felt that there was moderation in all things, and as he was parting with his best water from the Jordan, he would only send some of his second best wine.

Before he went to Battersby he stayed a day or two in London, which he now seldom did, being over seventy years old, and having practically retired from business. The John Pontifexes, who kept a sharp eye on him, discovered to their dismay that he had had an interview with his solicitors.

Chapter Eighteen

For the first time in his life Theobald felt that he had done something right, and could look forward to meeting his father without alarm. The old gentleman, indeed, had written him a most cordial letter, announcing his intention of standing godfather to the boy – nay, I may as well give it in full, as it shows the writer at his best. It runs:

'Dear Theobald, – Your letter gave me very sincere pleasure, the more so because I had made up my mind for the worst; pray accept my most hearty congratulations for my daughter-in-law and for yourself.

'I have long preserved a phial of water from the Jordan for the christening of my first grandson, should it please God to grant me one. It was given me by my old friend Dr Jones. You will agree with me that though the efficacy of the sacrament does not depend upon the source of the baptismal waters, yet, *ceteris paribus*, there is a sentiment attaching to the waters of the Jordan which should not be despised. Small matters like this sometimes influence a child's whole future career.

'I shall bring my own cook, and have told him to get everything ready for the christening dinner. Ask as many of your best neighbours as your table will hold. By the way, I have told Lesueur *not to get a lobster* – you had better drive over yourself and get one from Saltness (for Battersby was only fourteen or fifteen miles from the sea coast); they are better there, at least I think so, than anywhere else in England.

'I have put your boy down for something in the event of his attaining the age of twenty-one years. If your brother John continues to have nothing but girls I may do more later on, but I have many claims upon me, and am not as well off as you may imagine. – Your affectionate father,

'G. Pontifex.'

A few days afterwards the writer of the above letter made his appearance in a fly which had brought him from Gildenham to Battersby, a distance of fourteen miles. There was Lesueur, the cook, on the box with the driver, and as many hampers as the fly could carry were disposed upon the roof and elsewhere. Next day the John Pontifexes had to come, and Eliza and Maria, as well as Alethea, who, by her own special request, was godmother to the boy, for Mr Pontifex had decided that they were to form a happy family party; so come they all must, and be happy they all must, or it would be the worse for them. Next day the author of all this hubbub was actually christened. Theobald had proposed to call him George after old Mr Pontifex, but strange to say, Mr Pontifex overruled him in favour of the name Ernest. The word 'earnest' was just beginning to come into fashion, and he thought the possession of such a name might, like his having been baptised in water from the Jordan, have a permanent effect upon the boy's character, and influence him for good during the more critical periods of his life.

I was asked to be his second godfather, and was rejoiced to have an opportunity of meeting Alethea, whom I had not seen for some few years, but with whom I had been in constant correspondence. She and I had always been friends from the time we had played together as children onwards. When the death of her grandfather and grandmother severed her connection with Paleham my intimacy with the Pontifexes was kept up by my having been at school and college with Theobald, and each time I saw her I admired her more and more as the best, kindest, wittiest, most lovable, and to my mind, handsomest woman whom I had ever seen. None of the Pontifexes were deficient in good looks;

they were a well-grown shapely family enough, but Alethea was the flower of the flock even as regards good looks, while in respect of all other qualities that make a woman lovable, it seemed as though the stock that had been intended for three daughters, and would have been about sufficient for them, had all been allotted to herself, her sisters getting none, and she all.

It is impossible for me to explain how it was that she and I never married. We two knew exceedingly well, and that must suffice for the reader. There was the most perfect sympathy and understanding between us; we knew that neither of us would marry anyone else. I had asked her to marry me a dozen times over; having said this much I will say no more upon a point which is in no way necessary for the development of my story. For the last few years there had been difficulties in the way of our meeting, and I had not seen her, though, as I have said, keeping up a close correspondence with her. Naturally I was overjoyed to meet her again; she was now just thirty years old, but I thought she looked handsomer than ever.

Her father, of course, was the lion of the party, but seeing that we were all meek and quite willing to be eaten, he roared to us rather than at us. It was a fine sight to see him tucking his napkin under his rosy old gills, and letting it fall over his capacious waist-coat while the high light from the chandelier danced about the bump of benevolence on his bald old head like a star of Bethlehem.

The soup was real turtle; the old gentleman was evidently well pleased and he was beginning to come out. Gelstrap stood behind his master's chair. I sat next Mrs Theobald on her left hand, and was thus just opposite her father-in-law, whom I had every opportunity of observing.

During the first ten minutes or so, which were taken up with the soup and the bringing of the fish, I should probably have thought, if I had not long since made up my mind about him, what a fine old man he was and how proud his children should be of him; but suddenly as he was helping himself to lobster sauce, he flushed crimson, a look of extreme vexation suffused his face, and he darted two furtive but fiery glances to the two ends of the table, one for Theobald and one for Christina. They, poor simple souls, of course, saw that something was exceedingly wrong, and so did I, but I couldn't guess what it was till I heard the old man hiss in Christina's ear: 'It was not made with a hen lobster. What's the use,' he continued, 'of my calling the boy Ernest, and getting him christened in water from the Jordan, if his own father does not know a cock from a hen lobster?'

This cut me too, for I felt that till that moment I had not so much as known that there were cocks and hens among lobsters, but had vaguely thought that in the matter of matrimony they were even as the angels in heaven, and grew up almost spontaneously from rocks and seaweed.

Before the next course was over Mr Pontifex had recovered his temper, and from that time to the end of the evening he was at his best. He told us all about the water from the Jordan; how it had been brought by Dr Jones along with some stone jars of water from the Rhine, the Rhone, the Elbe and the Danube, and what trouble he had had with them at the Custom Houses, and how the intention had been to make punch with waters from all the greatest rivers in Europe; and how he, Mr Pontifex, had saved the Jordan water from going into the bowl, etc., etc. 'No, no, no,' he continued, 'it wouldn't have done at all, you know; very profane idea; so we each took a pint bottle of it home with us, and the punch was much better without it. I had a narrow escape with mine, though, the other day; I fell over a hamper in the cellar, when I was getting it up to bring to Battersby, and if I had not taken the greatest care the bottle would certainly have been broken, but I saved it.' And Gelstrap was standing behind the chair all the time!

Nothing more happened to ruffle Mr Pontifex, so we had a delightful evening, which has often recurred to me while watching the after career of my godson.

I called a day or two afterwards and found Mr Pontifex still at Battersby, laid up with one of those attacks of liver and depression to which he was becoming more and more subject. I stayed to luncheon. The old gentleman was cross and very difficult; he could eat nothing – had no appetite at all. Christina tried to coax him with a little bit of the fleshy part of a mutton chop. 'How in the name of reason can I be asked to eat a mutton chop?' he exclaimed angrily; 'you forget, my dear Christina, that you have to deal with a stomach that is totally disorganised,' and he pushed the plate from him, pouting and frowning like a naughty old child. Writing as I do by the light of a later knowledge, I suppose I should have seen nothing in this but the world's growing pains, the disturbance inseparable from transition in human things. I suppose in reality not a leaf goes yellow in autumn without ceasing to care about its sap and making the parent tree very uncomfortable by long growling and grumbling – but surely nature might find some less irritating way of carrying on business if she would give her mind to it. Why should the generations overlap one another at all? Why cannot we be buried as eggs in neat little cells with ten or twenty thousand pounds each wrapped round us in Bank of England notes, and wake up, as the sphex wasp does, to find that its papa and mamma have not only left ample provision at its elbow, but have been eaten by sparrows some weeks before it began to live consciously on its own account?

About a year and a half afterwards the tables were turned on Battersby – for Mrs John Pontifex was safely delivered of a boy. A year or so later still, George Pontifex was himself struck down suddenly by a fit of paralysis, much as his mother had been, but he did not see the years of his mother. When his will was opened, it was found that the original bequest of £20,000 to Theobald himself (over and above the sum that had been settled upon him and Christina at the time of his marriage) had been cut down to £17,500 when Mr Pontifex left 'something' to Ernest. The 'something' proved to be £2,500, which was to accumulate in the hands of trustees. The rest of the property went to John Pontifex, except that each of the daughters was left with about £15,000 over and above £5,000 apiece which they inherited from their mother.

Theobald's father then had told him the truth but not the whole truth. Nevertheless, what right had Theobald to complain? Certainly it was rather hard to make him think that he and his were to be gainers, and get the honour and glory of the bequest, when all the time the money was virtually being taken out of Theobald's own pocket. On the other hand the father doubtless argued that he had never told Theobald he was to have anything at all; he had a full right to do what he liked with his own money; if Theobald chose to indulge in unwarrantable expectations that was no affair of his; as it was he who was providing for him liberally; and if he did take £2,500 of Theobald's share he was still leaving it to Theobald's son, which, of course, was much the same thing in the end.

No one can deny that the testator had strict right upon his side; nevertheless the reader will agree with me that Theobald and Christina might not have considered the christening dinner so great a success if all the facts had been before them. Mr Pontifex had during his own lifetime set up a monument in Elmhurst Church to the memory of his wife (a slab with urns and cherubs like illegitimate children of King George the Fourth, and all the rest of it), and had left space for his own epitaph underneath that of his wife. I do not know whether it was written by one of his children, or whether they got some friend to write it for them. I do not believe that any satire was intended. I believe that it was the intention to convey that nothing short of the Day of Judgment could give anyone an idea how good a man Mr Pontifex had been, but at first I found it hard to think that it was free from guile.

The epitaph begins by giving dates of birth and death; then

sets out that the deceased was for many years head of the firm of Fairlie and Pontifex, and also resident in the parish of Elmhurst. There is not a syllable of either praise or dispraise. The last lines run as follows: –

HE NOW LIES AWAITING A JOYFUL RESURRECTION

AT THE LAST DAY.

WHAT MANNER OF MAN HE WAS

THAT DAY WILL DISCOVER.

Chapter Nineteen

This much, however, we may say in the meantime, that having lived to be nearly seventy-three years old and died rich he must have been in very fair harmony with his surroundings. I have heard it said sometimes that such and such a person's life was a lie; but no man's life can be a very bad lie; as long as it continues at all it is at worst nine-tenths of it true.

Mr Pontifex's life not only continued a long time, but was prosperous right up to the end. Is not this enough? Being in this world is it not our most obvious business to make the most of it – to observe what things do *bona fide* tend to long life and comfort, and to act accordingly? All animals, except man, know that the principal business of life is to enjoy it – and they do enjoy it as much as man and other circumstances will allow. He has spent his life best who has enjoyed it most; God will take care that we do not enjoy it any more than is good for us. If Mr Pontifex is to be blamed it is for not having eaten and drunk less and thus suffered less from his liver, and lived perhaps a year or two longer.

Goodness is naught unless it tends towards old age and sufficiency of means. I speak broadly and *exceptis excipiendis*. So the psalmist says, 'The righteous shall not lack anything that is good.' Either this is mere poetical license, or it follows that he who lacks anything that is good is not righteous; there is a presumption also that he who has passed a long life without lacking anything that is good has himself also been good enough for practical purposes.

Mr Pontifex never lacked anything he much cared about. True, he might have been happier than he was if he had cared about things which he did not care for, but the gist of this lies in the 'if he had cared.' We have all sinned and come short of the glory of making ourselves as comfortable as we easily might have done, but in this particular case Mr Pontifex did not care, and would not have gained much by getting what he did not want.

There is no casting of swine's meat before men worse than that which would flatter virtue as though her true origin were not good enough for her, but she must have a lineage, deduced as it were by spiritual heralds, from some stock with which she has nothing to do. Virtue's true lineage is older and more respectable than any that can be invented for her. She springs from man's experience concerning his own well-being – and this, though not infallible, is still the least fallible thing we have. A system which cannot stand without a better foundation than this must have something unstable within itself that it will topple over on whatever pedestal we place it.

The world has long ago settled that morality and virtue are what bring men peace at the last. 'Be virtuous,' says the copybook, 'and you will be happy.' Surely if a reputed virtue fails often in this respect it is only an insidious form of vice, and if a reputed vice brings no very serious mischief on a man's later years it is not so bad a vice as it is said to be. Unfortunately though we are all of a mind about the main opinion that virtue is what tends to happiness, and vice what ends in sorrow, we are not so unanimous about details – that is to say as to whether any given course, such, we will say, as smoking, has a tendency to happiness or the reverse.

I submit it as the result of my own poor observation, that a good deal of unkindness and selfishness on the part of parents towards children is not generally followed by ill consequences to the parents themselves. They may cast a gloom over their children's lives for many years without having to suffer anything that will hurt them. I should say, then, that it shows no great moral obliquity on the part of parents if within certain limits they make their children's lives a burden to them.

Granted that Mr Pontifex's was not a very exalted character, ordinary men are not required to have very exalted characters. It is enough if we are of the same moral and mental stature as the 'main' or 'mean' part of men – that is to say as the average.

It is involved in the very essence of things that rich men who die old shall have been mean. The greatest and wisest of mankind will be almost always found to be the meanest – the ones who have kept the 'mean' best between excess either of virtue or vice. They hardly ever have been prosperous if they have not done this, and considering how many miscarry altogether, it is no small feather in a man's cap if he has been no worse than his neighbours. Homer tells us about some one who made it his business αἰὲν ἀριστεύειν ϰαὶ ὑπείϱοχον ἔμμεναι ἄλλων – always to excel and to stand higher than other people. What an uncompanionable, disagreeable person he must have been! Homer's heroes generally came to a bad end, and I doubt not that this gentleman, whoever he was, did so sooner or later.

A very high standard, again, involves the possession of rare virtues, and rare virtues are like rare plants or animals, things that have not been able to hold their own in the world. A virtue to be serviceable must, like gold, be alloyed with some commoner but more durable metal.

People divide off vice and virtue as though they were two things, neither of which had with it anything of the other. This is not so. There is no useful virtue which has not some alloy of vice, and hardly any vice, if any, which carries not with it a little dash of virtue; virtue and vice are like life and death, or mind and matter – things which cannot exist without being qualified by their opposite. The most absolute life contains death, and the corpse is still in many respects living; so also it has been said, 'If thou, Lord, wilt be extreme to mark what is done amiss,' which shows that even the highest ideal we can conceive will yet admit so much compromise with vice as shall countenance the poor abuses of the time, if they are not too outrageous. That vice pays homage to virtue is notorious; we call this hypocrisy; there should be a word found for the homage which virtue not unfrequently pays, or at any rate would be wise in paying, to vice.

I grant that some men will find happiness in having what we all feel to be a higher moral standard than others. If they go in for this, however, they must be content with virtue as her own reward, and not grumble if they find lofty Quixotism an expensive luxury, whose rewards belong to a kingdom that is not of this world. They must not wonder if they cut a poor figure in trying to make the most of both worlds. Disbelieve as we may the details of the accounts which record the growth of the Christian religion, yet a great part of Christian teaching will remain as true as though we accepted the details. We cannot serve God and Mammon; strait is the way and narrow is the gate which leads to what those who live by faith hold to be best worth having, and there is no way of saying this better than the Bible has done. It is well there should be some who think thus, as it is well there should be speculators in commerce, who will often burn their fingers – but it is not well that the majority should leave the 'mean' and beaten path.

For most men, and most circumstances, pleasure – tangible material prosperity in this world – is the safest test of virtue. Progress has ever been through the pleasures rather than through the extreme sharp virtues, and the most virtuous have leaned to excess rather than to asceticism. To use a commercial metaphor, competition is so keen, and the margin of profits has been cut down so closely that virtue cannot afford to throw any *bona fide* chance away, and must base her action rather on the actual moneying out of conduct that on a flattering prospectus. She will not therefore neglect – as some do who are prudent and economical enough in other matters – the important factor of our chance of escaping detection, or at any rate of our dying first. A reasonable virtue will give this chance its due value, neither more nor less.

Pleasure, after all, is a safer guide than either right or duty. For hard as it is to know what gives us pleasure, right and duty are often still harder to distinguish and, if we go wrong with them, will lead us into just as sorry a plight as a mistaken opinion concerning pleasure. When men burn their fingers through following after pleasure they find out their mistake and get to see where they have gone wrong more easily than when they have burnt them through following after a fancied duty, or a fancied idea concerning right virtue. The devil, in fact, when he dresses himself in angel's clothes, can only be detected by experts of exceptional skill, and so often does he adopt this disguise that it is hardly safe to be seen talking to an angel at all, and prudent people will follow after pleasure as a more homely but more respectable and on the whole much more trustworthy guide.

Returning to Mr Pontifex, over and above his having lived long and prosperously, he left numerous offspring, to all of whom he communicated not only his physical and mental characteristics, with no more than the usual amount of modification, but also no small share of characteristics which are less easily transmitted – I mean his pecuniary characteristics. It may be said that he acquired these by sitting still and letting money run, as it were, right up against him, but against how many does not money run who do not take it when it does, or who, even if they hold it for a little while, cannot so incorporate it with themselves that it shall descend through them to their offspring? Mr Pontifex did this. He kept what he may be said to have made, and money is like a reputation for ability – more easily made than kept.

Take him, then, for all in all, I am not inclined to be so severe upon him as my father was. Judge him according to any very lofty standard, and he is nowhere. Judge him according to a fair average standard, and there is not much fault to be found with him. I have said what I have said in the foregoing chapter once for all, and shall not break my thread to repeat it. It should go without saying in modification of the verdict which the reader may be inclined to pass too hastily, not only upon Mr George Pontifex, but also upon Theobald and Christina. And now I will continue my story.

Chapter Twenty

The birth of his son opened Theobald's eyes to a good deal which he had but faintly realised hitherto. He had had no idea how great a nuisance a baby was. Babies come into the world so suddenly at the end, and upset everything so terribly when they do come: why cannot they steal in upon us with less of a shock to the domestic system? His wife, too, did not recover rapidly from her confinement; she remained an invalid for months; here was another nuisance and an expensive one, which interfered with the amount which Theobald liked to put by out of his income against, as he said, a rainy day, or to make provision for his family if he should have one. Now he was getting a family, so that it became all the more necessary to put money by, and here was the baby hindering him. Theorists may say what they like about a man's children being a continuation of his own identity, but it will generally be found that those who talk this way have no children of their own. Practical family men know better.

About twelve months after the birth of Ernest there came a second, also a boy, who was christened Joseph, and in less than twelve months afterwards, a girl, to whom was given the name of Charlotte. A few months before this girl was born Christina paid a visit to the John Pontifexes in London, and, knowing her condition, passed a good deal of time at the Royal Academy exhibition looking at the types of female beauty portrayed by the Academicians, for she had made up her mind that the child this time was to be a girl. Alethea warned her not to do this, but she persisted, and certainly the child turned out plain, but whether the pictures caused this or no I cannot say.

Theobald had never liked children. He had always got away

from them as soon as he could, and so had they from him; oh, why, he was inclined to ask himself, could not children be born into the world grown-up? If Christina could have given birth to a few full-grown clergymen in priest's orders – of moderate views, but inclining rather to Evangelicalism, with comfortable livings and in all respects facsimiles of Theobald himself – why, there might have been more sense in it; or if people could buy ready-made children at a shop of whatever age and sex they liked, instead of always having to make them at home and to begin at the beginning with them – that might do better, but as it was he did not like it. He felt as he had felt when he had been required to come and be married to Christina – that he had been going on for a long time quite nicely, and would much rather continue things on their present footing. In the matter of getting married he had been obliged to pretend he liked it; but times were changed, and if he did not like a thing now, he could find a hundred unexceptionable ways of making his dislike apparent.

It might have been better if Theobald in his younger days had kicked more against his father: the fact that he had not done so encouraged him to expect the most implicit obedience from his own children. He could trust himself, he said (and so did Christina), to be more lenient than perhaps his father had been to himself; his danger, he said (and so again did Christina), would be rather in the direction of being too indulgent; he must be on his guard against this, for no duty could be more important than that of teaching a child to obey its parents in all things.

He had read not long since of an Eastern traveller, who, while exploring somewhere in the more remote parts of Arabia and Asia Minor, had come upon a remarkably hardy, sober, industrious little Christian community – all of them in the best of health – who had turned out to be the actual living descendants of Jonadab, the son of Rechab; and two men in European costume, indeed, but speaking English with a broken accent, and by their colour evidently Oriental, had come begging to Battersby soon afterwards, and represented themselves as belonging to this people; they had said they were collecting funds to promote the conversion of their fellow tribesmen to the English branch of the Christian religion. True, they turned out to be imposters, for when he gave them a pound and Christina five shillings from her private purse, they went and got drunk with it in the next village but one to Battersby; still, this did not invalidate the story of the Eastern traveller. Then there were the Romans – whose greatness was probably due to the wholesome authority exercised by the head of a family over all its members. Some Romans had even killed their children; this was going too far, but then the Romans were not Christians, and knew no better.

The practical outcome of the foregoing was a conviction in Theobald's mind, and if in his, then in Christina's, that it was their duty to begin training up their children in the way they should go, even from their earliest infancy. The first signs of self-will must be carefully looked for, and plucked up by the roots at once before they had time to grow. Theobald picked up this numb serpent of a metaphor and cherished it in his bosom.

Before Ernest could well crawl he was taught to kneel; before he could well speak he was taught to lisp the Lord's prayer, and the general confession. How was it possible that these things could be taught too early? If his attention flagged or his memory failed him, here was an ill weed which would grow apace, unless it were plucked out immediately, and the only way to pluck it out was to whip him, or shut him up in a cupboard, or dock him of some of the small pleasures of childhood. Before he was three years old he could read and, after a fashion, write. Before he was four he was learning Latin, and could do rule of three sums.

As for the child himself, he was naturally of an even temper, he doted upon his nurse, on kittens and puppies, and on all things that would do him the kindness of allowing him to be fond of them. He was fond of his mother, too, but as regards his father, he has told me in later life he could remember no feeling but fear and shrinking. Christina did not remonstrate with Theobald concerning the severity of the tasks imposed upon their boy, nor yet as to the continual whippings that were found necessary at lesson times. Indeed, when during any absence of Theobald's the lessons were entrusted to her, she found to her sorrow that it was the only thing to do, and she did it no less effectually than Theobald himself; nevertheless she was fond of her boy, which Theobald never was, and it was long before she could destroy all affection for herself in the mind of her first-born. But she persevered.

Chapter Twenty-One

Strange! for she believed she doted upon him, and certainly she loved him better than either of her other children. Her version of the matter was that there had never yet been two parents so self-denying and devoted to the highest welfare of their children as Theobald and herself. For Ernest, a very great future – she was certain of it – was in store. This made severity all the more necessary, so that from the first he might have been kept pure from every taint of evil. She could not allow herself the scope for castle building which, we read, was indulged in by every Jewish matron before the appearance of the Messiah, for the Messiah had now come, but there was to be a millennium shortly, certainly not later than 1866, when Ernest would be just about the right age for it, and a modern Elias would be wanted to herald its approach. Heaven would bear her witness that she had never shrunk from the idea of martyrdom for herself and Theobald, nor would she avoid it for her boy, if his life was required of her in her Redeemer's service. Oh, no! If God told her to offer up her first-born, as He had told Abraham, she would take him up to Pigbury Beacon and plunge the – no, that she could not do, but it would be unnecessary – some one else might do that. It was not for nothing that Ernest had been baptised in water from the Jordan. It had not been her doing, nor yet Theobald's. They had not sought it. When water from the sacred stream was wanted for a sacred infant, the channel had been found through which it was to flow from far Palestine over land and sea to the door of the house where the child was lying. Why, it was a miracle! It was! It was! She saw it all now. The Jordan had left its bed and flowed into her own house. It was idle to say that this was not a miracle. No miracle was effected without means of some kind; the difference between the faithful and the unbeliever consisted in the very fact that the former could see a miracle where the latter could not. The Jews could see no miracle even in the raising of Lazarus and the feeding of the five thousand. The John Pontifexes would see no miracle in this matter of the water from the Jordan. The essence of a miracle lay not in the fact that means had been dispensed with, but in the adoption of means to a great end that had not been available without interference; and no one would suppose that Dr Jones would have brought the water unless he had been directed. She would tell this to Theobald, and get him to see it in the . . . and yet perhaps it would be better not. The insight of women upon matters of this sort was deeper and more unerring than that of men. It was a woman and not a man who had been filled most completely with the whole fulness of the Deity. But why had they not treasured up the water after it was used? It ought never, never to have been thrown away, but it had been. Perhaps, however, this was for the best too – they might have been tempted to set too much store by it, and it might have become a source of spiritual danger to them – perhaps even of spiritual pride, the very sin of all others which she most abhorred. As for the channel through which the Jordan had flowed to Battersby, that mattered not more than the earth through which the river ran in Palestine itself. Dr Jones was certainly worldly – very worldly; so, she regretted to feel, had been her father-in-law, though in a less degree; spiritual, at heart, doubtless, and becoming more and more spiritual continually as he grew older, still he was tainted with the world, till a very few hours, probably, before his death, whereas she and Theobald had given up all for Christ's sake. *They* were not worldly. At least Theobald was not. She had been, but she was sure she had grown in grace since she had left off eating things strangled and blood – this was as the washing in Jordan as against Abana and Pharpar, rivers of Damascus. Her boy should never touch a strangled fowl nor a black pudding –

that, at any rate, she could see to. He should have a coral from the neighbourhood of Joppa – there were coral insects on those coasts, so that the thing could easily be done with a little energy; she would write to Dr Jones about it, etc. And so on for hours together day after day for years. Truly, Mrs Theobald loved her child according to her lights with an exceeding great fondness, but the dreams she had dreamed in sleep were sober realities in comparison with those she indulged in while awake.

When Ernest was in his second year, Theobald, as I have already said, began to teach him to read. He began to whip him two days after he had begun to teach him.

'It was painful,' as he said to Christina, but it was the only thing to do and it was done. The child was puny, white and sickly, so they sent continually for the doctor who dosed him with calomel and James's powder. All was done in love, anxiety, timidity, stupidity, and impatience. They were stupid in little things; and he that is stupid in little will be stupid also in much.

Presently old Mr Pontifex died, and then came the revelation of the little alteration he had made in his will simultaneously with his bequest to Ernest. It was rather hard to bear, especially as there was no way of conveying a bit of their minds to the testator now that he could no longer hurt them. As regards the boy himself anyone must see that the bequest would be an unmitigated misfortune to him. To leave him a small independence was perhaps the greatest injury which one could inflict upon a young man. It would cripple his energies, and deaden his desire for active employment. Many a youth was led into evil courses by the knowledge that on arriving at majority he would come into a few thousands. They might surely have been trusted to have their boy's interests at heart, and must be better judges of those interests than he, at twenty-one, could be expected to be: besides if Jonadab, the son of Rechab's father – or perhaps it might be simpler under the circumstances to say Rechab at once – if Rechab, then, had left handsome legacies to his grandchildren – why,

Jonadab might not have found those children so easy to deal with, etc. 'My dear,' said Theobald, after having discussed the matter with Christina for the twentieth time, 'my dear, the only thing to guide and console us under misfortunes of this kind is to take refuge in practical work. I will go and pay a visit to Mrs Thompson.'

On those days Mrs Thompson would be told that her sins were all washed white, etc., a little sooner and a little more peremptorily than on others.

Chapter Twenty-Two

I used to stay at Battersby for a day or two sometimes, while my godson and his brother and sister were children. I hardly know why I went, for Theobald and I grew more and more apart, but one gets into grooves sometimes, and the supposed friendship between myself and the Pontifexes continued to exist, though it was now little more than rudimentary. My godson pleased me more than either of the other children, but he had not much of the buoyancy of childhood, and was more like a puny, sallow little old man than I liked. The young people, however, were very ready to be friendly.

I remember Ernest and his brother hovered round me on the first day of one of these visits with their hands full of fading flowers, which they at length proffered me. On this I did what I suppose was expected: I inquired if there was a shop near where they could buy sweeties. They said there was, so I felt in my pockets, but only succeeded in finding two pence halfpenny in small money. This I gave them, and the youngsters, aged four and three, toddled off alone. Ere long they returned, and Ernest said, 'We can't get sweeties for all this money' (I felt rebuked, but no rebuke was intended); 'we can get sweeties for this' (showing a penny), 'and for this' (showing another penny), 'but we cannot get them for all this,' and he added the halfpenny to the two pence. I suppose they had wanted a twopenny cake, or something like that. I was amused, and left them to solve the difficulty their own way, being anxious to see what they would do.

Presently Ernest said, 'May we give you back this' (showing the halfpenny) 'and not give you back this and this?' (showing the pence). I assented, and they gave a sigh of relief and went on their way rejoicing. A few more presents of pence and small toys completed the conquest, and they began to take me into their confidence.

They told me a good deal which I am afraid I ought not to have listened to. They said that if grandpapa had lived longer he would most likely have been made a Lord, and that then papa would have been the Honourable and Reverend, but that grandpapa was now in heaven singing beautiful hymns with grandmamma Allaby to Jesus Christ, who was very fond of them; and that when Ernest was ill, his mamma had told him he need not be afraid of dying, for he would go straight to heaven, if he would only be sorry for having done his lessons so badly and vexed his dear papa, and if he would promise never, never to vex him any more; and that when he got to heaven grandpapa and grandmamma Allaby would meet him, and he would be always with them, and they would be very good to him and teach him to sing ever such beautiful hymns, more beautiful by far than those which he was now so fond of, etc., etc.; but he did not wish to die, and was glad when he got better, for there were no kittens in heaven, and he did not think there were cowslips to make a cowslip tea with.

Their mother was plainly disappointed in them. 'My children are none of them geniuses, Mr Overton,' she said to me at breakfast one morning. 'They have fair abilities, and, thanks to Theobald's tuition, they are forward for their years, but they have nothing like genius: genius is a thing apart from this, is it not?'

Of course I said it was 'a thing quite apart from this,' but if my thoughts had been laid bare, they would have appeared as 'Give me my coffee immediately, ma'am, and don't talk nonsense.' I have no idea what genius is, but so far as I can form any conception about it, I should say it was a stupid word which cannot be too soon abandoned to scientific and literary *claqueurs*.

I do not know exactly what Christina expected, but I should imagine it was something like this: 'My children ought to be all geniuses, because they are mine and Theobald's, and it is naughty of them not to be; but, of course, they cannot be so good and clever as Theobald and I were, and if they show signs of being so it will be naughty of them. Happily, however, they are not this, and yet it is very dreadful that they are not. As for genius – hoity-toity, indeed – why, a genius should turn intellectual somersaults as soon as it is born, and none of my children have yet been able to get into the newspapers. I will not have children of mine give themselves airs – it is enough for them that Theobald and I should do so.'

She did not know, poor woman, that the true greatness wears an invisible cloak, under cover of which it goes in and out among men without being suspected; if its cloak does not conceal it from itself always, and from all others for many years, its greatness will ere long shrink to very ordinary dimensions. What, then, it may be asked, is the good of being great? The answer is that you may understand greatness better in others, whether alive or dead, and choose better company from these and enjoy and understand that company better when you have chosen it – also that you may be able to give pleasure to the best people and live in the lives of those who are yet unborn. This, one would think, was substantial gain enough for greatness without its wanting to ride rough-shod over us, even when disguised as humility.

I was there on a Sunday, and observed the rigour with which the young people were taught to observe the Sabbath; they might not cut out things, nor use their paint-box on a Sunday, and this they thought rather hard, because their cousins the John Pontifexes might do these things. Their cousins might play with their toy train on Sunday, but though they had promised that they would run none but Sunday trains, all traffic had been prohibited. One treat only was allowed them – on Sunday evenings they might choose their own hymns.

In the course of the evening they came into the drawing-room, and, as an especial treat, were to sing some of their hymns to me, instead of saying them, so that I might hear how nicely they sang. Ernest was to choose the first hymn, and he chose one about some people who were to come to the sunset tree. I am no botanist, and do not know what kind of tree a sunset tree is, but the words began, 'Come, come, come; come to the sunset tree for the day is past and gone.' The tune was rather pretty and had taken Ernest's fancy, for he was unusually fond of music and had a sweet little child's voice which he liked using.

He was, however, very late in being able to sound a hard 'c' or 'k,' and, instead of saying 'Come,' he said 'Tum, tum, tum.'

'Ernest,' said Theobald, from the arm-chair in front of the fire, where he was sitting with his hands folded before him, 'don't you think it would be very nice if you were to say "come" like other people, instead of "tum"?'

'I do say tum,' replied Ernest, meaning that he had said 'come.'

Theobald was always in a bad temper on Sunday evening. Whether it is that they are as much bored with the day as their neighbours, or whether they are tired, or whatever the cause may be, clergymen are seldom at their best on Sunday evening; I had already seen signs that evening that my host was cross, and was a little nervous at hearing Ernest say so promptly 'I do say tum,' when his papa had said he did not say it as he should.

Theobald noticed the fact that he was being contradicted in a moment. He got up from his arm-chair and went to the piano.

'No, Ernest, you don't,' he said, 'you say nothing of the kind, you say "tum," not "come." Now say "come" after me, as I do.'

'Tum,' said Ernest, at once; 'Is that better?' I have no doubt he thought it was, but it was not.

'Now, Ernest, you are not taking pains: you are not trying as you ought to do. It is high time you learned to say "come," why, Joey can say "come," can't you, Joey?'

'Yeth, I can,' replied Joey, and he said something which was not far off 'come.'

'There, Ernest, do you hear that? There's no difficulty about it, nor shadow of difficulty. Now, take your own time, think about it, and say "come" after me.'

The boy remained silent for a few seconds and then said 'tum' again.

I laughed, but Theobald turned to me impatiently and said, 'Please do not laugh, Overton; it will make the boy think it does not matter, and it matters a great deal;' then turning to Ernest, he said, 'Now, Ernest. I will give you one more chance, and if you don't say "come," I shall know that you are self-willed and naughty.'

He looked very angry, and a shade came over Ernest's face, like that which comes upon the face of a puppy when it is being scolded without understanding why. The child saw well what was coming now, was frightened, and, of course, said 'tum' once more.

'Very well, Ernest,' said his father, catching him angrily by the shoulder, 'I have done my best to save you, but if you will have it so, you will,' and he lugged the little wretch, crying by anticipation, out of the room. A few minutes more and we could hear screams coming from the dining-room, across the hall which separated the drawing-room from the dining-room, and knew that poor Ernest was being beaten.

'I have sent him to bed,' said Theobald, as he returned to the drawing-room, 'and now, Christina, I think we will have the servants in to prayers,' and he rang the bell for them, red-handed as he was.

Chapter Twenty-Three

The man-servant William came and set the chairs for the maids, and presently they filed in. First Christina's maid, then the cook, then the housemaid, then William, and then the coachman. I sat opposite them, and watched their faces as Theobald read a chapter from the Bible. They were nice people, but more absolute vacancy I never saw upon the countenances of human beings.

Theobald began by reading a few verses from the Old Testament, according to some system of his own. On this occasion the passage came from the fifteenth chapter of Numbers: it had no particular bearing that I could see upon anything which was going on just then, but the spirit which breathed throughout the whole seemed to me to be so like that of Theobald himself, that I could understand better after hearing it, how he came to think as he thought, and act as he acted.

The verses are as follows:

'But the soul that doeth aught presumptuously, whether he be born in the land or a stranger, the same reproacheth the Lord; and that soul shall be cut off from among his people.

'Because he hath despised the word of the Lord, and hath broken His commandments, that soul shall be utterly cut off; his iniquity shall be upon him.

'And while the children of Israel were in the wilderness they found a man that gathered sticks upon the Sabbath day.

'And they that found him gathering sticks brought him unto Moses and Aaron, and unto all the congregation.

'And they put him in ward because it was not declared what should be done to him.

'And the Lord said unto Moses, the man shall be surely put to death; all the congregation shall stone him with stones without the camp.

'And all the congregation brought him without the camp, and stoned him with stones, and he died; as the Lord commanded Moses.

'And the Lord spake unto Moses, saying,

'Speak unto the children of Israel, and bid them that they make them fringes in the borders of their garments throughout their generations, and that they put upon the fringe of the borders a ribband of blue.

'And it shall be unto you for a fringe, that ye may look upon it and remember all the commandments of the Lord, and do them, and that ye seek not after your own heart and your own eyes.

'That ye may remember and do all my commandments and be holy unto your God.

'I am the Lord your God which brought you out of the land of Egypt, to be your God: I am the Lord your God.'

My thoughts wandered while Theobald was reading the above, and reverted to a little matter which I had observed in the course of the afternoon.

It happened that some years previously, a swarm of bees had taken up their abode in the roof of the house under the slates, and had multiplied so that the drawing-room was a good deal frequented by these bees during the summer, when the windows were open. The drawing-room paper was of a pattern which consisted of bunches of red and white roses, and I saw several bees at different times fly up to these bunches and try them, under the impression that they were real flowers; having tried one bunch, they tried the next, and the next, and the next, till they reached the one that was nearest the ceiling, then they went down bunch by bunch as they had ascended, till they were stopped by the back of the sofa; on this they ascended bunch by bunch to the ceiling again; and so on, and so on till I was tired of watching them. As I thought of the family prayers being repeated night and morning, week by week, month by month, and year by year, I could not help thinking how like it was to the way in which the bees went up the wall and down the wall, bunch by bunch, without ever suspecting that so many of the associated ideas could be present, and yet the main idea be wanting hopelessly, and for ever.

When Theobald had finished reading we all knelt down and the Carlo Dolci and the Sassoferrato looked down upon a sea of upturned backs, as we buried our faces in our chairs. I noted that Theobald prayed that we might be made 'truly honest and conscientious' in all our dealings, and smiled at the introduction of the 'truly.' Then my thoughts ran back to the bees and I reflected that, after all, it was perhaps as well at any rate for Theobald that our prayers were seldom marked by any very encouraging degree of response, for if I had thought there was the slightest chance of my being heard I should have prayed that some one might ere long treat him as he had treated Ernest.

Then my thoughts wandered on to those calculations which people make about waste of time and how much one can get done if one gives ten minutes a day to it, and I was thinking what improper suggestion I could make in connection with this and the time spent in family prayers which should at the same time be just tolerable, when I heard Theobald beginning 'The grace of our Lord Jesus Christ' and in a few seconds the ceremony was over, and the servants filed out again as they had filed in.

As soon as they had left the drawing-room, Christina, who was a little ashamed of the transaction to which I had been a witness, imprudently returned to it, and began to justify it, saying that it cut her to the heart, and that it cut Theobald to the heart and a good deal more, but that 'it was the only thing to be done.'

I received this as coldly as I decently could, and by my silence during the rest of the evening showed that I disapproved of what I had seen.

Next day I was to go back to London, but before I went I said I should like to take some new-laid eggs back with me, so Theobald took me to the house of a labourer in the village who lived a stone's throw from the Rectory as being likely to supply me with them. Ernest, for some reason or other, was allowed to come too. I think the hens had begun to sit, but at any rate eggs were scarce, and the cottager's wife could not find me more than seven or eight, which we proceeded to wrap up in separate pieces of paper so that I might take them to town safely.

This operation was carried on upon the ground in front of the cottage door, and while we were in the midst of it the cottager's little boy, a lad much about Ernest's age, trod upon one of the eggs that was wrapped up in paper and broke it.

'There now, Jack,' said his mother, 'see what you've done, you've broken a nice egg and cost me a penny – here, Emma,' she added, calling to her daughter, 'take the child away, there's a dear.'

Emma came at once, and walked off with the youngster, taking him out of harm's way.

'Papa,' said Ernest, after we had left the house, 'why didn't Mrs Heaton whip Jack when he trod on the egg?'

I was spiteful enough to give Theobald a grim smile which said as plainly as words could have done that I thought Ernest had hit him rather hard.

Theobald coloured and looked angry. 'I dare say,' he said quickly, 'that his mother will whip him now that we are gone.'

I was not going to have this and said I did not believe it, and so the matter dropped, but Theobald did not forget it and my visits to Battersby were henceforth less frequent.

On our return to the house we found the postman had arrived and had brought a letter appointing Theobald to a rural deanery which had lately fallen vacant by the death of one of the neighbouring clergy who had held the office for many years. The bishop wrote to Theobald most warmly, and assured him that he valued him as among the most hard-working and devoted of his parochial clergy. Christina, of course, was delighted, and gave me to understand that it was only an instalment of the much higher dignities which were in store for Theobald when his merits were more widely known.

I did not then foresee how closely my godson's life and mine were in after years to be bound up together; if I had, I should doubtless have looked upon him with different eyes and noted much to which I paid no attention at the time. As it was, I was glad to get away from him, for I could do nothing for him, or chose to say that I could not, and the sight of so much suffering was painful to me. A man should not only have his own way as far as possible, but he should only consort with such things that are getting their own way so far as they are at any rate comfortable. Unless for short times under exceptional circumstances, he should not even see things that have been stunted or starved, much less should he eat meat that has been vexed by having been over-driven, or underfed, or afflicted with any disease; nor should he touch vegetables that have not been well grown. For all these things cross a man; whatever a man comes in contact with in any way forms a cross with him which will leave him better or worse, and the better things he is crossed with the more likely he is to live long and happily. All things must be crossed a little or they would cease to live – but holy things, such, for example, as Giovanni Bellini's saints, have been crossed with nothing but what is good of its kind.

Chapter Twenty-Four

The storm which I have described in the previous chapter was a sample of those that occurred daily for many years. No matter how clear the sky, it was always liable to cloud over now in one quarter now in another, and the thunder and lightning were upon the young people before they knew where they were.

'And then, you know,' said Ernest to me, when I asked him not long since to give me more of his childish reminiscences for the benefit of my story, 'we used to learn Mrs Barbould's hymns; they were in prose, and there was one about the lion which began, "Come, and I will show you what is strong. The lion is strong; when he raiseth himself from his lair, when he shaketh his mane, when the voice of his roaring is heard the cattle of the field fly, and the beasts of the desert hide themselves, for he is very terrible." I used to say this to Joey and Charlotte about my father himself when I got a little older, but they were always didactic, and said it was naughty of me.

'One great reason why clergymen's households are generally unhappy is because the clergyman is so much at home or close about the house. The doctor is out visiting patients half his time: the lawyer and the merchant have offices away from home, but the clergyman has no official place of business which shall ensure his being away from home for many hours together at stated times. Our great days were when my father went for a day's shopping to Gildenham. We were some miles from this place, and commissions used to accumulate on my father's list till he would make a day of it and go and do the lot. As soon as his back was turned the air felt lighter; as soon as the hall door opened to let him in again, the law with its all-reaching "touch not, taste not, handle not," was upon us again. The worst of it was that I could never trust Joey and Charlotte; they would go a good way with me and then turn back, or even the whole way, and then their consciences would compel them to tell papa and mamma. They liked running with the hare up to a certain point, but their instinct was towards the hounds.

'It seems to me,' he continued, 'that the family is a survival of the principle which is more logically embodied in the compound animal – and the compound animal is a form of life which has been found incompatible with high development. I would do with the family among mankind what nature has done with the compound animal, and confine it to the lower and less progressive races. Certainly there is no inherent love for the family system on the part of nature herself. Poll the forms of life and you will find it in a ridiculously small minority. The fishes know it not, and they get along quite nicely. The ants and the bees, who far outnumber man, sting their fathers to death as a matter of course, and are given to the atrocious mutilation of nine-tenths of the offspring committed to their charge, yet where shall we find communities more universally respected? Take the cuckoo again – is there any bird which we like better?'

I saw he was running off from his own reminiscences and tried to bring him back to them, but it was no use.

'What a fool,' he said, 'a man is to remember anything that happened more than a week ago unless it was pleasant, or unless he wants to make some use of it.

'Sensible people get the greater part of their own dying done during their own life-time. A man at five and thirty should no more regret not having had a happier childhood than he should regret not having been born a prince of the blood. He might be happier if he had been more fortunate in childhood, but, for aught he knows, if he had, something else might have happened which might have killed him long ago. If I had to be born again I would be born at Battersby of the same father and mother as before, and I would not alter anything that has ever happened to me.'

The most amusing incident that I can remember about his childhood was that when he was about seven years old he told me he was going to have a natural baby. I asked him his reasons for thinking this, and he explained that papa and mamma had always told him that nobody had children till they were married, and as long as he had believed this, of course, he had had no idea of having a child till he was grown up; but not long since he had been reading Mrs Markham's history of England and had come upon the words 'John of Gaunt had several natural children,' he had therefore asked his governess what a natural child was – were not all children natural?

'Oh, my dear,' said she, 'a natural child is a child a person has before he is married.' On this it seemed to follow logically that if John of Gaunt had had children before he was married, he, Ernest Pontifex, might have them also, and he would be obliged to me if I would tell him what he had better do under the circumstances.

I inquired how long ago he had made this discovery. He said about a fortnight, and he did not know where to look for the child, for it might come at any moment. 'You know,' he said, 'babies come so suddenly; one goes to bed one night and next morning there is a baby. Why, it might die of cold if we are not on the look-out for it. I hope it will be a boy.'

'And you have told your governess about this?'

'Yes, but she puts me off and does not help me: she says it will not come for many years, and she hopes not then.'

'Are you quite sure that you have not made any mistake in all this?'

'Oh, no; because Mrs Burne, you know, called here a few days ago, and I was sent for to be looked at. And mamma held me out at arm's length and said, "Is he Mr Pontifex's child, Mrs Burne, or is he mine?" Of course, she couldn't have said this if papa had not had some of the children himself. I did think the gentleman had all the boys and the lady all the girls; but it can't be like this, or else mamma would not haved asked Mrs Burne to guess; but then Mrs Burne said, "Oh, he's Mr Pontifex's child, of course,"; and I didn't quite know what she meant by saying "of course"; it seemed as though I was right in thinking that the husband has all the boys and the wife all the girls; I wish you would explain to me all about it.'

This I could hardly do, so I changed the conversation, after reassuring him as best I could.

Chapter Twenty-Five

Three or four years after the birth of her daughter, Christina had had one more child. She had never been strong since she married, and had a presentiment that she should not survive this last confinement. She accordingly wrote the following letter, which was to be given, as she endorsed upon it, to her sons when Ernest was sixteen years old. It reached him on his mother's death many years later, for it was the baby who died now, and not Christina. It was found among papers which she had repeatedly and carefully arranged, with the seal already broken. This, I am afraid, shows that Christina had read it and thought it too creditable to be destroyed when the occasion that had called it forth had gone by. It is as follows:

'Battersby, *March* 15th, 1841.

'My Two Dear Boys, – When this is put into your hands will you try to bring to mind the mother whom you lost in your childhood and whom, I fear, you will almost have forgotten? You, Ernest, will remember her best, for you are past five years old, and the many, many times that she has taught you your prayers and hymns and sums and told you stories, and our happy Sunday evenings will not quite have passed from your mind, and you, Joey, though only four, will perhaps recollect some of these things. My dear, dear boys, for the sake of that mother who loved you very dearly – and for the sake of your own happiness for ever and ever – attend to and try to remember, and from time to time read over again the last words she can ever speak to you. When I think about leaving you all, two things press heavily upon me: one, your father's sorrow (for you, my darlings, after missing me a little while, will soon forget your loss), the other, the everlasting welfare of my children. I know how long and deep the former will be, and I know that he will look to his children to be almost his only earthly comfort. You know (for I am certain that it will have been so) how he has devoted his life to you and taught you and laboured to lead you to all that is right and good. Oh, then, be sure that you *are* his comforts. Let him find you obedient, affectionate and attentive to his wishes, upright, self-denying and diligent; let him never blush for or grieve over the sins and follies of those who owe him such a debt of gratitude, and whose first duty it is to study his happiness. You have both of you a name which must not be disgraced, a father and a grandfather of whom to show yourselves worthy; your respectability and well-doing in life rest mainly with yourselves, but far, far beyond earthly respectability and well-doing, and compared with which they are as nothing, your eternal happiness rests with yourselves. You *know* your duty, but snares and temptations from without beset you, and the nearer you approach to manhood the more strongly will you feel this. With God's help, with God's word, and with humble hearts you will stand in spite of everything, but should you leave off seeking in earnest for the first, and applying to the second, should you learn to trust in yourselves, or to the advice and example of too many around you, you will, you must fall. Oh, "let God be true and every man a liar." He says you *cannot* serve Him and Mammon. He says that strait is the gate that leads to eternal life. Many there are who seek to widen it; they will tell you that such and such self-indulgences are but venial offences – that this and that worldly compliance is excusable and even necessary. The thing *cannot* be; for in a hundred and a hundred places He tells you so – look to your Bibles and seek there whether such counsel is true – and if not, oh, "halt not between two opinions," if God is the Lord follow *Him*; only be strong and of a good courage, and He will never leave you nor forsake you.

Remember, there is not in the Bible one law for the rich and one for the poor – one for the educated and one for the ignorant. To *all* there is but one thing needful. *All* are to be living to God and their fellow-creatures, and not to themselves. *All* must seek first the Kingdom of God and His righteousness – must *deny themselves*, be pure and chaste and charitable in the fullest and widest sense – all, "forgetting those things that are behind," must "press forward towards the mark, for the prize of the high calling of God."

'And now I will add but two things more. Be true through life to each other, love as only brothers should do, strengthen, warn, encourage one another, and let who will be against you, let each feel that in his brother he has a firm and faithful friend who will be so to the end; and, oh! be kind and watchful over your dear sister; without mother or sisters she will doubly need her brothers' love and tenderness and confidence. I am certain she will seek them, and will love you and try to make you happy; be sure then that you do not fail her, and remember, that were she to lose her father and remain unmarried, she would doubly need protectors. To you, then, I especially commend her. Oh! my three darling children, be true to each other, your Father, and your God. May He guide and bless you, and grant that in a better and happier world I and mine may meet again. – Your most affectionate mother,

'Christina Pontifex.'

From inquiries I have made, I have satisfied myself that most mothers write letters like this shortly before their confinements, and that fifty per cent keep them afterwards, as Christina did.

Chapter Twenty-Six

The foregoing letter shows how much greater was Christina's anxiety for the eternal than for the temporal welfare of her sons. One would have thought she had sowed enough of such religious wild oats by this time, but she had plenty still to sow. To me it seems that those who are happy in this world are better and more lovable people than those who are not, and that thus in the event of a Resurrection and Day of Judgment, they will be the most likely to be deemed worthy of a heavenly mansion. Perhaps a dim unconscious perception of this was the reason why Christina was so anxious for Theobald's earthly happiness, or was it merely due to a conviction that his eternal welfare was so much a matter of course that it only remained to secure his earthly happiness? He was to 'find his sons obedient, affectionate, attentive to his wishes, self-denying and diligent,' a goodly string, forsooth, of all the virtues most convenient to parents; he was never to have to blush for the follies of those 'who owed him such a debt of gratitude,' and 'whose first duty it was to study his happiness.' How like maternal solicitude is this! Solicitude for the most part lest the offspring should come to have wishes and feelings of its own, which may occasion may difficulties, fancied or real. It is this that is at the bottom of the whole mischief; but whether this last proposition is granted or no, at any rate we observe that Christina had a sufficiently keen appreciation of the duties of children towards their parents, and felt the task of fulfilling them adequately to be so difficult that she was very doubtful how far Ernest and Joey would succeed in mastering it. It is plain, in fact, that her supposed parting glance upon them was one of suspicion. But there was no suspicion of Theobald; that he should have devoted his life to his children – why, this was such a mere platitude, as almost to go without saying.

How, let me ask, was it possible that a child only a little past five years old, trained in such an atmosphere of prayers and hymns and sums and happy Sunday evenings – to say nothing of daily repeated beatings over the said prayers and hymns, etc., about which our authoress is silent – how was it possible that a lad so trained should grow up in any healthy or vigorous develop-ment, even though in her own way his mother was undoubtedly very fond of him, and sometimes told him stories? Can the eye of any reader fail to detect the coming wrath of God as about to descend upon the head of him who should be nurtured under the shadow of such a letter as the foregoing?

I have often thought that the Church of Rome does wisely in not allowing her priests to marry. Certainly it is a matter of com-mon observation in England that the sons of clergymen are frequently unsatisfactory. The explanation is very simple, but is so often lost sight of that I may perhaps be pardoned for giving it here.

The clergyman is expected to be a kind of human Sunday. Things must not be done in him which are venial in the weekday classes. He is paid for this business of leading a stricter life than other people. It is his *raison d'être*. If his parishioners feel that he does this, they approve of him, for they look upon him as their own contribution towards what they deem a holy life. This is why the clergyman is so often called a vicar – he being the person whose vicarious goodness is to stand for that of those entrusted to his charge. But his home is his castle as much as that of any other Englishman, and with him, as with others, unnatural ten-sion in public is followed by exhaustion when tension is no longer necessary. His children are the most defenceless things he can reach, and it is on them in nine cases out of ten that he will relieve his mind.

A clergyman, again, can hardly ever allow himself to look facts fairly in the face. It is his profession to support one side; it is impossible, therefore, for him to make an unbiased examination of the other.

We forget that every clergyman with a living or curacy is as much a paid advocate as the barrister who is trying to persuade a jury to acquit a prisoner. We should listen to him with the same suspense of judgment, the same full consideration of the arguments of the opposing counsel, as a judge does when he is trying a case. Unless we know these, and can state them in a way that our opponents would admit to be a fair representation of their views, we have no right to claim that we have formed an opinion at all. The misfortune is that by the law of the land one side only can be heard.

Theobald and Christina were no exceptions to the general rule. When they came to Battersby they had every desire to fulfil the duties of their position, and to devote themselves to the honour and glory of God. But it was Theobald's duty to see the honour and glory of God through the eyes of a Church which had lived three hundred years without finding reason to change a single one of its opinions.

I should doubt whether he ever got as far as doubting the wisdom of his Church upon any single matter. His scent for possible mischief was tolerably keen; so was Christina's, and it is likely that if either of them detected in him or herself the first faint symptoms of a want of faith they were nipped no less peremptorily in the bud, than signs of self-will in Ernest were – and I should imagine more successfully. Yet Theobald considered himself, and was generally considered to be, and indeed perhaps was, an exceptionally truthful person; indeed he was generally looked upon as an embodiment of all those virtues which make the poor respectable and the rich respected. In the course of time he and his wife became persuaded even to unconsciousness, that no one could even dwell under their roof without deep cause for thankfulness. Their children, their servants, their parishioners must be fortunate *ipso facto* that they were theirs. There was no road to happiness here or hereafter, but the road that they had themselves travelled, no good people who did not think as they did upon every subject, and no reasonable person who had wants the gratification of which would be inconvenient to them – Theobald and Christina.

This was how it came to pass that their children were white and puny; they were suffering from *home-sickness*. They were starving, through being over-crammed with the wrong things. Nature came down upon them, but she did not come down on Theobald and Christina. Why should she? They were not leading a starved existence. There are two classes of people in this world, those who sin, and those who are sinned against; if a man must belong to either, he had better belong to the first than to the second.

Chapter Twenty-Seven

I will give no more of the details of my hero's earlier years. Enough that he struggled through them, and at twelve years old knew every page of his Latin and Greek grammar by heart. He had read the greater part of Virgil, Horace and Livy, and I do not know how many Greek plays: he was proficient in arithmetic, knew the first four books of Euclid thoroughly, and had a fair knowledge of French. It was now time he went to school, and to school he was accordingly to go, under the famous Dr Skinner of Roughborough.

Theobald had known Dr Skinner slightly at Cambridge. He had been a burning and shining light in every position he had filled from his boyhood upwards. He was a very great genius. Everyone knew this; they said, indeed, that he was one of the few people to whom the word genius could be applied without exaggeration. Had he not taken I don't know how many University Scholarships in his freshman's year? Had he not been afterwards Senior Wrangler, First Chancellor's Medallist, and I do not know how many more things besides? And then, he was such a wonderful speaker; at the Union Debating Club he had been without a rival, and had, of course, been president; his moral character – a point on which so many geniuses were weak – was absolutely irreproachable; foremost of all, however, among his many great qualities, and perhaps more remarkable even than his genius, was what biographers have called 'the simple-minded and child-like earnestness of his character,' an earnestness which might be perceived by the solemnity with which he spoke even about trifles. It is hardly necessary to say he was on the Liberal side in politics.

His personal appearance was not particularly prepossessing.

He was about the middle height, portly, and had a couple of fierce grey eyes, that flashed fire from beneath a pair of great bushy beetling eyebrows and overawed all who came near him. It was in respect of his personal appearance, however, that, if he was vulnerable at all, his weak place was to be found. His hair when he was a young man was red, but after he had taken his degree he had a brain fever which caused him to have his head shaved; when he reappeared he did so wearing a wig, and one which was a good deal further off red than his own hair had been. He not only had never discarded his wig, but year by year it had edged itself a little more and a little more off red, till by the time he was forty, there was not a trace of red remaining, and his wig was brown.

When Dr Skinner was a very young man, hardly more than five-and-twenty, the head-mastership of Roughborough Grammar School had fallen vacant, and he had been unhesitatingly appointed. The result justified the selection. Dr Skinner's pupils distinguished themselves at whichever University they went to. He moulded their minds after the model of his own, and stamped an impression upon them which was indelible in after-life; whatever else a Roughborough man might be, he was sure to make everyone feel that he was a God-fearing earnest Christian and a Liberal, if not a Radical, in politics. Some boys, of course, were incapable of appreciating the beauty and loftiness of Dr Skinner's nature. Some such boys, alas! there will be in every school; upon them Dr Skinner's hand was very properly a heavy one. His hand was against them, and theirs against him during the whole time of the connection between them. They not only disliked him, but they hated all that he more especially embodied, and throughout their lives disliked all that reminded them of him. Such boys, however, were in a minority, the spirit of the place being decidedly Skinnerian.

I once had the honour of playing a game of chess with this great man. It was during the Christmas holidays, and I had come down to Roughborough for a few days to see Alethea Pontifex (who was then living there) on business. It was very gracious of him to take notice of me, for if I was a light of literature at all it was of the very lightest kind.

It is true that in the intervals of business I had written a good deal but my works had been almost exclusively for the stage, and for those theatres that devoted themselves to extravaganza and burlesque. I had written many pieces of this description, full of puns and comic songs, and they had had a fair success, but my best piece had been a treatment of English history during the Reformation period, in the course of which I had introduced Cranmer, Sir Thomas More, Henry the Eighth, Catherine of Aragon, and Thomas Cromwell (in his youth better known as the *Malleus Monachorum*), and had made them dance a break-down. I had also dramatised *The Pilgrim's Progress* for a Christmas Pantomime, and made an important scene of Vanity Fair, with Mr Greatheart, Apollyon, Christiana, Mercy, and Hopeful as the principal characters. The orchestra played music taken from Handel's best known works, but the time was a good deal altered, and altogether the tunes were not exactly as Handel left them. Mr Greatheart was very stout and he had a red nose; he wore a capacious waistcoat, and a shirt with a huge frill down the middle of the front. Hopeful was up to as much mischief as I could give him; he wore the costume of a young swell of the period, and had a cigar in his mouth which was continually going out.

Christiana did not wear much of anything: indeed it was said that the dress which the Stage Manager had originally proposed for her had been considered inadequate even by the Lord Chamberlain, but this is not the case. With all these delinquencies upon my mind it was natural that I should feel convinced of sin while playing chess (which I hate) with the great Dr Skinner of Roughborough – the historian of Athens and editor of Demosthenes. Dr Skinner, moreover, was one of those who pride themselves on being able to set people at their ease at once, and I had been sitting on the edge of my chair all the evening. But I have always been very easily overawed by a schoolmaster.

The game had been a long one, and at half-past nine, when supper came in, we had each of us a few pieces remaining. 'What will you take for supper, Dr Skinner?' said Mrs Skinner in a silvery voice.

He made no answer for some time, but at last in a tone of almost superhuman solemnity, he said, first, 'Nothing,' and then 'Nothing whatever.'

By and by, however, I had a sense come over me as though I were nearer the consummation of all things than I had ever yet been. The room seemed to grow dark, as an expression came over Dr Skinner's face, which showed that he was about to speak. The expression gathered force, the room grew darker and darker. 'Stay,' he at length added, and I felt that here at any rate was an end to a suspense which was rapidly becoming unbearable. 'Stay – I may presently take a glass of cold water – and a small piece of bread and butter.'

As he said the word 'butter' his voice sank to a hardly audible whisper; then there was a sigh as though of relief when the sentence was concluded, and the universe this time was safe. Another ten minutes of solemn silence finished the game. The Doctor rose briskly from his seat and placed himself at the supper table. 'Mrs Skinner,' he exclaimed jauntily, 'what are those mysterious-looking objects surrounded by potatoes?'

'Those are oysters, Dr Skinner.'

'Give me some, and give Overton some.'

And so on till he had eaten a good plate of oysters, a scallop shell of minced veal nicely browned, some apple tart, and a hunk of bread and cheese. This was the small piece of bread and butter.

The cloth was now removed and tumblers with teaspoons in them, a lemon or two and a jug of boiling water were placed upon the table. Then the great man unbent. His face beamed. 'And what shall it be to drink?' he exclaimed persuasively. 'Shall it be brandy and water? No. It shall be gin and water. Gin is the more wholesome liquor.'

So gin it was, hot and stiff too.

Who can wonder at him or do anything but pity him? Was he not headmaster of Roughborough School? To whom had he owed money at any time? Whose ox had he taken, whose ass had he taken, or whom had he defrauded? What whisper had ever been breathed against his moral character? If he had become rich it was by the most honourable of all means – his literary attainments; over and above his great works of scholarship, his 'Meditations upon the Epistle and Character of St Jude' had placed him among the most popular of English theologians; it was so exhaustive that no one who bought it need ever meditate upon the subject again – indeed it exhausted all who had anything to do with it. He had made £5,000 by this work alone, and would very likely make another £5,000 before he died. A man who had done all this and wanted a piece of bread and butter had a right to announce the fact with some pomp and circumstance. Nor should his words be taken without searching for what he used to call a 'deeper and more hidden meaning.' Those who searched for this even in his lightest utterances would not be without their reward. They would find that 'bread and butter' was Skinnerese for oyster-patties and apple tart, and 'gin hot' the true translation of water.

But independently of their money value, his works had made him a lasting name in literature. So probably Gallio was under the impression that his fame would rest upon the treatises on natural history which we gather from Seneca that he compiled, and which for aught we know may have contained a complete theory of evolution; but the treatises are all gone and Gallio has become immortal for the very last reason in the world that he expected, and for the very last reason that would have flattered his vanity. He has become immortal because he cared nothing about the most important movement with which he was ever brought into connection (I wish people who are in search of immortality would lay the lesson to heart and not make so much noise about important movements) and so, if Dr Skinner becomes immortal, it will probably be for some reason very different from the one which he so fondly imagined.

Could it be expected to enter into the head of such a man as this that in reality he was making his money by corrupting youth; that it was his paid profession to make the worse appear the better reason in the eyes of those who were too young and inexperienced to be able to find him out; that he kept out of the sight of those whom he professed to teach material points of the argument, for the production of which they had a right to rely upon the honour of anyone who made professions of sincerity; that he was a passionate half-turkey-cock half-gander of a man whose sallow, bilious face and hobble-gobble voice could scare the timid, but who would take to his heels readily enough if he were met firmly; that his 'Meditations on St Jude,' such as they were, were cribbed without acknowledgement, and would have been beneath contempt if so many people did not believe them to have been written honestly? Mrs Skinner might have perhaps kept him a little more in his proper place if she had thought it worth while to try, but she had enough to attend to in looking after her household and seeing that the boys were well fed, and if they were ill, properly looked after – which she took good care they were.

Chapter Twenty-Eight

Ernest had heard awful accounts of Dr Skinner's temper, and of the bullying which the younger boys at Roughborough had to put up with at the hands of the bigger ones. He had got about as much as he could stand, and felt as though it must go hard with him if his burdens of whatever kind were to be increased. He did not cry on leaving home, but I am afraid he did on being told that he was getting near Roughborough. His father and mother were with him, having posted from home in their own carriage; Roughborough had as yet no railway, and as it was only some forty miles from Battersby, this was the easiest way of getting there.

On seeing him cry, his mother felt flattered and caressed him. She said she knew he must feel very sad at leaving such a happy home, and going among people who, though they would be very good to him, could never, never be as good as his dear papa and she had been; still, she was herself, if he only knew it, much more deserving of pity than he was, for the parting was more painful to her than it could possibly be to him, etc., and Ernest, on being told that his tears were for grief at leaving home, took it all on trust, and did not trouble to investigate the real cause of his tears. As they approached Roughborough he pulled himself together, and was fairly calm by the time he reached Dr Skinner's.

On their arrival they had luncheon with the Doctor and his wife, and then Mrs Skinner took Christina over the bedrooms, and showed her where her dear little boy was to sleep.

Whatever men may think about the study of man, women do really believe the noblest study for womankind to be woman, and Christina was too much engrossed with Mrs Skinner to pay much attention to anything else; I dare say Mrs Skinner, too, was taking pretty accurate stock of Christina. Christina was charmed, as indeed she generally was with any new acquaintance, for she found in them (and so must we all) something of the nature of a cross; as for Mrs Skinner, I imagine she had seen too many Christinas to find much regeneration in the sample now before her; I believe her private opinion echoed the dictum of a well-known headmaster who declared that all parents were fools, but more especially mothers; she was, however, all smiles and sweetness, and Christina devoured these graciously as tributes paid more particularly to herself, and such as no other mother would have been at all likely to have won.

In the meantime Theobald and Ernest were with Dr Skinner in his library – the room where new boys were examined and old ones had up for rebuke or chastisement. If the walls of that room could speak, what an account of blundering and capricious cruelty would they not bear witness to!

Like all houses, Dr Skinner's had its peculiar smell. In this case the prevailing odour was one of Russia leather, but along with it there was a subordinate savour as of a chemist's shop. This came from a small laboratory in one corner of the room – the possession of which, together with the free chattery and smattery use of such words as 'carbonate,' 'hyposulphate,' 'phosphate,' and 'affinity,' were enough to convince even the most sceptical that Dr Skinner had a profound knowledge of chemistry.

I may say in passing that Dr Skinner had dabbled in a great many other things as well as chemistry. He was a man of many small knowledges, and each of them dangerous. I remember Alethea Pontifex once said in her wicked way to me, that Dr Skinner put her in mind of the Bourbon princes on their return from exile after the battle of Waterloo, only that he was their exact converse; for whereas they had learned nothing and forgotten nothing, Dr Skinner had learned everything and forgotten everything. And this puts me in mind of another of her wicked sayings about Dr Skinner. She told me one day that he had the harmlessness of the serpent and the wisdom of the dove.

But to return to Dr Skinner's library; over the chimney-piece there was a Bishop's half-length portrait of Dr Skinner himself, painted by the elder Pickersgill, whose merit Dr Skinner had been among the first to discern and foster. There were no other pictures in the library, but in the dining-room there was a fine collection, which the doctor had got together with his usual consummate taste. He added to it largely in later life, and when it came to the hammer at Christie's, as it did not long since, it was found to comprise many of the latest and most matured works of Solomon Hart, O'Neil, Charles Landseer, and more of our recent Academicians than I can at the moment remember. There were thus brought together and exhibited at one view many works which had attracted attention at the Academy Exhibitions, and as to whose ultimate destiny there had been some curiosity. The prices realised were disappointing to the executors, but, then, these things are so much a matter of chance. An unscrupulous writer in a well-known weekly paper had written the collection down. Moreover there had been one or two large sales a short time before Dr Skinner's, so that at this last there was rather a panic, and a reaction against the high prices that had ruled lately.

The table of the library was loaded with books many deep; MSS. of all kinds were confusedly mixed up with them – boys' exercises, probably, and examination papers – but all littering untidily about. The room in fact was as depressing from its slatternliness as from its atmosphere of erudition. Theobald and Ernest, as they entered it, stumbled over a large hole in the Turkey carpet, and the dust that rose showed how long it was since it had been taken up and beaten. This, I should say, was no fault of Mrs Skinner's but was due to the Doctor himself, who declared that if his papers were once disturbed it would be the death of him. Near the window was a green cage containing a pair of turtle doves, whose plaintive cooing added to the melancholy of the place. The walls were covered with book shelves from floor to ceiling, and on every shelf the books stood in double rows. It was horrible. Prominent among the most prominent upon the most prominent shelf were a series of splendidly-bound volumes entitled *Skinner's Works*.

Boys are sadly apt to rush to conclusions, and Ernest believed that Dr Skinner knew all the books in this terrible library, and that he, if he were to be any good, should have to learn them too. His heart fainted within him.

He was told to sit on a chair against the wall and did so, while Dr Skinner talked to Theobald upon the topics of the day. He talked about the Hampden Controversy then raging, and discoursed learnedly about 'Praemunire'; then he talked about the revolution which had just broken out in Sicily, and rejoiced that the Pope had refused to allow foreign troops to pass through his dominions in order to crush it. Dr Skinner and the other masters took in the *Times* among them, and Dr Skinner echoed the *Times'* leaders. In those days there were no penny papers and Theobald only took in the *Spectator* – for he was at that time on the Whig side in politics; besides this he used to receive the *Ecclesiastical Gazette* once a month, but he saw no other papers, and was amazed at the ease and fluency with which Dr Skinner ran from subject to subject.

The Pope's action in the matter of the Sicilian revolution naturally led the Doctor to the reforms which his Holiness had introduced into his dominions, and he laughed consumedly over the joke which had not long since appeared in *Punch*, to the effect that Pio 'No, No,' should rather have been named Pio 'Yes, Yes,' because, as the doctor explained, he granted everything his subjects asked for. Anything like a pun went straight to Dr Skinner's heart.

Then he went on to the matter of these reforms themselves. They opened up a new era in the history of Christendom, and would have such momentous and far-reaching consequences, that they might even lead to a reconciliation between the Churches of England and Rome. Dr Skinner had lately published a pamphlet upon this subject, which had shown great learning, and had attacked the Church of Rome in a way which did not promise much hope of reconciliation. He had grounded his attack upon the letters A.M.D.G., which he had seen outside a Roman Catholic chapel, and which of course stood for *Ad Mariam Dei Genetricem*. Could anything be more idolatrous?

I am told, by the way, that I must have let my memory play me one of the tricks it often does play me, when I said the Doctor proposed *Ad Mariam Dei Genetricem* as the full harmonies, so to speak, which should be constructed upon the bass A.M.D.G., for that this is bad Latin, and that the doctor really harmonised the letters thus: *Ave Maria Dei Genetrix*. No doubt the doctor did what was right in the matter of Latinity – I have forgotten the little Latin I ever knew, and am not going to look the matter up, but I believe the doctor said *Ad Mariam Dei Genetricem*, and if so we may be sure that *Ad Mariam Dei Genetricem* is good enough Latin at any rate for ecclesiastical purposes.

The reply of the local priest had not yet appeared, and Dr Skinner was jubilant, but when the answer appeared, and it was solemnly declared that A.M.D.G. stood for nothing more dangerous than *Ad Majorem Dei Gloriam*, it was felt that though this subterfuge would not succeed with any intelligent Englishman, still it was a pity Dr Skinner had selected this particular point for his attack, for he had to leave his enemy in possession of the field. When people are left in possession of the field, spectators have an awkward habit of thinking that their adversary does not dare to come to the scratch.

Dr Skinner was telling Theobald all about his pamphlet, and I doubt whether this gentleman was much more comfortable than Ernest himself. He was bored, for in his heart he hated Liberalism, though he was ashamed to say so, and, as I have said,

professed to be on the Whig side. He did not want to be reconciled to the Church of Rome; he wanted to make all Roman
Catholics turn Protestants, and could never understand why they
would not do so; but the Doctor talked in such a truly liberal
spirit, and shut him up so sharply when he tried to edge in a word
or two, that he had to let him have it all his own way, and this was
not what he was accustomed to. He was wondering how he
could bring it to an end, when a diversion was created by the discovery that Ernest had begun to cry – doubtless through an
intense but inarticulate sense of a boredom greater than he could
bear. He was evidently in a highly nervous state, and a good deal
upset by the excitement of the morning. Mrs Skinner therefore,
who came in with Christina at this juncture, proposed that he
should spend the afternoon with Mrs Jay, the matron, and not be
introduced to his young companions until the following morning. His father and mother now bade him an affectionate farewell,
and the lad was handed over to Mrs Jay.

O schoolmasters – if any of you read this book – bear in mind
when any particularly timid drivelling urchin is brought by his
papa into your study, and you treat him with the contempt which
he deserves, and afterwards make his life a burden to him for
years – bear in mind that it is exactly in the disguise of such a boy
as this that your future chronicler will appear. Never see a
wretched little heavy-eyed mite sitting on the edge of a chair
against your study wall without saying to yourselves, 'perhaps
this boy is he who, if I am not careful, will one day tell the world
what manner of man I was.' If even two or three schoolmasters
learn this lesson and remember it, the preceding chapters will not
have been written in vain.

Chapter Twenty-Nine

Soon after his father and mother had left him Ernest dropped asleep over a book which Mrs Jay had given him, and he did not awake till dusk. Then he sat down on a stool in front of the fire, which showed pleasantly in the late January twilight, and began to muse. He felt weak, feeble, ill at ease and unable to see his way out of the innumerable troubles that were before him. Perhaps, he said to himself, he might even die, but this, far from being an end of his troubles, would prove the beginning of new ones; for at the best he would only go to Grandpapa Pontifex and Grandmamma Allaby, and though they would perhaps be more easy to get on with than Papa and Mamma, yet they were undoubtedly not so really good, and were more worldly; moreover they were grown-up people – especially Grandpapa Pontifex, who so far as he could understand had been very much grown-up, and he did not know why, but there was always something that kept him from loving any grown-up people very much – except one or two of the servants, who had indeed been as nice as anything that he could imagine. Besides even if he were to die and go to Heaven he supposed he should have to complete his education somewhere.

In the meantime his father and mother were rolling along the muddy roads, each in his or her own corner of the carriage, and each revolving many things which were and were not to come to pass. Times have changed since I last showed them to the reader as sitting together silently in a carriage, but except as regards their mutual relations, they have altered singularly little. When I was younger I used to think the Prayer Book was wrong in requiring us to say the General Confession twice a week from childhood to old age, without making provision for our not being quite such great sinners at seventy as we had been at seven; granted that we should go to the wash like tablecloths at least once a week, still I used to think a day ought to come when we should want rather less rubbing and scrubbing at. Now that I have grown older myself I have seen that the Church has estimated probabilities better than I had done.

The pair said not a word to one another, but watched the fading light and naked trees, the brown fields with here and there a melancholy cottage by the roadside, and the rain that fell fast upon the carriage windows. It was a kind of afternoon on which nice people for the most part like to be snug at home, and Theobald was a little snappish at reflecting how many miles he had to post before he could be at his own fireside again. However there was nothing for it, so the pair sat quietly and watched the roadside objects flit by them, and get greyer and grimmer as the light faded.

Though they spoke not to one another, there was one nearer to each of them with whom they could converse freely. 'I hope,' said Theobald to himself, 'I hope he'll work – or else that Skinner will make him. I don't like Skinner, I never did like him, but he is unquestionably a man of genius, and no one turns out so many pupils who succeed at Oxford and Cambridge, and that is the best test. I have done my share towards starting him well. Skinner said he had been well grounded and was very forward. I suppose he will presume upon it now and do nothing, for his nature is an idle one. He is not fond of me, I'm sure he is not. He ought to be after all the trouble I have taken with him, but he is ungrateful and selfish. It is an unnatural thing for a boy not to be fond of his own father. If he was fond of me I should be fond of him, but I cannot like a son who, I am sure, dislikes me. He shrinks out of my way whenever he sees me coming near him. He will not stay five minutes in the same room with me if he can help it. He is deceitful. He would not want to hide himself away so much if he were not deceitful. That is a bad sign and one which makes me fear he will grow up extravagant. I am sure he will grow up extravagant. I should have given him more pocket-money if I had not known this – but what is the good of giving him pocket-money? It is all gone directly. If he doesn't buy something with it he gives it away to the first little boy or girl he sees who takes his fancy. He forgets that it's my money he is giving away. I give him money that he may have money and learn to know its uses, not that he may go and squander it immediately. I wish he was not so fond of music, it will interfere with his Latin and Greek. I will stop it as much as I can. Why, when he was translating Livy the other day he slipped out Handel's name in mistake for Hannibal's, and his mother tells me he knows half the tunes in the "Messiah" by heart. What should a boy of his age know about the "Messiah"? If I had shown half as many dangerous tendencies when I was a boy, my father would have apprenticed me to a greengrocer, of that I'm very sure,' etc., etc.

Then his thoughts turned to Egypt and the tenth plague. It seemed to him that if the little Egyptians had been anything like Ernest, the plague must have been something very like a blessing in disguise. If the Israelites were to come to England now he should be greatly tempted not to let them go.

Mrs Theobald's thoughts ran in a different current. 'Lord Lonsford's grandson – it's a pity his name is Figgins; however, blood is blood as much through the female line as the male, indeed, perhaps even more so if the truth were known. I wonder who Mr Figgins was. I think Mrs Skinner said he was dead; however, I must find out all about him. It would be delightful if young Figgins were to ask Ernest home for the holidays. Who knows but he might meet Lord Lonsford himself, or at any rate some of Lord Lonsford's other descendants?'

Meanwhile the boy himself was still sitting moodily before the fire in Mrs Jay's room. 'Papa and Mamma,' he was saying to himself, 'are much better and cleverer than anyone else, but, I, alas! shall never be either good or clever!'

Mrs Pontifex continued –

'Perhaps it would be best to get young Figgins on a visit to our-selves first. That would be charming. Theobald would not like it, for he does not like children; I must see how I can manage it, for it would be so nice to have young Figgins – or stay! Ernest shall go and stay with Figgins and meet the future Lord Lonsford, who I should think must be about Ernest's age, and then if he and Ernest were to become friends Ernest might ask him to Battersby, and he might fall in love with Charlotte. I think we have done *most wisely* in sending Ernest to Dr Skinner's. Dr Skinner's piety is no less remarkable than his genius. One can tell these things at a glance, and he must have felt it about me no less strongly than I about him. I think he seemed much struck with Theobald and myself – indeed, Theobald's intellectual power must impress any one, and I was showing, I do believe, to my best advantage. When I smiled at him and said I left my boy in his hands with the most entire confidence that he would be as well cared for as if he were at my own house, I am sure he was greatly pleased. I should not think many of the mothers who bring him boys can impress him so favourably, or say such nice things to him as I did. My smile *is* sweet when I desire to make it so. I never was perhaps exactly pretty, but I was always admitted to be fascinating. Dr Skinner is a very handsome man – too good on the whole I should say for Mrs Skinner. Theobald says he is not handsome, but men are no judges, and he has such a pleasant bright face. I think my bonnet became me. As soon as I get home I will tell Chambers to trim my blue and yellow merino with –' etc., etc.

All this time the letter which has been given above was lying in Christina's private little Japanese cabinet, read and re-read and approved of many times over, not to say, if the truth were known, rewritten more than once, though dated as in the first instance – and this, too, though Christina was fond enough of a joke in a small way.

Ernest, still in Mrs Jay's room, mused onward. 'Grown-up

people,' he said to himself, 'when they were ladies and gentlemen, never did naughty things, but he was always doing them. He had heard that some grown-up people were worldly, which of course was wrong, still this was quite distinct from being naughty, and did not get them punished or scolded. His own Papa and Mamma were not even worldly; they had often explained to him that they were exceptionally unworldly; he well knew that they had never done anything naughty since they had been children, and that even as children they had been nearly faultless. Oh! how different from himself. When should he learn to love his Papa and Mamma as they had loved theirs? How could he hope ever to grow up to be as good and wise as they, or even tolerably good and wise? Alas! never. It could not be. He did not love his Papa and Mamma, in spite of all their goodness both in themselves and to him. He hated Papa, and did not like Mamma, and this was what none but a bad and ungrateful boy would do after all that had been done for him. Besides he did not like Sunday; he did not like anything that was really good; his tastes were low and such as he was ashamed of. He liked people best if they sometimes swore a little, so long as it was not at him. As for his Catechism and Bible readings he had no heart in them. He had never attended to a sermon in his life. Even when he had been taken to hear Mr Vaughan at Brighton, who, as everyone knew, preached such beautiful sermons for children, he had been very glad when it was all over, nor did he believe he could get through church at all if it was not for the voluntary upon the organ and the hymns and chanting. The Catechism was awful. He had never been able to understand what it was that he desired of his Lord God and Heavenly Father, nor had he yet got hold of a single idea in connection with the word Sacrament. His duty towards his neighbour was another bugbear. It seemed to him that he had duties towards everybody, lying in wait for him upon every side, but that nobody had any duties towards him. Then there was that awful and mysterious word "business." What did it all mean? What was "business"? His Papa was a wonderfully good man of business, his Mamma had often told him so – but he should never be one. It was hopeless, and very awful, for people were continually telling him that he would have to earn his own living. No doubt, but how – considering how stupid, idle, ignorant, self-indulgent, and physically puny he was? All grown-up people were clever, except servants – and even these were cleverer than ever he should be. Oh, why, why, why, could not people be born into the world as grown-up persons? Then he thought of Casabianca. He had been examined in that poem by his father not long before. "When only would he leave his position? To whom did he call? Did he get an answer? Why? How many times did he call upon his father? What happened to him? What was the noblest life that perished there? Do you think so? Why do you think so?" And all the rest of it. Of course he thought Casabianca's was the noblest life that perished there; there could be no two opinions about that; it never occurred to him that the moral of the poem was that young people cannot begin too soon to exercise discretion in the obedience they pay to their Papa and Mamma. Oh, no! the only thought in his mind was that he should never, never have been like Casabianca, and that Casabianca would have despised him so much, if he could have known him, that he would not have condescended to speak to him. There was nobody else in the ship worth reckoning at all: it did not matter how much they were blown up. Mrs Hemans knew them all and they were a very indifferent lot. Besides Casabianca was so good-looking and came of such a good family.'

And thus his small mind kept wandering on till he could follow it no longer, and again went off into a doze.

Chapter Thirty

Next morning Theobald and Christina arose feeling a little tired from their journey, but happy in that best of all happiness, the approbation of their consciences. It would be their boy's fault henceforth if he were not good, and as prosperous as it was at all desirable that he should be. What more could parents do than they had done? The answer 'Nothing' will rise as readily to the lips of the reader as to those of Theobald and Christina themselves.

A few days later the parents were gratified at receiving the following letter from their son –

> 'My Dear Mamma, – I am very well. Dr Skinner made me do
> about the horse free and exulting roaming in the wide fields in
> Latin verse, but as I had done it with Papa I knew how to do it,
> and it was nearly all right, and he put me in the fourth form
> under Mr Templer, and I have to begin a new Latin grammar
> not like the old, but much harder. I know you wish me to work,
> and I will try very hard. With best love to Joey and Charlotte,
> and to Papa, I remain, your affectionate son,
>
> 'Ernest.'

Nothing could be nicer or more proper. It really did seem as though he were inclined to turn over a new leaf. The boys had all come back, the examinations were over, and the routine of the half-year began; Ernest found that his fears about being kicked about and bullied were exaggerated. Nobody did anything very dreadful to him. He had to run errands between certain hours for the elder boys, and to take his turn at greasing the footballs, and so forth, but there was an excellent spirit in the school as regards bullying.

Nevertheless, he was far from happy, Dr Skinner was much too like his father. True, Ernest was not thrown in with him much yet, but he was always there; there was no knowing at what moment he might not put in an appearance, and whenever he did show, it was to storm about something. He was like the lion in the Bishop of Oxford's Sunday story – always liable to rush out from behind some bush and devour someone when he was least expected. He called Ernest 'an audacious reptile' and said he wondered the earth did not open and swallow him up because he pronounced Thalia with a short i. 'And this to me,' he thundered, 'who never made a false quantity in my life.' Surely he would have been a much nicer person if he had made false quantities in his youth like other people. Ernest could not imagine how the boys in Dr Skinner's form continued to live; but yet they did, and even throve, and, strange as it may seem, idolised him, or professed to do so in after life. To Ernest it seemed like living on the crater of Vesuvius.

He was himself, as has been said, in Mr Templer's form, who was snappish, but not downright wicked, and was very easy to crib under. Ernest used to wonder how Mr Templer could be so blind, for he supposed Mr Templer must have cribbed when he was at school, and would ask himself whether he should forget his youth when he got old, as Mr Templer had forgotten his. He used to think he never could possibly forget any part of it.

Then there was Mrs Jay, who was sometimes very alarming. A few days after the half-year had commenced, there being some little extra noise in the hall, she rushed in with her spectacles on her forehead and her cap strings flying, and called the boy whom Ernest had selected as his hero the 'rampingest-scampingest-rackety-tackety-tow-row-roaringest boy in the whole school.' But she used to say things that Ernest liked. If the Doctor went out to dinner, and there were no prayers, she would come in and say, 'Young gentlemen, prayers are excused this evening'; and, take her for all in all, she was a kindly old soul enough.

Most boys soon discover the difference between noise and actual danger, but to others it is so unnatural to menace, unless they mean mischief, that they are long before they leave off taking turkey-cocks and ganders *au sérieux*. Ernest was one of the latter sort, and found the atmosphere of Roughborough so gusty that he was glad to shrink out of sight and out of mind whenever he could. He disliked the games worse even than the squalls of the class-room and hall, for he was still feeble, not filling out and attaining his full strength till a much later age than most boys. This was perhaps due to the closeness with which his father had kept him to his books in childhood, but I think in part also to a tendency towards lateness in attaining maturity, hereditary in the Pontifex family, which was one also of unusual longevity. At thirteen or fourteen he was a mere bag of bones, with upper arms about as thick as the wrists of other boys of his age; his little chest was pigeon-breasted; he appeared to have no strength or stamina whatever, and finding he always went to the wall in physical encounters, whether undertaken in jest or earnest, even with boys shorter than himself, the timidity natural to childhood increased upon him to an extent that I am afraid amounted to cowardice. This rendered him even less capable than he might otherwise have been, for as confidence increases power, so want of confidence increases impotence. After he had had the breath knocked out of him and been well shinned half a dozen times in scrimmages at football – scrimmages in which he had become involved sorely against his will – he ceased to see any further fun in football, and shirked that noble game in a way that got him into trouble with the elder boys, who would stand no shirking on the part of the younger ones.

He was as useless and ill at ease with cricket as with football, nor in spite of all his efforts could he ever throw a ball or a stone. It soon became plain, therefore, to everyone, that Pontifex was a young muff, a molly coddle, not to be tortured, but still not to be rated highly. He was not, however, actively unpopular, for it was seen that he was quite square *inter pares*, not at all vindictive, easily pleased, perfectly free with whatever little money he had, no greater lover of his school work than of the games, and generally more inclinable to moderate vice than to immoderate virtue.

These qualities will prevent any boy from sinking very low in the opinion of his school-fellows; but Ernest thought he had fallen lower than he probably had, and hated and despised himself for what he, as much as anyone else, believed to be his cowardice. He did not like the boys whom he thought like himself. His heroes were strong and vigorous, and the less they inclined towards him the more he worshipped them. All this made him very unhappy, for it never occurred to him that the instinct which made him keep out of games for which he was ill-adapted, was more reasonable than the reason which would have driven him into them. Nevertheless he followed his instinct for the most part, rather than his reason. *Sapiens suam si sapientiam nōrit.*

Chapter Thirty-One

With the masters Ernest was ere long in absolute disgrace. He had more liberty now than he had known heretofore. The heavy hand and watchful eye of Theobald were no longer about his path and about his bed and spying out all his ways; and punishment by way of copying out lines of Virgil was a very different thing from the savage beatings of his father. The copying out, in fact, was often less trouble than the lesson. Latin and Greek had nothing in them which commended them to his instinct as likely to bring him peace even at the last; still less did they hold out any hope of doing so within some more reasonable time. The deadness inherent in these defunct languages themselves had never been artificially counteracted by a system of *bona fide* rewards for application. There had been any amount of punishments for want of application, but no good comfortable bribes had baited the hook which was to allure him to his good.

Indeed, the more pleasant side of learning to do this or that had always been treated as something with which Ernest had no concern. We had no business with pleasant things at all, at any rate very little business, at any rate not he, Ernest. We were put into this world not for pleasure but duty, and pleasure had in it something more or less sinful in its very essence. If we were doing anything we liked, we, or at any rate he, Ernest, should apologise and think he was being very mercifully dealt with, if not at once told to go and do something else. With what he did not like, however, it was different; the more he disliked a thing the greater the presumption that it was right. It never occurred to him that the presumption was in favour of the rightness of what was most pleasant, and that the onus of proving that it was not right lay with those who disputed its being so. I have said more than once that he believed in his own depravity; never was there a little mortal more ready to accept without cavil whatever he was told by those who were in authority over him: he thought, at least, that he believed it, for as yet he knew nothing of that other Ernest that dwelt within him, and was so much stronger and more real than the Ernest of which he was conscious. The dumb Ernest persuaded with inarticulate feelings too swift and sure to be translated into such debatable things as words, but practically insisted as follows –

'Growing is not the easy plain sailing business that it is commonly supposed to be: it is hard work – harder than any but a growing boy can understand; it requires attention, and you are not strong enough to attend to your bodily growth, and to your lessons too. Besides, Latin and Greek are great humbug; the more people know of them the more odious they generally are; the nice people whom you delight in either never knew any at all or forgot what they had learned as soon as they could; they never turned to the classics after they were no longer forced to read them; therefore they are nonsense, all very well in their own time and country, but out of place here. Never learn anything until you find you have been made uncomfortable for a good long while by not knowing it; when you find that you have occasion for this or that knowledge, or foresee that you will have occasion for it shortly, the sooner you learn it the better, but till then spend your time in growing bone and muscle; these will be much more useful to you than Latin and Greek, nor will you ever be able to make them if you do not do so now, whereas Latin and Greek can be acquired at any time by those who want them.

'You are surrounded on every side by lies which would deceive even the elect, if the elect were not generally so uncommonly wide awake; the self of which you are conscious, your reasoning and reflecting self, will believe these lies and bid you act in accordance with them. This conscious self of yours, Ernest, is a prig begotten of prigs and trained in priggishness; I will not allow it to shape your actions, though it will doubtless shape your words for many a year to come. Your Papa is not here to beat you now; this is a change in the conditions of your existence, and should be followed by changed actions. Obey *me*, your true self and things will go tolerably well with you, but only listen to that outward and visible old husk of yours which is called your father, and I will rend you in pieces even unto the third and fourth generation as one who has hated God; for I, Ernest, am the God who made you.'

How shocked Ernest would have been if he could have heard the advice he was receiving; what consternation too there would have been at Battersby; but the matter did not end here, for this same wicked inner self gave him bad advice about his pocket-money, the choice of his companions, and on the whole Ernest was attentive and obedient to its behests, more so than Theobald had been. The consequence was that he learned little, his mind growing more slowly and his body rather faster than heretofore: and when by and by his inner self urged him in directions where he met obstacles beyond his strength to combat, he took – though with passionate compunctions of conscience – the nearest course to the one from which he was debarred which circumstances would allow.

It may be guessed that Ernest was not the chosen friend of the more sedate and well-conducted youths then studying at Roughborough. Some of the less desirable boys used to go to public-houses and drink more beer than was good for them; Ernest's inner self can hardly have told him to ally himself to these young gentlemen, but he did so at an early age, and was sometimes made pitiably sick by an amount of beer which would have produced no effect upon a stronger boy. Ernest's inner self must have interposed at this point and told him that there was not much fun in this, for he dropped the habit ere it had taken firm hold of him, and never resumed it; but he contracted another at the disgracefully early age of between thirteen and fourteen which he did not relinquish, though to the present day his conscious self keeps dinging it into him that the less he smokes the better.

And so matters went on till my hero was nearly fourteen years old. If by that time he was not actually a young blackguard, he belonged to a debatable class between the sub-reputable and the upper disreputable, with perhaps rather more leaning to the latter except so far as vices of meanness were concerned, from which he was fairly free. I gather this partly from what Ernest has told me, and partly from his school bills, which I remember Theobald showed me with much complaining. There was an institution at Roughborough called the monthly merit money; the maximum sum which a boy of Ernest's age could get was four shillings and sixpence; several boys got four shillings and few less than sixpence, but Ernest never got more than half-a-crown and seldom more than eighteen pence; his average would, I should think, be about one and nine pence, which was just too much for him to rank among the downright bad boys, but too little to put him among the good ones.

Chapter Thirty-Two

I must now return to Miss Alethea Pontifex, of whom I have said perhaps too little hitherto, considering how great her influence upon my hero's destiny proved to be.

On the death of her father, which happened when she was about thirty-two years old, she parted company with her sisters, between whom and herself there had been little sympathy, and came up to London. She was determined, so she said, to make the rest of her life as happy as she could, and she had clearer ideas about the best way of setting to work to do this than women, or indeed men, generally have.

Her fortune consisted, as I have said, of £5,000, which had come to her by her mother's marriage settlements, and £15,000 left her by her father, over both which sums she had now absolute control. These brought her in about £900 a year, and the money being invested in none but the soundest securities, she had no anxiety about her income. She meant to be rich, so she formed a scheme of expenditure which involved an annual outlay of about £500, and determined to put the rest by. 'If I do this,' she said laughingly, 'I shall probably just succeed in living comfortably within my income.' In accordance with this scheme she took unfurnished apartments in a house in Gower Street, of which the lower floors were let out as offices. John Pontifex tried to get her to take a house to herself, but Alethea told him to mind his own business so plainly that he had to beat a retreat. She had never liked him, and from that time dropped him almost entirely.

Without going much into society she yet became acquainted with most of the men and women who had attained a position in the literary, artistic and scientific worlds, and it was singular how highly her opinion was valued in spite of her never having attempted in any way to distinguish herself. She could have written if she had chosen, but she enjoyed seeing others write and encouraging them better than taking a more active part herself. Perhaps literary people liked her all the better because she did not write.

I, as she very well knew, had always been devoted to her, and she might have had a score of other admirers if she had liked, but she had discouraged them all, and railed at matrimony as women seldom do unless they have a comfortable income of their own. She by no means, however, railed at man as she railed at matrimony, and though living after a fashion in which even the most censorious could find nothing to complain of, as far as she properly could she defended those of her own sex whom the world condemned most severely.

In religion she was, I should think, as nearly a free-thinker as anyone could be whose mind seldom turned upon the subject. She went to church, but disliked equally those who aired either religion or irreligion. I remember once hearing her press a late well-known philosopher to write a novel instead of pursuing his attacks upon religion. The philosopher did not much like this, and dilated upon the importance of showing people the folly of much that they pretended to believe. She smiled and said demurely, 'Have they not Moses and the prophets? Let them hear *them*.' But she would say a wicked thing quietly on her own account sometimes, and called my attention once to a note in her prayer-book which gave an account of the walk to Emmaus with the two disciples and how Christ had said to them 'O fools and slow of heart to believe ALL that the prophets have spoken' – the 'all' being printed in small capitals.

Though scarcely on terms with her brother John, she had kept up closer relations with Theobald and his family, and had paid a few days' visit to Battersby once in every two years or so. Alethea had always tried to like Theobald and join forces with him as much as she could (for they two were the hares of the family, the rest being all hounds), but it was no use. I believe her chief reason for maintaining relations with her brother was that she might keep an eye on his children and give them a lift if they proved nice.

When Miss Pontifex had come down to Battersby in old times the children had not been beaten, and their lessons had been made lighter. She easily saw that they were overworked and unhappy, but she could hardly guess how all-reaching was the régime under which they lived. She knew she could not interfere effectually then, and wisely forbore to make too many inquiries. Her time, if ever it was to come, would be when the children were no longer living under the same roof as their parents. It ended in her making up her mind to have nothing to do with either Joey or Charlotte, but to see so much of Ernest as should enable her to form an opinion about his disposition and abilities.

He had now been a year and a half at Roughborough and was nearly fourteen years old, so that his character had begun to shape. His aunt had not seen him for some little time and, thinking that if she was to exploit him she could do so now perhaps better than at any other time, she resolved to go down to Roughborough on some pretext which should be good enough for Theobald, and to take stock of her nephew under circumstances in which she could get him for some few hours to herself. Accordingly in August, 1849, when Ernest was just entering on his fourth half-year, a cab drove up to Dr Skinner's door with Miss Pontifex, who asked and obtained leave for Ernest to come and dine with her at the Swan Hotel. She had written to Ernest to say she was coming and he was of course on the look-out for her. He had not seen her for so long that he was rather shy at first, but her good nature soon set him at his ease. She was so strongly biased in favour of anything young that her heart warmed towards him at once, though his appearance was less prepossessing than she had hoped. She took him to a cake shop and gave him whatever he liked as soon as she had got him off the school premises; and Ernest felt at once that she contrasted favourably even with his aunts, the Misses Allaby, who were so very sweet and good. The Misses Allaby were very poor; sixpence was to them what five shillings was to Alethea. What chance had they against one who, if she had a mind, could put by out of her income twice as much as they, poor women, could spend?

The boy had plenty of prattle in him when he was not snubbed, and Alethea encouraged him to chatter about whatever came uppermost. He was always ready to trust anyone who was kind to him; it took many years to make him reasonably wary in this respect – if indeed, as I sometimes doubt, he ever will be as wary as he ought to be – and in a short time he had quite dissociated his aunt from his papa and mamma and the rest, with whom his instinct told him he should be on his guard. Little did he know how great, as far as he was concerned, were the issues that depended upon his behaviour. If he had known, he would per-haps have played his part less successfully.

His aunt drew from him more details of his home and school life than his papa and mamma would have approved of, but he had no idea that he was being pumped. She got out of him all about the happy Sunday evenings, and how he and Joey and Charlotte quarrelled sometimes, but she took no side and treated everything as though it were a matter of course. Like all the boys, he could mimic Dr Skinner, and when warmed with dinner, and two glasses of sherry which made him nearly tipsy, he favoured his aunt with samples of the Doctor's manner and spoke of him familiarly as 'Sam.'

'Sam,' he said, 'is an awful old humbug.' It was the sherry that brought out this piece of swagger, for whatever else he was Dr Skinner was a reality to Master Ernest, before which, indeed, he sank into his boots in no time. Alethea smiled and said, 'I must not say anything to that, must I?' Ernest said, 'I suppose not,' and was checked. By and by he vented a number of small secondhand priggishnesses which he had caught up believing them to be the correct thing, and made it plain that even at that early age Ernest believed in Ernest with a belief which was amusing from its absurdity. His aunt judged him charitably as she was sure to do; she knew very well where the priggishness came from, and seeing that the string of his tongue had been loosened sufficiently gave him no more sherry.

It was after dinner, however, that he completed the conquest of his aunt. She then discovered that, like herself, he was passionately fond of music, and that, too, of the highest class. He knew, and hummed or whistled to her all sorts of pieces out of the works of the great masters, which a boy of his age could hardly be expected to know, and it was evident that this was purely instinctive, inasmuch as music received no kind of encouragement at Roughborough. There was no boy in the school as fond of music as he was. He picked up his knowledge, he said, from the organist of St Michael's Church, who used to practise sometimes on a week-day afternoon. Ernest had heard the organ booming away as he was passing outside the church, and had sneaked inside and up into the organ loft. In the course of time the organist became accustomed to him as a familiar visitant, and the pair became friends.

It was this which decided Alethea that the boy was worth taking pains with. 'He likes the best music,' she thought, 'and he hates Dr Skinner. This is a very fair beginning.' When she sent him away at night with a sovereign in his pocket (and he had only hoped to get five shillings) she felt as though she had had a good deal more than her money's worth for her money.

Chapter Thirty-Three

Next day Miss Pontifex returned to town, with her thoughts full of her nephew and how she could best be of use to him.

It appeared to her that to do him any real service she must devote herself almost entirely to him; she must in fact give up living in London, at any rate for a long time, and live at Rough-borough where she could see him continually. This was a serious undertaking; she had lived in London for the last twelve years, and naturally disliked the prospect of a small country town such as Roughborough. Was it a prudent thing to attempt so much? Must not people take their chances in this world? Can anyone do much for anyone else unless by making a will in his favour and dying then and there? Should not each look after his own happiness, and will not the world be best carried on if everyone minds his own business and leaves other people to mind theirs? Life is not a donkey race in which everyone is to ride his neighbour's donkey and the last is to win, and the psalmist long since formulated a common experience when he declared that no man may deliver his brother nor make agreement unto God for him, for it cost more to redeem their souls, so that he must let that alone for ever.

All these excellent reasons for letting her nephew alone occurred to her, and many more, but against them there pleaded a woman's love for children, and her desire to find someone among the younger branches of her own family to whom she could become warmly attached, and whom she could attach warmly to herself.

Over and above this she wanted someone to leave her money to; she was not going to leave it to people about whom she knew very little, merely because they happened to be sons and daughters of brothers and sisters whom she had never liked. She knew the power and value of money exceedingly well, and how many lovable people suffer and die yearly for the want of it; she was little likely to leave it without being satisfied that her legatees were square, lovable, and more or less hard up. She wanted those to have it who would be most likely to use it genially and sensibly, and whom it would thus be likely to make most happy; if she could find one such among her nephews and nieces, so much the better; it was worth taking a great deal of pains to see whether she could or could not; but if she failed, she must find an heir who was not related to her by blood.

'Of course,' she had said to me, more than once, 'I shall make a mess of it. I shall choose some nice-looking, well-dressed screw, with gentlemanly manners which will take me in, and he will go and paint Academy pictures, or write for the *Times*, or do something just as horrid the moment the breath is out of my body.'

As yet, however, she had made no will at all, and this was one of the few things that troubled her. I believe she would have left most of her money to me if I had not stopped her. My father left me abundantly well off, and my mode of life has been always simple, so that I have never known uneasiness about money; moreover, I was especially anxious that there should be no occasion given for ill-natured talk; she knew well, therefore, that her leaving her money to me would be of all things the most likely to weaken the ties that existed between us, provided that I was aware of it, but I did not mind her talking about whom she should make her heir, so long as it was well understood that I was not to be the person.

Ernest had satisfied her as having enough in him to tempt her strongly to take him up, but it was not till after many days' reflection that she gravitated towards actually doing so, with all the break in her daily ways that this would entail. At least, she said it took her some days, and certainly it appeared to do so, but from the moment she had begun to broach the subject, I had guessed how things were going to end.

It was now arranged she should take a house at Roughborough, and go and live there for a couple of years. As a compromise, however, to meet some of my objections, it was also arranged that she should keep her rooms in Gower Street, and come to town for a week once in each month; of course, also, she would leave Roughborough for the greater part of the holidays. After two years, the thing was to come to an end, unless it proved a great success. She should by that time, at any rate, have made up her mind what the boy's character was, and would then act as circumstances might determine.

The pretext she put forward ostensibly was that her doctor said she ought to be a year or two in the country after so many years of London life, and had recommended Roughborough on account of the purity of its air, and its easy access to and from London – for by this time the railway had reached it. She was anxious not to give her brother and sister any right to complain, if on seeing more of her nephew she found she could not get on with him, and she was also anxious not to raise false hopes of any kind in the boy's own mind.

Having settled how everything was to be, she wrote to Theobald and said she meant to take a house in Roughborough from the Michaelmas then approaching, and mentioned, as though casually, that one of the attractions of the place would be that her nephew was at school there and she should hope to see more of him than she had done hitherto.

Theobald and Christina knew how dearly Alethea loved London, and thought it very odd that she should want to go and live at Roughborough but they did not suspect that she was going there solely on her nephew's account, much less that she had thought of making Ernest her heir. If they had guessed this they would have been so jealous that I half believe they would have asked her to go and live somewhere else. Alethea however was two or three years younger than Theobald; she was still some years short of fifty, and might very well live to eighty-five or ninety; her money, therefore, was not worth taking much trouble about, and her brother and sister-in-law had dismissed it, so to speak, from their minds with costs, assuming, however, that if anything did happen to her while they were still alive, the money would, as a matter of course, come to them.

The prospect of Alethea seeing much of Ernest was a serious matter. Christina smelt mischief from afar, as indeed she often did. Alethea was worldly – as worldly, that is to say, as a sister of Theobald's could be. In her letter to Theobald she had said she knew how much of his and Christina's thoughts were taken up with anxiety for the boy's welfare. Alethea had thought this handsome enough, but Christina had wanted something better and stronger. 'How can she know how much we think of our darling?' she had exclaimed, when Theobald showed her his sister's letter. 'I think, my dear, Alethea would understand these things better if she had children of her own.' The least that would have satisfied Christina was to have been told that there never yet had been any parents comparable to Theobald and herself. She did not feel easy that an alliance of some kind would not grow up between aunt and nephew, and neither she nor Theobald wanted Ernest to have any allies. Joey and Charlotte were quite as many allies as were good for him. After all, however, if Alethea chose to go and live at Roughborough, they could not well stop her, and must make the best of it.

In a few weeks' time Alethea did choose to go and live at Roughborough. A house was found with a field and a nice little garden which suited her very well. 'At any rate,' she said to herself, 'I will have fresh eggs and flowers.' She even considered the question of keeping a cow, but in the end decided not to do so. She furnished her house throughout anew, taking nothing whatever from her establishment in Gower Street, and by Michaelmas – for the house was empty when she took it – she was settled comfortably, and had begun to make herself at home.

One of Miss Pontifex's first moves was to ask a dozen of the smartest and most gentlemanly boys to breakfast with her. From her seat in church she could see the faces of the upper-form boys, and soon made up her mind which of them it would be best to cultivate. Miss Pontifex, sitting opposite the boys in church, and reckoning them up with her keen eyes from under her veil by all a woman's *criteria*, came to a truer conclusion about the greater number of those she scrutinised than ever Dr Skinner had done. She fell in love with one boy from seeing him put on his gloves.

Miss Pontifex, as I have said, got hold of some of these youngsters through Ernest, and fed them well. No boy can resist being fed well by a good-natured and still handsome woman. Boys are very like nice dogs in this respect – give them a bone and they will like you at once. Alethea employed every other little artifice which she thought likely to win their allegiance to herself, and through this their countenance for her nephew. She found the football club in a slight money difficulty and at once gave half a sovereign towards its removal. The boys had no chance against her, she shot them down one after another as easily as though they had been roosting pheasants. Nor did she escape scatheless herself, for, as she wrote to me, she quite lost her heart to half a dozen of them. 'How much nicer they are,' she said, 'and how much more they know than those who profess to teach them!'

I believe it has been lately maintained that it is the young and fair who are the truly old and truly experienced, inasmuch as it is they who alone have a living memory to guide them; 'the whole charm,' it has been said, 'of youth lies in its advantage over age in respect of experience, and when this has for some reason failed or been misapplied, the charm is broken. When we say that we are getting old, we should say rather that we are getting new or young, and are suffering from inexperience; trying to do things which we have never done before, and failing worse and worse, till in the end we are landed in the utter impotence of death.'

Miss Pontifex died many a long year before the above passage was written, but she had arrived independently at much the same conclusion.

She first, therefore, squared the boys. Dr Skinner was even more easily dealt with. He and Mrs Skinner called, as a matter of course, as soon as Miss Pontifex was settled. She fooled him to the top of his bent, and obtained the promise of a MS. copy of one of his minor poems (for Dr Skinner had the reputation of being quite one of our most facile and elegant minor poets) on the occasion of his first visit. The other masters and masters' wives were not forgotten. Alethea laid herself out to please, as indeed she did wherever she went, and if any woman lays herself out to do this, she generally succeeds.

Chapter Thirty-Four

Miss Pontifex soon found out that Ernest did not like games, but she saw also that he could hardly be expected to like them. He was perfectly well shaped but unusually devoid of physical strength. He got a fair share of this in after life, but it came much later with him than with other boys, and at the time of which I am writing he was a mere little skeleton. He wanted something to develop his arms and chest without knocking him about as much as the school games did. To supply this want by some means which should add also to his pleasure was Alethea's first anxiety. Rowing would have answered every purpose, but unfortunately there was no river at Roughborough.

Whatever it was to be, it must be something which he would like as much as other boys liked cricket or football, and he must think the wish for it to have come originally from himself; it was not very easy to find anything that would do, but ere long it occurred to her that she might enlist his love of music on her side, and asked him one day when he was spending a half-holiday at her house whether he would like her to buy an organ for him to play on. Of course the boy said yes; then she told him about her grandfather and the organs he had built. It had never entered into his head that he could make one, but when he gathered from what his aunt had said that this was not out of the question, he rose as eagerly to the bait as she could have desired, and wanted to begin learning to saw and plane so that he might make the wooden pipes at once.

Miss Pontifex did not see how she could have hit upon anything more suitable, and she liked the idea that he would incidentally get a knowledge of carpentering, for she was impressed, perhaps foolishly, with the wisdom of the German custom which gives every boy a handicraft of some sort.

Writing to me on this matter, she said, 'Professions are all very well for those who have connection and interest as well as capital, but otherwise they are white elephants. How many men do not you and I know who have talent, assiduity, excellent good sense, straightforwardness, every quality, in fact, which should command success, and who yet go on from year to year waiting and hoping against hope for the work which never comes? How, indeed, is it likely to come unless to those who either are born with interest, or who marry in order to get it? Ernest's father and mother have no interest, and if they had they would not use it. I suppose they will make him a clergyman, or try to do so – perhaps it is the best thing to do with him, for he could buy a living with the money his grandfather left him, but there is no knowing what the boy will think of it when the time comes, and for aught we know he may insist on going to the backwoods of America, as so many other young men are doing now.' . . . But, anyway, he would like making an organ, and this could do him no harm, so the sooner he began the better.

Alethea thought it would save trouble in the end if she told her brother and sister-in-law of this scheme. 'I do not suppose,' she wrote, 'that Dr Skinner will approve very cordially of my attempt to introduce organ-building into the *curriculum* of Roughborough, but I will see what I can do with him, for I have set my heart on owning an organ built by Ernest's own hands, which he may play on as much as he likes while it remains in my house and which I will lend him permanently as soon as he gets one of his own, but which is to be my property for the present, inasmuch as I mean to pay for it.' This was put in to make it plain to Theobald and Christina that they should not be out of pocket in the matter.

If Alethea had been as poor as the Misses Allaby, the reader may guess what Ernest's papa and mamma would have said to this proposal; but then, if she had been as poor as they, she would never have made it. They did not like Ernest's getting more and more into his aunt's good books, still it was perhaps better that he should do so than that she should be driven back upon the John Pontifexes. The only thing, said Theobald, which made him hesitate, was that the boy might be thrown with low associates later on if he were to be encouraged in his taste for music – a taste which Theobald had always disliked. He had observed with regret that Ernest had ere now shown rather a hankering after low company, and he might make acquaintance with those who would corrupt his innocence. Christina shuddered at this, but when they had aired their scruples sufficiently they felt (and when people begin to 'feel,' they are invariably going to take what they believe to be the more worldly course) that to oppose Alethea's proposal would be injuring their son's prospects more than was right, so they consented, but not too graciously.

After a time, however, Christina got used to the idea, and then considerations occurred to her which made her throw herself into it with characteristic ardour. If Miss Pontifex had been a railway stock she might have been said to have been buoyant in the Battersby market for some few days; buoyant for long together she could never be, still for a time there really was an upward movement. Christina's mind wandered to the organ itself; she seemed to have made it with her own hands; there would be no other in England to compare with it for combined sweetness and power. She already heard the famous Dr Walmisley of Cambridge mistaking it for a Father Smith. It would come, no doubt, in reality to Battersby Church, which wanted an organ, for it must be all nonsense about Alethea's wishing to keep it, and Ernest would not have a house of his own for ever so many years, and they could never have it at the Rectory. Oh, no! Battersby Church was the only proper place for it.

Of course they would have a grand opening, and the Bishop would come down, and perhaps young Figgins might be on a visit to them – she must ask Ernest if young Figgins had yet left

Roughborough – he might even persuade his grandfather, Lord Lonsford, to be present. Lord Lonsford and the Bishop and everyone else would then compliment her, and Dr Wesley or Dr Walmisley, who should preside (it did not much matter which), would say to her, 'My dear Mrs Pontifex, I never yet played upon so remarkable an instrument.' Then she would give him one of her sweetest smiles and say she feared he was flattering her, on which he would rejoin with some pleasant little trifle about remarkable men (the remarkable man being for the moment Ernest) having invariably had remarkable women for their mothers – and so on and so on. The advantage of doing one's praising to oneself is that one can lay it on so thick and exactly in the right places.

Theobald wrote Ernest a short and surly letter *à propos* of his aunt's intentions in this matter.

'I will not commit myself,' he said, 'to an opinion whether anything will come of it; this will depend entirely upon your own exertions; you have had singular advantages hitherto, and your kind aunt is showing every desire to befriend you, but you must give greater proof of stability and steadiness of character than you have given yet if this organ matter is not to prove in the end to be only one disappointment the more.

'I must insist on two things: firstly, that this new iron in the fire does not distract your attention from your Latin and Greek' – ('They aren't mine,' thought Ernest, 'and never have been') – 'and secondly, that you bring no smell of glue or shavings into the house here, if you make any part of the organ during your holidays.'

Ernest was still too young to know how unpleasant a letter he was receiving. He believed the innuendoes contained in it to be perfectly just. He knew he was sadly deficient in perseverance. He liked some things for a little while, and then found he did not like them any more – and this was as bad as anything well could be. His father's letter gave him one of his many fits of melancholy over his own worthlessness, but the thought of the organ consoled him, and he felt sure that here at any rate was something to which he could apply himself steadily without growing tired of it.

It was settled that the organ was not to be begun before the Christmas holidays were over, and that till then Ernest should do a little plain carpentering, so as to get to know how to use his tools. Miss Pontifex had a carpenter's bench set up in an outhouse upon her own premises, and made terms with the most respectable carpenter in Roughborough, by which one of his men was to come for a couple of hours twice a week and set Ernest on the right way; then she discovered she wanted this or that simple piece of work done, and gave the boy a commission to do it, paying him handsomely as well as finding him in tools and materials. She never gave him a syllable of good advice, or talked to him about everything's depending upon his own exertions, but she kissed him often, and would come into the workshop and act the part of one who took an interest in what was being done so cleverly as ere long to become really interested.

What boy would not take kindly to almost anything with such assistance? All boys like making things; the exercise of sawing, planing and hammering proved exactly what his aunt had wanted to find – something that should exercise, but not too much, and at the same time amuse him; when Ernest's sallow face was flushed with his work, and his eyes were sparkling with pleasure, he looked quite a different boy from the one his aunt had taken in hand only a few months earlier. His inner self never told him that this was humbug, as it did about Latin and Greek. Making stools and drawers was worth living for, and after Christmas there loomed the organ, which was scarcely ever absent from his mind.

His aunt let him invite his friends, encouraging him to bring those whom her quick sense told her were the most desirable. She smartened him up also in his personal appearance, always without preaching to him. Indeed she worked wonders during the short time that was allowed her, and if her life had been spared I cannot think that my hero would have come under the shadow of that cloud which cast so heavy a gloom over his younger manhood; but unfortunately for him his gleam of sunshine was too hot and too brilliant to last, and he had many a storm yet to weather before he became fairly happy. For the present, however, he was supremely so, and his aunt was happy and grateful for his happiness, the improvement she saw in him, and his unrepressed affection for herself. She became fonder of him from day to day in spite of his many faults and almost incredible foolishness. It was perhaps on account of these very things that she saw how much he had need of her; but at any rate, from whatever cause, she became strengthened in her determination to be to him in the place of parents, and to find in him a son rather than a nephew. But still she made no will.

Chapter Thirty-Five

All went well for the first part of the following half-year. Miss Pontifex spent the greater part of her holidays in London, and I also saw her at Roughborough, where I spent a few days, staying at the 'Swan.' I heard all about my godson in whom, however, I took less interest than I said I did. I took more interest in the stage at that time than in anything else, and as for Ernest, I found him a nuisance for engrossing so much of his aunt's attention, and taking her so much from London. The organ was begun, and made fair progress during the first two months of the half-year. Ernest was happier than he had ever been before, and was struggling upwards. The best boys took more notice of him for his aunt's sake, and he consorted less with those who led him into mischief.

But much as Miss Pontifex had done, she could not all at once undo the effect of such surroundings as the boy had at Battersby. Much as he feared and disliked his father (though he still knew not how much this was), he had caught much from him; if Theobald had been kinder Ernest would have modelled himself upon him entirely, and ere long would probably have become as thorough a little prig as could have easily been found.

Fortunately his temper had come to him from his mother, who, when not frightened, and when there was nothing on the horizon which might cross the slightest whim of her husband, was an amiable, good-natured woman. If it was not such an awful thing to say of anyone, I should say that she meant well.

Ernest had also inherited his mother's love of building castles in the air, and – so I suppose it must be called – her vanity. He was very fond of showing off, and, provided he could attract attention, cared little from whom it came, nor what it was for. He caught up, parrot-like, whatever jargon he heard from his elders, which he thought was the correct thing, and aired it in season and out of season, as though it were his own.

Miss Pontifex was old enough and wise enough to know that this is the way in which even the greatest men as a general rule begin to develop, and was more pleased with his receptiveness and reproductiveness than alarmed at the things he caught and reproduced.

She saw that he was much attached to herself, and trusted to this rather than to anything else. She saw also that his conceit was not very profound, and that his fits of self-abasement were as extreme as his exaltation had been. His impulsiveness and sanguine trustfulness in anyone who smiled pleasantly at him, or indeed was not absolutely unkind to him, made her more anxious about him than any other point in his character; she saw clearly that he would have to find himself rudely undeceived many a time and oft, before he would learn to distinguish friend from foe within reasonable time. It was her perception of this which led her to take the action which she was so soon called upon to take.

Her health was for the most part excellent, and she had never had a serious illness in her life. One morning, however, soon after Easter, 1850, she awoke feeling seriously unwell. For some little time there had been a talk of fever in the neighbourhood, but in those days the precautions that ought to be taken against the spread of infection were not so well understood as now, and nobody did anything. In a day or two it became plain that Miss Pontifex had got an attack of typhoid fever and was dangerously ill. On this she sent off a messenger to town, and desired him not to return without her lawyer and myself.

We arrived on the afternoon of the day on which we had been summoned, and found her still free from delirium: indeed, the cheery way in which she received us made it difficult to think she could be in danger. She at once explained her wishes, which had reference, as I expected, to her nephew, and repeated the substance of what I have already referred to as her main source of uneasiness concerning him. Then she begged me by our long and close intimacy, by the suddenness of the danger that had fallen on her and her powerlessness to avert it, to undertake what she said she well knew, if she died, would be an unpleasant and invidious trust.

She wanted to leave the bulk of her money ostensibly to me, but in reality to her nephew, so that I should hold it in trust for him till he was twenty-eight years old, but neither he nor anyone else, except her lawyer and myself, was to know anything about it. She would leave £5,000 in other legacies, and £15,000 to Ernest – which by the time he was twenty-eight would have accumulated to, say, £30,000. 'Sell out the debentures,' she said, 'where the money now is – and put it into Midland Ordinary.'

'Let him make his mistakes,' she said, 'upon the money his grandfather left him. I am no prophet, but even I can see that it will take that boy many years to see things as his neighbours see them. He will get no help from his father and mother, who would never forgive him for his good luck if I left him the money outright; I dare say I am wrong, but I think he will have to lose the greater part or all of what he has, before he will know how to keep what he will get from me.'

Supposing he went bankrupt before he was twenty-eight years old, the money was to be mine absolutely, but she could trust me, she said, to hand it over to Ernest in due time.

'If,' she continued, 'I am mistaken, the worst that can happen is that he will come into a larger sum at twenty-eight instead of a smaller sum at, say, twenty-three, for I would never trust him with it earlier, and if he knows nothing about it he will not be unhappy for the want of it.'

She begged me to take £2,000 in return for the trouble I should have in taking charge of the boy's estate, and as a sign of the testratrix's hope that I would now and again look after him while he was still young. The remaining £3,000 I was to pay in legacies and annuities to friends and servants.

In vain both her lawyer and myself remonstrated with her on the unusual and hazardous nature of this arrangement. We told her that sensible people will not take a more sanguine view concerning human nature than the Courts of Chancery do. We said, in fact, everything that anyone else would say. She admitted everything, but urged that her time was short, that nothing would induce her to leave her money to her nephew in the usual way. 'It is an unusually foolish will,' she said, 'but he is an unusually foolish boy;' and she smiled quite merrily at her little sally. Like all the rest of her family, she was very stubborn when her mind was made up. So the thing was done as she wished it.

No provision was made for either my death or Ernest's – Miss Pontifex had settled it that we were neither of us going to die, and was too ill to go into details; she was so anxious, moreover, to sign her will while still able to do so that we had practically no alternative but to do as she told us. If she recovered we could see things put on a more satisfactory footing, and further discussion would evidently impair her chances of recovery; it seemed then only too likely that it was a case of this will or no will at all.

When the will was signed I wrote a letter in duplicate, saying that I held all Miss Pontifex had left me in trust for Ernest except as regards £5,000, but he was not to come into the bequest, and was to know nothing whatever about it directly or indirectly, till he was twenty-eight years old, and if he was bankrupt before he came into it the money was to be mine absolutely. At the foot of each letter Miss Pontifex wrote, 'The above was my understanding when I made my will,' and then signed her name. The solicitor and his clerk witnessed; I kept one copy myself and handed the other to Miss Pontifex's solicitor.

When all this had been done she became more easy in her mind. She talked principally about her nephew. 'Don't scold him,' she said, 'if he is volatile, and continually takes things up only to throw them down again. How can he find out his strength or weakness otherwise? A man's profession,' she said, and here she gave one of her wicked little laughs, 'is not like his wife, which he must take once for all, for better for worse, without proof beforehand. Let him go here and there, and learn his truest liking by finding out what, after all, he catches himself turning to most habitually – then let him stick to this; but I dare say Ernest will be forty or five and forty before he settles down. Then all his previous infidelities will work together to him for good if he is the boy I hope he is.

'Above all,' she continued, 'do not let him work up to his full strength, except once or twice in his lifetime; nothing is well done nor worth doing unless, take it all round, it has come pretty easily. Theobald and Christina would give him a pinch of salt and tell him to put it on the tails of the seven deadly virtues;' – here she laughed again in her old manner at once so mocking and so sweet – 'I think if he likes pancakes he had perhaps better eat them on Shrove Tuesday, but this is enough.' These were the last coherent words she spoke. From that time she grew continually worse, and was never free from delirium till her death – which took place less than a fortnight afterwards, to the inexpressible grief of those who knew and loved her.

Chapter Thirty-Six

Letters had been written to Miss Pontifex's brothers and sisters, and one and all came post-haste to Roughborough. Before they arrived the poor lady was already delirious, and for the sake of her own peace at the last I am half glad she never recovered consciousness.

I had known these people all their lives, as none can know each other but those who have played together as children; I knew how they had all of them – perhaps Theobald least, but all of them more or less – made her life a burden to her until the death of her father had made her her own mistress, and I was displeased at their coming one after the other to Roughborough, and inquiring whether their sister had recovered consciousness sufficiently to be able to see them. It was known that she had sent for me on being taken ill, and that I remained at Roughborough, and I own I was angered by the mingled air of suspicion, defiance and inquisitiveness with which they regarded me. They would all, except Theobald, I believe, have cut me downright if they had not believed me to know something they wanted to know themselves, and might have some chance of learning from me – for it was plain I had been in some way concerned with the making of their sister's will. None of them suspected what the ostensible nature of this would be, but I think they feared Miss Pontifex was about to leave money for public uses. John said to me in his blandest manner that he fancied he remembered to have heard his sister say that she thought of leaving money to found a college for the relief of dramatic authors in distress; to this I made no rejoinder, and I have no doubt his suspicions were deepened.

When the end came, I got Miss Pontifex's solicitor to write and tell her brothers and sisters how she had left her money: they were not unnaturally furious, and went each to his or her separate home without attending the funeral, and without paying any attention to myself. This was perhaps the kindest thing they could have done by me, for their behaviour made me so angry that I became almost reconciled to Alethea's will out of pleasure at the anger it had aroused. But for this I should have felt the will keenly, as having been placed by it in the position which of all others I had been most anxious to avoid, and as having saddled me with a very heavy responsibility. Still it was impossible for me to escape, and I could only let things take their course.

Miss Pontifex had expressed a wish to be buried at Paleham; in the course of the next few days I therefore took the body thither. I had not been to Paleham since the death of my father some six years earlier. I had often wished to go there, but had shrunk from doing so though my sister had been two or three times. I could not bear to see the house which had been my home for so many years of my life in the hands of strangers; to ring ceremoniously at a bell which I had never yet pulled except as a boy in jest; to feel that I had nothing to do with a garden in which I had in childhood gathered so many a nosegay, and which had seemed my own for many years after I had reached man's estate; to see the rooms bereft of every familiar feature, and made so unfamiliar in spite of their familiarity. Had there been any sufficient reason, I should have taken these things as a matter of course, and should no doubt have found them much worse in anticipation than in reality, but as there had been no special reason why I should go to Paleham I had hitherto avoided doing so. Now, however, my going was a necessity, and I confess I never felt more subdued than I did on arriving there with the dead playmate of my childhood.

I found the village more changed than I had expected. The railway had come there, and a brand new yellow brick station was on the site of old Mr and Mrs Pontifex's cottage. Nothing but the carpenter's shop was now standing. I saw many faces I knew, but even in six years they seemed to have grown wonderfully older. Some of the very old were dead, and the old were getting very old in their stead. I felt like the changeling in the fairy story who came back after a seven years' sleep. Everyone seemed glad to see me, though I had never given them particular cause to be so, and everyone who remembered old Mr and Mrs Pontifex spoke warmly of them and were pleased at their granddaughter's wishing to be laid near them. Entering the churchyard and standing in the twilight of a gusty cloudy evening on the spot close beside old Mrs Pontifex's grave which I had chosen for Alethea's, I thought of the many times that she, who would lie there henceforth, and I, who must surely lie one day in some such another place though when and where I knew not, had romped over this very spot as childish lovers together.

Next morning I followed her to the grave, and in due course set up a plain upright slab to her memory as like as might be to those over the graves of her grandmother and grandfather. I gave the dates and places of her birth and death, but added nothing except that this stone was set up by one who had known and loved her. Knowing how fond she had been of music I had been half-inclined at one time to inscribe a few bars of music, if I could find any which seemed suitable to her character, but I knew how much she would have disliked anything singular in connection with her tombstone and did not do it.

Before, however, I had come to this conclusion, I had thought that Ernest might be able to help me to the right thing, and had written to him upon the subject. The following is the answer I received:

'Dear Godpapa, – I send you the best bit I can think of; it is the subject of the last of Handel's six grand fugues and goes thus:

Grave

It would do better for a man, especially for an old man who was very sorry for things, than for a woman, but I cannot think of anything better; if you do not like it for Aunt Alethea I shall keep it for myself. – Your affectionate Godson,

'Ernest Pontifex.'

Was this the little lad who could get sweeties for two-pence but not for two-pence-halfpenny? Dear, dear me, I thought to myself, how these babes and sucklings do give us the go-by surely. Choosing his own epitaph at fifteen as for a man who 'had been very sorry for things,' and such a strain as that – why, it might have done for Leonardo da Vinci himself. Then I set the boy down as a conceited young jackanapes, which no doubt he was – but so are a great many other young people of Ernest's age.

Chapter Thirty-Seven

If Theobald and Christina had not been too well pleased when Miss Pontifex first took Ernest in hand, they were still less so when the connection between the two was interrupted so prematurely. They said they had made sure from what their sister had said that she was going to make Ernest her heir. I do not think she had given them so much as a hint to this effect. Theobald indeed gave Ernest to understand that she had done so in a letter which will be given shortly, but if Theobald wanted to make himself disagreeable, a trifle light as air would forthwith assume in his imagination whatever form was most convenient to him. I do not think they had even made up their minds what Alethea was to do with her money before they knew of her being at the point of death, and as I have said already, if they had thought it likely that Ernest would be made heir over their own heads without their having at any rate a life interest in the bequest, they would have soon thrown obstacles in the way of further intimacy between aunt and nephew.

This, however, did not bar their right to feeling aggrieved now that neither they nor Ernest had taken anything at all, and they could profess disappointment on their boy's behalf which they would have been too proud to admit upon their own. In fact, it was only amiable of them to be disappointed under these circumstances.

Christina said that the will was simply fraudulent, and was convinced that it could be upset if she and Theobald went the right way to work. Theobald, she said, should go before the Lord Chancellor, not in full court but in chambers, where he could explain the whole matter; or, perhaps it would be even better if she were to go herself – and I dare not trust myself to describe the reverie to which this last idea gave rise. I believe in the end Theobald died, and the Lord Chancellor (who had become a widower a few weeks earlier) made her an offer, which, however, she firmly but not ungratefully declined; she should ever, she said, continue to think of him as a friend – at this point the cook came in, saying the butcher had called, and what would she please to order.

I think Theobald must have had an idea that there was something behind the bequest to me, but he said nothing about it to Christina. He was angry and felt wronged, because he could not get at Alethea to give her a piece of his mind any more than he had been able to get at his father. 'It is so mean of people,' he exclaimed to himself, 'to inflict an injury of this sort, and then shirk facing those whom they have injured; let us hope that, at any rate, they and I may meet in Heaven.' But of this it was doubtful, for when people had done so great a wrong as this, it was hardly to be supposed that they would go to Heaven at all – and as for his meeting them in another place, the idea never so much as entered his mind.

One so angry and, of late, so little used to contradiction might be trusted, however, to avenge himself upon someone, and Theobald had long since developed the organ by means of which he might vent spleen with least risk and greatest satisfaction to himself. This organ, it may be guessed, was nothing else than Ernest; to Ernest, therefore, he proceeded to unburden himself, not personally, but by letter.

'You ought to know,' he wrote, 'that your Aunt Alethea had given your mother and me to understand that it was her wish to make you her heir – in the event, of course, of your conducting yourself in such a manner as to give her confidence in you; as a matter of fact, however, she has left you nothing, and the whole of her property has gone to your godfather, Mr Overton. Your mother and I are willing to hope that if she had lived longer you would yet have succeeded in winning her good opinion, but it is too late to think of this now.

The carpentering and organ-building must at once be discontinued. I never believed in the project, and have seen no reason to alter my original opinion. I am not sorry for your own sake, that it is to be at an end, nor, I am sure, will you regret it yourself in after years.

'A few words more as regards your own prospects. You have, as I believe you know, a small inheritance, which is yours legally under your grandfather's will. This bequest was made inadvertently, and, I believe, entirely through a misunderstanding on the lawyer's part. The bequest was probably intended not to take effect till after the death of your mother and myself; nevertheless, as the will is actually worded, it will now be at your command if you live to be twenty-one years old. From this, however, large deductions must be made. There will be legacy duty, and I do not know whether I am not entitled to deduct the expenses of your education and maintenance from birth to your coming of age; I shall not in all likelihood insist on this right to the full, if you conduct yourself properly, but a considerable sum should certainly be deducted, there will therefore remain very little – say £1,000 or £2,000 at the outside, as what will be actually yours – but the strictest account shall be rendered you in due time.

'This, let me warn you most seriously, is all that you must expect from me' (even Ernest saw that it was not from Theobald at all) 'at any rate till after my death, which for aught any of us know may be yet many years distant. It is not a large sum, but it is sufficient if supplemented by steadiness and earnestness of purpose. Your mother and I gave you the name Ernest, hoping that it would remind you continually of –' but I really cannot copy more of this effusion. It was all the same old will-shaking game and came practically to this, that Ernest was no good, and that if he went on as he was going on now, he would probably have to go about the streets begging without any shoes or stockings soon after he had left school, or at any rate, college; and that he, Theobald, and Christina were almost too good for this world altogether.

After he had written this Theobald felt quite good-natured, and sent to the Mrs Thompson of the moment even more soup and wine than her usual not illiberal allowance.

Ernest was deeply, passionately upset by his father's letter; to think that even his dear aunt, the one person of his relations whom he really loved, should have turned against him and thought badly of him after all. This was the unkindest cut of all. In the hurry of her illness Miss Pontifex, while thinking only of his welfare, had omitted to make such small present mention of him as would have made his father's innuendoes stingless; and her illness being infectious, she had not seen him after its nature was known. I myself did not know of Theobald's letter, nor think enough about my godson to guess what might easily be his state. It was not till many years afterwards that I found Theobald's letter in the pocket of an old portfolio which Ernest had used at school, and in which other old letters and school documents were collected which I have used in this book. He had forgotten that he had it, but told me when he saw it that he remembered it as the first thing that made him begin to rise against his father in a rebellion which he recognised as righteous, though he dared not openly avow it. Not the least serious thing was that it would, he feared, be his duty to give up the legacy his grandfather had left him; for if it was his only through a mistake, how could he keep it?

During the rest of the half-year Ernest was listless and unhappy. He was very fond of some of his school-fellows, but afraid of those whom he believed to be better than himself, and prone to idealise everyone into being his superior except those who were obviously a good deal beneath him. He held himself much too cheap, and because he was without that physical strength and vigour which he so much coveted, and also because he knew he shirked his lessons, he believed that he was without anything which could deserve the name of a good quality; he was naturally bad, and one of those for whom there was no place for repentance, though he sought it even with tears. So he shrank out of sight of those whom in his boyish way he idolised, never for a moment suspecting that he might have capacities to the full as high as theirs though of a different kind, and fell in more with those who were reputed of the baser sort, with whom he could at any rate be upon equal terms. Before the end of the half-year he had dropped from the estate to which he had been raised during his aunt's stay at Roughborough, and his old dejection, varied, however, with bursts of conceit rivalling those of his mother, resumed its sway over him. 'Pontifex,' said Dr Skinner, who had fallen upon him in hall one day like a moral landslip, before he had time to escape, 'do you never laugh? Do you always look so preternaturally grave?' The doctor had not meant to be unkind, but the boy turned crimson, and escaped.

There was one place only where he was happy, and that was in the old church of St Michael, when his friend the organist was practising. About this time cheap editions of the great oratorios began to appear, and Ernest got them all as soon as they were published; he would sometimes sell a school-book to a second-hand dealer, and buy a number or two of the 'Messiah,' or the 'Creation,' or 'Elijah,' with the proceeds. This was simply cheating his papa and mamma, but Ernest was falling low again – or thought he was – and he wanted the music much, and the Sallust, or whatever it was, little. Sometimes the organist would go home, leaving his keys with Ernest, so that he could play by himself and lock up the organ and the church in time to get back for calling over. At other times, while his friend was playing, he would wander round the church, looking at the monuments and the old stained-glass windows, enchanted as regards both ears and eyes, at once. Once the old rector got hold of him as he was watching a new window being put in, which the rector had bought in Germany – the work, it was supposed, of Albert Dürer. He questioned Ernest, and finding that he was fond of music, he said in his old trembling voice (for he was over eighty), 'Then you should have known Dr Burney who wrote the history of music. I knew him exceedingly well when I was a young man.' That made Ernest's heart beat, for he knew that Dr Burney, when a boy at school at Chester, used to break bounds that he might watch Handel smoking his pipe in the Exchange coffee house – and now he was in the presence of one who, if he had not seen Handel himself, had at least seen those who had seen him.

These were oases in his desert, but, as a general rule, the boy looked thin and pale, and as though he had a secret which depressed him, which no doubt he had, but for which I cannot blame him. He rose, in spite of himself, higher in the school, but fell ever deeper and deeper in disgrace with the masters, and did not gain in the opinion of those boys about whom he was persuaded that they could assuredly never know what it was to have a secret weighing upon their minds. This was what Ernest felt so keenly; he did not much care about the boys who liked him, and idolised some who kept him as far as possible at a distance, but this is pretty much the case with all boys everywhere.

At last things reached a crisis, below which they could not very well go, for at the end of the half-year but one after his aunt's death, Ernest brought back a document in his portmanteau, which Theobald stigmatised as 'infamous and outrageous.' I need hardly say I am alluding to his school bill.

This document was always a source of anxiety to Ernest, for it was gone into with scrupulous care, and he was a good deal cross-examined about it. He would sometimes 'write in' for articles necessary for his education, such as a portfolio, or a dictionary, and sell the same, as I have explained, in order to eke out his pocket money, probably to buy either music or tobacco. These frauds were sometimes, as Ernest thought, in imminent danger of being discovered, and it was a load off his breast when the cross-examination was safely over. This time Theobald had made a great fuss about the extras, but had grudgingly passed them; it was another matter, however, with the character and the moral statistics, with which the bill concluded.

The page on which these details were to be found was as follows:

REPORT OF THE CONDUCT AND PROGRESS OF ERNEST PONTIFEX, UPPER FIFTH FORM, HALF-YEAR ENDING MIDSUMMER, 1851

Classics – Idle, listless and unimproving.
Mathematics   "   "
Divinity   "   "
Conduct in house – Orderly.
General Conduct – Not satisfactory, on account of his great unpunctuality and inattention to duties.

Monthly merit money	1s.	6d.	6d.	0d.	6d.	Total 2s.	6d.
Number of merit marks	2	0	1	1	0	Total	4
Number of penal marks	26	20	25	30	25	Total	126
Number of extra penals	9	6	10	12	11	Total	48

I recommend that his pocket money be made to depend upon his merit money.

S. Skinner, Headmaster.

Chapter Thirty-Eight

Ernest was thus in disgrace from the beginning of the holidays, but an incident soon occurred which led him into delinquencies compared with which all his previous sins were venial.

Among the servants at the Rectory was a remarkably pretty girl named Ellen. She came from Devonshire, and was the daughter of a fisherman who had been drowned when she was a child. Her mother set up a small shop in the village where her husband had lived, and just managed to make a living. Ellen remained with her till she was fourteen, when she first went out to service. Four years later, when she was about eighteen, but so well grown that she might have passed for twenty, she had been strongly recommended to Christina, who was then in want of a housemaid, and had now been at Battersby about twelve months.

As I have said, the girl was remarkably pretty; she looked the perfection of health and good temper, indeed there was a serene expression upon her face which captivated almost all who saw her; she looked as if matters had always gone well with her and were always going to do so, and as if no conceivable combination of circumstances could put her for long together out of temper either with herself or with anyone else. Her complexion was clear, but high; her eyes were grey and beautifully shaped; her lips were full and restful, with something of an Egyptian Sphinx-like character about them. When I learned that she came from Devonshire I fancied I saw a strain of far away Egyptian blood in her, for I had heard, though I know not what foundation there was for the story, that the Egyptians made settlements on the coast of Devonshire and Cornwall long before the Romans conquered Britain. Her hair was a rich brown, and her figure – of about the middle height –

perfect, but erring if at all on the side of robustness. Altogether she was one of those girls about whom one is inclined to wonder how they can remain unmarried a week or a day longer.

Her face (as indeed faces generally are, though I grant they lie sometimes) was a fair index to her disposition. She was good nature itself, and everyone in the house, not excluding I believe even Theobald himself after a fashion, was fond of her. As for Christina she took the very warmest interest in her, and used to have her into the dining-room twice a week, and prepare her for confirmation (for by some accident she had never been confirmed) by explaining to her the geography of Palestine and the routes taken by St Paul on his various journeys in Asia Minor.

When Bishop Treadwell did actually come down to Battersby and hold a confirmation there (Christina had her wish, he slept at Battersby, and she had a grand dinner party for him, and called him 'My lord' several times), he was so much struck by her pretty face and modest demeanour when he laid his hands upon her that he asked Christina about her. When she replied that Ellen was one of her own servants, the bishop seemed, so she thought or chose to think, quite pleased that so pretty a girl should have found so exceptionally good a situation.

Ernest used to get up early during the holidays so that he might play the piano before breakfast without disturbing his papa and mamma – or rather, perhaps, without being disturbed by them. Ellen would generally be there sweeping the drawing-room floor and dusting while he was playing, and the boy, who was ready to make friends with most people, soon became very fond of her. He was not as a general rule sensitive to the charms of the fair sex, indeed he had hardly been thrown in with any woman except his Aunts Allaby, and his Aunt Alethea, his mother, his sister Charlotte and Mrs Jay; sometimes also he had to take off his hat to the Miss Skinners, and had felt as if he should sink into the earth on doing so, but his shyness had worn off with Ellen, and the pair had become fast friends.

Perhaps it was well that Ernest was not at home for very long together, but as yet his affection though hearty was quite Platonic. He was not only innocent, but deplorably – I might even say guiltily – innocent. His preference was based upon the fact that Ellen never scolded him, but was always smiling and good tempered; besides she used to like to hear him play, and this gave him additional zest in playing. The morning access to the piano was indeed the one distinct advantage which the holidays had in Ernest's eyes, for at school he could not get at a piano except quasi-surreptitiously at the shop of Mr Pearsall, the music-seller.

On returning this midsummer he was shocked to find his favourite looking pale and ill. All her good spirits had left her, the roses had fled from her cheek, and she seemed on the point of going into a decline. She said she was unhappy about her mother, whose health was failing, and was afraid she was herself not long for this world. Christina, of course, noticed the change. 'I have often remarked,' she said, 'that those very fresh-coloured, healthy-looking girls are the first to break up. I have given her calomel and James's powders repeatedly, and though she does not like it, I think I must show her to Dr Martin when he next comes here.'

'Very well, my dear,' said Theobald, so next time Dr Martin came Ellen was sent for. Dr Martin soon discovered what would probably have been apparent to Christina herself if she had been able to conceive of such an ailment in connection with a servant who lived under the same roof as Theobald and herself – the purity of whose married life should have preserved all unmarried people who came near them from any taint of mischief.

When it was discovered that in three or four months more Ellen would become a mother, Christina's natural good nature would have prompted her to deal as leniently with the case as she could, if she had not been panic-stricken lest any mercy on her and Theobald's part should be construed into toleration, however partial, of so great a sin; hereon she dashed off into the conviction that the only thing to do was to pay Ellen her wages, and pack her off on the instant bag and baggage out of the house which purity had more especially and particularly singled out for its abiding city. When she thought of the fearful contamination which Ellen's continued presence even for a week would occasion, she could not hesitate.

Then came the question – horrid thought! – as to who was the partner of Ellen's guilt? Was it, could it be, her own son, her darling Ernest? Ernest was getting a big boy now. She could excuse any young woman for taking a fancy to him; as for himself, why she was sure he was behind no young man of his age in appreciation of the charms of a nice-looking young woman. So long as he was innocent she did not mind this, but oh, if he were guilty!

She could not bear to think of it, and yet it would be mere cowardice not to look such a matter in the face – her hope was in the Lord, and she was ready to bear cheerfully and make the best of any suffering He might think fit to lay upon her. That the baby must be either a boy or girl – this much, at any rate, was clear. No less clear was it that the child, if a boy, would resemble Theobald, and if a girl, herself. Resemblance, whether of body or mind, generally leaped over a generation. The guilt of the parents must not be shared by the innocent offspring of shame – oh! no – and such a child as this would be . . . She was off in one of her reveries at once.

The child was in the act of being consecrated Archbishop of Canterbury when Theobald came in from a visit in the parish, and was told of the shocking discovery.

Christina said nothing about Ernest, and I believe was more than half angry when the blame was laid upon other shoulders. She was easily consoled, however, and fell back on the double reflection, firstly, that her son was pure, and secondly, that she was quite sure he would not have been so had it not been for his religious convictions which had held him back – as, of course, it was only to be expected they would.

Theobald agreed that no time must be lost in paying Ellen her wages and packing her off. So this was done, and less than two hours after Dr Martin had entered the house Ellen was sitting beside John the coachman, with her face muffled up so that it could not be seen, weeping bitterly as she was being driven to the station.

Chapter Thirty-Nine

Ernest had been out all the morning, but came into the yard of the Rectory from the spinney behind the house just as Ellen's things were being put into the carriage. He thought it was Ellen whom he then saw get into the carriage, but as her face had been hidden by her handkerchief he had not been able to see plainly who it was, and dismissed the idea as improbable.

He went to the back-kitchen window, at which the cook was standing peeling the potatoes for dinner, and found her crying bitterly. Ernest was much distressed, for he liked the cook, and, of course, wanted to know what all the matter was, who it was that had just gone off in the pony carriage, and why? The cook told him it was Ellen, but said that no earthly power should make it cross her lips why it was she was going away; when, however, Ernest took her *au pied de la lettre* and asked no further questions, she told him all about it after extorting the most solemn promises of secrecy.

It took Ernest some minutes to arrive at the facts of the case, but when he understood them he leaned against the pump, which stood near the back-kitchen window, and mingled his tears with the cook's.

Then his blood began to boil within him. He did not see that after all his father and mother could have done much otherwise than they actually did. They might perhaps have been less precipitate, and tried to keep the matter a little more quiet, but this would not have been easy, nor would it have mended things very materially. The bitter fact remains that if a girl does certain things she must do them at her peril, no matter how young and pretty she is nor to what temptation she has succumbed. This is the way of the world, and as yet there has been no help found for it.

Ernest could only see what he gathered from the cook, namely, that his favourite, Ellen, was being turned adrift with a matter of three pounds in her pocket, to go she knew not where, and to do she knew not what, and that she had said she should hang or drown herself, which the boy implicitly believed she would.

With greater promptitude than he had shown yet, he reckoned up his money and found he had two shillings and threepence at his command; there was his knife which might sell for a shilling, and there was the silver watch his Aunt Alethea had given him shortly before she died. The carriage had been gone now a full quarter of an hour, and it must have got some distance ahead, but he would do his best to catch it up, and there were short cuts which would perhaps give him a chance. He was off at once, and from the top of the hill just past the Rectory paddock he could see the carriage, looking very small, on a bit of road which showed perhaps a mile and a half in front of him.

One of the most popular amusements at Roughborough was an institution called 'the hounds' – more commonly known elsewhere as 'hare and hounds,' but in this case the hare was a couple of boys who were called foxes, and boys are so particular about correctness of nomenclature where their sports are concerned that I dare not say they played 'hare and hounds'; these were 'the hounds,' and that was all. Ernest's want of muscular strength did not tell against him here; there was no jostling up against boys who, though neither older nor taller than he, were yet more robustly built; if it came to mere endurance he was as good as anyone else, so when his carpentering was stopped he had naturally taken to 'the hounds' as his favourite amusement. His lungs thus exercised had become developed, and as a run of six or seven miles across country was not more than he was used to, he did not despair by the help of the short cuts of overtaking the carriage, or at the worst of catching Ellen at the station before the train left. So he ran and ran and ran till his first wind was gone and his second came, and he could breathe more easily. Never with 'the hounds' had he run so fast and with so few breaks as now, but with all his efforts and the help of the short cuts he did not catch up the carriage, and would probably not have done so had not John happened to turn his head and seen him running and making signs for the carriage to stop a quarter of a mile off. He was now about five miles from home, and was nearly done up.

He was crimson with his exertion; covered with dust, and with his trousers and coat sleeves a trifle short for him he cut a poor figure enough as he thrust on Ellen his watch, his knife, and the little money he had. The one thing he implored of her was not to do those dreadful things which she threatened – for his sake if for no other reason.

Ellen at first would not hear of taking anything from him, but the coachman, who was from the north country, sided with Ernest. 'Take it, my lass,' he said kindly, 'take what thou canst get whiles thou canst get it; as for Master Ernest here – he has run well after thee; therefore let him give thee what he is minded.'

Ellen did what she was told, and the two parted with many tears, the girl's last words being that she should never forget him, and that they should meet again hereafter, she was sure they should, and then she would repay him.

Then Ernest got into a field by the roadside, flung himself on the grass, and waited under the shadow of a hedge till the carriage should pass on its return from the station and pick him up, for he was dead beat. Thoughts which had already occurred to him with some force now came more strongly before him, and he saw that he had got himself into one mess – or rather into half a dozen messes – the more.

In the first place he should be late for dinner, and this was one of the offences on which Theobald had no mercy. Also he should have to say where he had been, and there was a danger of being found out if he did not speak the truth. Not only this, but sooner or later it must come out that he was no longer possessed of the beautiful watch which his dear aunt had given him and what, pray, had he done with it or how had he lost it? The reader will know very well what he ought to have done. He should have gone straight home, and if questioned should have said, 'I have been running after the carriage to catch our housemaid Ellen, whom I am very fond of; I have given her my watch, my knife and all my pocket-money, so that now I have no pocket-money at all and shall probably ask you for more sooner than I otherwise might have done, and you will also have to buy me a new watch and a knife.' But then fancy the consternation which such an announcement would have occasioned! Fancy the scowl and flashing eyes of the infuriated Theobald! 'You unprincipled young scoundrel,' he would exclaim, 'do you mean to vilify your own parents by implying that they have dealt harshly by one whose profligacy has disgraced their house?'

Or he might have taken it with one of those sallies of sarcastic calm, of which he believed himself to be a master.

'Very well, Ernest, very well: I shall say nothing; you can please yourself; you are not yet twenty-one, but pray act as if you were your own master; your poor aunt doubtless gave you the watch that you might fling it away upon the first improper character you came across; I think I can now understand, however, why she did not leave you her money; and, after all, your godfather may just as well have it as the kind of people on whom you would lavish it if it were yours.'

Then his mother would burst into tears and implore him to repent and seek the things belonging to his peace while there was yet time, by falling on his knees to Theobald and assuring him of his unfailing love for him as the kindest and tenderest father in the universe. Ernest could do all this just as well as they could, and now, as he lay on the grass, speeches, some one or other of which was as certain to come as the sun to set, kept running in his head till they confuted the idea of telling the truth by reducing it to an absurdity. Truth might be heroic, but it was not within the range of practical domestic politics.

Having settled then that he was to tell a lie, what lie should he tell? Should he say he had been robbed? He had enough imagination to know that he had not enough imagination to carry him out here. Young as he was, his instinct told him that the best liar is he who makes the smallest amount of lying go the longest way – who husbands it too carefully to waste it where it can be dispensed with. The simplest course would be to say that he had lost the watch, and was late for dinner because he had been looking for it. He had been out for a long walk – he chose the line across the fields that he had actually taken and the weather being very hot, he had taken off his coat and waistcoat; in carrying them over his arm his watch, his money, and his knife had dropped out of them. He had got nearly home when he found out his loss, and had run back as fast as he could, looking along the line he had followed, till at last he had given it up; seeing the carriage coming back from the station, he had let it pick him up and bring him home.

This covered everything, the running and all; for his face still showed that he must have been running hard; the only question was whether he had been seen about the Rectory by any but the servants for a couple of hours or so before Ellen had gone, and this he was happy to believe was not the case; for he had been out except during his few minutes' interview with the cook. His father had been out in the parish; his mother had certainly not come across him, and his brother and sister had also been out with the governess. He knew he could depend upon the cook and the other servants – the coachman would see to this; on the whole, therefore, both he and the coachman thought the story as proposed by Ernest would about meet the requirements of the case.

Chapter Forty

When Ernest got home and sneaked in through the back door, he heard his father's voice in its angriest tones, inquiring whether Master Ernest had already returned. He felt as Jack must have felt in the story of Jack and the Bean Stalk, when from the oven in which he was hidden he heard the ogre ask his wife what young children she had got for his supper. With much courage, and, as the event proved, with not less courage than discretion, he took the bull by the horns, and announced himself at once as having just come in after having met with a terrible misfortune. Little by little he told his story, and though Theobald stormed somewhat at his 'incredible folly and carelessness,' he got off better than he expected. Theobald and Christina had indeed at first been inclined to connect his absence from dinner with Ellen's dismissal, but on finding it clear, as Theobald said – everything was always clear with Theobald – that Ernest had not been in the house all the morning, and could therefore have known nothing of what had happened, he was acquitted on this account for once in a way, without a stain upon his character. Perhaps Theobald was in a good temper; he may have seen from the paper that morning that his stocks had been rising; it may have been this or twenty other things, but whatever it was, he did not scold so much as Ernest had expected, and, seeing the boy look exhausted, and believing him to be much grieved at the loss of his watch, Theobald actually prescribed a glass of wine after his dinner, which, strange to say, did not choke him, but made him see things more cheerfully than was usual with him.

That night when he said his prayers, he inserted a few paragraphs to the effect that he might not be discovered, and that things might go well with Ellen, but he was anxious and ill at ease. His guilty conscience pointed out to him a score of weak places in his story, through any one of which detection might even yet easily enter. Next day and for many days afterwards he fled when no man was pursuing, and trembled each time he heard his father's voice calling for him. He had already so many causes of anxiety that he could stand little more, and in spite of all his endeavours to look cheerful, even his mother could see that something was preying upon his mind. Then the idea returned to her that, after all, her son might not be innocent in the Ellen matter – and this was so interesting that she felt bound to get as near the truth as she could.

'Come here, my poor, pale-faced, heavy-eyed boy,' she said to him one day in her kindest manner; 'come and sit down by me, and we will have a little quiet confidential talk together, will we not?'

The boy went mechanically to the sofa. Whenever his mother wanted what she called a confidential talk with him she always selected the sofa as the most suitable ground on which to open her campaign. All mothers do this; the sofa is to them what the dining-room is to fathers. In the present case the sofa was particularly well adapted for a strategic purpose, being an old-fashioned one with a high back, mattress, bolsters and cushions. Once safely penned into one of its deep corners, it was like a dentist's chair, not too easy to get out of again. Here she could get at him better to pull him about, if this should seem desirable, or if she thought fit to cry she could bury her head in the sofa cushion and abandon herself to an agony of grief which seldom failed of its effect. None of her favourite manoeuvres were so easily adopted in her usual seat, the armchair on the right-hand side of the fireplace, and so well did her son know from his mother's tone that this was going to be a sofa conversation that he took his place like a lamb as soon as she began to speak and before she could reach the sofa herself.

'My dearest boy,' began his mother, taking hold of his hand

and placing it within her own, 'promise me never to be afraid either of your dear papa or of me; promise me this, my dear, as you love me, promise it to me,' and she kissed him again and again and stroked his hair. But with her other hand she still kept hold of his; she had got him and she meant to keep him.

The lad hung down his head and promised. What else could he do?

'You know there is no one, dear, dear Ernest, who loves you so much as your papa and I do; no one who watches so carefully over your interests or who is so anxious to enter into all your little joys and troubles as we are; but, my dearest boy, it grieves me to think sometimes that you have not that perfect love for and confidence in us which you ought to have. You know, my darling, that it would be as much our pleasure as our duty to watch over the development of your moral and spiritual nature, but alas! you will not let us see your moral and spiritual nature. At times we are almost inclined to doubt whether you have a moral and spiritual nature at all. Of your inner life, my dear, we know nothing beyond such scraps as we can glean in spite of you, from little things which escape you almost before you know that you have said them.'

The boy winced at this. It made him feel hot and uncomfortable all over. He knew well how careful he ought to be, and yet, do what he could, from time to time his forgetfulness of the part betrayed him into unreserve. His mother saw that he winced, and enjoyed the scratch which she had given him. Had she felt less confident of victory she had better have forgone the pleasure of touching as it were the eyes at the end of the snail's horns in order to enjoy seeing the snail draw them in again – but she knew that when she had got him well down into the sofa, and held his hand, she had the enemy almost absolutely at her mercy, and could do pretty much what she liked.

'Papa does not feel,' she continued, 'that you love him with that fulness and unreserve which would prompt you to have no concealment from him, and to tell him everything freely and fear-lessly as your most loving earthly friend next only to your Heavenly Father. Perfect love, as we know, casteth out fear: your father loves you perfectly, my darling, but he does not feel as though you love him perfectly in return. If you fear him it is because you do not love him as he deserves, and I know it some-times cuts him to the very heart to think that he has earned from you a deeper and more willing sympathy than you display towards him. Oh, Ernest, Ernest, do not grieve one who is so good and noble-hearted by conduct which I can call by no other name than ingratitude.'

Ernest could never stand being spoken to in this way by his mother: for he still believed that she loved him, and that he was fond of her and had a friend in her – up to a certain point. But his mother was beginning to come to the end of her tether; she had played the domestic confidence trick upon him times without number already. Over and over again had she wheedled from him all she wanted to know, and afterwards got him into the most horrible scrape by telling the whole to Theobald. Ernest had remonstrated more than once upon these occasions, and had pointed out to his mother how disastrous to him his confidences had been, but Christina had always joined issue with him and showed him in the clearest possible manner that in each case she had been right, and that he could not reasonably complain. Gen-erally it was her conscience that forbade her to be silent, and against this there was no appeal, for we are all bound to follow the dictates of our conscience. Ernest used to have to recite a hymn about conscience. It was to the effect that if you did not pay attention to its voice it would soon leave off speaking. 'My Mamma's conscience has not left off speaking,' said Ernest to one of his chums at Roughborough; 'it's always jabbering.'

When a boy has once spoken so disrespectfully as this about his mother's conscience it is practically all over between him and her. Ernest, through sheer force of habit, of the sofa, and of the return of the associated ideas, was still so moved by the siren's voice as to yearn to sail towards her, and fling himself into her arms, but it would not do; there were other associated ideas that returned also, and the mangled bones of too many murdered confessions were lying whitening round the skirts of his mother's dress, to allow him by any possibility to trust her further. So he hung his head and looked sheepish, but kept his own counsel.

'I see, my dearest,' continued his mother, 'either that I am mistaken, and that there is nothing on your mind, or that you will not unburden yourself to me: but oh, Ernest, tell me at least this much; is there nothing that you repent of, nothing which makes you unhappy in connection with that miserable girl Ellen?'

Ernest's heart failed him. 'I am a dead boy now,' he said to himself. He had not the faintest conception what his mother was driving at, and thought she suspected about the watch; but he held his ground.

I do not believe he was much more of a coward than his neighbours, only he did not know that all sensible people are cowards when they are off their beat, or when they think they are going to be roughly handled. I believe, that if the truth were known, it would be found that even the valiant St Michael himself tried hard to shirk from his famous combat with the dragon; he pretended not to see all sorts of misconduct on the dragon's part; shut his eyes to the eating up of I do not know how many hundreds of men, women and children whom he had promised to protect; allowed himself to be publicly insulted a dozen times over without resenting it; and in the end when even an angel could stand it no longer he shilly-shallied and temporised an unconscionable time before he would fix the day and hour for the encounter. As for the actual combat it was much such another *wurra-wurra* as Mrs Allaby had had with the young man who had in the end married her eldest daughter, till after a time behold, there was the dragon lying dead, while he was himself alive and not very seriously hurt after all.

'I do not know what you mean, mamma,' exclaimed Ernest anxiously and more or less hurriedly. His mother construed his manner into indignation at being suspected, and being rather frightened herself she turned tail and scuttled off as fast as her tongue could carry her.

'Oh!' she said, 'I see by your tone that you are innocent! Oh! oh! how I thank my heavenly Father for this; may He for His dear Son's sake keep you always pure. Your father, my dear' – (here she spoke hurriedly but gave him a searching look) 'was as pure as a spotless angel when he came to me. Like him, always be self-denying, truly truthful both in word and deed, never forgetful whose son and grandson you are, nor of the name we gave you, of the sacred stream in whose waters your sins were washed out of you through the blood and blessing of Christ,' etc.

But Ernest cut this – I will not say short – but a great deal shorter than it would have been if Christina had had her say out, by extricating himself from his mamma's embrace and showing a clean pair of heels. As he got near the purlieus of the kitchen (where he was more at ease) he heard his father calling for his mother, and again his guilty conscience rose against him. 'He has found all out now,' it cried, 'and he is going to tell mamma – this time I am done for.' But there was nothing in it; his father only wanted the key of the cellaret. Then Ernest slunk off into a coppice or spinney behind the Rectory paddock, and consoled himself with a pipe of tobacco. Here in the wood with the summer sun streaming through the trees and a book and his pipe the boy forgot his cares and had an interval of that rest without which I verily believe his life would have been insupportable.

Of course, Ernest was made to look for his lost property, and a reward was offered for it, but it seemed he had wandered a good deal off the path, thinking to find a lark's nest, more than once, and looking for a watch and purse on Battersby piewipes was very like looking for a needle in a bundle of hay: besides it might have been found and taken by some tramp, or by a magpie, of which there were many in the neighbourhood, so that after a week or ten days the search was discontinued, and the unpleasant fact had to be faced that Ernest must have another watch, another knife, and a small sum of pocket-money.

It was only right, however, that Ernest should pay half the cost of the watch; this should be made easy for him, for it should be deducted from his pocket-money in half-yearly instalments extending over two, or even it might be three years. In Ernest's own interests, then, as well as those of his father and mother, it would be well that the watch should cost as little as possible, so it was resolved to buy a second-hand one. Nothing was to be said to Ernest, but it was to be bought, and laid upon his plate as a surprise just before the holidays were over. Theobald would have to go to the county town in a few days and could then find some second-hand watch which would answer sufficiently well. In the course of time, therefore, Theobald went, furnished with a long list of household commissions, among which was the purchase of a watch for Ernest.

Those, as I have said, were always happy times, when Theobald was away for a whole day certain; the boy was beginning to feel easy in his mind as though God had heard his prayers, and he was not going to be found out. Altogether the day had proved an unusually tranquil one, but, alas! it was not to close as it had begun; the fickle atmosphere in which he lived was never more likely to breed a storm than after such an interval of brilliant calm, and when Theobald returned Ernest had only to look in his face to see that a hurricane was approaching.

Christina saw that something had gone very wrong, and was quite frightened lest Theobald should have heard of some serious money loss; he did not, however, at once unbosom himself, but rang the bell and said to the servant, 'Tell Master Ernest I wish to speak to him in the dining-room.'

Chapter Forty-One

Long before Ernest reached the dining-room his ill-divining soul had told him that his sin had found him out. What head of a family ever sends for any of its members into the dining-room if his intentions are honourable?

When he reached it he found it empty – his father having been called away for a few minutes unexpectedly upon some parish business – and he was left in the same kind of suspense as people are in after they have been ushered into their dentist's anteroom.

Of all the rooms in the house he hated the dining-room worst. It was here that he had had to do his Latin and Greek lessons with his father. It had a smell of some particular kind of polish or varnish which was used in polishing the furniture, and neither I nor Ernest can even now come within range of the smell of this kind of varnish without our hearts failing us.

Over the chimney-piece there was a veritable old master, one of the few original pictures which Mr George Pontifex had brought from Italy. It was supposed to be a Salvator Rosa and had been bought as a great bargain. The subject was Elijah or Elisha (whichever it was) being fed by the ravens in the desert. There were the ravens in the upper right-hand corner with bread and meat in their beaks and claws, and there was the prophet in question in the lower left-hand corner looking longingly up towards them. When Ernest was a very small boy it had been a constant matter of regret to him that the food which the ravens carried never actually reached the prophet; he did not understand the limitation of the painter's art, and wanted the meat and the prophet to be brought into direct contact. One day, with the help of some steps which had been left in the room, he had clambered up to the picture and with a piece of bread and butter traced a greasy line right across it from the ravens to Elisha's mouth, after which he had felt more comfortable.

Ernest's mind was drifting back to this youthful escapade when he heard his father's hand on the door, and in another second Theobald entered.

'Oh, Ernest,' said he, in an off-hand, rather cheery manner, 'there is a little matter which I should like you to explain to me, as I have no doubt you very easily can.' Thump, thump, thump, went Ernest's heart against his ribs; but his father's manner was so much nicer than usual that he began to think it might be after all only another false alarm.

'It had occurred to your mother and myself that we should like to set you up with a watch again before you went back to school' ('Oh, that's all,' said Ernest to himself quite relieved), 'and I have been to-day to look out for a second-hand one which should answer every purpose so long as you are at school.'

Theobald spoke as if watches had half a dozen purposes besides time-keeping, but he could hardly open his mouth without using one or other of his tags, and 'answering every purpose' was one of them.

Ernest was breaking out into the usual expressions of gratitude, when Theobald continued, 'You are interrupting me,' and Ernest's heart thumped again.

'You are interrupting me, Ernest. I have not yet done.' Ernest was instantly dumb.

'I passed several shops with second-hand watches for sale, but I saw none of a description and price which pleased me, till at last I was shown one which had, so the shopman said, been left with him recently for sale, and which I at once recognised as the one which had been given you by your Aunt Alethea. Even if I had failed to recognise it, as perhaps I might have done, I should have identified it directly it reached my hands, inasmuch as it had 'E. P., a present from A. P.' engraved upon the inside. I need say no more to show that this was the very watch which you told your mother and me that you had dropped out of your pocket.'

Up to this time Theobald's manner had been studiously calm, and his words had been uttered slowly, but here he suddenly quickened and flung off the mask as he added the words, 'or some such cock and bull story, which your mother and I were too truthful to disbelieve. You can guess what must be our feelings now.'

Ernest felt that this last home-thrust was just. In his less anxious moments he had thought his papa and mamma 'green' for the readiness with which they believed him, but he could not deny that their credulity was a proof of their habitual truthfulness of mind. In common justice he must own that it was very dreadful for two such truthful people to have a son as untruthful as he knew himself to be.

'Believing that a son of your mother and myself would be incapable of falsehood I at once assumed that some tramp had picked the watch up and was now trying to dispose of it.'

This to the best of my belief was not accurate. Theobald's first assumption had been that it was Ernest who was trying to sell the watch, and it was an inspiration of the moment to say that his magnanimous mind had at once conceived the idea of a tramp.

'You may imagine how shocked I was when I discovered that the watch had been brought for sale by that miserable woman Ellen' – here Ernest's heart hardened a little, and he felt as near an approach to an instinct to turn as one so defenceless could be expected to feel; his father quickly perceived this and continued, 'who was turned out of this house in circumstances which I will not pollute your ears by more particularly describing.

'I put aside the horrid conviction which was beginning to dawn upon me, and assumed that in the interval between her dismissal and her leaving this house, she had added theft to her other sin, and having found your watch in your bedroom had purloined it. It even occurred to me that you might have missed your watch after the woman was gone, and, suspecting who had taken it, had run after the carriage in order to recover it; but when I told the shopman of my suspicions he assured me that the person who left it with him had declared most solemnly that it had been given her by her master's son, whose property it was, and who had a perfect right to dispose of it.

'He told me further that, thinking the circumstances in which the watch was offered for sale somewhat suspicious, he had insisted upon the woman's telling him the whole story of how she came by it, before he would consent to buy it off her.

'He said that at first – as women of that stamp invariably do – she tried prevarication, but on being threatened that she should at once be given into custody if she did not tell the whole truth, she described the way in which you had run after the carriage, till as she said you were black in the face, and insisted on giving her all your pocket-money, your knife and your watch. She added that my coachman John – whom I shall instantly discharge – was witness to the whole transaction. Now, Ernest, be pleased to tell me whether this appalling story is true or false?'

It never occurred to Ernest to ask his father why he did not hit a man his own size, or to stop him midway in the story with a remonstrance against being kicked when he was down. The boy was too much shocked and shaken to be inventive; he could only drift and stammer out that the tale was true.

'So I feared,' said Theobald, 'and now, Ernest, be good enough to ring the bell.'

When the bell had been answered, Theobald desired that John should be sent for, and when John came Theobald calculated the wages due to him and desired him at once to leave the house.

John's manner was quiet and respectful. He took his dismissal as a matter of course, for Theobald had hinted enough to make him understand why he was being discharged, but when he saw Ernest sitting pale and awestruck on the edge of his chair against the dining-room wall, a sudden thought seemed to strike him, and turning to Theobald he said in a broad northern accent which I will not attempt to reproduce:

'Look here, master, I can guess what all this is about – now before I goes I want to have a word with you.'

'Ernest,' said Theobald, 'leave the room.'

'No, Master Ernest, you shan't,' said John, planting himself against the door. 'Now, master,' he continued, 'you may do as you please about me. I've been a good servant to you, and I don't mean to say as you've been a bad master to me, but I do say that if you bear hardly on Master Ernest here I have those in the village as 'll hear on't and let me know; and if I do hear on't I'll come back and break every bone in your skin, so there!'

John's breath came and went quickly, as though he would have been well enough pleased to begin the bone-breaking business at once. Theobald turned of an ashen colour – not, as he explained afterwards, at the idle threats of a detected and angry ruffian, but at such atrocious insolence from one of his own servants.

'I shall leave Master Ernest, John,' he rejoined proudly, 'to the reproaches of his own conscience.' ('Thank God and thank John,' thought Ernest.) 'As for yourself, I admit that you have been an excellent servant until this unfortunate business came on, and I shall have much pleasure in giving you a character if you want one. Have you anything more to say?'

'No more nor what I have said,' said John sullenly, 'but what I've said I means and I'll stick to – character or no character.'

'Oh, you need not be afraid about your character, John,' said Theobald kindly, 'and as it is getting late, there can be no occasion for you to leave the house before to-morrow morning.'

To this there was no reply from John who retired, packed up his things, and left the house at once.

When Christina heard what had happened she said she could condone all except that Theobald should have been subjected to such insolence from one of his own servants through the misconduct of his son. Theobald was the bravest man in the whole world, and could easily have collared the wretch and turned him out of the room, but how far more dignified, how far nobler had been his reply! How it would tell in a novel or upon the stage, for though the stage as a whole was immoral, yet there were doubtless some plays which were improving spectacles. She could fancy the whole house hushed with excitement at hearing John's menace, and hardly breathing by reason of their interest and expectation of the coming answer. Then the actor – probably the great and good Mr Macready – would say, 'I shall leave Master Ernest, John, to the reproaches of his own conscience.' Oh, it was sublime! What a roar of applause must follow! Then she should enter herself, and fling her arms about her husband's neck, and call him her lion-hearted husband. When the curtain dropped, it would be buzzed about the house that the scene just witnessed had been drawn from real life, and had actually occurred in the household of the Rev. Theobald Pontifex, who had married a Miss Allaby, etc., etc.

As regards Ernest the suspicions which had already crossed her mind were deepened, but she thought it better to leave the matter where it was. At present she was in a very strong position. Ernest's official purity was firmly established, but at the same time he had shown himself so susceptible that she was able to fuse two contradictory impressions concerning him into a single idea, and consider him as a kind of Joseph and Don Juan in one. This was what she had wanted all along, but her vanity being gratified by the possession of such a son, there was an end of it; the son himself was naught.

No doubt if John had not interfered, Ernest would have had to expiate his offence with ache, penury and imprisonment. As it was the boy was 'to consider himself' as undergoing these punishments, and as suffering pangs of unavailing remorse inflicted on him by his conscience into the bargain; but beyond the fact that Theobald kept him more closely to his holiday task, and the continued coldness of his parents, no ostensible punishment was meted out to him. Ernest, however, tells me that he looks back upon this as the time when he began to know that he had a cordial and active dislike for both his parents, which I suppose means that he was now beginning to be aware that he was reaching man's estate.

Chapter Forty-Two

About a week before he went back to school his father again sent for him into the dining-room, and told him that he should restore him his watch, but that he should deduct the sum he had paid for it – for he had thought it better to pay a few shillings rather than dispute the ownership of the watch, seeing that Ernest had undoubtedly given it to Ellen – from his pocket-money, in payments which should extend over two half-years. He would therefore have to go back to Roughborough this half-year with only five shillings' pocket-money. If he wanted more he must earn more merit money.

Ernest was not so careful about money as a pattern boy should be. He did not say to himself, 'Now I have got a sovereign which must last me fifteen weeks, therefore I may spend exactly one shilling and fourpence in each week" – and spend exactly one and fourpence in each week accordingly. He ran through his money at about the same rate as other boys did, being pretty well cleaned out a few days after he had got back to school. When he had no more money, he got a little into debt, and when as far in debt as he could see his way to repaying, he went without luxuries. Immediately he got any money he would pay his debts; if there was any over he would spend it; if there was not – and there seldom was – he would begin to go on tick again.

His finance was always based upon the supposition that he should go back to school with £1 in his pocket – of which he owed say a matter of fifteen shillings. There would be five shillings for sundry school subscriptions – but when these were paid the weekly allowance of sixpence given to each boy in hall, his merit money (which this half he was resolved should come to a good sum) and renewed credit, would carry him through the half.

The sudden failure of fifteen shillings was disastrous to my hero's scheme of finance. His face betrayed his emotions so clearly that Theobald said he was determined to 'learn the truth at once, and *this time* without days and days of falsehood' before he reached it. The melancholy fact was not long in coming out, namely, that the wretched Ernest added debt to the vices of idleness, falsehood, and possibly – for it was not impossible – immorality.

How had he come to get into debt? Did the other boys do so? Ernest reluctantly admitted that they did.

With what shops did they get into debt?

This was asking too much, Ernest said he didn't know!

'Oh, Ernest, Ernest,' exclaimed his mother, who was in the room, 'do not so soon a second time presume upon the forbearance of the tenderest-hearted father in the world. Give time for one stab to heal before you wound him with another.'

This was all very fine, but what was Ernest to do? How could he get the school shopkeepers into trouble by owning that they let some of the boys go on tick with them? There was Mrs Cross, a good old soul, who used to sell hot rolls and butter for breakfast, or eggs and toast, or it might be the quarter of a fowl with bread sauce and mashed potatoes for which she would charge sixpence. If she made a farthing out of the sixpence it was as much as she did. When the boys would come trooping into her shop after 'the hounds' how often had not Ernest heard her say to her servant girls, 'Now then, you wanches, git some cheers.' All the boys were fond of her, and was he, Ernest, to tell tales about her? It was horrible.

'Now look here, Ernest,' said his father with his blackest scowl, 'I am going to put a stop to this nonsense once for all. Either take me fully into your confidence, as a son should take a father, and trust me to deal with this matter as a clergyman and a man of the world – or understand distinctly that I shall take the whole story to Dr Skinner, who, I imagine, will take much sterner measures than I should.'

'Oh, Ernest, Ernest,' sobbed Christina, 'be wise in time, and trust those who have already shown you that they know but too well how to be forbearing.'

No genuine hero of romance should have hesitated for a moment. Nothing should have cajoled or frightened him into telling tales out of school. Ernest thought of his ideal boys: they, he well knew, would have let their tongues be cut out of them before information could have been wrung from any words of theirs. But Ernest was not an ideal boy, and he was not strong enough for his surroundings; I doubt how far any boy could withstand the moral pressure which was brought to bear upon him; at any rate he could not do so, and after a little more writhing he yielded himself a passive prey to the enemy. He consoled himself with the reflection that his papa had not played the confidence trick on him quite as often as his mamma had, and that probably it was better he should tell his father, than that his father should insist on Dr Skinner's making an inquiry. His papa's conscience 'jabbered' a good deal, but not as much as his mamma's. The little fool forgot that he had not given his father as many chances of betraying him as he had given to Christina.

Then it all came out. He owed this at Mrs Cross's, and this to Mrs Jones, and this at the 'Swan and Bottle' public house, to say nothing of another shilling or sixpence or two in other quarters. Nevertheless, Theobald and Christina were not satiated, but rather the more they discovered the greater grew their appetite for discovery; it was their obvious duty to find out everything, for though they might rescue their own darling from this hotbed of iniquity without getting to know more than they knew at present, were there not other papas and mammas with darlings whom also they were bound to rescue if it were possible? What boys, then, owed money to these harpies as well as Ernest?

Here, again, there was a feeble show of resistance, but the thumbscrews were instantly applied, and Ernest, demoralised as he already was, recanted and submitted himself to the powers that were. He told only a little less than he knew or thought he knew. He was examined, re-examined, cross-examined, sent to the retirement of his own bedroom and cross-examined again; the smoking in Mrs Jones' kitchen all came out; which boys smoked and which did not; which boys owed money and, roughly, how much and where; which boys swore and used bad language. Theobald was resolved that this time Ernest should, as he called it, take him into his confidence without reserve, so the school list which went with Dr Skinner's half-yearly bills was brought out, and the most secret character of each boy was gone through *seriatim* by Mr and Mrs Pontifex, so far as it was in Ernest's power to give information concerning it, and yet Theobald had on the preceding Sunday preached a less feeble sermon than he commonly preached, upon the horrors of the Inquisition. No matter how awful was the depravity revealed to them, the pair never flinched, but probed and probed, till they were on the point of reaching subjects more delicate than they had yet touched upon. Here Ernest's unconscious self took the matter up and made a resistance to which his conscious self was unequal, by tumbling him off his chair in a fit of fainting.

Dr Martin was sent for and pronounced the boy to be seriously unwell; at the same time he prescribed absolute rest and absence from nervous excitement. So the anxious parents were unwillingly compelled to be content with what they had got already – being frightened into leading him a quiet life for the short remainder of the holidays. They were not idle, but Satan can find as much mischief for busy hands as for idle ones, so he sent a little job in the direction of Battersby which Theobald and Christina undertook immediately. It would be a pity, they reasoned, that Ernest should leave Roughborough, now that he had been there three years; it would be difficult to find another school for him, and to explain

why he had left Roughborough. Besides, Dr Skinner and Theobald were supposed to be old friends, and it would be unpleasant
to offend him; these were all valid reasons for not removing the
boy. The proper thing to do, then, would be to warn Dr Skinner
confidently of the state of his school, and to furnish him with a
school list annotated with the remarks extracted from Ernest,
which should be appended to the name of each boy.

Theobald was the perfection of neatness; while his son was ill
upstairs, he copied out the school list so that he could throw his
comments into a tabular form, which assumed the following
shape – only that of course I have changed the names. One cross
in each square was to indicate occasional offence; two stood for
frequent, and three for habitual delinquency.

And thus through the whole school.

Of course, in justice to Ernest, Dr Skinner would be bound
over to secrecy before a word was said to him, but, Ernest being
thus protected, he could not be furnished with the facts too completely.

	Smoking	Drinking beer at the 'Swan and Bottle'	Swearing and Obscene Language	Notes
Robinson	O	O	X X	Will smoke next half
Brown	X X X	O	X	
Smith	X	X X	X X X	
Jones	X X	X X	X	

Chapter Forty-Three

So important did Theobald consider this matter that he made a special journey to Roughborough before the half-term began. It was a relief to have him out of the house, but though his destination was not mentioned, Ernest guessed where he had gone.

To this day he considers his conduct at this crisis to have been one of the most serious laches of his life – one which he can never think of without shame and indignation. He says he ought to have run away from home. But what good could he have done if he had? He would have been caught, brought back and examined two days later instead of two days earlier. A boy of barely sixteen cannot stand against the moral pressure of a father and mother who have always oppressed him any more than he can cope physically with a powerful full-grown man. True, he may allow himself to be killed rather than yield, but this is being so morbidly heroic as to come close round again to cowardice; for it is little else than suicide, which is universally condemned as cowardly.

On the re-assembling of the school it became apparent that something had gone wrong. Dr Skinner called the boys together, and with much pomp excommunicated Mrs Cross and Mrs Jones, by declaring their shops to be out of bounds. The street in which the 'Swan and Bottle' stood was also forbidden. The vices of drinking and smoking, therefore, were clearly aimed at, and before prayers Dr Skinner spoke a few impressive words about the abominable sin of using bad language. Ernest's feelings can be imagined.

Next day at the hour when the daily punishments were read out, though there had not yet been time for him to have offended, Ernest Pontifex was declared to have incurred every punishment which the school provided for evil-doers. He was placed on the idle list for the whole half-year, and on perpetual detentions; his bounds were curtailed; he was to attend Junior callings-over; in fact he was so hemmed in with punishments upon every side that it was hardly possible for him to go outside the school gates. This unparalleled list of punishments inflicted on the first day of the half-year, and intended to last till the ensuing Christmas holidays, was not connected with any specified offence. It required no great penetration, therefore, on the part of the boys to connect Ernest with the putting Mrs Cross's and Mrs Jones's shops out of bounds.

Great indeed was the indignation about Mrs Cross who, it was known, remembered Dr Skinner himself as a small boy only just got into jackets, and had doubtless let him have many a sausage and mashed potatoes upon deferred payment. The head boys assembled in conclave to consider what steps should be taken, but hardly had they done so before Ernest knocked timidly at the head-room door and took the bull by the horns by explaining the facts as far as he could bring himself to do so. He made a clean breast of everything except about the school list and the remarks he had made about each boy's character. This infamy was more than he could own to, and he kept his counsel concerning it. Fortunately he was safe in doing so, for Dr Skinner, pedant and more than pedant though he was, had still just sense enough to turn on Theobald in the matter of the school list. Whether he resented being told that he did not know the characters of his own boys, or whether he dreaded a scandal about the school I know not, but when Theobald had handed him the list, over which he had expended so much pains, Dr Skinner had cut him uncommonly short, and had then and there, with more suavity than was usual with him, committed it to the flames before Theobald's own eyes.

Ernest got off with the head boys easier than he expected. It was admitted that the offence, heinous though it was, had been committed under extenuating circumstances; the frankness with which the culprit had confessed all, his evidently unfeigned remorse, and the fury with which Dr Skinner was pursuing him tended to bring about a reaction in his favour, as though he had been more sinned against than sinning.

As the half-year wore on his spirits gradually revived, and when attacked by one of his fits of self-abasement he was in some degree consoled by having found out that even his father and mother, whom he had supposed so immaculate, were no better than they should be. About the fifth of November it was a school custom to meet on a certain common not far from Roughborough and burn somebody in effigy, this being the compromise arrived at in the matter of fireworks and Guy Fawkes festivities. This year it was decided that Pontifex's governor should be the victim, and Ernest, though a good deal exercised in mind as to what he ought to do, in the end saw no sufficient reason for holding aloof from proceedings which, as he justly remarked, could not do his father any harm.

It so happened that the bishop had held a confirmation at the school on the fifth of November. Dr Skinner had not quite liked the selection of this day, but the bishop was pressed by many engagements, and had been compelled to make the arrangement as it then stood. Ernest was among those who had to be confirmed, and was deeply impressed with the solemn importance of the ceremony. When he felt the huge old bishop drawing down upon him as he knelt in chapel he could hardly breathe, and when the apparition paused before him and laid its hands upon his head he was frightened almost out of his wits. He felt that he had arrived at one of the great turning points of his life, and that the Ernest of the future could resemble only very faintly the Ernest of the past.

This happened at about noon, but by the one o'clock dinner-hour the effect of the confirmation had worn off, and he saw no reason why he should forgo his annual amusement with the bon-fire; so he went with the others and was very valiant till the image was actually produced and was about to be burnt; then he felt a little frightened. It was a poor thing enough, made of paper, cal-ico and straw, but they had christened it The Rev Theobald Pontifex, and he had a revulsion of feeling as he saw it being car-ried towards the bonfire. Still he held his ground, and in a few minutes when all was over felt none the worse for having assisted at a ceremony which, after all, was prompted by a boyish love of mischief rather than by rancour.

I should say that Ernest had written to his father, and told him of the unprecedented way in which he was being treated; he even ventured to suggest that Theobald should interfere for his protec-tion and reminded him how the story had been got out of him, but Theobald had had enough of Dr Skinner for the present; the burning of the school list had been a rebuff which did not encour-age him to meddle a second time in the internal economics of Roughborough. He therefore replied that he must either remove Ernest from Roughborough altogether, which would for many reasons be undesirable, or trust to the discretion of the head mas-ter as regards the treatment he might think best for any of his pupils. Ernest said no more; he still felt that it was so discreditable to him to have allowed any confession to be wrung from him, that he could not press the promised amnesty for himself.

It was during the 'Mother Cross row,' as it was long styled among the boys, that a remarkable phenomenon was witnessed at Roughborough. I mean that of the head boys under certain conditions doing errands for their juniors. The head boys had no bounds and could go to Mrs Cross's whenever they liked; they actually, therefore, made themselves go-betweens, and would get anything from either Mrs Cross's or Mrs Jones's for any boy, no matter how low in the school, between the hours of a quarter to nine and nine in the morning, and a quarter to six and six in the afternoon. By degrees, however, the boys grew bolder, and the shops, though not openly declared in bounds again, were tacitly allowed to be so.

Chapter Forty-Four

I may spare the reader more details about my hero's school days. He rose, always in spite of himself, into the Doctor's form, and for the last two years or so of his time was among the praepostors, though he never rose into the upper half of them. He did little, and I think the Doctor rather gave him up as a boy whom he had better leave to himself, for he rarely made him construe, and he used to send in his exercises or not, pretty much as he liked. His tacit, unconscious obstinacy had in time effected more even than a few bold sallies in the first instance would have done. To the end of his career his position *inter pares* was what it had been at the beginning, namely, among the upper part of the less reputable class – whether of seniors or juniors – rather than among the lower part of the more respectable.

Only once in the whole course of his school life did he get praise from Dr Skinner for any exercise, and this he has treasured as the best example of guarded approval which he has ever seen. He had had to write a copy of Alcaics on 'The dogs of the monks of St Bernard,' and when the exercise was returned to him he found the Doctor had written on it: 'In this copy of Alcaics – which is still excessively bad – I fancy that I can discern some faint symptoms of improvement.' Ernest says that if the exercise was any better than usual it must have been by a fluke, for he is sure that he always liked dogs, especially St Bernard dogs, far too much to take any pleasure in writing Alcaics about them.

'As I look back upon it,' he said to me, but the other day, with a hearty laugh, 'I respect myself more for having never once got the best mark for an exercise than I should do if I had got it every time it could be got. I am glad nothing could make me do Latin and Greek verses; I am glad Skinner could never get any moral influence over me; I am glad I was idle at school, and I am glad my father overtasked me as a boy – otherwise, likely enough I should have acquiesced in the swindle, and might have written as good a copy of Alcaics about the dogs of the monks of St Bernard as my neighbours, and yet I don't know, for I remember there was another boy, who sent in a Latin copy of some sort, but for his own pleasure he wrote the following:

> The dogs of the monks of St Bernard go
> To pick little children out of the snow,
> And around their necks is the cordial gin
> Tied with a little bit of bob-bin.

I should like to have written that, and I did try, but I couldn't. I didn't like the last line, and tried to mend it, but I couldn't.'

I fancied I could see traces of bitterness against the instructors of his youth in Ernest's manner, and said something to this effect.

'Oh, no,' he replied, still laughing, 'no more than St Anthony felt towards the devils who had tempted him, when he met some of them casually a hundred or a couple of hundred years afterwards. Of course he knew they were devils, but that was all right enough; there must be devils. St Anthony probably liked these devils better than most others, and for old acquaintance sake showed them as much indulgence as was compatible with decorum.

'Besides, you know,' he added, 'St Anthony tempted the devils quite as much as they tempted him; for his peculiar sanctity was a greater temptation to tempt him than they could stand. Strictly speaking, it was the devils who were the more to be pitied, for they were led up by St Anthony to be tempted and fell, whereas St Anthony did not fall. I believe I was a disagreeable and unintelligible boy, and if ever I meet Skinner there is no one whom I would shake hands with, or do a good turn to more readily.'

At home things went on rather better; the Ellen and Mother Cross rows sank slowly down upon the horizon, and even at home he had quieter times now that he had become a praepostor. Nevertheless the watchful eye and protecting hand were still ever over him to guard his comings in and his goings out, and to spy on all his ways. Is it wonderful that the boy, though always trying to keep up appearances as though he were cheerful and contented – and at times actually being so – wore often an anxious, jaded look when he thought none were looking, which told of an almost incessant conflict within?

Doubtless Theobald saw these looks and knew how to interpret them, but it was his profession to know how to shut his eyes to things that were inconvenient – no clergyman could keep his benefice for a month if he could not do this; besides, he had allowed himself for so many years to say things he ought not to have said, and not to say the things he ought to have said, that he was little likely to see anything that he thought it more convenient not to see unless he was made to do so.

It was not much that was wanted. To make no mysteries where Nature has made none, to bring his conscience under something like reasonable control, to give Ernest his head a little more, to ask fewer questions, and to give him pocket money with a desire that it should be spent upon *menus plaisirs*. . . .

'Call that not much indeed,' laughed Ernest, as I read him what I have just written. 'Why, it is the whole duty of a father, but it is the mystery-making which is the worst evil. If people would dare to speak to one another unreservedly, there would be a good deal less sorrow in the world a hundred years hence.'

To return, however, to Roughborough. On the day of his leaving, when he was sent for into the library to be shaken hands with, he was surprised to feel that, though assuredly glad to leave, he did not do so with any especial grudge against the Doctor rankling in his breast. He had come to the end of it all, and was still alive, nor, take it all round, more seriously amiss than other people. Dr Skinner received him graciously, and was even frolic-some after his own heavy fashion. Young people are almost always placable, and Ernest felt as he went away that another such interview would not only have wiped off all old scores, but have brought him round into the ranks of the Doctor's admirers and supporters – among whom it is only fair to say that the greater number of the more promising boys were found.

Just before saying good-bye the Doctor actually took down a volume from those shelves which had seemed so awful six years previously, and gave it to him after having written his name in it, and the words φιλίας ℵαὶ εὐνοίας χάϱιν, which I believe written in Latin by a German – Schömann: *De comitiis Atheniensibus* – not exactly light and cheerful reading, but Ernest felt it was high time he got to understand the Athenian constitution and manner of voting; he had got them up a great many times already, but had forgotten them as fast as he had learned them; now, however, that the Doctor had given him this book, he would master the subject once for all. How strange it was! He wanted to remember these things very badly; he knew he did, but he could never retain them; in spite of himself they no sooner fell upon his mind than they fell off it again, he had such a dreadful memory; whereas, if anyone played him a piece of music and told him where it came from, he never forgot that, though he made no effort to retain it, and was not even conscious of trying to remember it at all. His mind must be badly formed and he was no good.

Having still a short time to spare, he got the keys of St Michael's church and went to have a farewell practice upon the organ, which he could now play fairly well. He walked up and down the aisle for a while in a meditative mood, and then, settling down to the organ, played 'They loathed to drink of the river' about six times over, after which he felt more composed and happier; then, tearing himself away from the instrument he loved so well, he hurried to the station.

As the train drew out he looked down from a high embankment

on to the little house his aunt had taken, and where it might be said she had died through her desire to do him a kindness. There were the two well-known bow windows, out of which he had often stepped to run across the lawn into the workshop. He reproached himself with the little gratitude he had shown towards this kind lady – the only one of his relations whom he had ever felt as though he could have taken into his confidence. Dearly as he loved her memory, he was glad she had not known the scrapes he had got into since she died; perhaps she might not have forgiven them – and how awful that would have been! But then, if she had lived, perhaps many of his ills would have been spared him. As he mused thus he grew sad again. Where, where, he asked himself, was it all to end? Was it to be always sin, shame and sorrow in the future, as it had been in the past, and the ever-watchful eye and protecting hand of his father laying burdens on him greater than he could bear – or was he, too, some day or another to come to feel that he was fairly well and happy?

There was a gray mist across the sun, so that the eye could bear its light, and Ernest, while musing as above, was looking right into the middle of the sun himself, as into the face of one whom he knew and was fond of. At first his face was grave, but kindly, as of a tired man who feels that a long task is over; but in a few seconds the more humorous side of his misfortunes presented itself to him, and he smiled half reproachfully, half merrily, as thinking how little all that had happened to him really mattered, and how small were his hardships as compared with those of most people. Still looking into the eye of the sun and smiling dreamily, he thought how he had helped to burn his father in effigy, and his look grew merrier, till at last he broke out into a laugh. Exactly at this moment the light veil of cloud parted from the sun, and he was brought to *terra firma* by the breaking forth of the sunshine. On this he became aware that he was being watched attentively by a fellow-traveller opposite to him, an elderly gentleman with a large head and iron-grey hair.

'My young friend,' said he, good-naturedly, 'you really must not carry on conversations with people in the sun, while you are in a public railway carriage.'

The old gentleman said not another word, but unfolded his *Times* and began to read it. As for Ernest, he blushed crimson. The pair did not speak during the rest of the time they were in the carriage, but they eyed each other from time to time, so that the face of each was impressed on the recollection of the other.

Chapter Forty-Five

Some people say that their school days were the happiest of their lives. They may be right, but I always look with suspicion upon those whom I hear saying this. It is hard enough to know whether one is happy or unhappy now, and still harder to compare the relative happiness or unhappiness of different times of one's life; the utmost that can be said is that we are fairly happy so long as we are not distinctly aware of being miserable. As I was talking with Ernest one day not so long since about this, he said he was so happy now that he was sure he had never been happier, and did not wish to be so, but that Cambridge was the first place where he had ever been consciously and continuously happy.

How can any boy fail to feel an ecstasy of pleasure on first finding himself in rooms which he knows for the next few years are to be his castle? Here he will not be compelled to turn out of the most comfortable place as soon as he has ensconced himself in it because papa or mamma happens to come into the room, and he should give it up to them. The most cosy chair here is for himself, there is no one even to share the room with him, or to interfere with his doing as he likes in it – smoking included. Why, if such a room looked out both back and front on to a blank dead wall it would still be a paradise, how much more then when the view is of some quiet grassy court or cloister or garden, as from the windows of the greater number of rooms at Oxford and Cambridge. Theobald as an old fellow and tutor of Emmanuel – at which college he had entered Ernest – was able to obtain from the present tutor a certain preference in the choice of rooms; Ernest's, therefore, were very pleasant ones, looking out upon the grassy court that is bounded by the Fellows' garden.

Theobald accompanied him to Cambridge, and was at his best while doing so. He liked the jaunt, and even he was not without a certain feeling of pride in having a full-blown son at the University. Some of the reflected rays of this splendour were allowed to fall upon Ernest himself. Theobald said he was 'willing to hope' – this was one of his tags – that his son would turn over a new leaf now that he had left school, and for his own part he was 'only too ready' – this was another tag – to let by-gones be by-gones.

Ernest, not yet having his name on the books, was able to dine with his father at the Fellows' table of one of the other colleges on the invitation of an old friend of Theobald's; he there made acquaintance with sundry of the good things of this life, the very names of which were new to him, and felt as he ate them that he was now indeed receiving a liberal education. When at length the time came for him to go to Emmanuel, where he was to sleep in his new rooms, his father came with him to the gates and saw him safe into college; a few minutes more and he found himself alone in a room for which he had a latch-key.

From this time he dated many days which, if not quite unclouded, were upon the whole very happy ones. I need not, however, describe them, as the life of a quiet steady-going undergraduate has been told in a score of novels better than I can tell it. Some of Ernest's schoolfellows came up to Cambridge at the same time as himself, and with these he continued on friendly terms during the whole of his college career. Other schoolfellows were only a year or two his seniors; these called on him, and he thus made a sufficiently favourable *entrée* into college life. A straightforwardness of character that was stamped upon his face, a love of humour, and a temper which was more easily appeased than ruffled made up for some awkwardness and want of *savoir faire*. He soon became a not unpopular member of the best set of his year, and though neither capable of becoming, nor aspiring to become, a leader, was admitted by the leaders as among their nearer hangers-on.

Of ambition he had at that time not one particle; greatness, or indeed superiority of any kind, seemed so far off and incomprehensible to him that the idea of connecting it with himself never crossed his mind. If he could escape the notice of all those with whom he did not feel himself *en rapport*, he conceived that he had triumphed sufficiently. He did not care about taking a good degree, except that it must be good enough to keep his father and mother quiet. He did not dream of being able to get a fellowship; if he had, he would have tried hard to do so, for he became so fond of Cambridge that he could not bear the thought of having to leave it; the briefness indeed of the season during which his present happiness was to last was almost the only thing that now seriously troubled him.

Having less to attend to in the matter of growing, and having got his head more free, he took to reading fairly well – not because he liked it, but because he was told he ought to do so, and his natural instinct, like that of all very young men who are good for anything, was to do as those in authority told him. The intention at Battersby was (for Dr Skinner had said that Ernest could never get a fellowship) that he should take a sufficiently good degree to be able to get a tutorship or mastership in some school preparatory to taking orders. When he was twenty-one years old his money was to come into his own hands, and the best thing he could do with it would be to buy the next presentation to a living, the rector of which was now old, and live on his mastership or tutorship till the living fell in. He could buy a very good living for the sum which his grandfather's legacy now amounted to, for Theobald had never had any serious intention of making deductions for his son's maintenance and education, and the money had accumulated till it was now about five thousand pounds! He had only talked about making deductions in order to stimulate the boy to exertion as far as possible, by making him think that this was his only chance of escaping starvation – or perhaps from pure love of teasing.

When Ernest had a living of £600 or £700 a year with a house, and not too many parishioners – why, he might add to his income by taking pupils, or even keeping a school, and then, say at thirty, he might marry. It was not easy for Theobald to hit on any much more sensible plan. He could not get Ernest into business, for he had no business connections – besides, he did not know what business meant; he had no interest, again, at the Bar; medicine was a profession which subjected its students to ordeals and temptations which these fond parents shrank from on behalf of their boy; he would be thrown among companions and familiar-ised with details which might sully him, and though he might stand, it was 'only too possible' that he would fall. Besides, ordin-ation was the road which Theobald knew and understood, and indeed the only road about which he knew anything at all, so not unnaturally it was the one he chose for Ernest.

The foregoing had been instilled into my hero from earliest boyhood, much as it had been instilled into Theobald himself, and with the same result – the conviction, namely, that he was certainly to be a clergyman, but that it was a long way off yet, and he supposed it was all right. As for the duty of reading hard, and taking as good a degree as he could, this was plain enough, so he set himself to work, as I have said, steadily, and to the sur-prise of everyone as well as himself got a college scholarship, of no great value, but still a scholarship, in his freshman's term. It is hardly necessary to say that Theobald stuck to the whole of this money, believing the pocket-money he allowed Ernest to be suf-ficient for him, and knowing how dangerous it was for young men to have money at command. I do not suppose it even occurred to him to try and remember what he had felt when his father took a like course in regard to himself.

Ernest's position in this respect was much what it had been at school except that things were on a larger scale. His tutor's and cook's bills were paid for him; his father sent him his wine; over and above this he had £50 a year with which to keep himself in clothes and all other expenses; this was about the usual thing at Emmanuel in Ernest's day, though many had much less than this. Ernest did as he had done at school – he spent what he could, soon after he received his money; he then incurred a few modest liabilities, and then lived penuriously till next term, when he would immediately pay his debts, and start new ones to much the same extent as those which he had just got rid of. When he came into his £5,000 and became independent of his father, £15 or £20 served to cover the whole of his unauthorised expenditure.

He joined the boat club, and was constant in his attendance at the boats. He still smoked, but never took more wine or beer than was good for him, except perhaps on the occasion of a boating supper, but even then he found the consequences unpleasant, and soon learned how to keep within safe limits. He attended chapel as often as he was compelled to do so; he communicated two or three times a year, because his tutor told him he ought to; in fact he set himself to live soberly and cleanly, as I imagine all his instincts prompted him to do, and when he fell – as who that is born of woman can help sometimes doing? – it was not till after a sharp tussle with a temptation that was more than his flesh and blood could stand; then he was very penitent and would go a fairly long while without sinning again; and this was how it had always been with him since he had arrived at years of indiscretion.

Even to the end of his career at Cambridge he was not aware that he had it in him to do anything, but others had begun to see that he was not wanting in ability and sometimes told him so. He did not believe it; indeed he knew very well that if they thought him clever they were being taken in, but it pleased him to have been able to take them in, and he tried to do so still further; he was therefore a good deal on the look-out for cants that he could catch and apply in season, and might have done himself some mischief thus if he had not been ready to throw over any cant as soon as he had come across another more nearly to his fancy; his friends used to say that when he rose he flew like a snipe, darting several times in various directions before he settled down to a steady straight flight, but when he had once got into this he would keep to it.

Chapter Forty-Six

When he was in this third year a magazine was founded at Cambridge, the contributions to which were exclusively by undergraduates. Ernest sent in an essay upon the Greek Drama, which he has declined to let me reproduce here without his being allowed to re-edit it. I have therefore been unable to give it in its original form, but when pruned of its redundancies (and this is all that has been done to it) it runs as follows:

'I shall not attempt within the limits at my disposal to make a *résumé* of the rise and progress of the Greek drama, but will confine myself to considering whether the reputation enjoyed by the three chief Greek tragedians, Æschylus, Sophocles and Euripides, is one that will be permanent, or whether they will one day be held to have been overrated.

'Why, I ask myself, do I see much that I can easily admire in Homer, Thucydides, Herodotus, Demosthenes, Aristophanes, Theocritus, parts of Lucretius, Horace's satires and epistles, to say nothing of other ancient writers, and yet find myself at once repelled by even those works of Æschylus, Sophocles and Euripides which are most generally admired.

'With the first-named writers I am in the hands of men who feel, if not as I do, still as I can understand their feeling, and as I am interested to see that they should have felt; with the second I have so little sympathy that I cannot understand how anyone can ever have taken any interest in them whatever. Their highest flights to me are dull, pompous and artificial productions, which, if they were to appear now for the first time, would, I should think, either fall dead or be severely handled by the critics. I wish to know whether it is I who am in fault in this matter, or whether part of the blame may not rest with the tragedians themselves.

'How far, I wonder, did the Athenians genuinely like these poets, and how far was the applause which was lavished upon them due to fashion or affectation? How far, in fact, did admiration for the orthodox tragedians take that place among the Athenians which going to church does among ourselves?

'This is a venturesome question considering the verdict now generally given for over two thousand years, nor should I have permitted myself to ask it if it had not been suggested to me by one whose reputation stands as high, and has been sanctioned for as long time as those of the tragedians themselves, I mean by Aristophanes.

'Numbers, weight of authority, and time, have conspired to place Aristophanes on as high a literary pinnacle as any ancient writer, with the exception perhaps of Homer, but he makes no secret of heartily hating Euripides and Sophocles, and I strongly suspect only praises Æschylus that he may run down the other two with greater impunity. For, after all, there is no such difference between Æschylus and his successors as will render the former very good and the latter very bad; and the thrusts at Æschylus which Aristophanes puts into the mouth of Euripides go home too well to have been written by an admirer.

'It may be observed that while Euripides accuses Æschylus of being "pomp-bundle-worded," which I suppose means bombastic and given to rodomontade, Æschylus retorts on Euripides that he is a "gossip gleaner, a describer of beggars, and a rag-stitcher," from which it may be inferred that he was truer to the life of his own times than Æschylus was. It happens, however, that a faithful rendering of contemporary life is the very quality which gives its most permanent interest to any work of fiction, whether in literature or painting, and it is a not unnatural consequence that while only seven plays by Æschylus, and the same number by Sophocles, have come down to us, we have no fewer than nineteen by Euripides.

'This, however, is a digression; the question before us is whether Aristophanes really liked Æschylus or only pretended to do so. It must be remembered that the claims of Æschylus, Sophocles and Euripides, to the foremost place amongst tragedians were held to be as incontrovertible as those of Dante, Petrarch, Tasso and Ariosto to be the greatest of Italian poets, are held among the Italians of to-day. If we can fancy some witty, genial writer, we will say in Florence, finding himself bored by all the poets I have named, we can yet believe he would be unwilling to admit that he disliked them without exception. He would prefer to think he could see something at any rate in Dante, whom he could idealise more easily, inasmuch as he was more remote; in order to carry his countrymen the farther with him, he would endeavour to meet them more than was consistent with his own instincts. Without some such palliation as admiration for one, at any rate, of the tragedians, it would be almost as dangerous for Aristophanes to attack them as it would be for an Englishman now to say that he did not think very much of the Elizabethan dramatists. Yet which of us in his heart likes any of the Elizabethan dramatists except Shakespeare? Are they in reality anything else than literary Struldbrugs?

'I conclude upon the whole that Aristophanes did not like any of the tragedians; yet no one will deny that this keen, witty, outspoken writer was as good a judge of literary value, and as able to see any beauties that the tragic dramas contained as nine-tenths, at any rate, of ourselves. He had, moreover, the advantage of thoroughly understanding the standpoint from which the tragedians expected their work to be judged, and what was his conclusion? Briefly, it was little else than this, that they were a fraud or something very like it. For my own part I cordially agree with him. I am free to confess that with the exception perhaps of some of the Psalms of David I know no writings which seem so little to deserve their reputation. I do not know that I should particularly mind my sisters reading them, but I will take good care never to read them myself.'

This last bit about the Psalms was awful, and there was a great fight with the editor as to whether or no it should be allowed to stand. Ernest himself was frightened at it, but he had once heard someone say that the Psalms were many of them very poor, and on looking at them more closely, after he had been told this, he found that there could hardly be two opinions on the subject. So he caught up the remark and reproduced it as his own, concluding that these psalms had probably never been written by David at all, but had got in among the others by mistake.

The essay, perhaps on account of the passage about the Psalms, created quite a sensation, and on the whole was well received. Ernest's friends praised it more highly than it deserved, and he was himself very proud of it, but he dared not show it at Battersby. He knew also that he was now at the end of his tether; this was his one idea (I feel sure he had caught more than half of it from other people), and now he had not another thing left to write about. He found himself cursed with a small reputation which seemed to him much bigger than it was and a consciousness that he could never keep it up. Before many days were over he felt his unfortunate essay to be a white elephant to him, which he must feed by hurrying into all sorts of frantic attempts to cap his triumph, and, as may be imagined, these attempts were failures.

He did not understand that if he waited and listened and observed, another idea of some kind would probably occur to him some day, and that the development of this would in its turn suggest still further ones. He did not yet know that the very worst way of getting hold of ideas is to go hunting expressly after them. The way to get them is to study something of which one is fond, and to note down whatever crosses one's mind in reference to it, either during study or relaxation, in a little notebook kept always in the waistcoat pocket. Ernest has come to know all about this now, but it took him a long time to find it out, for this is not the kind of thing that is taught at schools and universities.

Nor yet did he know that ideas, no less than the living beings in whose mind they arise, must be begotten by parents not very unlike themselves, the most original still differing but slightly from the parents that have given rise to them. Life is like a fugue, everything must grow out of the subject and there must be nothing new. Nor, again, did he see how hard it is to say where one idea ends and another begins, nor yet how closely this is paralleled in the difficulty of saying where life begins or ends, or an action or indeed anything, there being an unity in spite of infinite multitude, and an infinite multitude in spite of unity. He thought that ideas came into clever people's heads by a kind of spontaneous germination, without parentage in the thoughts of others or the course of observation; for as yet he believed in genius, of which he well knew that he had none, if it was the fine frenzied thing he thought it was.

Not very long before this he had come of age, and Theobald had handed him over his money, which amounted now to £5,000; it was invested to bring in 5 per cent and gave him, therefore, an income of £250 a year. He did not, however, realise the fact (he could realise nothing so foreign to his experience) that he was independent of his father till a long time afterwards; nor did Theobald make any difference in his manner towards him. So strong was the hold which habit and association held over both father and son, that the one considered he had as good a right as ever to dictate, and the other that he had as little right as ever to gainsay.

During his last year at Cambridge he overworked himself through this very blind deference to his father's wishes, for there was no reason why he should take more than a poll degree except that his father laid such stress upon his taking honours. He became so ill, indeed, that it was doubtful how far he would be able to go in for his degree at all; but he managed to do so, and when the list came out was found to be placed higher than either he or anyone else expected, being among the first three or four senior optimes, and a few weeks later, in the lower half of the second class of the Classical Tripos. Ill as he was when he got home, Theobald made him go over all the examination papers with him, and in fact reproduce as nearly as possible the replies that he had sent in. So little kick had he in him, and so deep was the groove into which he had got, that while at home he spent several hours a day in continuing his classical and mathematical studies as though he had not yet taken his degree.

Chapter Forty-Seven

Ernest returned to Cambridge for the May term of 1858, on the plea of reading for ordination, with which he was now face to face, and much nearer than he liked. Up to this time, though not religiously inclined, he had never doubted the truth of anything that had been told him about Christianity. He had never seen anyone who doubted, nor read anything that raised a suspicion in his mind as to the historical character of the miracles recorded in the Old and New Testaments.

It must be remembered that the year 1858 was the last of a term during which the peace of the Church of England was singularly unbroken. Between 1844, when *Vestiges of Creation* appeared, and 1859, when *Essays and Reviews* marked the commencement of that storm which raged until many years afterwards, there was not a single book published in England that caused serious commotion within the bosom of the Church. Perhaps Buckle's *History of Civilisation* and Mill's *Liberty* were the most alarming, but they neither of them reached the substratum of the reading public, and Ernest and his friends were ignorant of their very existence. The Evangelical movement, with the exception to which I shall revert presently, had become almost a matter of ancient history. Tractarianism had subsided into a tenth day's wonder; it was at work, but it was not noisy. The *Vestiges* were forgotten before Ernest went up to Cambridge; the Catholic aggression scare had lost its terrors; Ritualism was still unknown by the general provincial public, and the Gorham and Hampden controversies were defunct some years since; Dissent was not spreading; the Crimean war was the one engrossing subject, to be followed by the Indian Mutiny and the Franco-Austrian war.

These great events turned men's minds from speculative subjects, and there was no enemy to the faith which could arouse
even a languid interest. At no time probably since the beginning
of the century could an ordinary observer have detected less sign
of coming disturbance than at that of which I am writing.

I need hardly say that the calm was only on the surface. Older
men, who knew more than undergraduates were likely to do,
must have seen that the wave of scepticism which had already
broken over Germany was setting towards our own shores, nor
was it long, indeed, before it reached them. Ernest had hardly
been ordained before three works in quick succession arrested
the attention even of those who paid least heed to theological
controversy. I mean *Essays and Reviews*, Charles Darwin's *Origin
of Species*, and Bishop Colenso's *Criticisms on the Pentateuch*.

This, however, is a digression; I must revert to the one phase of
spiritual activity which had any life in it during the time Ernest
was at Cambridge, that is to say, to the remains of the Evangelical
awakening of more than a generation earlier, which was connected with the name of Simeon.

There were still a good many Simeonites, or as they were more
briefly called, 'Sims,' in Ernest's time. Every college contained
some of them, but their headquarters were at Caius, whither
they were attracted by Mr Clayton who was at that time senior
tutor, and among the sizars of St John's.

Behind the then chapel of this last-named college there was a
'labyrinth' (this was the name it bore) of dingy, tumbledown
rooms, tenanted exclusively by the poorest undergraduates, who
were dependent upon sizarships and scholarships for the means
of taking their degrees. To many, even at St John's, the existence
and whereabouts of the labyrinth in which the sizars chiefly lived
was unknown; some men in Ernest's time, who had rooms in the
first court, had never found their way through the sinuous passage which led to it.

In the labyrinth there dwelt men of all ages, from mere lads to grey-haired old men who had entered late in life. They were rarely seen except in hall or chapel or at lecture, where their manners of feeding, praying and studying, were considered alike objectionable; no one knew whence they came, whither they went, nor what they did, for they never showed at cricket or the boats; they were a gloomy, seedy-looking *confrérie*, who had as little to glory in in clothes and manners as in the flesh itself.

Ernest and his friends used to consider themselves marvels of economy for getting on with so little money, but the greater number of dwellers in the labyrinth would have considered one-half of their expenditure to be an exceeding measure of affluence, and so doubtless any domestic tyranny which had been experienced by Ernest was a small thing to what the average Johnian sizar had had to put up with.

A few would at once emerge on its being found after their first examination that they were likely to be ornaments to the college; these would win valuable scholarships that enabled them to live in some degree of comfort, and would amalgamate with the more studious of those who were in a better social position, but even these, with few exceptions, were long in shaking off the uncouthness they brought with them to the University, nor would their origin cease to be easily recognisable till they had become dons and tutors. I have seen some of these men attain high position in the world of politics or science, and yet still retain a look of labyrinth and Johnian sizarship.

Unprepossessing then, in feature, gait and manners, unkempt and ill-dressed beyond what can be easily described, these poor fellows formed a class apart, whose thoughts and ways were not as the thoughts and ways of Ernest and his friends, and it was among them that Simeonism chiefly flourished.

Destined most of them for the Church (for in those days 'holy orders' were seldom heard of), the Simeonites held themselves to have received a very loud call to the ministry, and were ready to pinch themselves for years so as to prepare for it by the necessary theological courses. To most of them the fact of becoming clergymen would be the *entrée* into a social position from which they were at present kept out by barriers they well knew to be impassable; ordination, therefore, opened fields for ambition which made it the central point in their thoughts, rather than as with Ernest, something which he supposed would have to be done some day, but about which, as about dying, he hoped there was no need to trouble himself as yet.

By way of preparing themselves more completely they would have meetings in one another's rooms for tea and prayer and other spiritual exercises. Placing themselves under the guidance of a few well-known tutors they would teach in Sunday Schools, and be instant, in season and out of season, in imparting spiritual instruction to all whom they could persuade to listen to them.

But the soil of the more prosperous undergraduates was not suitable for the seed they tried to sow. The small pieties with which they larded their discourse, if chance threw them into the company of one whom they considered worldly, caused nothing but aversion in the minds of those for whom they were intended. When they distributed tracts, dropping them by night into good men's letter boxes while they were asleep, their tracts got burnt, or met with even worse contumely; they were themselves also treated with the ridicule which they reflected proudly had been the lot of true followers of Christ in all ages. Often at their prayer meetings was the passage of St Paul referred to in which he bids his Corinthian converts note concerning themselves that they were for the most part neither well-bred nor intellectual people. They reflected with pride that they too had nothing to be proud of in these respects, and like St Paul, gloried in the fact that in the flesh they had not much to glory.

Ernest had several Johnian friends, and came thus to hear about the Simeonites and to see some of them, who were pointed out to him as they passed through the courts. They had a repellant attraction for him; he disliked them, but he could not bring himself to leave them alone. On one occasion he had gone so far as to parody one of the tracts they had sent round in the night, and to get a copy dropped into each of the leading Simeonites' boxes. The subject he had taken was 'Personal Cleanliness.' Cleanliness, he said, was next to godliness; he wished to know on which side it was to stand, and concluded by exhorting Simeonites to a freer use of the tub. I cannot commend my hero's humour in this matter; his tract was not brilliant, but I mention the fact as showing that at this time he was something of a Saul and took pleasure in persecuting the elect, not, as I have said, that he had any hankering after scepticism, but because, like the farmers in his father's village, though he would not stand seeing the Christian religion made light of, he was not going to see it taken seriously. Ernest's friends thought his dislike for Simeonites was due to his being the son of a clergyman who, it was known, bullied him; it is more likely, however, that it rose from an unconscious sympathy with them, which, as in St Paul's case, in the end drew him into the ranks of those whom he had most despised and hated.

Chapter Forty-Eight

Once, recently, when he was down at home after taking his degree, his mother had had a short conversation with him about his becoming a clergyman, set on hitherto by Theobald, who shrank from the subject himself. This time it was during a turn taken in the garden, and not on the sofa – which was reserved for supreme occasions.

'You know, my dearest boy,' she said to him, 'that papa' (she always called Theobald 'papa' when talking to Ernest) 'is so anxious you should not go into the Church blindly, and without fully realising the difficulties of a clergyman's position. He has considered all of them himself, and has been shown how small they are, when they are faced boldly, but he wishes you, too, to feel them as strongly and completely as possible before committing yourself to irrevocable vows, so that you may never, never have to regret the step you will have taken.'

This was the first time Ernest had heard that there were any difficulties, and he not unnaturally inquired in a vague way after their nature.

'That, my dear boy,' rejoined Christina, 'is a question which I am not fitted to enter upon either by nature or education. I might easily unsettle your mind without being able to settle it again. Oh, no! such questions are far better avoided by women, and, I should have thought, by men, but papa wished me to speak to you upon the subject, so that there might be no mistake hereafter, and I have done so. Now, therefore, you know all.'

The conversation ended here, so far as this subject was concerned, and Ernest thought he did know all. His mother would not have told him he knew all – not about a matter of that sort –

unless he actually did know it; well, it did not come to very much; he supposed there *were* some difficulties, but his father, who at any rate was an excellent scholar and a learned man, was probably quite right here, and he need not trouble himself more about them. So little impression did the conversation make on him, that it was not till long afterwards that, happening to remember it, he saw what a piece of sleight of hand had been practised upon him. Theobald and Christina, however, were satisfied that they had done their duty by opening their son's eyes to the difficulties of assenting to all a clergyman must assent to. This was enough; it was a matter for rejoicing that, though they had been put so fully and candidly before him, he did not find them serious. It was not in vain that they had prayed for so many years to be made 'truly honest and conscientious.'

'And now, my dear,' resumed Christina, after having disposed of all the difficulties that might stand in the way of Ernest's becoming a clergyman, 'there is another matter on which I should like to have a talk with you. It is about your sister Charlotte. You know how clever she is, and what a dear, kind sister she has been and always will be to yourself and Joey. I wish, my dearest Ernest, that I saw more chance of her finding a suitable husband that I do at Battersby, and I sometimes think you might do more than you do to help her.'

Ernest began to chafe at this, for he had heard it so often, but he said nothing.

'You know, my dear, a brother can do so much for his sister if he lays himself out to do it. A mother can do very little – indeed, it is hardly a mother's place to seek out young men; it is a brother's place to find a suitable partner for his sister; all that I can do is to try to make Battersby as attractive as possible to any of your friends whom you may invite. And in that,' she added, with a little toss of her head, 'I do not think I have been deficient hitherto.'

Ernest said he had already at different times asked several of his friends.

'Yes, my dear, but you must admit that they were none of them exactly the kind of young man whom Charlotte could be expected to take a fancy to. Indeed, I must own to having been a little disappointed that you should have yourself chosen any of these as your intimate friends.'

Ernest winced again.

'You never brought down Figgins when you were at Roughborough; now I should have thought Figgins would have been just the kind of boy whom you might have asked to come and see us.'

Figgins had been gone through times out of number already. Ernest had hardly known him, and Figgins, being nearly three years older than Ernest, had left long before he did. Besides, he had not been a nice boy, and had made himself unpleasant to Ernest in many ways.

'Now,' continued his mother, 'there's Towneley. I have heard you speak of Towneley as having rowed with you in a boat at Cambridge. I wish, my dear, you would cultivate your acquaintance with Towneley, and ask him to pay us a visit. The name has an aristocratic sound, and I think I have heard you say he is an eldest son.'

Ernest flushed at the sound of Towneley's name.

What had really happened in respect of Ernest's friends was briefly this. His mother liked to get hold of the names of the boys and especially of any who were at all intimate with her son; the more she heard, the more she wanted to know; there was no gorging her satiety; she was like a ravenous young cuckoo being fed upon a grass plot by a water wagtail, she would swallow all that Ernest could bring her, and yet be as hungry as before. And she always went to Ernest for her meals rather than to Joey, for Joey was either more stupid or more impenetrable – at any rate she could pump Ernest much the better of the two.

From time to time an actual live boy had been thrown to her, either by being caught and brought to Battersby, or by being asked to meet her if at any time she came to Roughborough. She had generally made herself agreeable, or fairly agreeable, as long as the boy was present, but as soon as she got Ernest to herself again she changed her note. Into whatever form she might throw her criticisms it came always in the end to this, that his friend was no good, that Ernest was not much better, and that he should have brought her someone else, for this one would not do at all.

The more intimate the boy had been or was supposed to be with Ernest the more he was declared to be naught, till in the end he had hit upon the plan of saying, concerning any boy whom he particularly liked, that he was not one of his especial chums, and that indeed he hardly knew why he had asked him; but he found he only fell on Scylla in trying to avoid Charybdis, for though the boy was declared to be more successful it was Ernest who was naught for not thinking more highly of him.

When she had once got hold of a name she never forgot it. 'And how is So-and-so?' she would exclaim, mentioning some former friend of Ernest's with whom he had either now quarrelled, or who had long since proved to be a mere comet and no fixed star at all. How Ernest wished he had never mentioned So-and-so's name, and vowed to himself that he would never talk about his friends in future, but in a few hours he would forget and would prattle away as imprudently as ever; then his mother would pounce noiselessly on his remarks as a barn-owl pounces upon a mouse, and would bring them up in a pellet six months afterwards when they were no longer in harmony with their surroundings.

Then there was Theobald. If a boy or college friend had been invited to Battersby, Theobald would lay himself out at first to be agreeable. He could do this well enough when he liked, and as regards the outside world he generally did like. His clerical neighbours, and indeed all his neighbours, respected him yearly more and more, and would have given Ernest sufficient cause to regret his imprudence if he had dared to hint that he had anything, however little, to complain of. Theobald's mind worked in this way: 'Now, I know Ernest has told this boy what a disagreeable person I am, and I will just show him that I am not disagreeable at all, but a good old fellow, a jolly old boy, in fact a regular old brick, and that it is Ernest who is in fault all through.'

So he would behave very nicely to the boy at first, and the boy would be delighted with him, and side with him against Ernest. Of course if Ernest had got the boy to come to Battersby he wanted him to enjoy his visit, and was therefore pleased that Theobald should behave so well, but at the same time he stood so much in need of moral support that it was painful to him to see one of his own familiar friends go over to the enemy's camp. For no matter how well we may know a thing – how clearly we may see a certain patch of colour, for example, as red, it shakes us and knocks us about to find another see it, or be more than half inclined to see it, as green.

Theobald had generally begun to get a little impatient before the end of the visit, but the impression formed during the earlier part was the one which the visitor had carried away with him. Theobald never discussed any of the boys with Ernest. It was Christina who did this. Theobald let them come, because Christina in a quiet, persistent way insisted on it; when they did come he behaved, as I have said, civilly, but he did not like it, whereas Christina did like it very much; she would have had half Rough-borough and half Cambridge to come and stay at Battersby if she could have managed it, and if it would not have cost so much money: she liked their coming, so that she might make a new acquaintance, and she liked tearing them to pieces and flinging the bits over Ernest as soon as she had had enough of them.

The worst of it was that she had so often proved to be right. Boys and young men are violent in their affections, but they are seldom very constant; it is not till they get older that they really know the kind of friend they want; in their earlier essays young men are simply learning to judge character. Ernest had been no exception to the general rule. His swans had one after the other proved to be more or less geese even in his own estimation, and he was beginning almost to think that his mother was a better judge of character than he was; but I think it may be assumed with some certainty that if Ernest had brought her a real young swan she would have declared it to be the ugliest and worst goose of all that she had yet seen.

At first he had not suspected that his friends were wanted with a view to Charlotte; it was understood that Charlotte and they might perhaps take a fancy for one another; and that would be so very nice, would it not? But he did not see that there was any deliberate malice in the arrangement. Now, however, that he had awoke to what it all meant, he was less inclined to bring any friend of his to Battersby. It seemed to his silly young mind almost dishonest to ask your friend to come and see you when all you really meant was 'Please, marry my sister.' It was like trying to obtain money under false pretences. If he had been fond of Charlotte it might have been another matter, but he thought her one of the most disagreeable young women in the whole circle of his acquaintance.

She was supposed to be very clever. All young ladies are either very pretty or very clever or very sweet; they may take their choice as to which category they will go in for, but go in for one of the three they must. It was hopeless to try and pass Charlotte off as either pretty or sweet. So she became clever as the only remaining alternative. Ernest never knew what particular branch of study it was in which she showed her talent, for she could neither play nor sing nor draw, but so astute are women that his mother and Charlotte really did persuade him into thinking that she, Charlotte, had something more akin to true genius than any other member of the family. Not one, however, of all the friends whom Ernest had been inveigled into trying to inveigle had shown the least sign of being so far struck with Charlotte's commanding powers as to wish to make them his own, and this may have had something to do with the rapidity and completeness with which Christina had dismissed them one after another and had wanted a new one.

And now she wanted Towneley. Ernest had seen this coming and had tried to avoid it, for he knew how impossible it was for him to ask Towneley, even if he had wished to do so.

Towneley belonged to one of the most exclusive sets in Cambridge, and was perhaps the most popular man among the whole number of undergraduates. He was big and very handsome – as it seemed to Ernest the handsomest man whom he had ever seen or ever could see, for it was impossible to imagine a more lively and agreeable countenance. He was good at cricket and boating, very good-natured, singularly free from conceit, not clever but very sensible, and, lastly, his father and mother had been drowned by the overturning of a boat when he was only two years old and had left him as their only child and heir to one of the finest estates in the South of England. Fortune every now and then does things handsomely by a man all round; Towneley was one of those to whom she had taken a fancy, and the universal verdict in this case was that she had chosen wisely.

Ernest had seen Towneley as everyone else in the University (except, of course, dons) had seen him, for he was a man of mark, and being very susceptible he had liked Towneley even more than most people did, but at the same time it never so much as entered his head that he should come to know him. He liked looking at him if he got a chance, and was very much ashamed of himself for doing so, but there the matter ended.

By a strange accident, however, during Ernest's last year, when the names of the crews for the scratch fours were drawn, he had found himself coxswain of a crew, among whom was none other than his especial hero Towneley; the three others were ordinary mortals, but they could row fairly well, and the crew on the whole was rather a good one.

Ernest was frightened out of his wits. When, however, the two met, he found Towneley no less remarkable for his entire want of anything like 'side,' and for his power of setting those whom he came across at their ease, than he was for outward accomplishments; the only difference he found between Towneley and other people was that he was so very much easier to get on with. Of course Ernest worshipped him more and more.

The scratch fours being ended the connection between the two came to an end, but Towneley never passed Ernest thenceforward without a nod and a few good-natured words. In an evil moment he had mentioned Towneley's name at Battersby, and now what was the result? Here was his mother plaguing him to ask Towneley to come down to Battersby and marry Charlotte. Why, if he had thought there was the remotest chance of Towneley's marrying Charlotte he would have gone down on his knees to him and told him what an odious young woman she was, and implored him to save himself while there was yet time.

But Ernest had not prayed to be made '*truly* honest and conscientious' for as many years as Christina had. He tried to conceal what he felt and thought as well as he could, and led the conversation back to the difficulties which a clergyman might feel to stand in the way of his being ordained – not because he had any misgivings, but as a diversion. His mother, however, thought she had settled all that, and he got no more out of her. Soon afterwards he found the means of escaping, and was not slow to avail himself of them.

Chapter Forty-Nine

On his return to Cambridge in the May term of 1858, Ernest and a few other friends who were also intended for orders came to the conclusion that they must now take a more serious view of their position. They therefore attended chapel more regularly than hitherto, and held evening meetings of a somewhat furtive character, at which they would study the New Testament. They even began to commit the Epistles of St Paul to memory in the original Greek. They got up Beveridge on the Thirty-nine Articles, and Pearson on the Creed; in their hours of recreation they read More's *Mystery of Godliness*, which Ernest thought was charming, and Taylor's *Holy Living and Dying*, which also impressed him deeply, through what he thought was the splendour of its language. They handed themselves over to the guidance of Dean Alford's notes on the Greek Testament, which made Ernest better understand what was meant by 'difficulties,' but also made him feel how shallow and impotent were the conclusions arrived at by German neologians, with whose works, being innocent of German, he was not otherwise acquainted. Some of the friends who joined him in these pursuits were Johnians, and the meetings were often held within the walls of St John's.

I do not know how tidings of these furtive gatherings had reached the Simeonites, but they must have come round to them in some way, for they had not been continued many weeks before a circular was sent to each of the young men who attended them, informing them that the Rev. Gideon Hawke, a well-known London Evangelical preacher, whose sermons were then much talked of, was about to visit his young friend Badcock of St John's, and would be glad to say a few words to any who might wish to hear them, in Badcock's rooms on a certain evening in May.

Badcock was one of the most notorious of all the Simeonites. Not only was he ugly, dirty, ill-dressed, bumptious, and in every way objectionable, but he was deformed and waddled when he walked, so that he had won the nickname which I can only reproduce by calling it 'Here's my back, and there's my back,' because the lower parts of his back emphasised themselves demonstratively as though about to fly off in different directions like the two extreme notes in the chord of the augmented sixth, with every step he took. It may be guessed, therefore, that the receipt of the circular had for a moment an almost paralysing effect on those to whom it was addressed, owing to the astonishment which it occasioned them. It certainly was a daring surprise, but like so many deformed people, Badcock was forward and hard to check; he was a pushing fellow to whom the present was just the opportunity he wanted for carrying war into the enemy's quarters.

Ernest and his friends consulted. Moved by the feeling that as they were now preparing to be clergymen they ought not to stand so stiffly on social dignity as heretofore, and also perhaps by the desire to have a good private view of a preacher who was then much upon the lips of men, they decided to accept the invitation. When the appointed time came they went with some confusion and self-abasement to the rooms of this man, on whom they had looked down hitherto as from an immeasurable height, and with whom nothing would have made them believe a few weeks earlier that they could ever come to be on speaking terms.

Mr Hawke was a very different-looking person from Badcock. He was remarkably handsome, or rather would have been but for the thinness of his lips, and a look of too great firmness and inflexibility. His features were a good deal like those of Leonardo da Vinci; moreover he was kempt, looked in vigorous health, and was of a ruddy countenance. He was extremely courteous in his manner, and paid a good deal of attention to Badcock, of whom he seemed to think highly. Altogether our young friends were taken aback, and inclined to think smaller beer of themselves and larger of Badcock than was agreeable to the old Adam who was still alive within them. A few well-known 'Sims' from St John's and other colleges were present, but not enough to swamp the Ernest set, as for the sake of brevity I will call them.

After a preliminary conversation in which there was nothing to offend, the business of the evening began by Mr Hawke's standing up at one end of the table, and saying 'Let us pray.' The Ernest set did not like this, but they could not help themselves, so they knelt down and repeated the Lord's Prayer and a few others after Mr Hawke, who delivered them remarkably well. Then, when all had sat down, Mr Hawke addressed them, speaking without notes and taking for his text the words, 'Saul, Saul, why persecutest thou me?' Whether owing to Mr Hawke's manner, which was impressive, or to his well-known reputation for ability, or whether from the fact that each one of the Ernest set knew that he had been more or less a persecutor of the 'Sims' and yet felt instinctively that the 'Sims' were after all much more like the early Christians than he was himself – at any rate the text, familiar though it was, went home to the consciences of Ernest and his friends as it had never yet done. If Mr Hawke had stopped here he would have almost said enough; as he scanned the faces turned towards him, and saw the impression he had made, he was perhaps minded to bring his sermon to an end before beginning it, but if so, he reconsidered himself and proceeded as follows. I give the sermon in full, for it is a typical one, and will explain a state of mind which in another generation or two will seem to stand sadly in need of explanation.

'My young friends,' said Mr Hawke, 'I am persuaded there is not one of you here who doubts the existence of a Personal God. If there were, it is to him assuredly that I should first address myself. Should I be mistaken in my belief that all here assembled accept the existence of a God who is present amongst us though we see him not, and whose eye is upon our most secret thoughts, let me implore the doubter to confer with me in private before we part; I will then put before him considerations through which God has been mercifully pleased to reveal himself to me, so far as man can understand him, and which I have found bring peace to the minds of others who have doubted.

'I assume also that there is none who doubts but that this God, after whose likeness we have been made, did in the course of time have pity upon man's blindness, and assume our nature, taking flesh and coming down and dwelling among us as a man indistinguishable physically from ourselves. He who made the sun, moon and stars, the world and all that therein is, came down from Heaven in the person of his Son, with the express purpose of leading a scorned life, and dying the most cruel, shameful death which fiendish ingenuity has invented.

'While on earth he worked many miracles. He gave sight to the blind, raised the dead to life, fed thousands with a few loaves and fishes, and was seen to walk upon the waves, but at the end of his appointed time he died, as was fore-determined, upon the cross, and was buried by a few faithful friends. Those, however, who had put him to death set a jealous watch over his tomb.

'There is no one, I feel sure, in this room who doubts any part of the foregoing, but if there is, let me again pray him to confer with me in private, and I doubt not that by the blessing of God his doubts will cease.

'The next day but one after our Lord was buried, the tomb being still jealously guarded by enemies, an angel was seen descending from Heaven with glittering raiment and a countenance that shone like fire. This glorious being rolled away the stone from the grave, and our Lord himself came forth, risen from the dead.

'My young friends, this is no fanciful story like those of the ancient deities, but a matter of plain history as certain as that you and I are now here together. If there is one fact better vouched

for than another in the whole range of certainties it is the Resurrection of Jesus Christ; nor is it less well assured that a few weeks
after he had risen from the dead, our Lord was seen by many
hundreds of men and women to rise amid a host of angels into
the air upon a heavenward journey till the clouds covered him
and concealed him from the sight of men.

'It may be said that the truth of these statements has been
denied, but what, let me ask you, has become of the questioners?
Where are they now? Do we see them or hear of them? Have
they been able to hold what little ground they made during the
supineness of the last century? Is there one of your fathers or
mothers or friends who does not see through them? Is there a
single teacher or preacher in this great University who has not
examined what these men had to say, and found it naught? Did
you ever meet one of them, or do you find any of their books
securing the respectful attention of those competent to judge
concerning them? I think not; and I think also you know as well
as I do why it is that they have sunk back into the abyss from
which they for a time emerged: it is because after the most careful and patient examination by the ablest and most judicial minds
of many countries, their arguments were found so untenable that
they themselves renounced them. They fled from the field routed,
dismayed, and suing for peace; nor have they again come to the
front in any civilised country.

'You know these things. Why, then, do I insist upon them? My
dear young friends, your own consciousness will have made the
answer to each one of you already; it is because, though you
know so well that these things did verily and indeed happen, you
know also that you have not realised them to yourselves as it was
your duty to do, nor heeded their momentous, awful import.

'And now let me go further. You all know that you will one day
come to die, or if not to die – for there are not wanting signs
which make me hope that the Lord may come again, while some
of us now present are alive – yet to be changed; for the trumpet

shall sound, and the dead shall be raised incorruptible, for this corruption must put on incorruption, and this mortal put on immortality, and the saying shall be brought to pass that is written. "Death is swallowed up in victory."

'Do you, or do you not believe that you will one day stand before the Judgment Seat of Christ? Do you, or do you not believe that you will have to give an account for every idle word that you have ever spoken? Do you, or do you not believe that you are called to live, not according to the will of man, but according to the will of that Christ who came down from Heaven out of love for you, who suffered and died for you, who calls you to him, and yearns towards you that you may take heed even in this your day – but who, if you heed not, will also one day judge you, and with whom there is no variableness nor shadow of turning?

'My dear young friends, strait is the gate, and narrow is the way which leadeth to Eternal Life, and few there be that find it. Few, few, few, for he who will not give up ALL for Christ's sake, has given up nothing.

'If you would live in the friendship of this world, if indeed you were not prepared to give up everything you most fondly cherish, should the Lord require it of you, then, I say, put the idea of Christ deliberately on one side at once. Spit upon him, buffet him, crucify him anew, do anything you like so long as you secure the friendship of this world while it is still in your power to do so; the pleasures of this brief life may not be worth paying for by the torments of eternity, but they are something while they last. If, on the other hand, you would live in the friendship of God, and be among the number of those for whom Christ has not died in vain; if, in a word, you value your eternal welfare, then give up the friendship of this world; of a surety you must make your choice between God and Mammon, for you cannot serve both.

'I put these considerations before you, if so homely a term may be pardoned, as a plain matter of business. There is nothing low or unworthy in this, as some lately have pretended, for all nature shows us that there is nothing more acceptable to God than an enlightened view of our own self-interest; never let anyone delude you here; it is a simple question of fact; did certain things happen or did they not? If they did happen, is it reasonable to suppose that you will make yourselves and others more happy by one course of conduct or by another?

'And now let me ask you what answer you have made to this question hitherto? Whose friendship have you chosen? If, knowing what you know, you have not yet begun to act according to the immensity of the knowledge that is in you, then he who builds his house and lays up his treasure on the edge of a crater of molten lava is a sane, sensible person in comparison with yourselves. I say this as no figure of speech or bugbear with which to frighten you, but as an unvarnished unexaggerated statement which will be no more disputed by yourselves than by me.'

And now Mr Hawke, who up to this time had spoken with singular quietness, changed his manner to one of greater warmth and continued –

'Oh! my young friends, turn, turn, turn now while it is called to-day – now from this hour, from this instant; stay not even to gird up your loins; look not behind you for a second, but fly into the bosom of that Christ who is to be found of all who seek him, and from that fearful wrath of God which lieth in wait for those who know not the things belonging to their peace. For the Son of Man cometh as a thief in the night, and there is not one of us can tell but what this day his soul may be required of him. If there is even one here who has heeded me,' – and he let his eye fall for an instant upon almost all his hearers, but especially on the Ernest set – 'I shall know that it was not for nothing that I felt the call of the Lord, and heard as I thought a voice by night that bade me come hither quickly, for there was a chosen vessel who had need of me.'

Here Mr Hawke ended rather abruptly; his earnest manner, striking countenance and excellent delivery had produced an effect greater than the actual words I have given can convey to the reader; the virtue lay in the man more than in what he said; as for the last few mysterious words about his having heard a voice by night, their effect was magical; there was not one who did not look down to the ground, nor who in his heart did not half believe that he was the chosen vessel on whose especial behalf God had sent Mr Hawke to Cambridge. Even if this were not so, each one of them felt that he was now for the first time in the actual presence of one who had had a direct communication from the Almighty, and they were thus suddenly brought a hundredfold nearer to the New Testament miracles. They were amazed, not to say scared, and as though by tacit consent they gathered together, thanked Mr Hawke for his sermon, said goodnight in a humble deferential manner to Badcock and the other Simeonites, and left the room together. They had heard nothing but what they had been hearing all their lives; how was it, then, that they were so dumbfounded by it? I suppose partly because they had lately begun to think more seriously, and were in a fit state to be impressed, partly from the greater directness with which each felt himself addressed, through the sermon being delivered in a room, and partly to the logical consistency, freedom from exaggeration, and profound air of conviction with which Mr Hawke had spoken. His simplicity and obvious earnestness had impressed them even before he had alluded to his special mission, but this clenched everything, and the words 'Lord, is it I?' were upon the hearts of each as they walked pensively home through moonlit courts and cloisters.

I do not know what passed among the Simeonites after the Ernest set had left them, but they would have been more than mortal if they had not been a good deal elated with the results of the evening. Why, one of Ernest's friends was in the University eleven, and he had actually been in Badcock's rooms and had slunk off on saying good-night as meekly as any of them. It was no small thing to have scored a success like this.

Chapter Fifty

Ernest felt now that the turning point of his life had come. He would give up all for Christ – even his tobacco.

So he gathered together his pipes and pouches, and locked them up in his portmanteau under his bed where they should be out of sight, and as much out of mind as possible. He did not burn them, because someone might come in who wanted to smoke, and though he might abridge his own liberty, yet, as smoking was not a sin, there was no reason why he should be hard on other people.

After breakfast he left his rooms to call on a man named Dawson, who had been one of Mr Hawke's hearers on the preceding evening, and who was reading for ordination at the forthcoming Ember Weeks, now only four months distant. This man had been always of a rather serious turn of mind – a little too much so for Ernest's taste; but times had changed, and Dawson's undoubted sincerity seemed to render him a fitting counsellor for Ernest at the present time. As he was going through the first court of John's on his way to Dawson's rooms, he met Badcock, and greeted him with some deference. His advance was received with one of those ecstatic gleams which shone occasionally upon the face of Badcock, and which, if Ernest had known more, would have reminded him of Robespierre. As it was, he saw it and unconsciously recognised the unrest and self-seekingness of the man, but could not yet formulate them; he disliked Badcock more than ever, but as he was going to profit by the spiritual benefits which he had put in his way, he was bound to be civil to him, and civil he therefore was.

Badcock told him that Mr Hawke had returned to town

immediately his discourse was over, but that before doing so he had inquired particularly who Ernest and two or three others were. I believe each one of Ernest's friends was given to understand that he had been more or less particularly inquired after. Ernest's vanity – for he was his mother's son – was tickled at this; the idea again presented itself to him that he might be the one for whose benefit Mr Hawke had been sent. There was something, too, in Badcock's manner which conveyed the idea that he could say more if he chose, but had been enjoined to silence.

On reaching Dawson's rooms, he found his friends in raptures over the discourse of the preceding evening. Hardly less delighted was he with the effect it had produced on Ernest. He had always known, he said, that Ernest would come round; he had been sure of it, but he had hardly expected the conversion to be so sudden. Ernest said no more had he, but now that he saw his duty so clearly he would get ordained as soon as possible, and take a curacy, even though the doing so would make him have to go down from Cambridge earlier, which would be a great relief to him. Dawson applauded this determination, and it was arranged that as Ernest was still more or less of a weak brother, Dawson should take him, so to speak, in spiritual tow for a while, and strengthen and confirm his faith.

An offensive and defensive alliance therefore was struck up between this pair (who were in reality singularly ill assorted), and Ernest set to work to master the books on which the Bishop would examine him. Others gradually joined them till they formed a small set or church (for these are the same thing), and the effect of Mr Hawke's sermon instead of wearing off in a few days, as might have been expected, became more and more marked, so much so that it was necessary for Ernest's friends to hold him back rather than urge him on, for he seemed likely to develop – as indeed he did for a time – into a religious enthusiast.

In one matter only did he openly backslide. He had, as I said above, locked up his pipes and tobacco so that he might not be tempted to use them. All day long on the day after Mr Hawke's sermon he let them lie in his portmanteau bravely; but this was not very difficult, as he had for some time given up smoking till after hall. After hall this day he did not smoke till chapel time, and then went to chapel in self-defence. When he returned he determined to look at the matter from a common-sense point of view. On this he saw that, provided tobacco did not injure his health – and he really could not see that it did – it stood much on the same footing as tea or coffee.

Tobacco had nowhere been forbidden in the Bible, but then it had not yet been discovered, and had probably only escaped proscription for this reason. We can conceive of St Paul or even our Lord Himself as drinking a cup of tea, but we cannot imagine either of them as smoking a cigarette or a churchwarden. Ernest could not deny this, and admitted that Paul would almost certainly have condemned tobacco in good round terms if he had known of its existence. Was it not then taking rather a mean advantage of the Apostle to stand on his not having actually forbidden it? On the other hand, it was possible that God knew Paul would have forbidden smoking, and had purposely arranged the discovery of tobacco for a period at which Paul should be no longer living. This might seem rather hard on Paul, considering all he had done for Christianity, but it would be made up to him in other ways.

These reflections satisfied Ernest that on the whole he had better smoke, so he sneaked to his portmanteau and brought out his pipes and tobacco again. There should be moderation, he felt, in all things, even in virtue; so for that night he smoked immoderately. It was a pity, however, that he had bragged to Dawson about giving up smoking. The pipes had better be kept in a cupboard for a week or two, till in other and easier respects Ernest should have proved his steadfastness. Then they might steal out again little by little – and so they did.

Ernest now wrote home a letter couched in a vein different

from his ordinary ones. His letters were usually all common form and padding, for as I have already explained, if he wrote about anything that really interested him, his mother always wanted to know more and more about it – every fresh answer being as the lopping off of a hydra's head and giving birth to half a dozen or more new questions – but in the end it came invariably to the same result, namely, that he ought to have done something else, or ought not to go on doing as he proposed. Now, however, there was a new departure, and for the thousandth time he concluded that he was about to take a course of which his father and mother would approve, and in which they would be interested, so that at last he and they might get on more sympathetically than heretofore. He therefore wrote a gushing impulsive letter which afforded much amusement to myself as I read it, but which was too long for reproduction. One passage ran: 'I am now going towards Christ; the greater number of my college friends are, I fear, going away from Him; we must pray for them that they might find the peace that is in Christ even as I have myself found it.' Ernest covered his face with his hands for shame as he read this extract from the bundle of letters he had put into my hands – they had been returned to him by his father on his mother's death, his mother having carefully preserved them.

'Shall I cut it out?' said I, 'I will if you like.'

'Certainly not,' he answered, 'and if good-natured friends have kept more records of my follies, pick out any plums that may amuse the reader, and let him have his laugh over them.' But fancy what effect a letter like this – so unled up to – must have produced at Battersby! Even Christina refrained from ecstasy over her son's having discovered the power of Christ's word, while Theobald was frightened out of his wits. It was well his son was not going to have any doubts or difficulties, and that he would be ordained without making a fuss over it, but he smelt mischief in this sudden conversion of one who had never yet shown any inclination towards religion. He hated people who did not know where to stop. Ernest was always so *outré* and strange; there was never any knowing what he would do next, except that it would be something unusual and silly. If he was to get the bit between his teeth after he had got ordained and bought his living, he would play more pranks than ever he, Theobald, had done. The fact, doubtless, of his being ordained and having bought a living would go a long way to steady him, and if he married, his wife must see to the rest; this was his only chance and, to do justice to his sagacity, Theobald in his heart did not think very highly of it.

When Ernest came down to Battersby in June, he imprudently tried to open up a more unreserved communication with his father than was his wont. The first of Ernest's snipe-like flights on being flushed by Mr Hawke's sermon was in the direction of ultra-Evangelicalism. Theobald himself had been much more Low than High Church. This was the normal development of the country clergyman during the first years of his clerical life, between, we will say, the years 1825 to 1850; but he was not prepared for the almost contempt with which Ernest now regarded the doctrines of baptismal regeneration and priestly absolution (Hoity toity, indeed, what business had he with such questions?), nor for his desire to find some means of reconciling Methodism and the Church. Theobald hated the Church of Rome, but he hated dissenters too, for he found them as a general rule troublesome people to deal with: he always found people who did not agree with him troublesome to deal with: besides, they set up for knowing as much as he did; nevertheless, if he had been let alone he would have leaned towards them rather than towards the High Church party. The neighbouring clergy, however, would not let him alone. One by one they had come under the influence, directly or indirectly, of the Oxford movement which had begun twenty years earlier. It was surprising how many practices he now tolerated which in his youth he would have considered Popish; he knew very well therefore which way things were going in Church matters, and saw that as usual Ernest was setting himself the other way. The opportunity for telling his son that he was a fool was too favourable not to be embraced, and Theobald was not slow to embrace it. Ernest was annoyed and surprised for had not his father and mother been wanting him to be more religious all his life? Now that he had become so they were still not satisfied. He said to himself that a prophet was not without honour save in his own country, but he had been lately – or rather until lately – getting into an odious habit of turning proverbs upside down, and it occurred to him that a country is sometimes not without honour save for its own prophet. Then he laughed, and for the rest of the day felt more as he used to feel before he had heard Mr Hawke's sermon.

He returned to Cambridge for the Long Vacation of 1858 – none too soon, for he had to go in for the Voluntary Theological Examination, which bishops were now beginning to insist upon. He imagined all the time he was reading that he was storing himself with the knowledge that would best fit him for the work he had taken in hand. In truth, he was cramming for a pass. In due time he did pass – creditably, and was ordained Deacon with half a dozen others of his friends in the autumn of 1858. He was then just twenty-three years old.

Chapter Fifty-One

Ernest had been ordained to a curacy in one of the central parts of London. He hardly knew anything of London yet, but his instincts drew him thither. The day after he was ordained he entered upon his duties – feeling much as his father had done when he found himself boxed up in the carriage with Christina on the morning of his marriage. Before the first three days were over, he became aware that the light of the happiness which he had known during his four years at Cambridge had been extinguished, and he was appalled by the irrevocable nature of the step which he now felt that he had taken much too hurriedly.

The most charitable excuse that I can make for the vagaries which it will now be my duty to chronicle is that the shock of change consequent upon his becoming suddenly religious, being ordained and leaving Cambridge, had been too much for my hero, and had for the time thrown him off an equilibrium which was yet little supported by experience, and therefore as a matter of course unstable.

Everyone has a mass of bad work in him which he will have to work off and get rid of before he can do better – and indeed, the more lasting a man's ultimate good work is, the more sure he is to pass through a time, and perhaps a very long one, in which there seems to be very little hope for him at all. We must all sow our spiritual wild oats. The fault I feel personally disposed to find with my godson is not that he had wild oats to sow, but that they were such an exceedingly tame and uninteresting crop. The sense of humour and tendency to think for himself, of which till a few months previously he had been showing fair promise, were nipped as though by a late frost, while his earlier habit of taking on trust everything that was told him by those in authority, and following everything out to the bitter end, no matter how preposterous, returned with redoubled strength. I suppose this was what might have been expected from anyone placed as Ernest now was, especially when his antecedents are remembered, but it surprised and disappointed some of his cooler-headed Cambridge friends who had begun to think well of his ability. To himself it seemed that religion was incompatible with half measures, or even with compromise. Circumstances had led to his being ordained; for the moment he was sorry they had, but he had done it and must go through with it. He therefore set himself to find out what was expected of him, and to act accordingly.

His rector was a moderate High Churchman of no very pronounced views – an elderly man who had had too many curates not to have long since found out that the connection between rector and curate, like that between employer and employed in every other walk of life, was a mere matter of business. He had now two curates, of whom Ernest was the junior; the senior curate was named Pryer, and when this gentleman made advances, as he presently did, Ernest in his forlorn state was delighted to meet them.

Pryer was about twenty-eight years old. He had been at Eton and at Oxford. He was tall, and passed generally for good-looking; I only saw him once for about five minutes, and then thought him odious both in manners and appearance. Perhaps it was because he caught me up in a way I did not like. I had quoted Shakespeare for lack of something better to fill up a sentence – and had said that one touch of nature made the whole world kin. 'Ah,' said Pryer, in a bold, brazen way which displeased me, 'but one touch of the unnatural makes it more kindred still,' and he gave me a look as though he thought me an old bore and did not care two straws whether I was shocked or not. Naturally enough, after this I did not like him.

This, however, is anticipating, for it was not till Ernest had been three or four months in London that I happened to meet his fellow-curate, and I must deal here rather with the effect he produced upon my godson than upon myself. Besides being what was generally considered good-looking, he was faultless in his get-up, and altogether the kind of man whom Ernest was sure to be afraid of and yet be taken in by. The style of his dress was very High Church, and his acquaintances were exclusively of the extreme High Church party, but he kept his views a good deal in the background in his rector's presence, and that gentleman, though he looked askance on some of Pryer's friends, had no such ground of complaint against him as to make him sever the connection. Pryer, too, was popular in the pulpit, and, take him all round, it was probable that many worse curates would be found for one better. When Pryer called on my hero, as soon as the two were alone together, he eyed him all over with a quick penetrating glance and seemed not dissatisfied with the result – for I must say here that Ernest had improved in personal appearance under the more genial treatment he had received at Cambridge. Pryer, in fact approved of him sufficiently to treat him civilly, and Ernest was immediately won by anyone who did this. It was not long before he discovered that the High Church party, and even Rome itself, had more to say for themselves than he had thought. This was his first snipe-like change of flight.

Pryer introduced him to several of his friends. They were all of them young clergymen, belonging as I have said to the highest of the High Church school, but Ernest was surprised to find how much they resembled other people when among themselves. This was a shock to him; it was ere long a still greater one to find that certain thoughts which he warred against as fatal to his soul, and which he had imagined he should lose once for all on ordination, were still as troublesome to him as they had been; he also saw plainly enough that the young gentlemen who formed the circle of Pryer's friends were in much the same unhappy predicament as himself.

This was deplorable. The only way out of it that Ernest could see was that he should get married at once. But then he did not know any one whom he wanted to marry. He did not know any woman, in fact, whom he would not rather die than marry. It had been one of Theobald's and Christina's main objects to keep him out of the way of women, and they had so far succeeded that women had become to him mysterious, inscrutable objects to be tolerated when it was impossible to avoid them, but never to be sought out or encouraged. As for any man loving, or even being at all fond of any woman, he supposed it was so, but he believed the greater number of those who professed such sentiments were liars. Now, however, it was clear that he had hoped against hope too long, and that the only thing to do was to go and ask the first woman who would listen to him to come and be married to him as soon as possible.

He broached this to Pryer, and was surprised to find that this gentleman, though attentive to such members of his flock as were young and good-looking, was strongly in favour of the celibacy of the clergy, as indeed were the other demure young clerics to whom Pryer had introduced Ernest.

Chapter Fifty-Two

'You know, my dear Pontifex,' said Pryer to him, some few weeks after Ernest had become acquainted with him, when the two were taking a constitutional one day in Kensington Gardens, 'You know, my dear Pontifex, it is all very well to quarrel with Rome, but Rome has reduced the treatment of the human soul to a science, while our own Church, though so much purer in many respects, has no organised system either of diagnosis or pathology – I mean, of course, spiritual diagnosis and spiritual pathology. Our Church does not prescribe remedies upon any settled system, and, what is still worse, even when her physicians have according to their lights ascertained the disease and pointed out the remedy, she has no discipline which will ensure its being actually applied. If our patients do not choose to do as we tell them, we cannot make them. Perhaps really under all the circumstances this is as well, for we are spiritually mere horse doctors as compared with the Roman priesthood, nor can we hope to make much headway against the sin and misery that surround us, till we return in some respects to the practice of our forefathers and of the greater part of Christendom.'

Ernest asked in what respects it was that his friend desired a return to the practice of our forefathers.

'Why, my dear fellow, can you really be ignorant? It is just this, either the priest is indeed a spiritual guide, as being able to show people how they ought to live better than they can find out for themselves, or he is nothing at all – he has no *raison d'être*. If the priest is not as much a healer and director of men's souls as a physician is of their bodies, what is he? The history of all ages has shown – and surely you must know this as well as I do – that as men cannot cure the bodies of their patients if they have not been properly trained in hospitals under skilled teachers, so neither can souls be cured of their more hidden ailments without the help of men who are skilled in soul-craft – or in other words, of priests. What do one half of our formularies and rubrics mean if not this? How in the name of all that is reasonable can we find out the exact nature of a spiritual malady, unless we have had experience of other similar cases? How can we get this without express training? At present we have to begin all experiments for ourselves, without profiting by the organised experience of our predecessors, inasmuch as that experience is never organised and co-ordinated at all. At the outset, therefore, each one of us must rain many souls which could be saved by knowledge of a few elementary principles.'

Ernest was very much impressed.

'As for men curing themselves,' continued Pryer, 'they can no more cure their own souls than they can cure their own bodies, or manage their own law affairs. In these two last cases they see the folly of meddling with their own cases clearly enough, and go to a professional adviser as a matter of course; surely a man's soul is at once a more difficult and intricate matter to treat, and at the same time it is more important to him that it should be treated rightly than that either his body or his money should be so. What are we to think of the practice of a Church which encourages people to rely on unprofessional advice in matters affecting their eternal welfare, when they would not think of jeopardising their worldly affairs by such insane conduct?'

Ernest could see no weak place in this. These ideas had crossed his own mind vaguely before now, but he had never laid hold of them or set them in an orderly manner before himself. Nor was he quick at detecting false analogies and the misuse of metaphors; in fact, he was a mere child in the hands of his fellow curate.

'And what,' resumed Pryer, 'does all this point to? Firstly, to the duty of confession – the outcry against which is absurd, as an outcry would be against dissection as part of the training of medical students. Granted these young men must see and do a great deal we do not ourselves even like to think of, but they should adopt some other profession unless they are prepared for this; they may even get inoculated with poison from a dead body and lose their lives, but they must stand their chance. So if we aspire to be priests in deed as well as name, we must familiarise ourselves with the minutest and most repulsive details of all kinds of sin, so that we may recognise it in all its stages. Some of us must doubtlessly perish spiritually in such investigations. We cannot help it; all science must have its martyrs, and none of these will deserve better of humanity than those who have fallen in the pursuit of spiritual pathology.'

Ernest grew more and more interested, but in the meekness of his soul said nothing.

'I do not desire this martyrdom for myself,' continued the other, 'on the contrary I will avoid it to the very utmost of my power, but if it be God's will that I should fall while studying what I believe most calculated to advance his glory – then, I say, not my will, oh, Lord, but thine be done.'

This was too much even for Ernest. 'I heard of an Irishwoman once,' he said, with a smile, 'who said she was a martyr to the drink.'

'And so she was,' rejoined Pryer with warmth; and he went on to show that this good woman was an experimentalist whose experiment, though disastrous in its effects upon herself, was pregnant with instruction to other people. She was thus a true martyr or witness to the frightful consequences of intemperance, to the saving, doubtless, of many who but for her martyrdom would have taken to drinking. She was one of a forlorn hope whose failure to take a certain position went to the proving it to be impregnable and therefore to the abandonment of all attempt to take it. This was almost as great a gain to mankind as the actual taking of the position would have been.

'Besides,' he added more hurriedly, 'the limits of vice and virtue are wretchedly ill-defined. Half the vices which the world
condemns most loudly have seeds of good in them and require
moderate use rather than total abstinence.'

Ernest asked timidly for an instance.

'No, no,' said Pryer, 'I will give you no instance, but I will give
you a formula that shall embrace all instances. It is this, that no
practice is entirely vicious which has not been extinguished
among the comeliest, most vigorous, and most cultivated races
of mankind in spite of centuries of endeavour to extirpate it. If a
vice in spite of such efforts can still hold its own among the most
polished nations, it must be founded on some immutable truth or
fact in human nature, and must have some compensatory advantage which we cannot afford altogether to dispense with.'

'But,' said Ernest timidly, 'is not this virtually doing away with
all distinction between right and wrong, and leaving people without any moral guide whatever?'

'Not the people,' was the answer: 'it must be our care to be
guides to these, for they are and always will be incapable of guid-
ing themselves sufficiently. We should tell them what they must
do, and in an ideal state of things should be able to enforce their
doing it: perhaps when we are better instructed the ideal state
may come about; nothing will so advance it as greater knowledge
of spiritual pathology on our own part. For this, three things are
necessary; firstly, absolute freedom in experiment for us the
clergy; secondly, absolute knowledge of what the laity think and
do, and of what thoughts and actions result in what spiritual conditions; and thirdly, a compacter organisation among ourselves.

'If we are to do any good we must be a closely united body,
and must be sharply divided from the laity. Also we must be free
from those ties which a wife and children involve. I can hardly
express the horror with which I am filled by seeing English priests
living in what I can only designate as 'open matrimony.' It is
deplorable. The priest must be absolutely sexless – if not in prac-

tice, yet at any rate in theory, absolutely – and that too, by a theory so universally accepted that none shall venture to dispute it.'

'But,' said Ernest, 'has not the Bible already told people what they ought and ought not to do, and is it not enough for us to insist on what can be found here, and let the rest alone?'

'If you begin with the Bible,' was the rejoinder, 'you are three parts gone on the road to infidelity, and will go the other part before you know where you are. The Bible is not without its value to us clergy, but for the laity it is a stumbling block which cannot be taken out of their way too soon or too completely. Of course, I mean on the supposition that they read it, which, happily, they seldom do. If people read the Bible as the ordinary British churchman or churchwoman reads it, it is harmless enough; but if they read it with any care – which we should assume they will if we give it them at all – it is fatal to them.'

'What do you mean?' said Ernest, more and more astonished, but more and more feeling that he was at least in the hands of a man who had definite ideas.

'Your question shows me that you have never read your Bible. A more unreliable book was never put upon paper. Take my advice and don't read it, not till you are a few years older, and may do so safely.'

'But surely you believe the Bible when it tells you of such things as that Christ died and rose from the dead? Surely you believe this?' said Ernest, quite prepared to be told that Pryer believed nothing of the kind.

'I do not believe it, I know it.'

'But how – if the testimony of the Bible fails?'

'On that of the living voice of the Church, which I know to be infallible and to be informed of Christ himself.'

Chapter Fifty-Three

The foregoing conversation and others like it made a deep impression upon my hero. If next day he had taken a walk with Mr Hawke, and heard what he had to say on the other side, he would have been just as much struck, and as ready to fling off what Pryer had told him, as he now was to throw aside all he had ever heard from anyone except Pryer; but there was no Mr Hawke at hand, so Pryer had everything his own way.

Embryo minds, like embryo bodies, pass through a number of strange metamorphoses before they adopt their final shape. It is no more to be wondered at that one who is going to turn out a Roman Catholic should have passed through the stages of being first a Methodist, and then a free-thinker, than that a man should at some former time have been a mere cell, and later on an invertebrate animal. Ernest, however, could not be expected to know this; embryos never do. Embryos think with each stage of their development that they have now reached the only condition which really suits them. This, they say, must certainly be their last, inasmuch as its close will be so great a shock that nothing can survive it. Every change is a shock; every shock is a *pro tanto* death. What we call death is only a shock great enough to destroy our power to recognise a past and a present as resembling one another. It is the making us consider the points of difference between our present and our past greater than the points of resemblance, so that we can no longer call the former of these two in any proper sense a continuation of the second, but find it less trouble to think of it as something that we choose to call new.

But, to let this pass, it was clear that spiritual pathology (I confess that I do not know myself what spiritual pathology means – but Pryer and Ernest doubtless did) was the great desideratum of the age. It seemed to Ernest that he had made this discovery himself and been familiar with it all his life, that he had never known, in fact, of anything else. He wrote long letters to his college friends expounding his views as though he had been one of the Apostolic fathers. As for the Old Testament writers, he had no patience with them. 'Do oblige me,' I find him writing to one friend, 'by reading the prophet Zechariah, and giving me your candid opinion upon him. He is poor stuff, full of Yankee bounce; it is sickening to live in an age when such balderdash can be gravely admired whether as poetry or prophecy.' This was because Pryer had set him against Zechariah. I do not know what Zechariah had done; I should think myself that Zechariah was a very good prophet; perhaps it was because he was a Bible writer, and not a very prominent one, that Pryer selected him as one through whom to disparage the Bible in comparison with the Church.

To his friend Dawson I find him saying a little later on: 'Pryer and I continue our walks, working out each other's thoughts. At first he used to do all the thinking, but I think I am pretty well abreast of him now, and rather chuckle at seeing that he is already beginning to modify some of the views he held most strongly when I first knew him.

'Then I think he was on the high road to Rome; now, however, he seems to be a good deal struck with a suggestion of mine, in which you, too, perhaps may be interested. You see we must infuse new life into the Church somehow; we are not holding our own against either Rome or infidelity.' (I may say in passing that I do not believe Ernest had as yet ever seen an infidel – not to speak to.) 'I proposed, therefore, a few days back to Pryer – and he fell in eagerly with the proposal as soon as he saw that I had the means of carrying it out – that we should set on foot a spiritual movement somewhat analogous to the Young England movement of twenty years ago, the aim of which shall be at once to outbid Rome on the one hand, and scepticism on the other. For this purpose I see nothing better than the foundation of an institution or college for placing the nature and treatment of sin on a more scientific basis than it rests at present. We want – to borrow a useful term of Pryer's – a College of Spiritual Pathology where young men' (I suppose Ernest thought he was no longer young by this time) 'may study the nature and treatment of the sins of the soul as medical students study those of the bodies of their patients. Such a college, as you will probably admit, will approach both Rome on the one hand, and science on the other – Rome, as giving the priesthood more skill, and therefore as paving the way for their obtaining greater power, and science, by recognising that even free thought has a certain kind of value in spiritual inquiries. To this purpose Pryer and I have resolved to devote ourselves henceforth heart and soul.

'Of course, my ideas are still unshaped, and all will depend upon the men by whom the college is first worked. I am not yet a priest, but Pryer is, and if I were to start the College, Pryer might take charge of it for a time and I work under him nominally as his subordinate. Pryer himself suggested this. Is it not generous of him?

'The worst of it is that we have not enough money; I have, it is true, £5,000, but we want at least £10,000, so Pryer says, before we can start; when we are fairly under weigh I might live at the college and draw a salary from the foundation, so that it is all one, or nearly so, whether I invest my money in this way or in buying a living; besides I want very little; it is certain that I shall never marry; no clergyman should think of this, and an unmarried man can live on next to nothing. Still I do not see my way to as much money as I want, and Pryer suggests that as we can hardly earn more now we must get it by a judicious series of investments. Pryer knows several people who make quite a handsome income out of very little or, indeed, I may say, nothing at all, by buying things at a place they call the Stock Exchange; I don't know much about it yet, but Pryer says I should soon learn; he thinks, indeed, that I have shown rather a talent in this direction, and under proper auspices should make a very good man of business. Others, of course, and not I, must decide this; but a man can do anything if he gives his mind to it, and though I should not care about having more money for my own sake, I care about it very much when I think of the good I could do with it by saving souls from such horrible torture hereafter. Why, if the thing succeeds, and I really cannot see what is to hinder it, it is hardly possible to exaggerate its importance, nor the proportions which it may ultimately assume,' etc., etc.

Again I asked Ernest whether he minded my printing this. He winced, but said, 'No, not if it helps you to tell your story: but don't you think it is too long?'

I said it would let the reader see for himself how things were going in half the time that it would take me to explain them to him.

'Very well, then, keep it by all means.'

I continue turning over my file of Ernest's letters and find as follows:

'Thanks for your last, in answer to which I send you a rough copy of a letter I sent to the *Times* a day or two back. They did not insert it, but it embodies pretty fully my ideas on the parochial visitation question, and Pryer fully approves of the letter. Think it carefully over and send it back to me when read, for it is so exactly my present creed that I cannot afford to lose it.

'I should very much like to have a *viva voce* discussion on these matters: I can only see for certain that we have suffered a dreadful loss in being no longer able to excommunicate. We should excommunicate rich and poor alike, and pretty freely too. If this power were restored to us we could, I think, soon put a stop to by far the greater part of the sin and misery with which we are surrounded.'

These letters were written only a few weeks after Ernest had been ordained, but they are nothing to others that he wrote a little later on.

In his eagerness to regenerate the Church of England (and through this the universe) by the means which Pryer had suggested to him, it occurred to him to try to familiarise himself with the habits and thoughts of the poor by going and living amongst them. I think he got this notion from Kingsley's *Alton Locke* which, High churchman though he for the nonce was, he had devoured as he had devoured Stanley's *Life of Arnold*, Dickens's novels, and whatever other literary garbage of the day was most likely to do him harm; at any rate he actually put his scheme into practice, and took lodgings in Ashpit Place, a small street in the neighbourhood of Drury Lane Theatre, in a house of which the landlady was the widow of a cabman.

This lady occupied the whole ground floor. In the front kitchen there was a tinker. The back kitchen was let to a bellows-mender. On the first floor came Ernest, with his two rooms which he furnished comfortably, for one must draw the line somewhere. The two upper floors were parcelled out among four different sets of lodgers: there was a tailor named Holt, a drunken fellow who used to beat his wife at night till her screams woke the house; above him there was another tailor with a wife but no children; these people were Wesleyans, given to drink but not noisy. The two back rooms were held by single ladies, who it seemed to Ernest must be respectably connected, for well-dressed gentlemanly-looking young men used to go up and down stairs past Ernest's rooms to call at any rate on Miss Snow – Ernest had heard her door slam after they had passed. He thought, too, that some of them went up to Miss Maitland's. Mrs Jupp, the landlady, told Ernest that these were brothers and cousins of Miss Snow's, and that she was herself looking out for a situation as a governess, but at present had an engagement as an actress at the Drury Lane Theatre. Ernest asked whether Miss Maitland in the top back was also looking out for a situation, and was told she was wanting an engagement as a milliner. He believed whatever Mrs Jupp told him.

Chapter Fifty-Four

This move on Ernest's part was variously commented upon by his friends, the general opinion being that it was just like Pontifex, who was sure to do something unusual wherever he went, but that on the whole the idea was commendable. Christina could not restrain herself when on sounding her clerical neighbours she found them inclined to applaud her son for conduct which they idealised into something much more self-denying than it really was. She did not quite like his living in such an unaristocratic neighbourhood; but what he was doing would probably get into the newspapers, and then great people would take notice of him. Besides, it would be very cheap; down among these poor people he could live for next to nothing, and might put by a great deal of his income. As for temptations, there could be few or none in such a place as that. This argument about cheapness was the one with which she most successfully met Theobald, who grumbled *more suo* that he had no sympathy with his son's extravagance and conceit. When Christina pointed out to him that it would be cheap he replied that there was something in that.

On Ernest himself the effect was to confirm the good opinion of himself which had been growing upon him ever since he had begun to read for orders, and to make him flatter himself that he was among the few who were ready to give up *all* for Christ. Ere long he began to conceive of himself as a man with a mission and a great future. His lightest and most hastily formed opinions began to be of momentous importance to him, and he inflicted them, as I have already shown, on his old friends, week by week becoming more and more *entêté* with himself and his own crotchets. I should like well enough to draw a veil over this part of my hero's career, but cannot do so without marring my story.

In the spring of 1859 I find him writing:

'I cannot call the visible Church Christian till its fruits are Christian, that is until the fruits of the members of the Church of England are in conformity, or something like conformity, with her teaching. I cordially agree with the teaching of the Church of England in most respects, but she says one thing and does another, and until excommunication – yes, and wholesale excommunication – be resorted to, I cannot call her a Christian institution. I should begin with our Rector, and if I found it necessary to follow him up by excommunicating the Bishop, I should not flinch even from this.

'The present London Rectors are hopeless people to deal with. My own is one of the best of them, but the moment Pryer and I show signs of wanting to attack an evil in a way not recognised by routine, or of remedying anything about which no outcry has been made, we are met with, "I cannot think what you mean by all this disturbance; nobody else among the clergy sees these things, and I have no wish to be the first to begin turning everything topsy-turvy." And then people call him a sensible man. I have no patience with them. However, we know what we want, and, as I wrote to Dawson the other day, have a scheme on foot which will, I think, fairly meet the requirements of the case. But we want more money, and my first move towards getting this has not turned out quite so satisfactorily as Pryer and I had hoped; we shall, however, I doubt not, retrieve it shortly.'

When Ernest came to London he intended doing a good deal of house-to-house visiting, but Pryer had talked him out of this even before he settled down in his new and strangely-chosen apartments. The line he now took was that if people wanted

Christ, they must prove their want by taking some little trouble, and the trouble required of them was that they should come and seek him, Ernest, out; there he was in the midst of them ready to teach; if people did not choose to come to him it was no fault of his.

'My great business here,' he writes again to Dawson, 'is to observe. I am not doing much in parish work beyond my share of the daily services. I have a man's Bible Class, and a boy's Bible Class, and a good many young men and boys to whom I give instruction one way or another; then there are the Sunday School children, with whom I fill my room on a Sunday evening as full as it will hold, and let them sing hymns and chants. They like this. I do a great deal of reading – chiefly of books which Pryer and I think most likely to help; we find nothing comparable to the Jesuits. Pryer is a thorough gentleman, and an admirable man of business – no less observant of the things of this world, in fact, than of the things above; by a brilliant *coup* he has retrieved, or nearly so, a rather serious loss which threatened to delay indefinitely the execution of our great scheme. He and I daily gather fresh principles. I believe great things are before me, and am strong in the hope of being able by and by to effect much.

'As for you I bid you God speed. Be bold but logical, speculative but cautious, daringly courageous, but properly circumspect withal,' etc., etc.

I think this may do for the present.

Chapter Fifty-Five

I had called on Ernest as a matter of course when he first came to London, but had not seen him. I had been out when he returned my call, so that he had been in town for some weeks before I actually saw him, which I did not very long after he had taken possession of his new rooms. I liked his face, but except for the common bond of music, in respect of which our tastes were singularly alike, I should hardly have known how to get on with him. To do him justice he did not air any of his schemes to me until I had drawn him out concerning them. I, to borrow the words of Ernest's landlady, Mrs Jupp, 'am not a very regular church-goer' – I discovered upon cross-examination that Mrs Jupp had been to church once when she was churched for her son Tom some five and twenty years since, but never either before or afterwards; not even, I fear, to be married, for though she called herself 'Mrs' she wore no wedding ring, and spoke of the person who should have been Mr Jupp as 'my poor dear boy's father,' not as 'my husband.' But to return. I was vexed at Ernest's having been ordained. I was not ordained myself and I did not like my friends to be ordained, nor did I like having to be on my best behaviour and to look as if butter would not melt in my mouth, and all for a boy whom I remembered when he knew yesterday and to-morrow and Tuesday, but not a day of the week more – not even Sunday itself – and when he said he did not like the kitten because it had pins in its toes.

I looked at him and thought of his aunt Alethea, and how fast the money she had left him was accumulating; and it was all to go to this young man, who would use it probably in the very last ways with which Miss Pontifex would have sympathised. I was annoyed. 'She always said,' I thought to myself, 'that she would make a mess of it, but I did not think she would have made as great a mess of it as this.' Then I thought that perhaps if his aunt had lived he would not have been like this.

Ernest behaved quite nicely to me and I own that the fault was mine if the conversation drew towards dangerous subjects. I was the aggressor, presuming, I suppose, upon my age and long acquaintance with him, as giving me a right to make myself unpleasant in a quiet way.

Then he came out, and the exasperating part of it was that up to a certain point he was so very right. Grant him his premises and his conclusions were sound enough, nor could I, seeing that he was already ordained, join issue with him about his premises as I should certainly have done if I had had a chance of doing so before he had taken orders. The result was that I had to beat a retreat and went away not in the best of humours. I believe the truth was that I liked Ernest, and was vexed at his being a clergyman, and at a clergyman having so much money coming to him.

I talked a little with Mrs Jupp on my way out. She and I had reckoned one another up at first sight as being neither of us 'very regular church-goers,' and the strings of her tongue had been loosened. She said Ernest would die. He was much too good for the world and he looked so sad, 'just like young Watkins of the "Crown" over the way who died a month ago, and his poor dear skin was white as alablaster; least-ways they say he shot hisself. They took him from the Mortimer, I met them just as I was going with my Rose to get a pint o' four ale, and she had her arm in splints. She told her sister she wanted to go to Perry's to get some wool, instead o' which it was only a stall to get me a pint o' ale, bless her heart; there's nobody else would do that much for poor old Jupp, and it's a horrid lie to say she is gay; not but what I like a gay woman, I do: I'd rather give a gay woman half-a-crown than stand a modest woman a pot o' beer, but I don't want to go associating with bad girls for all that. So they took him from the

Mortimer; they wouldn't let him go home no more; and he done it that artful, you know. His wife was in the country living with her mother, and she always spoke respectful o' my Rose. Poor dear, I hope his soul is in Heaven. Well, sir, would you believe it, there's that in Mr Pontifex's face which is just like young Watkins; he looks that worrited and scrunched up at times, but it's never for the same reason, for he don't know nothing at all, no more than a unborn babe, no he don't; why, there's not a monkey going about London with an Italian organ grinder but knows more than Mr Pontifex do. He don't know – well, I suppose –'

Here a child came in on an errand from some neighbour and interrupted her, or I can form no idea where or when she would have ended her discourse. I seized the opportunity to run away, but not before I had given her five shillings and made her write down my address, for I was a little frightened by what she said. I told her if she thought her lodger grew worse, she was to come and let me know.

Weeks went by and I did not see her again. Having done as much as I had, I felt absolved from doing more, and let Ernest alone, as thinking that he and I should only bore one another.

He had now been ordained a little over four months, but these months had not brought happiness or satisfaction with them. He had lived in a clergyman's house all his life, and might have been expected perhaps to have known pretty much what being a clergyman was like, and so he did – a country clergyman; he had formed an ideal, however, as regards what a town clergyman could do, and was trying in a feeble tentative way to realise it, but somehow or other it always managed to escape him.

He lived among the poor, but he did not find that he got to know them. The idea that they would come to him proved to be a mistaken one. He did indeed visit a few tame pets whom his rector desired him to look after. There was an old man and his wife who lived next door but one to Ernest himself; then there was a plumber of the name of Chesterfield; an aged lady of the name of Gover, blind and bedridden, who munched and munched her feeble old toothless jaws as Ernest spoke or read to her, but who could do little more; a Mr Brookes, a rag and bottle merchant in Birdsey's Rents in the last stage of dropsy, and perhaps half a dozen or so others. What did it all come to, when he did go to see them? The plumber wanted to be flattered, and liked fooling a gentleman into wasting his time by scratching his ears for him. Mrs Gover, poor old woman, wanted money; she was very good and meek, and when Ernest got her a shilling from Lady Anne Jones's bequest, she said it was 'small but seasonable,' and munched and munched in gratitude. Ernest sometimes gave her a little money himself, but not, as he says now, half what he ought to have given.

What could he do else that would have been of the smallest use to her? Nothing indeed; but giving occasional half-crowns to Mrs Gover was not regenerating the universe, and Ernest wanted nothing short of this. The world was all out of joint, and instead of feeling it to be a cursed spite that he was born to set it right, he thought he was just the kind of person that was wanted for the job, and was eager to set to work, only he did not exactly know how to begin, for the beginning he had made with Mr Chesterfield and Mrs Gover did not promise great developments.

Then poor Mr Brookes – he suffered very much, terribly indeed; he was not in want of money; he wanted to die and couldn't, just as we sometimes want to go to sleep and cannot. He had been a serious-minded man, and death frightened him as it must frighten anyone who believes that all his most secret thoughts will be shortly exposed in public. When I read Ernest the description of how his father used to visit Mrs Thompson at Battersby, he coloured and said: 'That's just what I used to say to Mr Brookes.' Ernest felt that his visits, so far from comforting Mr Brookes, made him fear death more and more, but how could he help it?

Even Pryer, who had been a curate a couple of years, did not know personally more than a couple of hundred people in the parish at the outside, and it was only at the houses of very few of these that he ever visited, but then Pryer had such a strong objection on principle to house visitations. What a drop in the sea were those with whom he and Pryer were brought into direct communication in comparison with those whom he must reach and move if he were to produce much effect of any kind, one way or the other. Why, there were between fifteen and twenty thousand poor in the parish, of whom but the merest fraction even attended a place of worship. Some few went to dissenting chapels, a few were Roman Catholics; by far the greater number, however, were practically infidels, if not actively hostile, at any rate indifferent to religion, while many were avowed Atheists – admirers of Tom Paine, of whom he now heard for the first time; but he never met and conversed with any of these.

Was he really doing everything that could be expected of him? It was all very well to say that he was doing as much as other young clergymen did; that was not the kind of answer which Jesus Christ was likely to accept; why, the Pharisees themselves in all probability did as much as the other Pharisees did. What he should do was to go into the highways and byways, and compel people to come in. Was he doing this? Or were not they rather compelling him to keep out – outside their doors at any rate? He began to have an uneasy feeling as though ere long, unless he kept a sharp look out, he should drift into being a sham.

True, all would be changed as soon as he could endow the College for Spiritual Pathology; matters, however, had not gone too well with 'the things that people bought in the place that was called the Stock Exchange.' In order to get on faster, it had been arranged that Ernest should buy more of these things than he could pay for, with the idea that in a few weeks, or even days, they would be much higher in value, and he could sell them at a tremendous profit; but, unfortunately, instead of getting higher, they had fallen immediately after Ernest had bought, and obstinately refused to get up again; so, after a few settlements, he had got frightened, for he read an article in some newspaper, which said they would go ever so much lower, and, contrary to Pryer's advice, he insisted on selling – at a loss of something like £500. He had hardly sold when up went the shares again, and he saw how foolish he had been, and how wise Pryer was, for if Pryer's advice had been followed he would have made £500 instead of losing it. However, he told himself he must live and learn.

Then Pryer made a mistake. They had bought some shares, and the shares went up delightfully for about a fortnight. This was a happy time indeed, for by the end of a fortnight the lost £500 had been recovered, and three or four hundred pounds had been cleared into the bargain. All the feverish anxiety of that miserable six weeks, when the £500 was being lost, was now being repaid with interest. Ernest wanted to sell and make sure of the profit, but Pryer would not hear of it; they would go ever so much higher yet, and he showed Ernest an article in some newspaper which proved that what he said was reasonable, and they did go up a little – but only a very little, for then they went down, down, and Ernest saw first his clear profit of three or four hundred pounds go, and then the £500 loss, which he thought he had recovered, slipped away by falls of a half and one at a time, and then he lost £200 more. Then a newspaper said that these shares were the greatest rubbish that had ever been imposed upon the English public, and Ernest could stand it no longer, so he sold out, again this time against Pryer's advice, so that when they went up, as they shortly did, Pryer scored off Ernest a second time.

Ernest was not used to vicissitudes of this kind, and they made him so anxious that his health was affected. It was arranged, therefore, that he had better know nothing of what was being done. Pryer was a much better man of business than he was, and would see to it all. This relieved Ernest of a good deal of trouble, and was better, after all, for the investments themselves; for, as

Pryer justly said, a man must not have a faint heart if he hopes to succeed in buying and selling upon the Stock Exchange, and seeing Ernest nervous made Pryer nervous too – at least, he said it did. So the money drifted more and more into Pryer's hands. As for Pryer himself, he had nothing but his curacy and a small allowance from his father.

Some of Ernest's friends got an inkling from his letters of what he was doing, and did their utmost to dissuade him, but he was as infatuated as a young lover of two and twenty. Finding that these friends disapproved, he dropped away from them, and they, being bored with his egotism and high-flown ideas, were not sorry to let him do so. Of course, he said nothing about his speculations – indeed, he hardly knew that anything done in so good a cause could be called speculation. At Battersby, when his father urged him to look out for a next presentation, and even brought one or two promising ones under his notice, he made objections and excuses, though always promising to do as his father desired very shortly.

Chapter Fifty-Six

By and by a subtle, indefinable *malaise* began to take possession of him. I once saw a very young foal trying to eat some most objectionable refuse, and unable to make up its mind whether it was good or no. Clearly it wanted to be told. If its mother had seen what it was doing she would have set it right in a moment and as soon as ever it had been told that what it was eating was filth, the foal would have recognised it and never have wanted to be told again; but the foal could not settle the matter for itself, or make up its mind whether it liked what it was trying to eat or no, without assistance from without. I suppose it would have come to do so by and by, but it was wasting time and trouble, which a single look from its mother would have saved, just as wort will in time ferment of itself, but will ferment much more quickly if a little yeast be added to it. In the matter of knowing what gives us pleasure we are all like wort, and if unaided from without can only ferment slowly and toilsomely.

My unhappy hero about this time was very much like the foal, or rather he felt much what the foal would have felt if its mother and all the other grown-up horses in the field had vowed that what it was eating was the most excellent and nutritious food to be found anywhere. He was so anxious to do what was right, and so ready to believe that every one knew better than himself, that he never ventured to admit to himself that he might be all the while on a hopelessly wrong tack. It did not occur to him that there might be a blunder anywhere, much less did it occur to him to try and find out where the blunder was. Nevertheless he became daily more full of *malaise,* and daily, only he knew it not, more ripe for an explosion should a spark fall upon him.

One thing, however, did begin to loom out of the general vagueness, and to this he instinctively turned as trying to seize it – I mean, the fact that he was saving very few souls, whereas there were thousands and thousands being lost hourly all around him which a little energy such as Mr Hawke's might save. Day after day went by, and what was he doing? Standing on professional *etiquette,* and praying that his shares might go up and down as he wanted them, so that they might give him money enough to enable him to regenerate the universe. But in the meantime the people were dying. How many souls would not be doomed to endless ages of the most frightful torments that the mind could think of, before he could bring his spiritual pathology engine to bear upon them? Why might he not stand and preach as he saw the Dissenters doing sometimes in Lincoln's Inn Fields and other thoroughfares? He could say all that Mr Hawke had said. Mr Hawke was a very poor creature in Ernest's eyes now, for he was a Low Churchman, but we should not be above learning from any one, and surely he could affect his hearers as powerfully as Mr Hawke had affected him if he only had the courage to set to work. The people whom he saw preaching in the squares sometimes drew large audiences. He could at any rate preach better than they.

Ernest broached this to Pryer, who treated it as something too outrageous to be even thought of. Nothing, he said, could more tend to lower the dignity of the clergy and bring the Church into contempt. His manner was brusque, and even rude.

Ernest ventured a little mild dissent; he admitted it was not usual, but something at any rate must be done, and that quickly. This was how Wesley and Whitfield had begun that great movement which had kindled religious life in the minds of hundreds of thousands. This was no time to be standing on dignity. It was just because Wesley and Whitfield had done what the Church would not that they had won men to follow them whom the Church had now lost.

Pryer eyed Ernest searchingly, and after a pause said, 'I don't know what to make of you, Pontifex; you are at once so very right and so very wrong. I agree with you heartily that something should be done, but it must not be done in a way which experience has shown leads to nothing but fanaticism and dissent. Do you approve of these Wesleyans? Do you hold your ordination vows so cheaply as to think, that it does not matter whether the services of the Church are performed in her churches and with all due ceremony or not? If you do – then, frankly, you had no business to be ordained; if you do not, then remember that one of the first duties of a young deacon is obedience to authority. Neither the Catholic Church, nor yet the Church of England allows her clergy to preach in the streets of cities where there is no lack of churches.'

Ernest felt the force of this, and Pryer saw that he wavered.

'We are living,' he continued more genially, 'in an age of transition, and in a country which, though it has gained much by the Reformation, does not perceive how much it has also lost. You cannot and must not hawk Christ about in the streets as though you were in a heathen country whose inhabitants had never heard of him. The people here in London have had ample warning. Every church they pass is a protest to them against their lives, and a call to them to repent. Every church-bell they hear is a witness against them, everyone of those whom they meet on Sundays going to or coming from church is a warning voice from God. If these countless influences produce no effect upon them, neither will the few transient words which they would hear from you. You are like Dives, and think that if one rose from the dead they would hear him. Perhaps they might; but then you cannot pretend that you have risen from the dead.'

Though the last few words were spoken laughingly, there was a sub-sneer about them which made Ernest wince; but he was quite subdued, and so the conversation ended. It left Ernest, however, not for the first time, consciously dissatisfied with Pryer, and inclined to set his friend's opinion on one side – not openly, but quietly, and without telling Pryer anything about it.

Chapter Fifty-Seven

He had hardly parted from Pryer before there occurred another incident which strengthened his discontent. He had fallen, as I have shown, among a gang of spiritual thieves or coiners, who passed the basest metal upon him without his finding it out, so childish and inexperienced was he in the ways of anything but those back eddies of the world, schools and universities. Among the bad threepenny pieces which had been passed off upon him, and which he kept for small hourly disbursement, was a remark that poor people were much nicer than the richer and better educated. Ernest now said that he travelled third class not because it was cheaper, but because the people whom he met in third class carriages were so much pleasanter and better behaved. As for the young men who attended Ernest's evening classes, they were pronounced to be more intelligent and better ordered generally than the average run of Oxford and Cambridge men. Our foolish young friend having heard Pryer talk to this effect, caught up all he said and reproduced it *more suo*.

One evening, however, about this time, whom should he see coming along a small street not far from his own but, of all persons in the world, Towneley, looking as full of life and good spirits as ever, and if possible even handsomer than he had been at Cambridge. Much as Ernest liked him he found himself shrinking from speaking to him, and was endeavouring to pass him without doing so when Towneley saw him and stopped him at once, being pleased to see an old Cambridge face. He seemed for the moment a little confused at being seen in such a neighbourhood, but recovered himself so soon that Ernest hardly noticed it, and then plunged into a few kindly remarks about old times.

Ernest felt that he quailed as he saw Towneley's eye wander to his white necktie and saw that he was being reckoned up, and rather disapprovingly reckoned up, as a parson. It was the merest passing shade upon Towneley's face, but Ernest had felt it.

Towneley said a few words of common form to Ernest about his profession as being what he thought would be most likely to interest him, and Ernest, still confused and shy, gave him for lack of something better to say his little threepenny-bit about poor people being so very nice. Towneley took this for what it was worth and nodded assent, whereon Ernest imprudently went further and said, 'Don't you like poor people very much yourself?'

Towneley gave his face a comical but good-natured screw, and said quietly, but slowly and decidedly, 'No, no, no,' and escaped.

It was all over with Ernest from that moment. As usual he did not know it, but he had entered none the less upon another reaction. Towneley had just taken Ernest's threepenny-bit into his hands, looked at it and returned it to him as a bad one. Why did he see in a moment that it was a bad one now, though he had been unable to see it when he had taken it from Pryer? Of course some poor people were very nice, and always would be so, but as though scales had fallen from his eyes he saw that no one was nicer for being poor, and that between the upper and lower classes there was a gulf which amounted practically to an impassable barrier.

That evening he reflected a good deal. If Towneley was right, and Ernest felt that the 'No' had applied, not to the remark about poor people only, but to the whole scheme and scope of his own recently adopted ideas, he and Pryer must surely be on a wrong track. Towneley had not argued with him; he had said one word only, and that one of the shortest in the language, but Ernest was in a fit state for inoculation, and the minute particle of virus set about working immediately.

Which did he now think was most likely to have taken the juster view of life and things, and whom would it be best to imitate, Towneley or Pryer? His heart returned answer to itself without a moment's hesitation. The faces of men like Towneley were open and kindly; they looked as if at ease themselves, and as though they would set all who had to do with them at ease as far as might be. The faces of Pryer and his friends were not like this. Why had he felt tacitly rebuked as soon as he had met Towneley? Was he not a Christian? Certainly; he believed in the Church of England as a matter of course. Then how could he be himself wrong in trying to act up to the faith that he and Towneley held in common? He was trying to lead a quiet, unobtrusive life of self-devotion, whereas Towneley was not, so far as he could see, trying to do anything of the kind; he was only trying to get on comfortably in the world, and to look and be as nice as possible. And he was nice, and Ernest knew that such men as himself and Pryer were not nice, and his old dejection came over him.

Then came an even worse reflection; how if he had fallen among material thieves as well as spiritual ones? He knew very little of how his money was going on; he had put it all now into Pryer's hands, and though Pryer gave him cash to spend whenever he wanted it, he seemed impatient of being questioned as to what was being done with the principal. It was part of the understanding, he said, that that was to be left to him, and Ernest had better stick to this, or he, Pryer would throw up the College of Spiritual Pathology altogether; and so Ernest was cowed into acquiescence, or cajoled, according to the humour in which Pryer saw him to be. Ernest thought that further questions would look as if he doubted Pryer's word, and also that he had gone too far to be able to recede in decency or honour. This, however, he felt was riding out to meet trouble unnecessarily. Pryer had been a little impatient, but he was a gentleman and an admirable man of business, so his money would doubtless come back to him all right some day.

Ernest comforted himself as regards this last source of anxiety, but as regards the other, he began to fed as though, if he was to be saved, a good Samaritan must hurry up from somewhere – he knew not whence.

Chapter Fifty-Eight

Next day he felt stronger again. He had been listening to the voice of the evil one on the night before, and would parley no more with such thoughts. He had chosen his profession, and his duty was to persevere with it. If he was unhappy it was probably because he was not giving up all for Christ. Let him see whether he could not do more than he was doing now, and then perhaps a light would be shed upon his path.

It was all very well to have made the discovery that he didn't very much like poor people, but he had got to put up with them, for it was among them that his work must lie. Such men as Towneley were very kind and considerate, but he knew well enough it was only on condition that he did not preach to them. He could manage the poor better, and, let Pryer sneer as he liked, he was resolved to go more among them, and try the effect of bringing Christ to them if they would not come and seek Christ of themselves. He would begin with his own house.

Who then should he take first? Surely he could not do better than begin with the tailor who lived immediately over his bead. This would be desirable, not only because he was the one who seemed to stand most in need of conversion, but also because, if he were once converted, he would no longer beat his wife at two o'clock in the morning, and the house would be much pleasanter in consequence. He would therefore go upstairs at once, and have a quiet talk with this man.

Before doing so, he thought it would be well if he were to draw up something like a plan of campaign; he therefore reflected over some pretty conversations which would do very nicely if Mr Holt would be kind enough to make the answers proposed for him in their proper places. But the man was a great hulking fellow, of a savage temper, and Ernest was forced to admit that unforeseen developments might arise to disconcert him. They say it takes nine tailors to make a man, but Ernest felt that it would take at least nine Ernests to make a Mr Holt. How if, as soon as Ernest came in, the tailor were to become violent and abusive? What could he do? Mr Holt was in his own lodging and had a right to be undisturbed. A legal right yes, but had he a moral right? Ernest thought not, considering his mode of life. But put this on one side; if the man were to be violent, what should he do? Paul had fought with wild beasts at Ephesus – that must indeed have been awful – but perhaps they were not very wild beasts; a rabbit and a canary are wild beasts; but formidable or not as wild beasts go, they would, nevertheless, stand no chance against St Paul, for he was inspired; the miracle would have been if the wild beasts escaped, not that St Paul should have done so; but, however all this might be, Ernest felt that he dared not begin to convert Mr Holt by fighting him. Why, when he had heard Mrs Holt screaming 'murder,' he had cowered under the bed clothes and waited, expecting to hear the blood dripping through the ceiling on to his own floor. His imagination translated every sound into a pat, pat, pat, and once or twice he thought he had felt it dropping on to his counterpane, but he had never gone upstairs to try and rescue poor Mrs Holt. Happily it had proved next morning that Mrs Holt was in her usual health.

Ernest was in despair about hitting on any good way of opening up spiritual communication with his neighbour, when it occurred to him that he had better perhaps begin by going upstairs, and knocking very gently at Mr Holt's door. He would then resign himself to the guidance of the Holy Spirit, and act as the occasion, which, I suppose, was another name for the Holy Spirit, suggested. Triply armed with this reflection, he mounted the stairs quite jauntily, and was about to knock when he heard Holt's voice inside swearing savagely at his wife. This made him pause to think whether after all the moment was an auspicious one, and while he was thus pausing, Mr Holt, who had heard that someone was on the stairs, opened the door and put his head out. When he saw Ernest, he made an unpleasant, not to say offensive movement, which might or might not have been directed at Ernest, and looked altogether so ugly that my hero had an instant-aneous and unequivocal revelation from the Holy Spirit to the effect that he should continue his journey upstairs at once, as though he had never intended arresting it at Mr Holt's room, and begin by converting Mr and Mrs Baxter, the Methodists in the top floor front. So this was what he did.

These good people received him with open arms, and were quite ready to talk. He was beginning to convert them from Methodism to the Church of England, when all at once he found himself embarrassed by discovering that he did not know what he was to convert them from. He knew the Church of England, or thought he did, but he knew nothing of Methodism beyond its name. When he found that, according to Mr Baxter, the Wesley-ans had a vigorous system of Church discipline (which worked admirably in practice) it appeared to him that John Wesley had anticipated the spiritual engine which he and Pryer were prepar-ing, and when he left the room he was aware that he had caught more of a spiritual Tartar than he had expected. But he must cer-tainly explain to Pryer that the Wesleyans had a system of Church discipline. This was very important.

Mr Baxter advised Ernest on no account to meddle with Mr Holt, and Ernest was much relieved at the advice. If an opportun-ity arose of touching the man's heart, he would take it; he would pat the children on the head when he saw them on the stairs, and ingratiate himself with them as far as he dared; they were sturdy youngsters, and Ernest was afraid even of them, for they were ready with their tongues, and knew much for their ages. Ernest felt that it would indeed be almost better for him that a millstone should be hanged about his neck, and he cast into the sea, than that he should offend one of the little Holts. However, he would try not to offend them; perhaps an occasional penny or two might square them. This was as much as he could do, for he saw that the attempt to be instant out of season, as well as in season, would, St Paul's injunction notwithstanding, end in failure.

Mrs Baxter gave a very bad account of Miss Emily Snow, who lodged in the second floor back next to Mr Holt. Her story was quite different from that of Mrs Jupp the landlady. She would doubtless be only too glad to receive Ernest's ministrations or those of any other gentleman, but she was no governess, she was in the ballet at Drury Lane, and besides this, she was a very bad young woman, and if Mrs Baxter was landlady would not be allowed to stay in the house a single hour, not she indeed.

Miss Maitland in the next room to Mrs Baxter's own was a quiet and respectable young woman to all appearance; Mrs Baxter had never known of any goings on in that quarter, but, bless you, still waters run deep, and these girls were all alike, one as bad as the other. She was out at all kinds of hours, and when you knew that you knew all.

Ernest did not pay much heed to these aspersions of Mrs Baxter's. Mrs Jupp had got round the greater number of his many blind sides, and had warned him not to believe Mrs Baxter, whose lip, she said, was something awful.

Ernest had heard that women were always jealous of one another, and certainly these young women were more attractive than Mrs Baxter was, so jealousy was probably at the bottom of it. If they were maligned there could be no objection to his making their acquaintance; if not maligned they had all the more need of his ministrations. He would reclaim them at once.

He told Mrs Jupp of his intention. Mrs Jupp at first tried to dissuade him, but seeing him resolute, suggested that she should herself see Miss Snow first, so as to prepare her and prevent her from being alarmed by his visit. She was not at home now, but in the course of the next day, it should be arranged. In the meantime he had better try Mr Shaw, the tinker, in the front kitchen. Mrs Baxter had told Ernest that Mr Shaw was from the North Country, and an avowed freethinker; he would probably, she said, rather like a visit, but she did not think Ernest would stand much chance of making a convert of him.

Chapter Fifty-Nine

Before going down into the kitchen to convert the tinker Ernest ran hurriedly over his analysis of Paley's evidences, and put into his pocket a copy of Archbishop Whateley's *Historic Doubts*. Then he descended the dark rotten old stairs and knocked at the tinker's door. Mr Shaw was very civil; he said he was rather throng just now, but if Ernest did not mind the sound of hammering he should be very glad of a talk with him. Our hero, assenting to this, ere long led the conversation to Whateley's *Historic Doubts* – a work which, as the reader may know, pretends to show that there never was any such person as Napoleon Buonaparte, and thus satires the arguments of those who have attacked the Christian miracles.

Mr Shaw said he knew *Historic Doubts* very well.

'And what do you think of it? said Ernest, who regarded the pamphlet as a masterpiece of wit and cogency.

'If you really want to know,' said Mr Shaw, with a sly twinkle, 'I think that he who was so willing and able to prove that what was was not, would be equally able and willing to make a case for thinking that what was not was, if it suited his purpose,' Ernest was very much taken aback. How was it that all the clever people of Cambridge had never put him up to this simple rejoinder? The answer is easy: they did not develop it for the same reason that a hen never developed webbed feet – that is to say, because they did not want to do so; but this was before the days of Evolution, and Ernest could not as yet know anything of the great principle that underlies it.

'You see,' continued Mr Shaw, 'these writers all get their living by writing in a certain way, and the more they write in that way, the more they are likely to get on. You should not call them dishonest for this any more than a judge should call a barrister dishonest for earning his living by defending one in whose innocence he does not seriously believe; but you should hear the barrister on the other side before you decide upon the case.'

This was another facer. Ernest could only stammer that he had endeavoured to examine these questions as carefully as he could.

'You think you have,' said Mr Shaw; 'you Oxford and Cambridge gentlemen think you have examined everything. I have examined very little myself except the bottoms of old kettles and saucepans, but if you will answer me a few questions, I will tell you whether or no you have examined much more than I have.'

Ernest expressed his readiness to be questioned.

'Then,' said the tinker, 'give me the story of the Resurrection of Jesus Christ as told in St John's gospel.'

I am sorry to say that Ernest mixed up the four accounts in a deplorable manner; he even made the angel come down and roll away the stone and sit upon it. He was covered with confusion when the tinker first told him without the book of some of his many inaccuracies, and then verified his criticisms by referring to the New Testament itself.

'Now.' said Mr Shaw good-naturedly, 'I am an old man and you are a young one, so perhaps you'll not mind my giving you a piece of advice. I like you, for I believe you mean well, but you've been real bad brought up, and I don't think you have ever had so much as a chance yet. You know nothing of our side of the question, and I have just shown you that you do not know much more of your own, but I think you will make a kind of Carlyle sort of a man some day. Now go upstairs and read the accounts of the Resurrection correctly without mixing them up, and have a clear idea of what it is that each writer tell us, then if you feel inclined to pay me another visit I shall be glad to see you, for I shall know you have made a good beginning and mean business. Till then, sir, I must wish you a very good morning.'

Ernest retreated abashed. An hour sufficed him to perform the task enjoined upon him by Mr Shaw; and at the end of that hour the 'No, no, no,' which still sounded in his ears as he heard it from Towneley, came ringing up more loudly still from the very pages of the Bible itself, and in respect of the most important of all the events which are recorded in it. Surely Ernest's first day's attempt at more promiscuous visiting, and at carrying out his principles more thoroughly, had not been unfruitful. But he must go and have a talk with Pryer. He therefore got his lunch and went to Pryer's lodgings. Pryer not being at home, he lounged to the British Museum Reading Room, then recently opened, sent for the *Vestiges of Creation,* which he had never yet seen, and spent the rest of the afternoon in reading it. Ernest did not see Pryer on the day of his conversation with Mr Shaw, but he did so next morning and found him in a good temper, which of late he had rarely been. Sometimes, indeed, he had behaved to Ernest in a way which did not bode well for the harmony with which the College of Spiritual Pathology would work when it had once been founded. It almost seemed as though he were trying to get a moral ascendency over him, so as to make him a creature of his own.

He did not think it possible that he could go too far, and indeed, when I reflect upon my hero's folly and inexperience, there is much to be said in excuse for the conclusion which Pryer came to.

As a matter of fact, however, it was not so. Ernest's faith in Pryer had been too great to be shaken down all in a moment, but it had been weakened lately more than once. Ernest had fought hard against allowing himself to see this, nevertheless any third person who knew the pair would have been able to see that the connection between the two might end at any moment, for when the time for one of Ernest's snipe-like changes of flight came, he was quick in making it; the time, however, was not yet come, and the intimacy between the two was apparently all that it had ever been. It was only that horrid money business (so said Ernest to himself) that caused any unpleasantness between them, and no doubt Pryer was right, and he, Ernest, much too nervous. However, that might stand over for the present.

In like manner, though he had received a shock by reason of his conversation with Mr Shaw, and by looking at the *Vestiges,* he was as yet too much stunned to realise the change which was coming over him. In each case the momentum of old habits carried him forward in the old direction. He therefore called on Pryer, and spent an hour and more with him.

He did not say that he had been visiting among his neighbours; this to Pryer would have been like a red rag to a bull. He only talked in much his usual vein about the proposed College, the lamentable want of interest in spiritual things which was characteristic of modern society, and other kindred matters; he concluded by saying that for the present he feared Pryer was indeed right, and that nothing could be done.

'As regards the laity,' said Pryer, 'nothing; not until we have a discipline which we can enforce with pains and penalties. How can a sheep dog work a flock of sheep unless he can bite occasionally as well as bark? But as regards ourselves we can do much.'

Pryer's manner was strange throughout the conversation, as though he were thinking all the time of something else. His eyes wandered curiously over Ernest, as Ernest had often noticed them wander before: the words were about Church discipline, but somehow or other the discipline part of the story had a knack of dropping out after having been again and again emphatically declared to apply to the laity and not to the clergy: once indeed Pryer had pettishly exclaimed: 'Oh, bother the College of Spiritual Pathology.' As regards the clergy, glimpses of a pretty large cloven hoof kept peeping out from under the saintly robe of Pryer's conversation, to the effect, that so long as they were theoretically perfect, practical peccadilloes – or even peccadaccios, if there is such a word, were of less importance. He was restless, as though wanting to approach a subject which he did not quite venture to touch upon, and kept harping (he did this about every third day) on the wretched lack of definition concerning the limits of vice and virtue, and the way in which half the vices wanted regulating rather than prohibiting. He dwelt also on the advantages of complete unreserve, and hinted that there were mysteries into which Ernest had not yet been initiated, but which would enlighten him when he got to know them, as he would be allowed to do when his friends saw that he was strong enough.

Pryer had often been like this before, but never so nearly, as it seemed to Ernest, coming to a point – though what the point was he could not fully understand. His inquietude was communicating itself to Ernest, who would probably ere long have come to know as much as Pryer could tell him, but the conversation was abruptly interrupted by the appearance of a visitor. We shall never know how it would have ended, for this was the very last time that Ernest ever saw Pryer. Perhaps Pryer was going to break to him some bad news about his speculations.

Chapter Sixty

Ernest now went home and occupied himself till luncheon with studying Dean Alford's notes upon the various Evangelistic records of the Resurrection, doing as Mr Shaw had told him, and trying to find out not that they were all accurate, but whether they were all accurate or no. He did not care which result he should arrive at, but he was resolved that he would reach one or the other. When he had finished Dean Alford's notes he found them come to this, namely, that no one yet had succeeded in bringing the four accounts into tolerable harmony with each other, and that the Dean, seeing no chance of succeeding better than his predecessors had done, recommended that the whole story should be taken on trust – and this Ernest was not prepared to do.

He got his luncheon, went out for a long walk, and returned to dinner at half-past six. While Mrs Jupp was getting him his dinner – a steak and a pint of stout – she told him that Miss Snow would be very happy to see him in about an hour's time. This disconcerted him, for his mind was too unsettled for him to wish to convert anyone just then. He reflected a little, and found that, in spite of the sudden shock to his opinions, he was being irresistibly drawn to pay the visit as though nothing had happened. It would not look well for him not to go, for he was known to be in the house. He ought not to be in too great a hurry to change his opinions on such a matter as the evidence for Christ's Resurrection all of a sudden – besides he need not talk to Miss Snow about this subject today – there were other things he might talk about. What other things? Ernest felt his heart beat fast and fiercely, and an inward monitor warned him that he was thinking of anything rather than of Miss Snow's soul.

What should he do? Fly, fly, fly – it was the only safety. But would Christ have fled? Even though Christ had not died and risen from the dead there could be no question that He was the model whose example we were bound to follow. Christ would not have fled from Miss Snow; he was sure of that, for He went about more especially with prostitutes and disreputable people. Now, as then, it was the business of the true Christian to call not the righteous but sinners to repentance. It would be inconvenient to him to change his lodgings, and he could not ask Mrs Jupp to turn Miss Snow and Miss Maitland out of the house. Where was he to draw the line? Who would be just good enough to live in the same house with him, and who not just good enough?

Besides, where were these poor girls to go? Was he to drive them from house to house till they had no place to lie in? It was absurd; his duty was clear: he would go and see Miss Snow at once; and try if he could not induce her to change her present mode of life; if he found temptation too strong for him he would fly then – so he went upstairs with his Bible under his arm, and a consuming fire in his heart.

He found Miss Snow looking very pretty in a neatly, not to say demurely, furnished room. I think she had bought an illuminated text or too, and pinned it up over her fireplace that morning. Ernest was very much pleased with her, and mechanically placed his Bible upon the table. He had just opened a timid conversation and was deep in blushes, when a hurried step came bounding up the stairs as though of one over whom the force of gravity had little power, and a man burst into the room saying. 'I'm come before my time.' It was Towneley.

His face dropped as he caught sight of Ernest. 'What *you* here, Pontifex! Well, upon my word!'

I cannot describe the hurried explanations that passed quickly between the three – enough that in less than a minute Ernest, blushing more scarlet than ever, slunk off, Bible and all, deeply humiliated as he contrasted himself and Towneley. Before he had reached the bottom of the staircase leading to his own room he heard Towneley's hearty laugh through Miss Snow's door, and cursed the hour that he was born.

Then it flashed upon him that if he could not see Miss Snow he could at any rate see Miss Maitland. He knew well enough what he wanted now, and as for the Bible, he pushed it from him to the other end of his table. It fell over on the floor, and he kicked it into a corner, it was the Bible given him at his christening by his affectionate aunt, Elizabeth Allaby. True, he knew very little of Miss Maitland, but ignorant young fools in Ernest's state do not reflect or reason closely. Mrs Baxter had said that Miss Maitland and Miss Snow were birds of a feather, and Mrs Baxter probably knew better than that old liar, Mrs Jupp. Shakespeare says:

> O opportunity, thy guilt is great
> 'Tis thou that execut'st the traitor treason:
> Thou sett'st the wolf where he the lamb may get;
> Whoever plots the sin, thou 'point'st the season;
> 'Tis thou that spurn'st at right, at law, at reason;
> > And in thy shady cell, where none may spy him,
> > Sits Sin, to seize the souls that wander by him.

If the guilt of opportunity is great, how much greater is the guilt of that which is believed to be opportunity, but in reality is no opportunity at all. If the better part of valour is discretion, how much more is not discretion the better part of vice?

About ten minutes after we last saw Ernest, a scared, insulted girl, flushed and trembling, was seen hurrying from Mrs Jupp's house as fast as her agitated state would let her, and in another ten minutes two policemen were seen also coming out of Mrs Jupp's, between whom there shambled rather than walked our unhappy friend Ernest, with staring eyes, ghastly pale, and with despair branded upon every line of his face.

Chapter Sixty-One

Pryer had done well to warn Ernest against promiscuous house to house visitation. He had not gone outside Mrs Jupp's street door, and yet what had been the result? Mr Holt had put him in bodily fear; Mr and Mrs Baxter had nearly made a Methodist of him; Mr Shaw had undermined his faith in the Resurrection; Miss Snow's charms had ruined – or would have done so but for an accident – his moral character. As for Miss Maitland, he had done his best to ruin hers, and had damaged himself gravely and irretrievably in consequence. The only lodger who had done him no harm was the bellows' mender, whom he had not visited.

Other young clergymen, much greater fools in many respects than he, would not have got into these scrapes. He seemed to have developed an aptitude for mischief almost from the day of his having been ordained. He could hardly preach without making some horrid *faux pas*. He preached one Sunday morning when the Bishop was at his Rector's church, and made his sermon turn upon the question what kind of little cake it was that the widow of Zarephath had intended making when Elijah found her gathering a few sticks. He demonstrated that it was a seed cake. The sermon was really very amusing, and more than once he saw a smile pass over the sea of faces underneath him. The Bishop was very angry, and gave my hero a severe reprimand in the vestry after service was over; the only excuse he could make was that he was preaching *ex tempore*, had not thought of this particular point till he was actually in the pulpit, and had then been carried away by it.

Another time he preached upon the barren fig-tree, and described the hopes of the owner as he watched the delicate blossom unfold, and give promise of such beautiful fruit in autumn. Next day he received a letter from a botanical member of his congregation who explained to him that this could hardly have been, inasmuch as the fig produces its fruit first and blossoms inside the fruit, or so nearly so that no flower is perceptible to an ordinary observer. This last, however, was an accident which might have happened to anyone but a scientist or an inspired writer.

The only excuse I can make for him is that he was very young – not yet four and twenty – and that in mind as in body, like most of those who in the end come to think for themselves, he was a slow grower. By far the greater part, moreover, of his education had been an attempt, not so much to keep him in blinkers as to gouge his eyes out altogether.

But to return to my story. It transpired afterwards that Miss Maitland had had no intention of giving Ernest in charge when she ran out of Mrs Jupp's house. She was running away because she was frightened, but almost the first person whom she ran against had happened to be a policeman of a serious turn of mind, who wished to gain a reputation for activity. He stopped her, questioned her, frightened her still more, and it was he rather than Miss Maitland, who insisted on giving my hero in charge to himself and another constable.

Towneley was still in Mrs Jupp's house when the policeman came. He had heard a disturbance, and going down to Ernest's room while Miss Maitland was out of doors, had found him lying, as it were, stunned at the foot of the moral precipice over which he had that moment fallen. He saw the whole thing at a glance, but before he could take action, the policeman came in and action became impossible.

He asked Ernest who were his friends in London. Ernest at first wanted not to say, but Towneley soon gave him to understand that he must do as he was bid, and selected myself from the few whom he had named. 'Writes for the stage, does he?' said Towneley. 'Does he write comedy?' Ernest thought Towneley meant that I ought to write tragedy, and said he was afraid I wrote burlesque. 'Oh, come, come,' said Towneley, 'that will do famously. I will go and see him at once.' But on second thoughts he determined to stay with Ernest and go with him to the police court. So he sent Mrs Jupp for me. Mrs Jupp hurried so fast to fetch me, that in spite of the weather's being still cold she was 'giving out,' as she expressed it, in streams. The poor old wretch would have taken a cab, but she had no money and did not like to ask Towneley to give her some. I saw that something very serious had happened, but was not prepared for anything so deplorable as what Mrs Jupp actually told me. As for Mrs Jupp, she said her heart had been jumping out of its socket and back again ever since.

I got her into a cab with me, and we went off to the police station. She talked without ceasing.

'And if the neighbours do say cruel things about me, I'm sure it ain't no thanks to *him* if they're true. Mr Pontifex never took a bit o' notice of me no more than I had been his sister. Oh, it's enough to make anyone's back bone curdle. Then I thought perhaps my Rose might get on better with him, so I set her to dust him and clean him as though I were busy, and gave her such a beautiful clean new pinny, but he never took no notice of her no more than he did of me, and she didn't want no compliment neither, she wouldn't have taken not a shilling from him, though he had offered it, but he didn't seem to know anything at all. I can't make out what the young men are a-coming to; I wish the horn may blow for me and the worms take me this very night, if it's not enough to make a woman stand before God and strike the one half on 'em silly to see the way they goes on, and many an honest girl has to go home night after night without so much as a fourpenny bit and paying three and sixpence a week rent, and not a shelf nor cupboard in the place and a dead wall in front of the window.

'It's not Mr Pontifex,' she continued, 'that's so bad, he's good at heart. He never says nothing unkind. And then there's his dear eyes – but when I speak about that to my Rose she calls me an old fool and says I ought to be pole-axed. It's that Pryer as I can't abide. Oh he! He likes to wound a woman's feelings he do, and to chuck anything in her face, he do – he likes to wind a woman up and to wound her down.' (Mrs Jupp pronounced 'wound' as though it rhymed to 'sound.') 'It's a gentleman's place to soothe a woman, but he, he'd like to tear her hair out by handfuls. Why, he told me to my face that I was a-getting old; old indeed! there's not a woman in London knows my age except Mrs Davis down in the Old Kent Road, and beyond a haricot vein in one of my legs I'm as young as ever I was. Old indeed! There's many a good tune played on an old fiddle. I hate his nasty insinuendos.'

Even if I had wanted to stop her, I could not have done so. She said a great deal more than I have given above. I have left out much because I could not remember it, but still more because it was really impossible for me to print it.

When we got to the police station I found Towneley and Ernest already there. The charge was one of assault, but not aggravated by serious violence. Even so, however, it was lamentable enough, and we both saw that our young friend would have to pay dearly for his inexperience. We tried to bail him out for the night, but the Inspector would not accept bail, so we were forced to leave him.

Towneley then went back to Mrs Jupp's to see if he could find Miss Maitland and arrange matters with her. She was not there, but he traced her to the house of her father, who lived at Camberwell. The father was furious and would not hear of any intercession on Towneley's part. He was a Dissenter, and glad to make the most of any scandal against a clergyman; Towneley, therefore, was obliged to return unsuccessful.

Next morning, Towneley – who regarded Ernest as a drowning man, who must be picked out of the water somehow or other if possible, irrespective of the way in which he got into it – called on me, and we put the matter into the hands of one of the best known attorneys of the day. I was greatly pleased with Towneley, and thought it due to him to tell him what I had told no one else. I mean that Ernest would come into his aunt's money in a few years' time, and would therefore then be rich.

Towneley was doing all he could before this, but I knew that the knowledge I had imparted to him would make him feel as though Ernest was more one of his own class, and had therefore a greater claim upon his good offices. As for Ernest himself, his gratitude was greater than could be expressed in words. I have heard him say that he can call to mind many moments, each one of which might well pass for the happiest in his life, but that this night stands clearly out as the most painful that he ever passed, yet so kind and considerate was Towneley that it was quite bearable.

But with all the best wishes in the world neither Towneley nor I could do much to help beyond giving our moral support. Our attorney told us that the magistrate before whom Ernest would appear was very severe on cases of this description, and that the fact of his being a clergyman would tell against him. 'Ask for no remand,' he said, 'and make no defence. We will call Mr Pontifex's rector and you two gentlemen as witness for previous good character. These will be enough. Let us then make a profound apology and beg the magistrate to deal with the case summarily instead of sending it for trial. If you can get this, believe me, your young friend will be better out of it than he has any right to expect.'

Chapter Sixty-Two

This advice, besides being obviously sensible, would end in saving Ernest both time and suspense of mind, so we had no hesitation in adopting it. The case was called on about eleven o'clock, but we got it adjourned till three, so as to give time for Ernest to set his affairs as straight as he could, and to execute a power of attorney enabling me to act for him as I should think fit while he was in prison.

Then all came out about Pryer and the College of Spiritual Pathology. Ernest had even greater difficulty in making a clean breast of this than he had had in telling us about Miss Maitland, but he told us all, and the upshot was that he had actually handed over to Pryer every halfpenny that he had then possessed with no other security than Pryer's I.O.U.'s for the amount. Ernest, though still declining to believe that Pryer could be guilty of dishonourable conduct, was becoming alive to the folly of what he had been doing; he still made sure, however, of recovering, at any rate, the greater part of his property as soon as Pryer should have had time to sell. Towneley and I were of a different opinion, but we did not say what we thought.

It was dreary work waiting all the morning amid such unfamiliar and depressing surroundings. I thought how the Psalmist had exclaimed with quiet irony, 'One day in thy courts is better than a thousand,' and I thought that I could utter a very similar sentiment in respect of the Courts in which Towneley and I were compelled to loiter. At last, about three o'clock the case was called on, and we went round to the part of the court which is reserved for the general public, while Ernest was taken into the prisoner's dock. As soon as he collected himself sufficiently he recognised the magistrate as the old gentleman who had spoken to him in the train on the day he was leaving school, and saw, or thought he saw, to his great grief, that he too was recognised.

Mr Ottery, for this was our attorney's name, took the line he had proposed. He called no other witnesses than the rector, Towneley and myself, and threw himself on the mercy of the magistrate. When he had concluded, the magistrate spoke as follows: 'Ernest Pontifex, yours is one of the most painful cases that I have ever had to deal with. You have been singularly favoured in your parentage and education. You have had before you the example of blameless parents, who doubtless instilled into you from childhood the enormity of the offence which by your own confession you have committed. You were sent to one of the best public schools in England. It is not likely that in the healthy atmosphere of such a school as Roughborough you can have come across contaminating influences; you were probably, I may say certainly, impressed at school with the heinousness of any attempt to depart from the strictest chastity until such time as you had entered into a state of matrimony. At Cambridge you were shielded from impurity by every obstacle which virtuous and vigilant authorities could devise, and even had the obstacles been fewer, your parents probably took care that your means should not admit of your throwing money away upon abandoned characters. At night proctors patrolled the street and dogged your steps if you tried to go into any haunt where the presence of vice was suspected. By day the females who were admitted within the college walls were selected mainly on the score of age and ugliness. It is hard to see what more can be done for any young man than this. For the last four or five months you have been a clergyman, and if a single impure thought had still remained within your mind, ordination should have removed it: nevertheless, not only does it appear that your mind is as impure as though none of the influences to which I have referred had been brought to bear upon it, but it seems as though their only result had been this – that you have not even the common sense to be able to distinguish between a respectable girl and a prostitute.

'If I were to take a strict view of my duty I should commit you for trial, but in consideration of this being your first offence, I shall deal leniently with you and sentence you to imprisonment with hard labour for six calendar months.'

Towneley and I both thought there was a touch of irony in the magistrate's speech, and that he could have given a lighter sentence if he would, but that was neither here nor there. We obtained leave to see Ernest for a few minutes before he was removed to Coldbath Fields, where he was to serve his term, and found him so thankful to have been summarily dealt with that he hardly seemed to care about the miserable plight in which he was to pass the next six months. When he came out, he said, he would take what remained of his money, go off to America or Australia and never be heard of more.

We left him full of this resolve, I to write to Theobald, and also to instruct my solicitor to get Ernest's money out of Pryer's hands, and Towneley to see the reporters and keep the case out of the newspapers. He was successful as regards all the higher-class papers. There was only one journal, and that of the lowest class, which was incorruptible.

Chapter Sixty-Three

I saw my solicitor at once, but when I tried to write to Theobald, I found it better to say I would run down and see him. I therefore proposed this, asking him to meet me at the station, and hinting that I must bring bad news about his son. I knew he would not get my letter more than a couple of hours before I should see him, and thought the short interval of suspense might break the shock of what I had to say.

Never do I remember to have halted more between two opinions than on my journey to Battersby upon this unhappy errand. When I thought of the little sallow-faced lad whom I had remembered years before, of the long and savage cruelty with which he had been treated in childhood – cruelty none the less real for having been due to ignorance and stupidity rather than to deliberate malice; of the atmosphere of lying and self-laudatory hallucination in which he had been brought up; of the readiness the boy had shown to love anything that would be good enough to let him, and of how affection for his parents, unless I am much mistaken, had only died in him because it had been killed anew, again and again and again, each time that it had tried to spring. When I thought of all this I felt as though, if the matter had rested with me, I would have sentenced Theobald and Christina to mental suffering even more severe than that which was about to fall upon them. But on the other hand, when I thought of Theobald's own childhood, of that dreadful old George Pontifex his father, of John and Mrs John, and of his two sisters, when again I thought of Christina's long years of hope deferred that maketh the heart sick, before she was married, of the life she must have led at Crampsford, and of the surroundings in the midst of which she and her husband both lived at Battersby, I felt as though the wonder was that misfortunes so persistent had not been followed by even graver retribution.

Poor people! They had tried to keep their ignorance of the world from themselves by calling it the pursuit of heavenly things, and then shutting their eyes to anything that might give them trouble. A son having been born to them they had shut his eyes also as far as was practicable. Who could blame them? They had chapter and verse for everything they had either done or left undone; there is no better thumbed precedent than that for being a clergyman and a clergyman's wife. In what respect had they differed from their neighbours? How did their household differ from that of any other clergyman of the better sort from one end of England to the other? Why then should it have been upon them, of all people in the world, that this tower of Siloam had fallen?

Surely it was the tower of Siloam that was naught rather than those who stood under it; it was the system rather than the people that was at fault. If Theobald and his wife had but known more of the things that are therein, they would have done little harm to anyone. Selfish they would have always been, but not more so than may very well be pardoned, and not more than other people would be. As it was, the case was hopeless; it would be no use their even entering into their mothers' wombs and being born again. They must not only be born again but they must be born again each one of them of a new father and of a new mother and of a different line of ancestry for many generations before their minds could become supple enough to learn anew. The only thing to do with them was to humour them and make the best of them till they died – and be thankful when they did so.

Theobald got my letter as I had expected, and met me at the station nearest to Battersby. As I walked back with him towards his own house I broke the news to him as gently as I could.

I pretended that the whole thing was in great measure a mistake, and that though Ernest no doubt had had intentions which he ought to have resisted, he had not meant going anything like the length which Miss Maitland supposed. I said we had felt how much appearances were against him, and had not dared to set up this defence before the magistrate, though we had no doubt about its being the true one.

Theobald acted with a readier and acuter moral sense than I had given him credit for.

'I will have nothing more to do with him,' he exclaimed promptly, 'I will never see his face again; do not let him write either to me or his mother; we know of no such person. Tell him you have seen me, and that from this day forward I shall put him out of my mind as though he had never been born. I have been a good father to him, and his mother idolised him; selfishness and ingratitude have been the only return we have ever had from him; my hope henceforth must be in my remaining children.'

I told him how Ernest's fellow curate had got hold of his money, and hinted that he might very likely be penniless, or nearly so, on leaving prison. Theobald did not seem displeased at this, but added soon afterwards: 'If this proved to be the case, tell him from me that I will give him a hundred pounds if he will tell me through you when he will have it paid, but tell him not to write and thank me, and say that if he attempts to open up direct communication either with his mother or myself, he shall not have a penny of the money.'

Knowing what I knew, and having determined on violating Miss Pontifex's instructions should the occasion arise, I did not think Ernest would be any the worse for a complete estrangement from his family, so I acquiesced more readily in what Theobald had proposed than that gentleman may have expected.

Thinking it better that I should not see Christina, I left Theobald near Battersby and walked back to the station. On my way I was pleased to reflect that Ernest's father was less of a fool than I had taken him to be, and had the greater hopes, therefore, that his son's blunders might be due to postnatal, rather than congenital misfortunes. Accidents which happen to a man before he is born, in the persons of his ancestors, will, if he remembers them at all, leave an indelible impression on him; they will have moulded his character so that, do what he will, it is hardly possible for him to escape their consequences. If a man is to enter into the Kingdom of Heaven, he must do so, not only as a little child, but as a little embryo, or rather a little zoosperm – and not only this, but as one that has come of zoosperms which have entered into the Kingdom of Heaven before him for many generations. Accidents which occur for the first time, and belong to the period since a man's last birth, are not, as a general rule, so permanent in their effects, though of course they may sometimes be so. At any rate, I was not displeased at the view which Ernest's father took of the situation.

Chapter Sixty-Four

After Ernest had been sentenced, he was taken back to the cells to wait for the van which should take him to Coldbath Fields, where he was to serve his term.

He was still too stunned and dazed by the suddenness with which events had happened during the last twenty-four hours to be able to realise his position. A great chasm had opened between his past and future; nevertheless, he breathed, his pulse beat, he could think and speak. It seemed to him that he ought to be prostrated by the blow that had fallen on him, but he was not prostrated; he had suffered from many small laches far more acutely. It was not until he thought of the pain his disgrace would inflict on his father and mother that he felt how readily he would have given up all he had, rather than have fallen into his present plight. It would break his mother's heart. It must, he knew it would – and it was he who had done this.

He had had a headache coming on all the forenoon, but a thought of his father and mother, his pulse quickened, and the pain in his head suddenly became intense. He could hardly walk to the van, and he found its motion insupportable. On reaching the prison he was too ill to walk without assistance across the hall to the corridor or gallery where prisoners were marshalled on their arrival. The prison warder, seeing at once that he was a clergyman, did not suppose he was shamming, as he might have done in the case of an old gaol-bird; he therefore sent for the doctor. When this gentleman arrived, Ernest was declared to be suffering from an incipient attack of brain fever, and was taken away to the infirmary. Here he hovered for the next two months between life and death, never in full possession of his reason and often delirious, but at last, contrary to the expectation of both doctor and nurse, he began slowly to recover.

It is said that those who have been nearly drowned find the return to consciousness much more painful than the loss of it had been, and so it was with my hero. As he lay helpless and feeble, it seemed to him a refinement of cruelty that he had not died once for all during his delirium. He thought he should still most likely recover only to sink a little later on from shame and sorrow; nevertheless from day to day he mended, though so slowly that he could hardly realise it to himself. One afternoon, however, about three weeks after he had regained consciousness, the nurse who tended him, and who had been very kind to him, made some little rallying sally which amused him; he laughed, and as he did so, she clapped her hands and told him he would be a man again. The spark of hope was kindled, and again he wished to live. Almost from that moment his thoughts began to turn less to the horrors of the past, and more to the best way of meeting the future.

His worst pain was on behalf of his father and mother, and how he should again face them. It still seemed to him that the best thing both for him and them would be that he should sever himself from them completely, take whatever money he could recover from Pryer, and go to some place in the uttermost parts of the earth, where he should never meet anyone who had known him at school or college, and start afresh. Or perhaps he might go to the gold fields in California or Australia, of which such wonderful accounts were then heard; there he might even make his fortune, and return as an old man many years hence, unknown to everyone, and if so, he would live at Cambridge. As he built these castles in the air, the spark of life became a flame, and he longed for health, and for the freedom which, now that so much of his sentence had expired, was not after all very far distant.

Then things began to shape themselves more definitely. Whatever happened he would be a clergyman no longer. It would have been practically impossible for him to have found another curacy, even if he had been so minded, but he was not so minded. He hated the life he had been leading ever since he had begun to read for orders; he could not argue about it, but simply he loathed it and would have no more of it. As he dwelt on the prospect of becoming a layman again, however disgraced, he rejoiced at what had befallen him, and found a blessing in this very imprisonment which had at first seemed such an unspeakable misfortune.

Perhaps the shock of so great a change in his surroundings had accelerated changes in his opinions, just as the cocoons of silkworms, when sent in baskets by rail, hatch before their time through the novelty of heat and jolting. But however this may be, his belief in the stories concerning the Death, Resurrection and Ascension of Jesus Christ, and hence his faith in all other Christian miracles, had dropped off him once and for ever. The investigation he had made in consequence of Mr Shaw's rebuke, hurried though it was, had left a deep impression upon him, and now he was well enough to read he made the New Testament his chief study, going through it in the spirit which Mr Shaw had desired of him, that is to say as one who wished neither to believe nor disbelieve, but cared only about finding out whether he ought to believe or no. The more he read in this spirit the more the balance seemed to lie in favour of unbelief, till, in the end, all further doubt became impossible, and he saw plainly enough that, whatever else might be true, the story that Christ had died, come to life again, and been carried from earth through clouds into the heavens could not now be accepted by unbiassed people. It was well he had found it out so soon. In one way or another it was sure to meet him sooner or later. He would probably have seen it years ago if he had not been hoodwinked by people who were paid for hoodwinking him. What should he have done, he asked himself, if he had not made his present discovery till years later, when he was more deeply committed to the life of a clergyman?

Should he have had the courage to face it, or would he not more probably have evolved some excellent reason for continuing to think as he had thought hitherto? Should he have had the courage to break away even from his present curacy?

He thought not, and knew not whether to be more thankful for having been shown his error or for having been caught up and twisted round so that he could hardly err farther, almost at the very moment of his having discovered it. The price he had had to pay for this boon was light as compared with the boon itself. What is too heavy a price to pay for having duty made at once clear and easy of fulfilment instead of very difficult? He was sorry for his father and mother, and he was sorry for Miss Maitland, but he was no longer sorry for himself.

It puzzled him, however, that he should not have known how much he had hated being a clergyman till now. He knew that he did not particularly like it, but if anyone had asked him whether he actually hated it, he would have answered no. I suppose people almost always want something external to themselves, to reveal to them their own likes and dislikes. Our most assured likings have for the most part been arrived at neither by introspection nor by any process of conscious reasoning, but by the bounding forth of the heart to welcome the gospel proclaimed to it by another. We hear some say that such and such a thing is thus or thus, and in a moment the train that has been laid within us, but whose presence we knew not, flashes into consciousness and perception.

Only a year ago he had bounded forth to welcome Mr Hawke's sermon; since then he had bounded after a College of Spiritual Pathology; now he was in full cry after rationalism pure and simple; how could he be sure that his present state of mind would be more lasting than his previous ones? He could not be certain, but he felt as though he were now on firmer ground than he had ever been before, and no matter how fleeting his present opinions might prove to be, he could not but act according to them till he saw reason to change them. How impossible, he reflected, it would have been for him to do this, if he had remained surrounded by people like his father and mother, or Pryer and Pryer's friends, and his rector. He had been observing, reflecting, and assimilating all these months with no more consciousness of mental growth than a schoolboy has of growth of body, but should he have been able to admit his growth to himself, and to act up to his increased strength if he had remained in constant close connection with people who assured him solemnly that he was under a hallucination? The combination against him was greater than his unaided strength could have broken through, and he felt doubtful how far any shock less severe than the one from which he was suffering would have sufficed to free him.

Chapter Sixty-Five

As he lay on his bed day after day slowly recovering, he woke up to the fact which most men arrive at sooner or later, I mean that very few care two straws about truth, or have any confidence that it is righter and better to believe what is true than what is untrue, even though belief in the untruth may seem at first sight most expedient. Yet it is only these few who can be said to believe anything at all; the rest are simply unbelievers in disguise. Perhaps, after all, these last are right. They have numbers and prosperity on their side. They have all which the rationalist appeals to as his tests of right and wrong. Right, according to him, is what seems right to the majority of sensible, well-to-do people; we know of no safer criterion than this, but what does the derision thus arrived at involve? Simply this, that a conspiracy of silence about things whose truth would be immediately apparent to disinterested inquirers is not only tolerable but righteous on the part of those who profess to be and take money for being *par excellence* guardians and teachers of truth.

Ernest saw no logical escape from this conclusion. He saw that belief on the part of the early Christians in the miraculous nature of Christ's Resurrection was explicable, without any supposition of miracle. The explanation lay under the eyes of anyone who chose to take a moderate degree of trouble; it had been put before the world again and again, and there had been no serious attempt to refute it. How was it that Dean Alford, for example, who had made the New Testament his speciality, could not or would not see what was so obvious to Ernest himself? Could it be for any other reason than that he did not want to see it, and if so was he not a traitor to the cause of truth? Yes, but was he not also a respectable and successful man, and were not the vast majority of respectable and successful men, such, for example, as all the bishops and archbishops, doing exactly as Dean Alford did, and did not this make their action right, no matter though it had been cannibalism or infanticide, or even habitual untruthfulness of mind?

Monstrous, odious falsehood! Ernest's feeble pulse quickened and his pale face flushed as this hateful view of life presented itself to him in all its logical consistency. It was not the fact of most men being liars that shocked him – that was all right enough; but even the momentary doubt whether the few who were not liars ought not to become liars too. There was no hope left if this were so; if this were so, let him die, the sooner the better. 'Lord,' he exclaimed inwardly, 'I don't believe one word of it. Strengthen Thou and confirm my disbelief.' It seemed to him that he could never henceforth see a bishop going to consecration without saying to himself: 'There, but for the grace of God, went Ernest Pontifex.' It was no doing of his. He could not boast; if he had lived in the time of Christ he might himself have been an early Christian, or even an Apostle for aught he knew. On the whole he felt that he had much to be thankful for.

The conclusion, then, that it might be better to believe error than truth, should be ordered out of court at once, no matter by how clear a logic it had been arrived at; but what was the alternative? It was this, that our criterion of truth – *i.e.* that truth is what commends itself to the great majority of sensible successful people – is not infallible. The rule is sound, and covers by far the greater number of eases, but it has its exceptions.

He asked himself, what were they? Ah, that was a difficult matter; there were so many, and the rules which governed them were sometimes so subtle, that mistakes always had and always would be made; it was just this that made it impossible to reduce life to an exact science. There was a rough and ready rule-of-thumb test of truth, and a number of rules as regards exceptions which could be mastered without much trouble, yet there was a residue of cases in which decision was difficult – so difficult that a man had better follow his instinct than attempt to decide them by any process of reasoning.

Instinct then is the ultimate court of appeal. And what is instinct? It is a mode of faith in the evidence of things not actually seen. And so my hero returned almost to the point from which he had started originally, namely that the just shall live by faith.

And this is what the just – that is to say reasonable people – do as regards those daily affairs of life which most concern them. They settle smaller matters by the exercise of their own deliberation. More important ones, such as the cure of their own bodies and the bodies of those whom they love, the investment of their money, the extrication of their affairs from any serious mess – these things they generally entrust to others of whose capacity they know little save from general report; they act therefore on the strength of faith, not of knowledge. So the English nation entrusts the welfare of its fleet and naval defences to a First Lord of the Admiralty, who, not being a sailor can know nothing about these matters except by acts of faith. There can be no doubt about faith and not reason being the *ultima ratio*.

Even Euclid, who has laid himself as little open to the charge of credulity as any writer who ever lived, cannot get beyond this. He has no demonstrable first premise. He requires postulates and axioms which transcend demonstration, and without which he can do nothing. His superstructure indeed is demonstration, but his ground is faith. Nor again can he get further than telling a man he is a fool if he persists in differing from him. He says 'which is absurd,' and declines to discuss the matter further. Faith and authority, therefore, prove to be as necessary for him as for anyone else. 'By faith in what, then,' asked Ernest of himself, 'shall a just man endeavour to live at this present time?' He answered to himself, 'At any rate not by faith in the supernatural element of the Christian religion.'

And how should he best persuade his fellow-countrymen to leave off believing in this supernatural element? Looking at the matter from a practical point of view, he thought the Archbishop of Canterbury afforded the most promising key to the situation. It lay between him and the Pope. The Pope was perhaps best in theory, but in practice the Archbishop of Canterbury would do sufficiently well. If he could only manage to sprinkle a pinch of salt, as it were, on the Archbishop's tail, he might convert the whole Church of England to free thought by a *coup de main*. There must be an amount of cogency which even an Archbishop – an Archbishop whose perceptions had never been quickened by imprisonment for assault – would not be able to withstand. When brought face to face with the facts, as he, Ernest, could arrange them, his Grace would have no resource but to admit them; being an honourable man he would at once resign his Archbishopric, and Christianity would become extinct in England within a few months' time. This, at any rate, was how things ought to be. But all the time Ernest had no confidence in the Archbishop's not hopping off just as the pinch was about to fall on him, and this seemed so unfair that his blood boiled at the thought of it. If this was to be so, he must try if he could not fix him by the judicious use of bird-lime or a snare, or throw the salt on his tail from an ambuscade.

To do him justice it was not himself that he greatly cared about. He knew he had been humbugged, and he knew also that the greater part of the ills which had afflicted him were due, indirectly, in chief measure to the influence of Christian teaching; still, if the mischief had ended with himself, he should have thought little about it, but there was his sister, and his brother Joey, and the hundreds and thousands of young people throughout England whose lives were being blighted through the lies told them by people whose business it was to know better, but who scamped their work and shirked difficulties instead of facing them. It was this which made him think it worth while to be angry, and to consider whether he could not at least do something towards saving others from such years of waste and misery as he had had to pass himself. If there was no truth in the miraculous accounts of Christ's Death and Resurrection, the whole of the religion founded upon the historic truth of those events tumbled to the ground. 'Why,' he exclaimed, with all the arrogance of youth, 'they put a gipsy or fortune-teller into prison for getting money out of silly people who think they have supernatural power; why should they not put a clergyman in prison for pretending that he can absolve sins, or turn bread and wine into the flesh and blood of One who died two thousand years ago? What,' he asked himself, 'could be more pure 'hanky-panky' than that a bishop should lay his hands upon a young man and pretend to convey to him the spiritual power to work this miracle? It was all very well to talk about toleration; toleration, like everything else, had its limits; besides, if it was to include the bishop let it include the fortune-teller too.' He would explain all this to the Archbishop of Canterbury by and by, but as he could not get hold of him just now, it occurred to him that he might experimentalise advantageously upon the viler soul of the prison chaplain. It was only those who took the first and most obvious step in their power who ever did great things in the end, so one day, when Mr Hughes – for this was the chaplain's name – was talking to him, Ernest introduced the question of Christian evidences, and tried to raise a discussion upon them. Mr Hughes had been very kind to him, but he was more than twice my hero's age, and had long taken the measure of such objections as Ernest tried to put before him. I do not suppose he believed in the actual objective truth of the stories about Christ's Resurrection and Ascension any more than Ernest did, but he knew that this was a small matter, and that the real issue lay much deeper than this.

Mr Hughes was a man who had been in authority for many

years, and he brushed Ernest on one side as if he had been a fly. He did it so well that my hero never ventured to tackle him again, and confined his conversation with him for the future to such matters as what he had better do when he got out of prison; and here Mr Hughes was ever ready to listen to him with sympathy and kindness.

Chapter Sixty-Six

Ernest was now so far convalescent as to be able to sit up for the greater part of the day. He had been three months in prison, and, though not strong enough to leave the infirmary, was beyond all fear of a relapse. He was talking one day with Mr Hughes about his future, and again expressed his intention of emigrating to Australia or New Zealand with the money he should recover from Pryer. Whenever he spoke of this he noticed that Mr Hughes looked grave and was silent: he had thought that perhaps the chaplain wanted him to return to his profession, and disapproved of his evident anxiety to turn to something else; now, however, he asked Mr Hughes point blank why it was that he disapproved of his idea of emigrating.

Mr Hughes endeavoured to evade him, but Ernest was not to be put off. There was something in the chaplain's manner which suggested that he knew more than Ernest did, but did not like to say it. This alarmed him so much that he begged him not to keep him in suspense; after a little hesitation Mr Hughes, thinking him now strong enough to stand it, broke the news as gently as he could that the whole of Ernest's money had disappeared.

The day after my return from Battersby I called on my solicitor, and was told that he had written to Pryer, requiring him to refund the monies for which he had given his I.O.U.'s. Pryer replied that he had given orders to his broker to close his operations, which unfortunately had resulted so far in heavy loss, and that the balance should be paid to my solicitor on the following settling day, then about a week distant. When the time came, we heard nothing from Pryer, and going to his lodgings found that he had left with his few effects on the very day after he had heard from us, and had not been seen since.

I had heard from Ernest the name of the broker who had been employed, and went at once to see him. He told me Pryer had closed all his accounts for cash on the day that Ernest had been sentenced, and had received £2,315, which was all that remained of Ernest's original £5,000. With this he had decamped, nor had we enough clue as to his whereabouts to be able to take any steps to recover the money. There was, in fact, nothing to be done but to consider the whole as lost. I may say here that neither I nor Ernest ever heard of Pryer again, nor have any idea what became of him.

This placed me in a difficult position. I knew, of course, that in a few years Ernest would have many times over as much money as he had lost, but I knew also that he did not know this, and feared that the supposed loss of all he had in the world might be more than he could stand when coupled with his other misfortunes.

The prison authorities had found Theobald's address from a letter in Ernest's pocket, and had communicated with him more than once concerning his son's illness, but Theobald had not written to me, and I supposed my godson to be in good health. He would be just twenty-four years old when he left prison, and if I followed out his aunt's instructions, would have to battle with fortune for another four years as well as he could. The question before me was whether it was right to let him run so much risk, or whether I should not to some extent transgress my instructions – which there was nothing to prevent my doing if I thought Miss Pontifex would have wished it – and let him have the same sum that he would have recovered from Pryer.

If my godson had been an older man, and more fixed in any definite groove, this is what I should have done, but he was still very young, and more than commonly unformed for his age. If, again, I had known of his illness I should not have dared to lay any heavier burden on his back than he had to bear already; but not being uneasy about his health, I thought a few years of rough-ing it and of experience concerning the importance of not playing tricks with money would do him no harm. So I decided to keep a sharp eye upon him as soon as he came out of prison, and to let him splash about in deep water as best he could till I saw whether he was able to swim, or was about to sink. In the first case I would let him go on swimming till he was nearly eight-and-twenty, when I would prepare him gradually for the good fortune that awaited him; in the second I would hurry up to the rescue. So I wrote to say that Pryer had absconded, and that he could have £100 from his father when he came out of prison. I then waited to see what effect these tidings would have, not expecting to receive an answer for three months, for I had been told on inquiry that no letter could be received by a prisoner till after he had been three months in gaol. I also wrote to Theobald and told him of Pryer's disappearance.

As a matter of fact, when my letter arrived the governor of the gaol read it, and in a case of such importance would have relaxed the rules if Ernest's state had allowed it; his illness prevented this, and the governor left it to the chaplain and the doctor to break the news to him when they thought him strong enough to bear it, which was now the case. In the meantime I received a formal official document saying that my letter had been received and would be communicated to the prisoner in due course; I believe it was simply through a mistake on the part of a clerk that I was not informed of Ernest's illness, but I heard nothing of it till I saw him by his own desire a few days after the chaplain had broken to him the substance of what I had written. Ernest was terribly shocked when he heard of the loss of his money, but his ignor-ance of the world prevented him from seeing the full extent of the mischief. He had never been in serious want of money yet, and did not know what it meant. In reality, money losses are the hardest to bear of any by those who are old enough to compre-hend them.

A man can stand being told that he must submit to a severe surgical operation, or that he has some disease which will shortly kill him, or that he will be a cripple or blind for the rest of his life; dreadful as such tidings must be, we do not find that they unnerve the greater number of mankind; most men, indeed, go coolly enough even to be hanged, but the strongest quail before financial ruin, and the better men they are, the more complete, as a general rule, is their prostration. Suicide is a common consequence of money losses; it is rarely sought as a means of escape from bodily suffering. If we feel that we have a competence at our backs, so that we can die warm and quietly in our beds, with no need to worry about expense, we live our lives out to the dregs, no matter how excruciating our torments. Job probably felt the loss of his flocks and herds more than that of his wife and family, for he could enjoy his flocks and herds without his family, but not his family – not for long – if he had lost all his money. Loss of money indeed is not only the worst pain in itself, but it is the parent of all others. Let a man have been brought up to a moderate competence, and have no specialty; then let his money be suddenly taken from him, and how long is his health likely to survive the change in all his little ways which loss of money will entail? How long again is the esteem and sympathy of friends likely to survive ruin? People may be very sorry for us, but their attitude towards us hitherto has been based upon the supposition that we were situated thus or thus in money matters; when this breaks down there must be a restatement of the social problem so far as we are concerned; we have been obtaining esteem under false pretences. Granted, then, that the three most serious losses which a man can suffer are those affecting money, health and reputation – loss of money is far the worst, then comes ill-health, and then loss of reputation; loss of reputation is a bad third, for, if a man keeps health and money unimpaired, it will be generally found that his loss of reputation is due to breaches of parvenu conventions only, and not to violations of those older, better established canons whose authority is unquestionable. In this case a man may grow a new reputation as easily as a lobster grows a new claw, or, if he have health and money, may thrive in great peace of mind without any reputation at all. The only chance for a man who has lost his money is that he shall still be young enough to stand uprooting and transplanting without more than temporary derangement, and this I believed my godson still to be.

By the prison rules he might receive and send a letter after he had been in gaol three months, and might also receive one visit from a friend. When he received my letter, he at once asked me to come and see him, which of course I did. I found him very much changed, and still so feeble, that the exertion of coming from the infirmary to the cell in which I was allowed to see him, and the agitation of seeing me were too much for him. At first he quite broke down, and I was so pained at the state in which I found him, that I was on the point of breaking my instructions then and there. I contented myself, however, for the time, with assuring him that I would help him as soon as he came out of prison, and that, when he had made up his mind what he would do, he was to come to me for what money might be necessary, if he could not get it from his father. To make it easier for him I told him that his aunt, on her death-bed, had desired me to do something of this sort should an emergency arise, so that he would only be taking what his aunt had left him.

'Then,' said he, 'I will not take the £100 from my father, and I will never see him or my mother again.'

I said: 'Take the £100, Ernest, and as much more as you can get, and then do not see them again if you do not like.'

This Ernest would not do. If he took money from them, he could not cut them and he wanted to cut them. I thought my godson would get on a great deal better if he would only have the firmness to do as he proposed, as regards breaking completely with his father and mother, and said so. 'Then don't you like them?' said he, with a look of surprise.

'Like them!' said I, 'I think they're horrid.'

'Oh, that's the kindest thing of all you have done for me,' he exclaimed, 'I thought all – all middle-aged people liked my father and mother.'

He had been about to call me old, but I was only fifty-seven, and was not going to have this, so I made a face when I saw him hesitating, which drove him into 'middle-aged.'

'If you like it,' said I, 'I will say all your family are horrid except yourself and your aunt Alethea. The greater part of every family is always odious; if there are one or two good ones in a very large family, it is as much as can be expected.'

'Thank you,' he replied, gratefully, 'I think I can now stand almost anything. I will come and see you as soon as I come out of gaol. Good-bye.' For the warder had told us that the time allowed for our interview was at an end.

Chapter Sixty-Seven

As soon as Ernest found that he had no money to look to upon leaving prison he saw that his dreams about emigrating and farming must come to an end, for he knew that he was incapable of working at the plough or with the axe for long together himself. And now it seemed he should have no money to pay any one else for doing so. It was this that resolved him to part once and for all with his parents. If he had been going abroad he could have kept up relations with them, for they would have been too far off to interfere with him.

He knew his father and mother would object to being cut; they would wish to appear kind and forgiving; they would also dislike having no further power to plague him; but he knew also very well that so long as he and they ran in harness together they would be always pulling one way and he another. He wanted to drop the gentleman and go down into the ranks, beginning on the lowest rung of the ladder, where no one would know of his disgrace or mind it if he did know; his father and mother on the other hand would wish him to clutch on to the fag-end of gentility at a starvation salary and with no prospect of advancement. Ernest had seen enough in Ashpit Place to know that a tailor, if he did not drink and attended to his business, could earn more money than a clerk or a curate, while much less expense by way of show was required of him. The tailor also had more liberty, and a better chance of rising. Ernest resolved at once, as he had fallen so far, to fall still lower – promptly, gracefully and with the idea of rising again, rather than cling to the skirts of a respectability which would permit him to exist on sufferance only, and make him pay an utterly extortionate price for an article which he could do better without.

He arrived at this result more quickly than he might otherwise have done through remembering something he had once heard his aunt say about 'kissing the soil.' This had impressed him and stuck by him perhaps by reason of its brevity; when later on he came to know the story of Hercules and Antæus, he found it one of the very few ancient fables which had a hold over him – his chiefest debt to classical literature. His aunt had wanted him to learn carpentering, as a means of kissing the soil should his or her Hercules ever throw him. It was too late for this now – or he thought it was – but the mode of carrying out his aunt's idea was a detail; there were a hundred ways of kissing the soil besides becoming a carpenter.

He had told me this during our interview, and I had encouraged him to the utmost in my power. He showed so much more good sense than I had given him credit for that I became comparatively easy about him, and determined to let him play his own game, being always, however, ready to hand in case things went too far wrong. It was not simply because he disliked his father and mother that he wanted to have no more to do with them; if it had been only this he would have put up with them; but a warning voice within told him distinctly enough that if he was clean cut away from them he might still have a chance of success, whereas if they had anything whatever to do with him, or even knew where he was, they would hamper him and in the end ruin him. Absolute independence he believed to be his only chance of very life itself.

Over and above this if this were not enough – Ernest had a faith in his own destiny such as most young men, I suppose, feel, but the grounds of which were not apparent to any one but himself. Rightly or wrongly, in a quiet way he believed he possessed a strength which, if he were only free to use it in his own way, might do great things some day. He did not know when, nor where, nor how his opportunity was to come, but he never doubted that it would come in spite of all that had happened, and above all else he cherished the hope that he might know how to seize it if it came, for whatever it was it would be something that no one else could do so well as he could. People said there were no dragons and giants for adventurous men to fight with nowadays; it was beginning to dawn upon him that there were just as many now as at any past time.

Monstrous as such a faith may seem in one who was qualifying himself for a high mission by a term of imprisonment, he could no more help it than he could help breathing; it was innate in him, and it was even more with a view to this than for other reasons that he wished to sever the connection between himself and his parents; for he knew that if ever the day came in which it should appear that before him too there was a race set in which it might be an honour to have run among the foremost, his father and mother would be the first to let him and hinder him in running it. They had been the first to say that he ought to run such a race; they would also be the first to trip him up if he took them at their word, and then afterwards upbraid him for not having won. Achievement of any kind would be impossible for him unless he was free from those who would be for ever dragging him back into the conventional. The conventional had been tried already and had been found wanting.

He had an opportunity now, if he chose to take it, of escaping once for all from those who had at once tormented him and would hold him earthward should a chance of soaring open before him. He should never have had it but for his imprisonment; but for this the force of habit and routine would have been too strong for him; he should hardly have had it if he had not lost all his money; the gap would not have been so wide but that he might have been inclined to throw a plank across it. He rejoiced now, therefore, over his loss of money as well as over his imprisonment, which had made it more easy for him to follow his truest and most lasting interests.

At times he wavered, when he thought of how his mother,

who in her way, as he thought, had loved, him, would weep and think sadly over him, or how perhaps she might even fall ill and die, and how the blame would rest with him. At these times his resolution was near breaking, but when he found I applauded his design, the voice within, which bade him see his father's and mother's faces no more, grew louder and more persistent. If he could not cut himself adrift from those who he knew would hamper him, when so small an effort was wanted, his dream of a destiny was idle; what was the prospect of a hundred pounds from his father in comparison with jeopardy to this? He still felt deeply the pain his disgrace had inflicted upon his father and mother, but he was getting stronger, and reflected that as he had run his chance with them for parents, so they must run theirs with him for a son.

He had nearly settled down to this conclusion when he received a letter from his father which made his decision final. If the prison rules had been interpreted strictly, he would not have been allowed to have this letter for another three months, as he had already heard from me, but the governor took a lenient view, and considered the letter from me to be a business communication hardly coming under the category of a letter from friends. Theobald's letter, therefore, was given to his son. It ran as follows:

'My Dear Ernest, – My object in writing is not to upbraid you with the disgrace and shame you have inflicted upon your mother and myself, to say nothing of your brother Joey, and your sister. Suffer of course we must, but we know to whom to look in our affliction, and are filled with anxiety rather on your behalf than our own. Your mother is wonderful. She is pretty well in health, and desires me to send you her love.

'Have you considered your prospects on leaving prison? I understand from Mr Overton that you have lost the legacy which your grandfather left you, together with all the interest that accrued during your minority, in the course of speculation upon the Stock Exchange! If you have indeed been guilty of such appalling folly it is difficult to see what you can turn your hand to, and I suppose you will try to find a clerkship in an office. Your salary will doubtless be low at first, but you have made your bed and must not complain if you have to lie upon it. If you take pains to please your employers they will not be backward in promoting you.

'When I first heard from Mr Overton of the unspeakable calamity which had befallen your mother and myself, I had resolved not to see you again. I am unwilling, however, to have recourse to a measure which would deprive you of your last connecting link with respectable people. Your mother and I will see you as soon as you come out of prison; not at Battersby – we do not wish you to come down here at present – but somewhere else, probably in London. You need not shrink from seeing us; we shall not reproach you. We will then decide about your future.

'At present our impression is that you will find a fairer start probably in Australia or New Zealand than here, and I am prepared to find you £75 or even if necessary so far as £100 to pay your passage money. Once in the colony you must be dependent upon your own exertions.

'May Heaven prosper them and you, and restore you to us years hence a respected member of society. – Your affectionate father,

'T. Pontifex.'

Then there was a postscript in Christina's writing.

'My darling, darling boy, pray with me daily and hourly that we may yet again become a happy, united, God-fearing family as we were before this horrible pain fell upon us. – Your sorrowing but ever loving mother,

'C. P.'

This letter did not produce the effect on Ernest that it would have done before his imprisonment began. His father and mother thought they could take him up as they had left him off. They forgot the rapidity with which development follows misfortune, if the sufferer is young and of a sound temperament. Ernest made no reply to his father's letter, but his desire for a total break developed into something like a passion. 'There are orphanages,' he exclaimed to himself, 'for children who have lost their parents – oh! why, why, why are there no harbours of refuge for grown men who have not yet lost them?' And he brooded over the bliss of Melchisedek who had been born an orphan, without father, without mother, and without descent.

Chapter Sixty-Eight

When I think over all that Ernest told me about his prison meditations, and the conclusions he was drawn to, it occurs to me that in reality he was wanting to do the very last thing which it would have entered into his head to think of wanting. I mean that he was trying to give up father and mother for Christ's sake. He would have said he was giving them up because he thought they hindered him in the pursuit of his truest and most lasting happiness. Granted, but what is this if it is not Christ? What is Christ if He is not this? He who takes the highest and most self-respecting view of his own welfare which it is in his power to conceive, and adheres to it in spite of conventionality, is a Christian whether he knows it and calls himself one, or whether he does not. A rose is not the less a rose because it does not know its own name.

What if circumstances had made his duty more easy for him than it would be to most men? That was his luck, as much as it is other people's luck to have other duties made easy for them by accident of birth. Surely if people are born rich or handsome they have a right to their good fortune. Some, I know, will say that one man has no right to be born with a better constitution than another; others again will say that luck is the only righteous object of human veneration. Both, I dare say, can make out a very good case, but whichever may be right surely Ernest had as much right to the good luck of finding a duty made easier as he had had to the bad fortune of falling into the scrape which had got him into prison. A man is not to be sneered at for having a trump card in his hand; he is only to be sneered at if he plays his trump card badly.

Indeed, I question whether it is ever much harder for anyone to give up father and mother for Christ's sake than it was for Ernest. The relations between the parties will have almost always been severely strained before it comes to this. I doubt whether anyone was ever yet required to give up those to whom he was tenderly attached for a mere matter of conscience: he will have ceased to be tenderly attached to them long before he is called upon to break with them; for differences of opinion concerning any matter of vital importance spring from differences of constitution, and these will already have led to so much other disagreement that the 'giving up' when it comes, is like giving up an aching but very loose and hollow tooth. It is the loss of those whom we are not required to give up for Christ's sake which is really painful to us. Then there is a wrench in earnest. Happily, no matter how light the task that is demanded from us, it is enough if we do it; we reap our reward, much as though it were a Herculean labour.

But to return, the conclusion Ernest came to was that he would be a tailor. He talked the matter over with the chaplain, who told him there was no reason why he should not be able to earn his six or seven shillings a day by the time he came out of prison, if he chose to learn the trade during the remainder of his term – not quite three months; the doctor said he was strong enough for this, and that it was about the only thing he was as yet fit for; so he left the infirmary sooner than he would otherwise have done and entered the tailor's shop, overjoyed at the thoughts of seeing his way again, and confident of rising some day if he could only get a firm foothold to start from.

Everyone whom he had to do with saw that he did not belong to what are called the criminal classes, and finding him eager to learn and to save trouble always treated him kindly and almost respectfully. He did not find the work irksome; it was far more pleasant than making Latin and Greek verses at Roughborough; he felt that he would rather be here in prison than at Roughborough again – yes, or even at Cambridge itself. The only trouble he was ever in danger of getting into was through exchanging words or looks with the more decent-looking of his fellow-prisoners. This was forbidden, but he never missed a chance of breaking the rules in this respect.

Any man of his ability who was at the same time anxious to learn would of course make rapid progress, and before he left prison the warder said he was as good a tailor with his three months' apprenticeship as many a man was with twelve. Ernest had never before been so much praised by any of his teachers. Each day as he grew stronger in health and more accustomed to his surroundings he saw some fresh advantage in his position, an advantage which he had not aimed at, but which had come almost in spite of himself, and he marvelled at his own good fortune, which had ordered things so greatly better for him than he could have ordered them for himself.

His having lived six months in Ashpit Place was a case in point. Things were possible to him which to others like him would be impossible. If such a man as Towneley were told he must live henceforth in a house like those in Ashpit Place it would be more than he could stand. Ernest could not have stood it himself if he had gone to live there of compulsion through want of money. It was only because he had felt himself able to run away at any minute that, he had not wanted to do so; now, however, that he had become familiar with life in Ashpit Place he no longer minded it, and could live gladly in lower parts of London than that so long as he could pay his way. It was from no prudence or forethought that he had served this apprenticeship to life among the poor. He had been trying in a feeble way to be thorough in his work: he had not been thorough, the whole thing had been a *fiasco*; but he had made a little puny effort in the direction of being genuine, and behold, in his hour of need it had been returned to him with a reward far richer than he had deserved. He could not have faced becoming one of the very poor unless he had had such a bridge to conduct him over to them as he had found unwittingly in

Ashpit Place. True, there had been drawbacks in the particular house he had chosen, but he need not live in a house where there was a Mr Holt and he should no longer be tied to the profession which he so much hated; if there were neither screams nor scripture readings he could be happy in a garret at three shillings a week, such as Miss Maitland lived in.

As he thought further he remembered that all things work together for good to them that love God; was it possible, he asked himself, that he too, however imperfectly, had been trying to love Him? He dared not answer Yes, but he would try hard that it should be so. Then there came into his mind that noble air of Handel's: 'Great God, who yet but darkly known,' and he felt it as he had never felt it before. He had lost his faith in Christianity, but his faith in something – he knew not what, but that there was a something as yet but darkly known, which made right right and wrong wrong – his faith in this grew stronger and stronger daily.

Again there crossed his mind thoughts of the power which he felt to be in him, and of how and where it was to find its vent. The same instinct which had led him to live among the poor because it was the nearest thing to him which he could lay hold of with any clearness came to his assistance here too. He thought of the Australian gold and how those who lived among it had never seen it though it abounded all around them: 'There is gold everywhere,' he exclaimed inwardly, 'to those who look for it.' Might not his opportunity be close upon him if he looked carefully enough at his immediate surroundings? What was his position? He had lost all. Could he not turn his having lost all into an opportunity? Might he not, if he too sought the strength of the Lord, find, like St Paul, that it was perfected in weakness?

He had nothing more to lose; money, friends, character, all were gone for a very long time if not for ever; but there was something else also that had taken its flight along with these. I mean the fear of that which man could do unto him. *Cantabit Vacuus.* Who could hurt him more than he had been hurt already?

Let him but be able to earn his bread, and he knew of nothing which he dared not venture if it would make the world a happier place for those who were young and lovable. Herein he found so much comfort that he almost wished he had lost his reputation even more completely – for he saw that it was like a man's life which may be found of them that lose it and lost of them that would find it. He should not have had the courage to give up all for Christ's sake, but now Christ had mercifully taken all, and lo! it seemed as though all were found.

As the days went slowly by he came to see that Christianity and the denial of Christianity after all met as much as any other extremes do; it was a fight about names – not about things; practically the Church of Rome, the Church of England, and the freethinker have the same ideal standard and meet in the gentleman; for he is the most perfect saint who is the most perfect gentleman. Then he saw also that it matters little what profession, whether of religion or irreligion, a man may make, provided only he follows it out with charitable inconsistency, and without insisting on it to the bitter end. It is in the uncompromisingness with which dogma *is* held and not in the dogma or want of dogma that the danger lies. This was the crowning point of the edifice; when he had got here he no longer wished to molest even the Pope. The Archbishop of Canterbury might have hopped about all round him and even picked crumbs out of his hand without running risk of getting a sly sprinkle of salt. That wary prelate himself might perhaps have been of a different opinion, but the robins and thrushes that hop about our lawns are not more needlessly distrustful of the hand that throws them out crumbs of bread in winter, than the Archbishop would have been of my hero.

Perhaps he was helped to arrive at the foregoing conclusion by an event which almost thrust inconsistency upon him. A few days after he had left the infirmary the chaplain came to his cell and told him that the prisoner who played the organ in chapel had just finished his sentence and was leaving the prison; he therefore offered the post to Ernest, who he already knew played the organ. Ernest was at first in doubt whether it would be right for him to assist at religious services more than he was actually compelled to do, but the pleasure of playing the organ, and the privileges which the post involved, made him see excellent reasons for not riding consistency to death. Having, then, once introduced an element of inconsistency into his system, he was far too consistent not to be inconsistent consistently, and he lapsed ere long into an amiable indifferentism which to outward appearance differed but little from the indifferentism from which Mr Hawke had aroused him.

By becoming organist he was saved from the treadmill, for which the doctor had said he was unfit as yet, but which he would probably have been put to in due course as soon as he was stronger. He might have escaped the tailor's shop altogether and done only the comparatively light work of attending to the chaplain's rooms if he had liked, but he wanted to learn as much tailoring as he could, and did not therefore take advantage of this offer; he was allowed, however, two hours a day in the afternoon for practice. From that moment his prison life ceased to be monotonous, and the remaining two months of his sentence slipped by almost as rapidly as they would have done if he had been free. What with music, books, learning his trade, and conversation with the chaplain, who was just the kindly, sensible person that Ernest wanted in order to steady him a little, the days went by so pleasantly that when the time came for him to leave prison, he did so, or thought he did so, not without regret.

Chapter Sixty-Nine

In coming to the conclusion that he would sever the connection between himself and his family once for all Ernest had reckoned without his family. Theobald wanted to be rid of his son, it is true, in so far as he wished him to be no nearer at any rate than the Antipodes; but he had no idea of entirely breaking with him. He knew his son well enough to have a pretty shrewd idea that this was what Ernest would wish himself, and perhaps as much for this reason as for any other he was determined to keep up the connection, provided it did not involve Ernest's coming to Battersby nor any recurring outlay.

When the time approached for him to leave prison, his father and mother consulted as to what course they should adopt.

'We must never leave him to himself,' said Theobald impressively; 'we can neither of us wish that.'

'Oh, no! no! dearest Theobald,' exclaimed Christina. 'Whoever else deserts him, and however distant he may be from us, he must still feel that he has parents whose hearts beat with affection for him no matter how cruelly he has pained them.'

'He has been his own worst enemy,' said Theobald. 'He has never loved us as we deserved, and now he will be withheld by false shame from wishing to see us. He will avoid us if he can.'

'Then we must go to him ourselves,' said Christina, 'whether he likes it or not we must be at his side to support him as he enters again upon the world.'

'If we do not want him to give us the slip we must catch him as he leaves prison.'

'We will, we will; our faces shall be the first to gladden his eyes as he comes out, and our voices the first to exhort him to return to the paths of virtue.'

'I think,' said Theobald, 'if he sees us in the street he will turn round and run away from us. He is intensely selfish.'

'Then we must get leave to go inside the prison, and see him before he gets outside.'

After a good deal of discussion this was the plan they decided on adopting, and having so decided, Theobald wrote to the governor of the gaol asking whether he could be admitted inside the gaol to receive Ernest when his sentence had expired. He received answer in the affirmative, and the pair left Battersby the day before Ernest was to come out of prison.

Ernest had not reckoned on this, and was rather surprised on being told a few minutes before nine that he was to go into the receiving room before he left the prison as there were visitors waiting to see him. His heart fell, for he guessed who they were, but he screwed up his courage and hastened to the receiving room. There, sure enough, standing at the end of the table nearest the door were the two people whom he regarded as the most dangerous enemies he had in all the world – his father and mother. He could not fly, but he knew that if he wavered he was lost.

His mother was crying, but she sprang forward to meet him and clasped him in her arms. 'Oh, my boy, my boy,' she sobbed, and she could say no more.

Ernest was as white as a sheet. His heart beat so that he could hardly breathe. He let his mother embrace him, and then withdrawing himself stood silently before her with the tears falling from his eyes. At first he could not speak. For a minute or so the silence on all sides was complete. Then, gathering strength, he said in a low voice:

'Mother' (it was the first time he had called her anything but 'mamma'), 'we must part.' On this, turning to the warder, he said: 'I believe I am free to leave the prison if I wish to do so. You cannot compel me to remain here longer. Please take me to the gates.'

Theobald stepped forward. 'Ernest, you must not, shall not, leave us in this way.'

'Do not speak to me,' said Ernest, his eyes flashing with a fire that was unwonted in them. Another warder then came up and took Theobald aside, while the first conducted Ernest to the gates.

'Tell them,' said Ernest, 'from me that they must think of me as one dead, for I am dead to them. Say that my greatest pain is the thought of the disgrace I have inflicted upon them, and that above all things else I will study to avoid paining them hereafter; but say also that if they write to me I will return their letters unopened, and that if they come and see me I will protect myself in whatever way I can.'

By this time he was at the prison gate, and in another moment was at liberty. After he had got a few steps out he turned his face to the prison wall, leant against it for support, and wept as though his heart would break.

Giving up father and mother for Christ's sake was not such an easy matter after all. If a man has been possessed by devils for long enough they will rend him as they leave him, however imperatively they may have been cast out. Ernest did not stay long where he was, for he feared each moment that his father and mother would come out. He pulled himself together and turned into the labyrinth of small streets which opened out in front of him.

He had crossed his Rubicon – not perhaps very heroically or dramatically, but then it is only in dramas that people act dramatically. At any rate, by hook or by crook, he had scrambled over, and was out upon the other side. Already he thought of much which he would gladly have said, and blamed his want of presence of mind; but, after all, it mattered very little. Inclined though he was to make very great allowances for his father and mother, he was indignant at their having thrust themselves upon him without warning at a moment when the excitement of leaving prison was already as much as he was fit for. It was a mean advantage to have taken over him, but he was glad they had taken it, for it made him realise more fully than ever that his one chance lay in separating himself completely from them.

The morning was grey, and the first signs of winter fog were beginning to show themselves, for it was now the 30th of September. Ernest wore the clothes in which he had entered prison, and was therefore dressed as a clergyman. No one who looked at him would have seen any difference between his present appearance and his appearance six months previously; indeed, as he walked slowly through the dingy crowded lane called Eyre Street Hill (which he well knew, for he had clerical friends in that neighbourhood), the months he had passed in prison seemed to drop out of his life, and so powerfully did association carry him away that, finding himself in his old dress and in his old surroundings, he felt dragged back into his old self – as though his six months of prison life had been a dream from which he was now waking to take things up as he had left them. This was the effect of unchanged surroundings upon the unchanged part of him. But there was a changed part, and the effect of unchanged surroundings upon this was to make everything seem almost as strange as though he had never had any life but his prison one, and was now born into a new world.

All our lives long, every day and every hour, we are engaged in the process of accommodating our changed and unchanged selves to changed and unchanged surroundings; living, in fact, in nothing else than this process of accommodation; when we fail in it a little we are stupid, when we fail flagrantly we are mad, when we suspend it temporarily we sleep, when we give up the attempt altogether we die. In quiet, uneventful lives the changes internal and external are so small that there is little or no strain in the process of fusion and accommodation; in other lives there is great strain, but there is also great fusing and accommodating power; in others great strain with little accommodating power. A life will be successful or not according as the power of accommodation is equal to or unequal to the strain of fusing and adjusting internal and external changes.

The trouble is that in the end we shall be driven to admit the unity of the universe so completely as to be compelled to deny that there is either an external or an internal, but must see everything both as external and internal at one and the same time, subject and object – external and internal – being unified as much as everything else. This will knock our whole system over, but then every system has got to be knocked over by something.

Much the best way out of this difficulty is to go in for separation between internal and external – subject and object – when we find this convenient, and unity between the same when we find unity convenient. This is illogical, but extremes are alone logical, and they are always absurd, the mean is alone practicable and it is always illogical. It is faith and not logic which is the supreme arbiter. They say all roads lead to Rome, and all philosophies that I have ever seen lead ultimately either to some gross absurdity, or else to the conclusion already more than once insisted on in these pages, that the just shall live by faith, that is to say that sensible people will get through life by rule of thumb as they may interpret it most conveniently without asking too many questions for conscience sake. Take any fact, and reason upon it to the bitter end, and it will ere long lead to this as the only refuge from some palpable folly.

But to return to my story. When Ernest got to the top of the street and looked back, he saw the grimy, sullen walls of his prison filling up the end of it. He paused for a minute or two. 'There,' he said to himself, 'I was hemmed in by bolts which I could see and touch; here I am barred by others which are none the less real – poverty and ignorance of the world. It was no part of my business to try to break the material bolts of iron and escape from prison, but now that I am free I must surely seek to break these others.'

He had read somewhere of a prisoner who had made his

escape by cutting up his bedstead with an iron spoon. He admired and marvelled at the man's mind, but could not even try to imitate him; in the presence of immaterial barriers, however, he was not so easily daunted, and felt as though, even if the bed were iron and the spoon a wooden one, he could find some means of making the wood cut the iron sooner or later.

He turned his back upon Eyre Street Hill and walked down Leather Lane into Holborn. Each step he took, each face or object that he knew, helped at once to link him on to the life he had led before his imprisonment, and at the same time to make him feel how completely that imprisonment had cut his life into two parts, the one of which could bear no resemblance to the other.

He passed down Fetter Lane into Fleet Street and so to the Temple, to which I had just returned from my summer holiday. It was about half-past nine, and I was having my breakfast, when I heard a timid knock at the door and opened it to find Ernest.

Chapter Seventy

I had begun to like him on the night Towneley had sent for me, and on the following day I thought he had shaped well. I had liked him also during our interview in prison, and wanted to see more of him, so that I might make up my mind about him. I had lived long enough to know that some men who do great things in the end are not very wise when they are young; knowing that he would leave prison on the 30th, I had expected him, and, as I had a spare bedroom, pressed him to stay with me, till he could make up his mind what he would do.

Being so much older than he was, I anticipated no trouble in getting my own way, but he would not hear of it. The utmost he would assent to was that he should be my guest till he could find a room for himself, which he would set about doing at once.

He was still much agitated, but grew better as he ate a breakfast, not of prison fare and in a comfortable room. It pleased me to see the delight he took in all about him; the fireplace with a fire in it; the easy-chairs, the *Times*, my cat, the red geraniums in the window, to saying nothing of coffee, bread and butter, sausages, marmalade, etc. Everything was pregnant with the most exquisite pleasure to him. The plane trees were full of leaf still; he kept rising from the breakfast table to admire them; never till now, he said, had he known what the enjoyment of these things really was. He ate, looked, laughed and cried by turns, with an emotion which I can neither forget nor describe.

He told me how his father and mother had lain in wait for him, as he was about to leave prison. I was furious and applauded him heartily for what he had done. He was very grateful to me for this. Other people, he said, would tell him he ought to think of his father and mother rather than of himself, and it was such a comfort to find someone who saw things as he saw them himself. Even if I had differed from him I should not have said so, but I was of his opinion, and was almost as much obliged to him for seeing things as I saw them, as he to me for doing the same kind office by himself. Cordially as I disliked Theobald and Christina, I was in such a hopeless minority in the opinion I had formed concerning them that it was pleasant to find someone who agreed with me.

Then there came an awful moment for both of us.

A knock, as of a visitor and not a postman, was heard at my door.

'Goodness gracious,' I exclaimed, 'why didn't we sport the oak? Perhaps it is your father. But surely he would hardly come at this time of day! Go at once into my bedroom.'

I went to the door, and, sure enough, there were both Theobald and Christina. I could not refuse to let them in and was obliged to listen to their version of the story, which agreed substantially with Ernest's. Christina cried bitterly – Theobald stormed. After about ten minutes, during which I assured them that I had not the faintest conception where their son was, I dismissed them both. I saw they looked suspiciously upon the manifest signs that someone was breakfasting with me, and parted from me more or less defiantly, but I got rid of them, and poor Ernest came out again, looking white, frightened and upset. He had heard voices, but no more, and did not feel sure that the enemy might not be gaining over me. We sported the oak now, and before long he began to recover.

After breakfast we discussed the situation. I had taken away his wardrobe and books from Mrs Jupp's, but had left his furniture, pictures and piano, giving Mrs Jupp the use of these, so that she might let her room furnished, in lieu of charge for taking care of the furniture. As soon as Ernest heard that his wardrobe was at hand, he got out a suit of clothes he had had before he had been ordained, and put it on at once, much, as I thought, to the improvement of his personal appearance.

Then we went into the subject of his finances. He had had ten pounds from Pryer only a day or two before he was apprehended, of which between seven and eight were in his purse when he entered the prison. This money was restored to him on leaving. He had always paid cash for whatever he bought, so that there was nothing to be deducted for debts. Besides this, he had his clothes, books and furniture. He could, as I have said, have had £100 from his father if he had chosen to emigrate, but this both Ernest and I (for he brought me round to his opinion) agreed it would be better to decline. This was all he knew of as belonging to him.

He said he proposed at once taking an unfurnished top back attic in as quiet a house as he could find, say at three or four shillings a week, and looking out for work as a tailor. I did not think it much mattered what he began with, for I felt pretty sure he would ere long find his way to something that suited him, if he could get a start with anything at all. The difficulty was how to get him started. It was not enough that he should be able to cut out and make clothes – that he should have the organs, so to speak, of a tailor; he must be put into a tailor's shop and guided for a little while by someone who knew how and where to help him.

The rest of the day he spent in looking for a room, which he soon found, and in familiarising himself with liberty. In the evening I took him to the Olympic, where Robson was then acting in a burlesque on Macbeth, Mrs Keley, if I remember rightly, taking the part of Lady Macbeth. In the scene before the murder, Macbeth had said he could not kill Duncan when he saw his boots upon the landing. Lady Macbeth put a stop to her husband's hesitation by whipping him up under her arm, and carrying him off the stage, kicking and screaming. Ernest laughed till he cried. 'What rot Shakespeare is after this,' he exclaimed, involuntarily.

I remembered his essay on the Greek tragedians, and was more *épris* with him than ever.

Next day he set about looking for employment, and I did not see him till about five o'clock, when he came and said that he had had no success. The same thing happened the next day and the day after that. Wherever he went he was invariably refused and often ordered point blank out of the shop; I could see by the expression of his face, though he said nothing, that he was getting frightened, and began to think I should have come to the rescue. He said he had made a great many inquiries and had always been told the same story. He found that it was easy to keep on in an old line, but very hard to strike out into a new one.

He talked to the fishmonger in Leather Lane, where he went to buy a bloater for his tea, casually as though from curiosity and without any interested motive. 'Sell,' said the master of the shop. 'Why, nobody wouldn't believe what can be sold by penn'orths and twopenn'orths if you go the right way to work. Look at whelks, for instance. Last Saturday night me and my little Emma here, we sold £7 worth of whelks between eight and half-past eleven o'clock – and almost all in penn'orths and twopenn'orths – a few hap'orths, but not many. It was the steam that did it. We kept a-boiling of 'em hot and hot, and whenever the steam came strong up from the cellar on to the pavement, the people bought, but whenever the steam went down they left off buying; so we boiled them over and over again till they was all sold. That's just where, it is; if you know your business you can sell, if you don't you'll soon make a mess of it. Why, but for the steam, I should not have sold IOS. worth of whelks all the night through.'

This, and many another yarn of kindred substance which he heard from, other people determined Ernest more than ever to stake on tailoring as the one trade about which he knew anything at all; nevertheless, here were three or four days gone by and employment seemed as far off as ever.

I now did what I ought to have done before, that is to say,

I called on my own tailor whom I had dealt with for over a quarter of a century and asked his advice. He declared Ernest's plan to be hopeless. 'If,' said Mr Larkins, for this was my tailor's name, 'he had begun at fourteen, it might have done, but no man of twenty-four could stand being turned to work, into a workshop full of tailors; he would not get on with the men, nor the men with him; you could not expect him to be "hail fellow, well met," with them, and you could not expect his fellow-workmen to like him if he was not. A man must have sunk low through drink or natural taste for low company, before he could get on with those who have had such a different training from his own.'

Mr Larkins said a great deal more and wound up by taking me to see the place where his own men worked. 'This is a paradise,' he said, 'compared to most workshops. What gentleman could stand this air, think you, for a fortnight?'

I was glad enough to get out of the hot, fetid atmosphere in five minutes, and saw that there was no brick of Ernest's prison to be loosened by going and working among tailors in a work-shop.

Mr Larkins wound up by saying that even if my *protégé* were a much better workman than he probably was, no master would give him employment, for fear of creating a bother among the men.

I left, feeling that I ought to have thought of all this myself, and was more than ever perplexed as to whether I had not better let my young friend have a few thousand pounds and send him out to the colonies, when, on my return home at about five o'clock, I found him waiting for me, radiant, and declaring that he had found all he wanted.

Chapter Seventy-One

It seems he had been patrolling the streets for the last three or four nights – I suppose in search of something to do – at any rate knowing better what he wanted to get than how to get it. Nevertheless, what he wanted was in reality so easily to be found that it took a highly educated scholar like himself to be unable to find it. But, however this may be, he had been scared, and now saw lions where there were none, and was shocked and frightened, and night after night his courage had failed him and he had returned to his lodgings in Laystall Street without accomplishing his errand. He had not taken me into his confidence upon this matter, and I had not inquired what he did with himself in the evenings. At last he had concluded that, however painful it might be to him, he would call on Mrs Jupp, who he thought would be able to help him if anyone could. He had been walking moodily from seven till about nine, and now resolved to go straight to Ashpit Place and make a mother confessor of Mrs Jupp without more delay.

Of all tasks that could be performed by mortal woman there was none which Mrs Jupp would have liked better than the one Ernest was thinking of imposing upon her; nor do I know that in his scared and broken-down state he could have done much better than he now proposed. Mrs Jupp would have made it very easy for him to open his grief to her; indeed, she would have coaxed it all out of him before he knew where he was; but the fates were against Mrs Jupp, and the meeting between my hero and his former landlady was postponed *sine die*, for his determination had hardly been formed and he had not gone more than a hundred yards in the direction of Mrs Jupp's house, when a woman accosted him.

He was turning from her, as he had turned from so many others, when she started back with a movement that aroused his curiosity. He had hardly seen her face, but being determined to catch sight of it, followed her as she hurried away, and passed her; then turning round he saw that she was none other than Ellen, the housemaid who had been dismissed by his mother eight years previously.

He ought to have assigned Ellen's unwillingness to see him to its true cause, but a guilty conscience made him think she had heard of his disgrace and was turning away from him in contempt. Brave as had been his resolution about facing the world, this was more than he was prepared for; 'What! you too shun me, Ellen?' he exclaimed.

The girl was crying bitterly and did not understand him. 'Oh, Master Ernest', she sobbed, 'let me go; you are too good for the likes of me to speak to now.'

'Why, Ellen,' said he, 'what nonsense you talk; you haven't been in prison, have you?'

'Oh, no, no, no, not as bad as that,' she exclaimed passionately.

'Well, I have,' said Ernest, with a forced laugh, 'I came out three or four days ago after six months with hard labour.'

Ellen did not believe him, but she looked at him with a 'Lor'! Master Ernest,' and dried her eyes at once. The ice was broken between them, for as a matter of fact Ellen had been in prison several times, and though she did not believe Ernest, his merely saying he had been in prison made her feel more at ease with him. For her there were two classes of people, those who had been in prison and those who had not. The first she looked upon as fellow-creatures and more or less Christians, the second, with few exceptions, she regarded with suspicion, not wholly unmingled with contempt.

Then Ernest told her what had happened to him during the last six months, and by-and-by she believed him.

'Master Ernest,' said she, after they had talked for a quarter of an hour or so, 'there's a place over the way where they sell tripe and onions. I know you was always very fond of tripe and onions, let's go over and have some, and we can talk better there.'

So the pair crossed the street and entered the tripe shop; Ernest ordered supper.

'And how is your pore dear mamma, and your dear papa, Master Ernest?' said Ellen, who had now recovered herself and was quite at home with my hero. 'Oh, dear, dear me,' she said. 'I did love your pa; he was a good gentleman, he was, and your ma too; it would do anyone good to live with her, I'm sure.'

Ernest was surprised and hardly knew what to say. He had expected to find Ellen indignant at the way she had been treated, and inclined to lay the blame of her having fallen to her present state at his father's and mother's door. It was not so. Her only recollection of Battersby was as of a place where she had had plenty to eat and drink, not too much hard work, and where she had not been scolded. When she heard that Ernest had quarrelled with his father and mother she assumed as a matter of course that the fault must lie entirely with Ernest.

'Oh, your pore, pore ma!' said Ellen. 'She was always so very fond of you. Master Ernest: you was always her favourite; I can't abear to think of anything between you and her. To think now of the way she used to have me into the dining-room and teach me my catechism, that she did! Oh, Master Ernest, you really must go and make it all up with her; indeed you must.'

Ernest felt rueful, but he had resisted so valiantly already that the devil might have saved himself the trouble of trying to get at him through Ellen in the matter of his father and mother. He changed the subject, and the pair warmed to one another as they had their tripe and pots of beer. Of all people in the world Ellen was perhaps the one to whom Ernest could have spoken most freely at this juncture. He told her what he thought he could have told to no one else.

'You know, Ellen.' he concluded, 'I had learnt as a boy things that I ought not to have learnt, and had never had a chance of that which would have set me straight.'

'Gentlefolks is always like that,' said Ellen musingly.

'I believe you are right, but I am no longer a gentleman, Ellen, and I don't see why I should be "like that" any longer, my dear. I want you to help me to be like something else as soon as possible.'

'Lor'! Master Ernest, whatever can you be meaning?'

The pair soon afterwards left the eating-house and walked up Fetter Lane together.

Ellen had had hard times since she had left Battersby, but they had left little trace upon her.

Ernest saw only the fresh-looking smiling face, the dimpled cheek, the clear blue eyes and lovely sphinx-like lips which he had remembered as a boy. At nineteen she had looked older than she was, now she looked much younger; indeed she looked hardly older than when Ernest had last seen her, and it would have taken a man of much greater experience than he possessed to suspect how completely she had fallen from her first estate. It never occurred to him that the poor condition of her wardrobe was due to her passion for ardent spirits, and that first and last she had served five or six times as much time in gaol as he had. He ascribed the poverty of her attire to the attempts to keep herself respectable, which Ellen during supper had more than once alluded to. He had been charmed with the way in which she had declared that a pint of beer would make her tipsy, and had only allowed herself to be forced into drinking the whole after a good deal of remonstrance. To him she appeared a very angel dropped from the sky, and all the more easy to get on with for being a fallen one.

As he walked up Fetter Lane with her towards Laystall Street, he thought of the wonderful goodness of God towards him in throwing in his way the very person of all others whom he was most glad to see, and whom, of all others, in spite of her living so near him, he might have never fallen in with but for happy-accident.

When people get it into their heads that they are being specially favoured by the Almighty, they had better as a general rule mind their p's and q's, and when they think they see the devil's drift with more special clearness, let them remember that he has had much more experience than they have, and is probably meditating mischief.

Already during supper the thought that in Ellen at last he had found a woman whom he could love well enough to wish to live with and marry had flitted across his mind, and the more they had chatted the more reasons kept suggesting themselves for thinking that what might be folly in ordinary cases would not be folly in his.

He must marry someone; that was already settled. He could not marry a lady; that was absurd. He must marry a poor woman. Yes, but a fallen one? Was he not fallen himself? Ellen would fall no more. He had only to look at her to be sure of this. He could not live with her in sin, not for more than the shortest time that could elapse before their marriage; he no longer believed in the supernatural element of Christianity, but the Christian morality at any rate was indisputable. Besides, they might have children, and a stigma would rest upon them. Whom had he to consult but himself now? His father and mother never need know, and even if they did, they should be thankful to see him married to any woman who would make him happy as Ellen would. As for not being able to afford marriage, how did poor people do? Did not a good wife rather help matters than not? Where one could live two could do so, and if Ellen was three or four years older than he was – well, what was that?

Have you, gentle reader, ever loved at first sight? When you fell in love at first sight, how long, let me ask, did it take you to become ready to fling every other consideration to the winds except that of obtaining possession of the loved one? Or rather, how long would it have taken you if you had had no father or mother, nothing to lose in the way of money, position, friends, professional advancement, or what not, and if the object of your affections was as free from all these *impedimenta* as you were yourself?

If you were a young John Stuart Mill, perhaps it would have taken you some time, but suppose your nature was quixotic, impulsive, altruistic, guileless; suppose you were a hungry man starving for something to love and lean upon, for one whose burdens you might bear, and who might help you to bear yours. Suppose you were down on your luck, still stunned by a horrible shock, and this bright vista of a happy future floated suddenly before you, how long under these circumstances do you think you would reflect before you would decide on embracing what chance had thrown in your way?

It did not take my hero long, for before he got past the ham and beef shop near the top of Fetter Lane, he had told Ellen that she must, come home with him and live with him till they could get married, which they would do upon the first day that the law allowed.

I think the devil must have chuckled and made tolerably sure of his game this time.

Chapter Seventy-Two

Ernest told Ellen of his difficulty about finding employment.

'But what do you think of going into a shop for, my dear,' said Ellen. 'Why not take a little shop yourself?'

Ernest asked how much this would cost. Ellen told him that he might take a house in some small street, say near the 'Elephant and Castle,' for 17s. or 18s. a week, and let off the two top floors for 10s., keeping the back parlour and shop for themselves. If he could raise five or six pounds to buy some second-hand clothes to stock the shop with, they could mend them and clean them, and she could look after the women's clothes while he did the men's. Then he could mend and make, if he could get the orders.

They could soon make a business of £2 a week in this way; she had a friend who began like that and had now moved to a better shop, where she made £5 or £6 a week at least – and she, Ellen, had done the greater part of the buying and selling herself.

Here was a new light indeed. It was as though he had got his £5,000 back again all of a sudden, and perhaps ever so much more later on into the bargain. Ellen seemed more than ever to be his good genius.

She went out and got a few rashers of bacon for his and her breakfast. She cooked them much more nicely than he had been able to do, and laid breakfast for him and made coffee, and some nice brown toast. Ernest had been his own cook and housemaid for the last few days and had not given himself satisfaction. Here he suddenly found himself with someone to wait on him again. Not only had Ellen pointed out to him how he could earn a living when no one except himself had known how to advise him, but here she was so pretty and smiling, looking after even his comforts, and restoring him practically in all respects that he much cared about to the position which he had lost – or rather putting him in one that he already liked much better. No wonder he was radiant when he came to explain his plans to me.

He had some difficulty in telling all that had happened. He hesitated, blushed, hummed and hawed. Misgivings began to cross his mind when he found himself obliged to tell his story to someone else. He felt inclined to slur things over, but I wanted to get at the facts, so I helped him over the bad places, and questioned him till I had got out pretty nearly the whole story as I have given it above.

I hope I did not show it, but I was very angry. I had begun to like Ernest. I don't know why, but I never have heard that any young man to whom I had become attached was going to get married without hating his intended instinctively, though I had never seen her; I have observed that most bachelors feel the same thing, though we are generally at some pains to hide the fact. Perhaps it is because we know we ought to have got married ourselves. Ordinarily we say we are delighted – in the present case I did not feel obliged to do this, though I made an effort to conceal my vexation. That a young man of much promise who was heir also to what was now a handsome fortune, should fling himself away upon such a person as Ellen was quite too provoking, and the more so because of the unexpectedness of the whole affair.

I begged him not to marry Ellen yet – not at least until he had known her for a longer time. He would not hear of it; he had given his word, and if he had not given it he should go and give it at once. I had hitherto found him upon most matters singularly docile and easy to manage, but on this point I could do nothing with him. His recent victory over his father and mother had increased his strength, and I was nowhere. I would have told him of his true position, but I knew very well that this would only make him more bent on having his own way – for with so much money why should he not please himself? I said nothing, therefore, on this head, and yet all that I could urge went for very little with one who believed himself to be an artisan or nothing.

Really from his own standpoint there was nothing very outrageous in what he was doing. He had known and been very fond of Ellen years before. He knew her to come of respectable people, and to have borne a good character, and to have been universally liked at Battersby. She was then a quick, smart, hardworking girl – and a very pretty one. When at last they met again she was on her best behaviour, in fact she was modesty and demureness itself. What wonder, then, that his imagination should fail to realise the changes that eight years must have worked? He knew too much against himself, and was too bankrupt in love to be squeamish; if Ellen had been only what he thought her, and if his prospects had been in reality no better than he believed they were, I do not know that there is anything much more imprudent in what Ernest proposed than there is in half the marriages that take place every day.

There was nothing for it, however, but to make the best of the inevitable, so I wished my young friend good fortune, and told him he could have whatever money he wanted to start his shop with, if what he had in hand was not sufficient. He thanked me, asked me to be kind enough to let him do all my mending and repairing, and to get him any other like orders that I could, and left, me to my own reflections.

I was even more angry when he was gone than I had been while he was with me. His frank, boyish face had beamed with a happiness that had rarely visited it. Except at Cambridge he had hardly known what happiness meant, and even there his life had been clouded as of a man for whom wisdom at the greatest of its entrances was quite shut out. I had seen enough of the world and of him to have observed this, but it was impossible, or I thought it had been impossible, for me to have helped him.

Whether I ought to have tried to help him or not I do not

know, but I am sure that the young of all animals often do want help upon matters about which anyone would say *a priori* that there should be no difficulty. One would think that a young seal would want no teaching how to swim, nor yet a bird to fly, but in practice a young seal drowns if put out of its depth before its parents have taught it to swim; and so again, even the young hawk must be taught to fly before it can do so.

I grant that the tendency of the times is to exaggerate the good which teaching can do, but in trying to teach too much, in most matters, we have neglected others in respect of which a little sensible teaching would do no harm.

I know it is the fashion to say that young people must find out things for themselves, and so they probably would if they had fair play to the extent of not having obstacles put in their way. But they seldom have fair play; as a general rule they meet with foul play, and foul play from those who live by selling them stones made into a great variety of shapes and sizes so as to form a tolerable imitation of bread.

Some are lucky enough to meet with few obstacles, some are plucky enough to override them, but in the greater number of cases, if people are saved at all they are saved so as by fire.

While Ernest was with me Ellen was looking out for a shop on the south side of the Thames near the 'Elephant and Castle,' which was then almost a new and a very rising neighbourhood. By one o'clock she had found several from which a selection was to be made, and before night the pair had made their choice.

Ernest brought Ellen to me. I did not want to see her, but could not well refuse. He had laid out a few of his shillings upon her wardrobe, so that she was neatly dressed, and, indeed, she looked very pretty and so good that I could hardly be surprised at Ernest's infatuation when the other circumstances of the case were taken into consideration. Of course we hated one another instinctively from the first moment we set eyes on one another, but we each told Ernest that we had been favourably impressed.

Then I was taken to see the shop. An empty house is like a stray dog or a body from which life has departed. Decay sets in at once in every part of it, and what mould and wind and weather would spare, street boys commonly destroy. Ernest's shop in its untenanted state was a dirty unsavoury place enough. The house was not old, but it had been run up by a jerry-builder and its constitution had no stamina whatever. It was only by being kept warm and quiet that it would remain in health for many months together. Now it had been empty for some weeks and the cats had got in by night, while the boys had broken the windows by day. The parlour floor was covered with stones and dirt, and in the area was a dead dog which had been killed in the street and been thrown down into the first unprotected place that could be found. There was a strong smell throughout the house, but whether it was bugs, or rats, or cats, or drains, or a compound of all four, I could not determine. The sashes did not fit, the flimsy doors hung badly; the skirting had gone in several places, and there were not a few holes in the floor; the locks were loose, the paper was torn and dirty; the stairs were weak and one felt the treads give as one went up them.

Over and above these drawbacks the house had an ill name, by reason of the fact that the wife of the last occupant had hanged herself in it not very many weeks previously. She had set down a bloater before the fire for her husband's tea, and had made him a round of toast. She then left the room as though about to return to it shortly, but instead of doing so she went into the back kitchen and hanged herself without a word. It was this which had kept the house empty so long in spite of its excellent position as a corner shop. The last tenant had left immediately after the inquest, and if the owner had had it done up then people would have got over the tragedy that had been enacted in it, but the combination of bad condition and bad fame had hindered many from taking it, who like Ellen, could see that it had great business capabilities. Almost anything would have sold there, but it happened also that there was no second-hand clothes shop in close proximity so that everything combined in its favour, except its filthy state and its reputation.

When I saw it, I thought I would rather die than live in such an awful place – but then I had been living in the Temple for the last five and twenty years. Ernest was lodging in Laystall Street and had just come out of prison; before this he had lived in Ashpit Place so that this house had no terrors for him provided he could get it done up. The difficulty was that the landlord was hard to move in this respect. It ended in my finding the money to do everything that was wanted, and taking a lease of the house for five years at the same rental as that paid by the last occupant. I then sublet it to Ernest, of course taking care that it was put more efficiently into repair than his landlord was at all likely to have put it.

A week later I called and found everything so completely trans-formed that I should hardly have recognised the house. All the ceilings had been whitewashed, all the rooms papered, the broken glass hacked out and reinstated, the defective woodwork renewed, all the sashes, cupboards and doors had been painted. The drains had been thoroughly overhauled; everything, in fact, that could be done had been done, and the rooms now looked as cheerful as they had been forbidding when I had last seen them. The people who had done the repairs were supposed to have cleaned the house down before leaving, but Ellen had given it another scrub from top to bottom herself after they were gone, and it was as clean as a new pin. I almost felt as though I could have lived in it myself, and as for Ernest, he was in the seventh heaven. He said it was all my doing and Ellen's.

There was already a counter in the shop and a few fittings, so that nothing now remained but to get some stock and set them out for sale. Ernest said he could not begin better than by selling his clerical wardrobe and his books, for though the shop was intended especially for the sale of second-hand clothes, yet Ellen said there was no reason why they should not sell a few books too; so a beginning was to be made by selling the books he had had at school and college at about one shilling a volume, taking them all round, and I have heard him say that he learned more that proved of practical use to him through stocking his books on a bench in front of his shop and selling them, than he had done from all the years of study which he had bestowed upon their contents.

For the inquiries that were made of him whether he had such and such a book taught him what he could sell and what he could not; how much he could get for this, and how much for that. Having made ever such a little beginning with books, he took to attending book sales as well as clothes sales, and ere long this branch of his business became no less important than the tailoring, and would, I have no doubt, have been the one which he would have settled down to exclusively, if he had been called upon to remain a tradesman; but this is anticipating.

I made a contribution and a stipulation. Ernest wanted to sink the gentleman completely, until such time as he could work his way up again. If he had been left to himself he would have lived with Ellen in the shop back-parlour and kitchen, and have let out both the upper floors according to his original programme. I did not want him, however, to cut himself adrift from music, letters and polite life, and feared that unless he had some kind of den into which he could retire he would ere long become the tradesman and nothing else. I therefore insisted on taking the first floor front and back myself, and furnishing them with the things which had been left at Mrs Jupp's. I bought these things off him for a small sum and had them moved into his present abode. I went to Mrs Jupp's to arrange all this, as Ernest did not like going to Ashpit Place. I had half expected to find the furniture sold and Mrs Jupp gone, but it was not so; with all her faults the woman was perfectly honest.

I told her that Pryer had taken all Ernest's money and run

away with it. She hated Pryer. 'I never knew anyone,' she exclaimed, 'as white-livered in the face as that Pryer; he hasn't got an upright vein in his whole body. Why, all that time when he used to come breakfasting with Mr Pontifex morning after morning, it took me to a perfect shadow the way he carried on. There was no doing anything to please him right. First I used to get them eggs and bacon, and he didn't like that; and then I got him a bit of fish, and he didn't like that, or else it was too dear, and you know fish is dearer than ever; and then I got him a bit of German, and he said it rose on him; then I tried sausages, and he said they hit him in the eye worse even than German; oh! how I used to wander my room and fret about it inwardly and cry for hours, and all about them paltry breakfasts – and it wasn't Mr Pontifex; he'd like anything that anyone chose to give him.

'And so the piano's to go,' she continued, 'What beautiful tunes Mr Pontifex did play upon it, to be sure; and there was one I liked better than any I ever heard. I was in the room when he played it once and when I said, "Oh, Mr Pontifex, that's the kind of woman I am," he said, "No, Mrs Jupp, it isn't, for this tune is old, but no one can say you are old," But, bless you, he meant nothing by it, it was only his mucky flattery.'

Like myself, she was vexed at his getting married. She didn't like his being married, and she didn't like his not being married – but, anyhow, it was Ellen's fault, not his, and she hoped he would be happy. 'But after all,' she concluded, 'it ain't you and it ain't me, and it ain't him and it ain't her. It's what you must call the fortunes of matterimony, for there ain't no other word for it.'

In the course of the afternoon the furniture arrived at Ernest's new abode. In the first floor we placed the piano, table, pictures, bookshelves, a couple of armchairs, and all the little household gods which he had brought from Cambridge. The back room was furnished exactly as his bedroom at Ashpit Place had been – new things being got for the bridal appartment downstairs. These two first-floor rooms I insisted on retaining as my own, but Ernest was to use them whenever he pleased; he was never to sublet even the bedroom, but was to keep it for himself in case his wife should be ill at any time, or in case he might be ill himself.

In less than a fortnight from the time of his leaving prison all these arrangements had been completed, and Ernest felt that he had again linked himself on to the life which he had led before his imprisonment – with a few important differences, however, which were greatly to his advantage. He was no longer a clergy-man; he was about to marry a woman to whom he was much attached, and he had parted company for ever with his father and mother.

True, he had lost all his money, his reputation, and his position as a gentleman; he had, in fact, had to burn his house down in order to get his roast sucking pig; but if asked whether he would rather be as he was new, or as he was on the day before his arrest, he would not have had a moment's hesitation in preferring his present to his past. If his present could only have been purchased at the expense of all that he had gone through, it was still worth purchasing at the price, and he would go through it all again if necessary. The loss of the money was the worst, but Ellen said she was sure they would get on, and she knew all about it. As for the loss of reputation – considering that he had Ellen and me left, it did not come to much.

I saw the house on the afternoon of the day on which all was finished, and there remained nothing but to buy some stock and begin selling. When I was gone, after he had had his tea, he stole up to his castle – the first floor front. He lit his pipe and sat down to the piano. He played Handel for an hour or so, and then set himself to the table to read and write. He took all his sermons and all the theological works he had begun to compose during the time he had been clergyman and put them in the fire; as he saw them consume he felt as though he had got rid of another incubus. Then he took up some of the little pieces he had begun to write during the latter part of his undergraduate life at Cambridge and began to cut them about and re-write them. As he worked quietly at these till he heard the clock strike ten and it was time to go to bed, he felt that he was now not only happy but supremely happy.

Next day Ellen took him to Debenham's auction rooms, and they surveyed the lots of clothes which were hung up all round the auction room to be viewed. Ellen had had sufficient experience to know about how much each lot ought to fetch; she overhauled lot after lot, and valued it; in a very short time Ernest himself began to have a pretty fair idea what each lot should go for, and before the morning was over valued a dozen lots running at prices about which Ellen said he would not hurt if he could get them for that.

So far from disliking this work or finding it tedious he liked it very much, indeed he would have liked anything which did not overtax his physical strength, and which held out a prospect of bringing him in money. Ellen would not let him buy anything on the occasion of this sale; she said he had better see one sale first and watch how prices actually went. So at twelve o'clock when the sale began, he saw the lots sold which he and Ellen had marked, and by the time the sale was over he knew enough to be able to bid with safety whenever he should actually want to buy. Knowledge of this sort is very easily acquired by anyone who is in *bone fide* want of it.

But Ellen did not want him to buy at auctions – not much at least at present. Private dealing, she said, was best. If I, for example, had any cast-off clothes, he was to buy them from my laundress, and get a connection with other laundresses, to whom he might give a trifle more than they got at present for whatever clothes their masters might give them, and yet make a good profit. If gentlemen sold their things, he was to try and get them to sell to him. He flinched at nothing; perhaps he would have flinched if he had had any idea how *outré* his proceedings were, but the very ignorance of the world which had ruined him up till now, by a happy irony began to work its own cure. If some malignant fairy had meant to curse him in this respect, she had overdone her malice. He did not know he was doing anything strange. He only knew that he had no money, and must provide for himself, a wife, and a possible family. More than this, he wanted to have some leisure in an evening, so that he might read and write and keep up his music. If anyone would show him how he could do better than he was doing, he should be much obliged to them, but to himself it seemed that he was doing sufficiently well; for at the end of the first week the pair found they had made a clear profit of £3. In a few weeks this had increased to £4, and by the New Year they had made a profit of £5 in one week.

Ernest had by this time been married some two months, for he had stuck to his original plan of marrying Ellen on the first day he could legally do so. This date was a little delayed by the change of abode from Laystall Street to Blackfriars, but on the first day that it could be done it was done. He had never had more than £250 a year, even in the times of his affluence, so that a profit of £5 a week, if it could be maintained steadily, would place him where he had been as far as income went, and, though he should have to feed two mouths instead of one, yet his expenses in other ways were so much curtailed by his changed social position, that, take it all round, his income was practically what it had been a twelvemonth before. The next thing to do was to increase it, and put by money.

Prosperity depends, as we all know, in great measure upon energy and good sense, but it also depends not a little upon pure luck – that is to say, upon connections which are in such a tangle that it is more easy to say that they do not exist, than to try to trace them. A neighbourhood may have an excellent reputation as being likely to be a rising one, and yet may become suddenly eclipsed by another, which no one would have thought so promising. A fever hospital may divert the stream of business, or a new station attract it; so little, indeed, can be certainly known, that it is better not to try to know more than is in everybody's mouth, and to leave the rest to chance.

Luck, which certainly had not been too kind to my hero hitherto, now seemed to have taken him under her protection. The neighbourhood prospered, and he with it. It seemed as though he no sooner bought a thing and put it into his shop, than it sold with a profit of from thirty to fifty per cent. He learned book-keeping, and watched his accounts carefully, following up any success immediately; he began to buy other things besides clothes – such as books, music, odds and ends of furniture, etc. Whether it was luck or business aptitude, or energy, or the politeness with which he treated all his customers, I cannot say – but to the surprise of no one more than himself, he went ahead faster than he had anticipated, even in his wildest dreams, and by Easter was established in a strong position as the owner of a business which was bringing him in between four and five hundred a year, and which he understood how to extend.

Chapter Seventy-Three

Ellen and he got on capitally, all the better, perhaps, because the disparity between them was so great, that neither did Ellen want to be elevated, nor did Ernest want to elevate her. He was very fond of her, and very kind to her; they had interests which they could serve in common; they had antecedents with a good part of which each was familiar; they had each of them excellent tempers, and this was enough. Ellen did not seem jealous at Ernest's preferring to sit the greater part of his time after the day's work was done in the first floor front where I occasionally visited him. She might have come and sat with him if she had liked, but, somehow or other, she generally found enough to occupy her down below. She had the tact also to encourage him to go out of an evening whenever he had a mind, without in the least caring that he should take her too – and this suited Ernest very well. He was, I should say, much happier in his married life than people generally are.

At first it had been very painful to him to meet any of his old friends, as he sometimes accidentally did, but this soon passed; either they cut him, or he cut them; it was not nice being cut for the first time or two, but after that, it became rather pleasant than not, and when he began to see that he was going ahead, he cared very little what people might say about his antecedents. The ordeal was a painful one, but if a man's moral and intellectual constitution are naturally sound, there is nothing which will give him so much strength of character as having been well cut.

It was easy for him to keep his expenditure down, for his tastes were not luxurious. He liked theatres, outings into the country on a Sunday, and tobacco, but he did not care for much else, except writing and music. As for the usual run of concerts, he hated them. He worshipped Handel; he liked Offenbach, and the airs that went about the streets, but he cared nothing between these two extremes. Music, therefore, cost him little. As for theatres, I got him and Ellen as many orders as they liked, so these cost them nothing. The Sunday outings were a small item; for a shilling or two he could get a return ticket to some place far enough out of town to give him a good walk and a thorough change for the day. Ellen went with him the first few times, but she said she found it too much for her, there were a few of her old friends whom she should sometimes like to see, and they and he, she said, would not hit it off perhaps too well, so it would be better for him to go alone. This seemed so sensible, and suited Ernest so exactly that he readily fell into it, nor did he suspect dangers which were apparent enough to me when I heard how she had treated the matter. I kept silence, however, and for a time all continued to go well. As I have said, one of his chief pleasures was in writing. If a man carries with him a little sketch book and is continually jotting down sketches, he has the artistic instinct; a hundred things may hinder his due development, but the instinct is there. The literary instinct may be known by a man's keeping a small notebook in his waistcoat pocket, into which he jots down anything that strikes him, or any good thing that he hears said, or a reference to any passage which he thinks will come in useful to him. Ernest had such a notebook always with him. Even when he was at Cambridge he had begun the practice without anyone's having suggested it to him. These notes he copied out from time to time into a book, which as they accumulated he was driven into indexing approximately as he went along. When I found out this, I knew that he had the literary instinct, and when I saw his notes I began to hope great things of him.

For a long time I was disappointed. He was kept back by the nature of the subjects he chose – which were generally metaphysical. In vain I tried to get him away from these to matters which had a greater interest for the general public. When I begged him to try his hand at some pretty, graceful, little story which should be full of whatever people knew and liked best, he would immediately set to work upon a treatise to show the grounds on which all belief rested.

'You are stirring mud,' said I, 'or poking at a sleeping dog. You are trying to make people resume consciousness about things, which, with sensible men, have already passed into the unconscious stage. The men whom you would disturb are in front of you, and not, as you fancy, behind you; it is you who are the lagger, not they.'

He could not see it. He said he was engaged on an essay upon the famous *quod semper, quod ubique, quod ab omnibus** of St Vincent de Lerins. This was the more provoking because he showed himself able to do better things if he had liked.

I was then at work upon my burlesque 'The Impatient Griselda,' and was sometimes at my wits' end for a piece of business or a situation; he gave me many suggestions, all of which were marked by excellent good sense. Nevertheless, I could not prevail with him to put philosophy on one side, and was obliged to leave him to himself.

For a long time, as I have said, his choice of subjects continued to be such as I could not approve. He was continually studying scientific and metaphysical writers, in the hope of either finding or making for himself a philosopher's stone in the shape of a system which should, go on all fours under all circumstances, instead of being liable to be upset at every touch and turn, as every system yet promulgated has turned out to be. He kept to the pursuit of this will-o'-the-wisp so long that I gave up hope, and set him down as another fly that had been caught, as it were, by a piece of paper daubed over with some sticky stuff that had not even the merit of being sweet, but to my surprise he at last declared that he was satisfied, and had found what he wanted.

I supposed that he had only hit upon some new 'Lo, here!'

* 'what [has been accepted] always, everywhere, and by all'.

when to my relief he told me that he had concluded that no system which should go perfectly upon all fours was possible, inasmuch as no one could get behind Bishop Berkeley, and therefore no absolutely incontrovertible first premise could ever be laid. Having found this he was just as well pleased as if he had found the most perfect system imaginable. All he wanted, he said, was to know which way it was to be – that is to say whether a system was possible or not, and if possible then what the system was to be. Having found out that no system based on absolute certainty was possible he was contented.

I had only a very vague idea who Bishop Berkeley was, but was thankful to him for having defended us from an incontrovertible first premise. I am afraid I said a few words implying that after a great deal of trouble he had arrived at the conclusion which sensible people reach without bothering their brains so much.

He said: 'Yes, but I was not born sensible. A child of ordinary powers learns to walk at a year or two old without knowing much about it; failing ordinary powers he had better learn laboriously than never learn at all. I am sorry I was not stronger, but to do as I did was my only chance.'

He looked so meek that I was vexed with myself for having said what I had, more especially when I remembered his bringing-up, which had doubtless done much to impair his power of taking a commonsense view of things. He continued –

'I see it all now. The people like Towneley are the only ones who know anything that is worth knowing, and like that of course I can never be. But to make Towneleys possible there must be hewers of wood and drawers of water – men, in fact, through whom conscious knowledge must pass before it can reach those who can apply it gracefully and instinctively as the Towneleys can. I am a hewer of wood, but if I accept the position frankly and do not set up to be a Towneley, it does not matter.'

He still, therefore, stuck to science instead of turning to literature proper as I hoped he would have done, but he confined himself henceforth to inquiries on specific subjects concerning which an increase of our knowledge – as he said – was possible.

Having, in fact, after infinite vexation of spirit, arrived at a conclusion which cut at the roots of all knowledge, he settled contentedly down to the pursuit of knowledge, and has pursued it ever since in spite of occasional excursions into the regions of literature proper.

But this is anticipating, and may perhaps also convey a wrong impression, for from the outset he did occasionally turn his attention to work which must be more properly called literary than either scientific or metaphysical.

Chapter Seventy-Four

About six months after he had set up his shop his prosperity had reached its climax. It seemed even then as though he were likely to go ahead no less fast then heretofore, and I doubt not that he would have done so, if success or non-success had depended upon himself alone. Unfortunately he was not the only person to be reckoned with.

One morning he had gone out to attend some sales, leaving his wife perfectly well, as usual in good spirits and looking very pretty. When he came back he found her sitting on a chair in the back parlour, with her hair over her face, sobbing and crying as though her heart would break. She said she had been frightened in the morning by a man who had pretended to be a customer, and had threatened her unless she gave him some things, and she had to give them to him in order to save herself from violence; she had been in hysterics ever since the man had gone. This was her story, but her speech was so incoherent that it was not easy to make out what she said. Ernest knew she was with child, and thinking this might have something to do with the matter would have sent for a doctor if Ellen had not begged him not to do so.

Anyone who had had experience of drunken people would have seen at a glance what the matter was, but my hero knew nothing about them – nothing, that is to say, about the drunkenness of the habitual drunkard, which shows itself very differently from that of one who gets drunk only once in a way. The idea that his wife could drink had never even crossed his mind, indeed she always made a fuss about taking more than a very little beer and never touched spirits. He did not know much more about hysterics than he did about drunkenness, but he had always heard that women who were about to become mothers were liable to be easily upset and were often rather flighty, so he was not greatly surprised, and thought he had settled the matter by registering the discovery that being about to become a father has its troublesome as well as its pleasant side.

The great change in Ellen's life consequent upon her meeting Ernest and getting married had for a time actually sobered her by shaking her out of her old ways. Drunkenness is so much a matter of habit, and habit so much a matter of surroundings, and if you completely change the surroundings you will sometimes get rid of the drunkenness altogether. Ellen had intended remaining always sober henceforward, and never having had so long a steady fit before, believed she was now cured. So she perhaps would have been if she had seen none of her old acquaintances. When, however, her new life was beginning to lose its newness, and when her old acquaintances came to see her, her present surroundings became more like her past, and on this she herself began to get like her past too. At first she only got a little tipsy and struggled against a relapse; but it was no use, she soon lost the heart to fight, and now her object was not to try and keep sober, but to get gin without her husband's finding out.

So the hysterics continued, and she managed to make her husband still think they were due to her being about to become a mother. The worse her attacks were, the more devoted he became in his attention to her. At last he insisted that a doctor should see her. The doctor, of course, took in the situation at a glance, but said nothing to Ernest except in such a guarded way that he did not understand the hints that were thrown out to him. He was much too downright and matter of fact to be quick at taking hints of this sort. He hoped that as soon as his wife's confinement was over she would regain her health, and had no thought save how to spare her as far as possible till that happy time should come.

In the mornings she was generally better, as long that is to say as Ernest remained at home; but he had to go out buying, and on his return would generally find that she had had another attack as soon as he had left the house. At times she would laugh and cry for half an hour together, at others she would lie in a semi-comatose state upon the bed, and when he came back he would find that the shop had been neglected and all the work of the household left undone. Still he took it for granted that this was all part of the usual course when women were going to become mothers, and when Ellen's share of the work settled down more and more upon his own shoulders he did it all and drudged away without a murmur. Nevertheless, he began to feel in a vague way more as he had felt in Ashpit Place, at Roughborough or at Battersby, and to lose the buoyancy of spirits which had made another man of him during the first six months of his married life.

It was not only that he had to do so much household work, for even the cooking, cleaning up slops, bed-making and fire-lighting ere long devolved upon him, but his business no longer prospered. He could buy as hitherto, but Ellen seemed unable to sell as she had sold at first. The fact was that she sold as well as ever, but kept back part of the proceeds in order to buy gin, and she did this more and more till even the unsuspecting Ernest ought to have seen that she was not telling the truth. When she sold better – that is to say when she did not think it safe to keep back more than a certain amount, she got money out of him on the plea that she had a longing for this or that, and that it would perhaps irreparably damage the baby if her longing was denied her. All seemed right, reasonable, and unavoidable, nevertheless Ernest saw that until the confinement was over he was likely to have a hard time of it. All, however, would then come right again.

Chapter Seventy-Five

In the month of September, 1860, a girl was born, and Ernest was proud and happy. The birth of the child, and a rather alarming talk which the doctor had given to Ellen sobered her for a few weeks, and it really seemed as though his hopes were about to be fulfilled. The expenses of his wife's confinement were heavy, and he was obliged to trench upon his savings, and he had no doubt about soon recouping this now that Ellen was herself again; for a time indeed his business did revive a little, nevertheless it seemed as though the interruption to his prosperity had in some way broken the spell of good luck which had attended him in the outset; he was still sanguine, however, and worked night and day with a will, but there was no more music, or reading, or writing now. His Sunday outings were put a stop to, and but for the first floor being let to myself, he would have lost his citadel there too, but he seldom used it, for Ellen had to wait more and more upon the baby, and, as a consequence, Ernest had to wait more and more upon Ellen.

One afternoon, about a couple of months after the baby had been born, and just as my happy hero was beginning to feel more hopeful and therefore better able to bear his burdens, he returned from a sale, and found Ellen in the same hysterical condition that he had found her in the spring. She said she was again with child, and Ernest still believed her.

All the troubles of the preceding six months began again then and there, and grew worse and worse continually. Money did not come in quickly, for Ellen cheated him by keeping it back and dealing improperly with the goods he bought. When it did come in she got it out of him as before on pretexts which it seemed inhuman to inquire into. It was always the same story. By and by a new feature began to show itself. Ernest had inherited his father's punctuality and exactness as regards money; he liked to know the worst of what he had to pay at once; he hated having expenses sprung upon him which if not foreseen might and ought to have been so, but now bills began to be brought to him for things ordered by Ellen without his knowledge, or for which he had already given her the money. This was awful, and even Ernest turned. When he remonstrated with her – not for having bought the things, but for having said nothing to him about the moneys being owing – Ellen met him with hysteria and there was a scene. She had now pretty well forgotten the hard times she had known when she had been on her own resources and reproached him downright with having married her – on that moment the scales fell from Ernest's eyes as they had fallen when Towneley had said, 'No, no, no.' He said nothing, but he woke up once for all to the fact that he had made a mistake in marrying. A touch had again come which had revealed him to himself.

He went upstairs to the disused citadel, flung himself into the arm-chair, and covered his face with his hands.

He still did nor know that his wife drank, but he could no longer trust her, and his dream of happiness was over. He had been saved from the Church – so as by fire, but still saved – but what could now save him from his marriage? He had made the same mistake that he had made in wedding himself to the Church, but with a hundred times worse results. He had learnt nothing by experience: he was an Esau – one of those wretches, whose hearts the Lord had hardened, who, having ears, heard not, having eyes saw not, and who should find no place for repentance though they sought it even with tears.

Yet had he not on the whole tried to find out what the ways of God were, and to follow them in singleness of heart? To a certain extent, yes; but he had not been thorough; he had not given up all for God. He knew that very well; he had done little as compared with what he might and ought to have done, but still if he was being punished for this, God was a hard taskmaster, and one, too, who was continually pouncing out upon his unhappy creatures from ambuscades. In marrying Ellen he had meant to avoid a life of sin, and to take the course he believed to be moral and right. With his antecedents and surroundings it was the most natural thing in the world for him to have done, yet in what a frightful position had not his morality landed him. Could any amount of immorality have placed him in a much worse one? What was morality worth if it was not that which on the whole brought a man peace at the last, and could anyone have reasonable certainty that marriage would do this? It seemed to him that in his attempt to be moral he had been following a devil which had disguised itself as an angel of light. But if so, what ground was there on which a man might rest the sole of his foot and tread in reasonable safety?

He was still too young to reach the answer, 'On common sense' – an answer which he would have felt to be unworthy of anyone who had an ideal standard.

However this might be, it was plain that he had now done for himself. It had been thus with him all his life. If there had come at any time a gleam of sunshine and hope, it was to be obscured immediately – why, prison was happier than this! There, at any rate, he had had no money anxieties, and these were beginning to weigh upon him now with all their horrors. He was happier even now than he had been at Battersby or at Roughborough, and would not now go back, even if he could, to his Cambridge life, but for all that the outlook was so gloomy, in fact so hopeless, that he felt as if he could have only too gladly gone to sleep and died in his arm-chair once for all.

As he was musing thus and looking upon the wreck of his hopes – for he saw well enough that as long as he was linked to Ellen he should never rise as he had dreamed of doing – he heard a noise below, and presently a neighbour ran upstairs and entered his room hurriedly –

'Good gracious, Mr Pontifex,' she exclaimed, 'for goodness' sake come down quickly and help. Mrs Pontifex is took with the horrors – and she's orkard.'

The unhappy man came down as he was bid and found his wife mad with *delirium tremens.*

He knew all now. The neighbours thought he must have known that his wife drank all along, but Ellen had been so artful, and he so simple, that, as I have said, he had had no suspicion. 'Why,' said the woman who had summoned him, 'she'll drink anything she can stand up and pay her money for.' Ernest could hardly believe his ears, but when the doctor had seen his wife and she had become more quiet, he went over to the public-house hard by and made inquiries, the result of which rendered further doubt impossible. The publican took the opportunity to present my hero with a bill of several pounds for bottles of spirits supplied to his wife, and what with his wife's confinement and the way business had fallen off, he had not the money to pay with for the sum exceeded the remnant of this savings.

He came to me – not for money, but to tell me his miserable story. I had seen for some time that there was something wrong, and had suspected pretty shrewdly what the matter was, but of course I said nothing. Ernest and I had been growing apart for some time. I was vexed at his having married, and he knew I was vexed, though I did my best to hide it.

A man's friendships are, like his will, invalidated by marriage – but they are also no less invalidated by the marriage of his friends. The rift in friendship which invariably makes its appearance on the marriage of either of the parties to it was fast widening, as it no less invariably does, to the great gulf which is fixed between the married and the unmarried, and I was beginning to leave my *protégé* to a fate with which I had neither right nor power to meddle. In fact, I had begun to feel him rather a burden; I did not so much mind this when I could be of use, but I grudged it when I could be of none. He had made his bed and he must lie upon it.

Ernest had felt all this and had seldom come near me till now, one evening late in 1860, he called on me, and with a very woe-begone face told me his troubles.

As soon as I found that he no longer liked his wife I forgave him at once and was as much interested in him as ever. There is nothing an old bachelor likes better than to find a married man who wishes he had not got married – especially when the case is such an extreme one that he need not pretend to hope that matters will come all right again, or encourage his young friend to make the best of it.

I was myself in favour of a separation, and said I would make Ellen an allowance myself – of course intending that it should come out of Ernest's money; but he would not hear of this. He had married Ellen, he said, and he must try to reform her. He hated it, but he must try; and finding him as usual very obstinate I was obliged to acquiesce, though with little confidence as to the result. I was vexed at seeing him waste himself upon such a barren task, and again began to feel him burdensome. I am afraid I showed this, for he again avoided me for some time, and, indeed, for many months I hardly saw him at all. Ellen remained very ill for some days, and then gradually recovered. Ernest hardly left her till she was out of danger. When she had recovered he got the doctor to tell her that if she had another attack she would certainly die; this so frightened her that she took the pledge.

Then he became more hopeful again. When she was sober she was just what she was during the first days of her married life, and so quick was he to forget pain that after a few days he was as fond of her as ever. But Ellen could not forgive him for knowing what he did. She knew that he was on the watch to shield her from temptation, and though he did his best to make her think that he had no further uneasiness about her, she found the burden of her union with respectability grow more and more heavy upon her, and looked back more and more longingly upon the lawless freedom of the life she had led before she met her husband.

I will dwell no longer on this part of my story. During the spring months of 1861 she kept straight – she had had her fling of dissipation, and this, together with the impression made upon her by her having taken the pledge, tamed her for a while. The shop went fairly well, and enabled Ernest to make the two ends meet. In the spring and summer of 1861 he even put by a little money again. In the autumn his wife was confined of a boy – a very fine one, so everybody said. She soon recovered, and Ernest was beginning to breathe freely and be almost sanguine when, without a word of warning, the storm broke again. He returned one afternoon about two years after his marriage, and found his wife lying upon the floor insensible.

From this time he became hopeless, and began to go visibly down hill. He had been knocked about too much, and the luck had gone too long against him. The wear and tear of the last three years had told on him, and though not actually ill he was over-worked, below part, and unfit for any further burden.

He struggled for a while to prevent himself from finding this out, but the facts were too strong for him. Again he called on me and told me what had happened. I was glad the crisis had come; I was sorry for Ellen, but a complete separation from her was the only chance for her husband. Even after this last outbreak he was unwilling to consent to this, and talked nonsense about dying at his post, till I got tired of him. Each time I saw him the old gloom had settled more and more deeply upon his face, and I had about made up my mind to put an end to the situation by a *coup de main*, such as bribing Ellen to run away with somebody else, or something of that kind, when matters settled themselves as usual in a way which I had not anticipated.

Chapter Seventy-Six

The winter had been a trying one. Ernest had only paid his way by selling his piano. With this he seemed to cut away the last link that connected him with his earlier life, and to sink once for all into the small shopkeeper. It seemed to him that however low he might sink his pain could not last much longer, for he should simply die if it did.

He hated Ellen now, and the pair lived in open want of harmony with each other. If it had not been for her children, he would have left her and gone to America, but he could not leave his children with Ellen, and as for taking them with him he did not know how to do it, nor what to do with them when he had got them to America. If he had not lost energy he would probably in the end have taken the children and gone off, but his nerve was shaken, so day after day went by and nothing was done.

He had only got a few shillings in the world now, except the value of his stock, which was very little; he could get perhaps £3 or £4 by selling his music and what few pictures and pieces of furniture still belonged to him. He thought of trying to live by his pen, but his writing had dropped off long ago; he no longer had an idea in his head. Look which way he would he saw no hope; the end, if it had not actually come, was within easy distance and he was almost face to face with actual want. When he saw people going about poorly clad, or even without shoes and stockings, he wondered whether within a few months' time he too should not have to go about in this way. The remorseless, resistless hand of fate had caught him in its grip and was dragging him down, down, down. Still he staggered on, going his daily rounds, buying second-hand clothes, and spending his evenings in cleaning and mending them.

One morning, as he was returning from a house at the West End where he had bought some clothes from one of the servants, he was struck by a small crowd which had gathered round a space that had been railed off on the grass near one of the paths in the Green Park.

It was a lovely soft spring morning at the end of March, and unusually balmy for the time of year; even Ernest's melancholy was relieved for a while by the look of spring that pervaded earth and sky; but it soon returned, and smiling sadly he said to himself: 'It may bring hope to others, but for me there can be no hope henceforth.'

As these words were in his mind he joined the small crowd who were gathered round the railings, and saw that they were looking at three sheep with very small lambs only a day or two old, which had been penned off for shelter and protection from the others that ranged the park.

They were very pretty, and Londoners so seldom get a chance of seeing lambs that it was no wonder every one stopped to look at them. Ernest observed that no one seemed fonder of them than a great lubberly butcher boy, who leaned up against the railings with a tray of meat upon his shoulder. He was looking at this boy and smiling at the grotesqueness of his admiration, when he became aware that he was being watched intently by a man in coachman's livery, who had also stopped to admire the lambs, and was leaning against the opposite side of the enclosure. Ernest knew him in a moment as John, his father's old coachman at Battersby, and went up to him at once.

'Why, Master Ernest,' said he, with his strong northern accent, 'I was thinking of you only this very morning,' and the pair shook hands heartily. John was in an excellent place at the West End. He had done very well, he said, ever since he had left Battersby, except for the first year or two, and that, he said with a screw of the face, had well nigh broke him.

Ernest asked how this was.

'Why, you see,' said John, 'I was always main fond of that lass Ellen, whom you remember running after, Master Ernest, and giving your watch to. I expect you haven't forgotten that day, have you?' And here he laughed. 'I don't know as I be the father of the child she carried away with her from Battersby, but I very easily may have been. Anyhow, after I had left your papa's place a few days I wrote to Ellen to an address we had agreed upon, and told her I would do what I ought to do, and so I did, for I married her within a month afterwards. Why, Lord love the man, whatever is the matter with him?' – for as he had spoken the last few words of his story Ernest had turned white as a sheet, and was leaning against the railings.

'John,' said my hero, gasping for breath, 'are you sure of what you say – are you quite sure you really married her?'

'Of course I am,' said John, 'I married her before the registrar at Letchbury on the 15th of August, 1851.'

'Give me your arm,' said Ernest, 'and take me into Piccadilly, and put me into a cab, and come with me at once, if you can spare time, to Mr Overton's at the Temple.'

Chapter Seventy-Seven

I do not think Ernest himself was much more pleased at finding that he had never been married than I was. To him, however, the shock of pleasure was positively numbing in its intensity. As he felt his burden removed, he reeled for the unaccustomed lightness of his movements; his position was so shattered that his identity seemed to have been shattered also; he was one waking up from a horrible nightmare to find himself safe and sound in bed, but who can hardly even yet believe that the room is not full of armed men who are about to spring upon him.

'And it is I,' he said, 'who not an hour ago complained that I was without hope. It is I, who for weeks have been railing at fortune, and saying that though she smiled on others she never smiled at me. Why, never was anyone half so fortunate as I am.'

'Yes,' said I, 'you have been inoculated for marriage, and have recovered.'

'And yet,' he said, 'I was very fond of her till she took to drinking.'

'Perhaps; but is it not Tennyson who has said: "'Tis better to have loved and lost, than never to have lost at all"?'

'You are an inveterate bachelor,' was the rejoinder.

Then we had a long talk with John, to whom I gave a £5 note upon the spot. He said, 'Ellen had used to drink at Battersby; the cook had taught her; he had known it, but was so fond of her that he had chanced it and married her to save her from the streets and in the hope of being able to keep her straight. She had done with him just as she had done with Ernest – made him an excellent wife as long as she kept sober, but a very bad one afterwards.'

'There isn't,' said John, 'a sweeter-tempered, handier, prettier girl than she was in all England, nor one as knows better what a man likes, and how to make him happy, if you can keep her from drink; but you can't keep her; she's that artful she'll get it under your very eyes, without you knowing it. If she can't get any more of your things to pawn or sell, she'll steal her neighbours'. That's how she got into trouble first when I was with her. During the six months she was in prison I should have felt happy if I had not known she would come out again. And then she did come out, and before she had been free a fortnight, she began shop-lifting and going on the loose again – and all to get money to drink with. So seeing I could do nothing with her and that she was just a-killing of me, I left her, and came up to London, and went into service again, and I did not know what had become of her till you and Mr Ernest told me. I hope you'll neither of you say you've seen me.'

We assured him we would keep his counsel, and then he left us, with many protestations of affection towards Ernest, to whom he had been always much attached.

We talked the situation over, and decided first to get the children away, and then to come to terms with Ellen concerning their future custody; as for herself, I proposed that we should make her an allowance of, say, a pound a week to be paid so long as she gave no trouble. Ernest did not see where the pound a week was to come from, so I eased his mind by saying I would pay it myself. Before the day was two hours older we had got the children, about whom Ellen had always appeared to be indifferent, and had confided them to the care of my laundress, a good motherly sort of woman, who took to them and to whom they took at once.

Then came the odious task of getting rid of their unhappy mother. Ernest's heart smote him at the notion of the shock the break-up would be to her. He was always thinking that people had a claim upon him for some inestimable service they had rendered him, or for some irreparable mischief done to them by himself; the case, however, was so clear, that Ernest's scruples did not offer serious resistance.

I did not see why he should have the pain of another interview with his wife, so I got Mr Ottery to manage the whole business. It turned out that we need not have harrowed ourselves so much about the agony of mind which Ellen would suffer on becoming an outcast again. Ernest saw Mrs Richards, the neighbour who had called him down on the night when he had first discovered his wife's drunkenness, and got from her some details of Ellen's opinions upon the matter. She did not seem in the least conscience-stricken; she said: 'Thank goodness, at last!' And although aware that her marriage was not a valid one, evidently regarded this as a mere detail which it would not be worth anybody's while to go into more particularly. As regards his breaking with her, she said it was a good job both for him and for her.

'This life,' she continued, 'don't suit me. Ernest is too good for me; he wants a woman as shall be a bit better than me, and I want a man that shall be a bit worse than him. We should have got on all very well if we had not lived together as married folks, but I've been used to have a little place of my own, however small, for a many years, and I don't want Ernest, or any other man, always hanging about it. Besides, he is too steady: his being in prison hasn't done him a bit of good – he's just as grave as those as have never been in prison at all, and he never swears nor curses, come what may; it makes me afeared of him, and therefore I drink the worse. What us poor girls wants is not to be jumped up all of a sudden and made honest women of; this is too much for us and throws us off our perch; what we wants is a regular friend or two, who'll just keep us from starving, and force us to be good for a bit together now and again. That's about as much as we can stand. He may have the children; he can do better for them than I can; and as for his money, he may give it or keep it as he likes, he's never done me any harm, and I shall let him alone; but if he means me to have it, I suppose I'd better have it.' – And have it she did.

'And I,' thought Ernest to himself again when the arrangement was concluded, 'am the man who thought himself unlucky!'

I may as well say here all that need be said further about Ellen. For the next three years she used to call regularly at Mr Ottery's every Monday morning for her pound. She was always neatly dressed, and looked so quiet and pretty that no one would have suspected her antecedents. At first she wanted sometimes to anticipate, but after three or four ineffectual attempts – on each of which occasions she told a most pitiful story – she gave it up and took her money regularly without a word. Once she came with a bad black eye, 'which a boy had throwed a stone and hit her by mistake'; but on the whole she looked pretty much the same at the end of the three years as she had done at the beginning. Then she explained that she was going to be married again. Mr Ottery saw her on this, and pointed out to her that she would very likely be again committing bigamy by doing so. 'You may call it what you like,' she replied, 'but I am going off to America with Bill the butcher's man, and we hope Mr Pontifex won't be too hard on us and stop the allowance.' Ernest was little likely to do this, so the pair went in peace. I believe it was Bill who had blacked her eye, and she liked him all the better for it.

From one or two little things I have been able to gather that the couple got on very well together, and that in Bill she has found a partner better suited to her than either John or Ernest. On his birthday Ernest generally receives an envelope with an American post-mark containing a book-marker with a flaunting text upon it, or a moral kettleholder, or some other similar small token of recognition, but no letter. Of the children she has taken no notice.

Chapter Seventy-Eight

Ernest was now well turned twenty-six years old, and in little more than another year and a half would come into possession of his money. I saw no reason for letting him have it earlier than the date fixed by Miss Pontifex herself; at the same time I did not like his continuing the shop at Blackfriars after the present crisis. It was not till now that I fully understood how much he had suffered nor how nearly his supposed wife's habits had brought him to actual want.

I had indeed noted the old wan worn look settling upon his face, but was either too indolent or too hopeless of being able to sustain a protracted and successful warfare with Ellen to extend the sympathy and make the inquiries which I suppose I ought to have made. And yet I hardly know what I could have done, for nothing short of his finding out what he had found out would have detached him from his wife, and nothing could do him much good as long as he continued to live with her.

After all I suppose I was right; I suppose things did turn out all the better in the end for having been left to settle themselves – at any rate whether they did or did not, the whole thing was in too great a muddle for me to venture to tackle it so long as Ellen was upon the scene; now, however, that she was removed, all my interest in my godson revived, and I turned over many times in my mind what I had better do with him.

It was now three and a half years since he had come up to London and begun to live, so to speak, upon his own account. Of these years, six months had been spent as a clergyman, six months in gaol, and for two and a half years he had been acquiring two-fold experience in the ways of business and of marriage. He had failed, I may say, in everything that he had undertaken, even as a prisoner; yet his defeats had been always, as it seemed to me, something so like victories, that I was satisfied of his being worth all the pains I could bestow upon him; my only fear was lest I should meddle with him when it might be better for him to be let alone. On the whole I concluded that a three and a half years' apprenticeship to a rough life was enough; the shop had done much for him; it had kept him going after a fashion, when he was in great need; it had thrown him upon his own resources, and taught him to see profitable openings all around him, where a few months before he would have seen nothing but insuperable difficulties; it had enlarged his sympathies by making him understand the lower classes, and not confining his view of life to that taken by gentlemen only. When he went about the streets and saw the books outside the second-hand book-stalls, the bric-a-brac in the curiosity shops, and the infinite commercial activity which is omnipresent around us, he understood it and sympathised with it as he could never have done if he had not kept a shop himself.

He has often told me that when he used to travel on a railway that overlooked populous suburbs, and looked down upon street after street of dingy houses, he used to wonder what kind of people lived in them, what they did and felt, and how far it was like what he did and felt himself. Now, he said he knew all about it. I am not very familiar with the writer of the Odyssey (who, by the way, I suspect strongly of having been a clergyman) but he assuredly hit the right nail on the head when he epitomised his typical wise man as knowing 'the ways and farings of many men.' What culture is comparable to this? What a lie, what a sickly debilitating debauch did not Ernest's school and university career now seem to him, in comparison with his life in prison and as a tailor in Blackfriars. I have heard him say he would have gone through all he had suffered if it were only for the deeper insight it gave him into the spirit of the Grecian and the Surrey pantomimes. What confidence again in his own power to swim if thrown into deep waters had not he won through his experiences during the last three years!

But, as I have said, I thought my godson had now seen as much of the undercurrents of life as was likely to be of use to him, and that it was time he began to live in a style more suitable to his prospects. His aunt had wished him to kiss the soil, and he had kissed it with a vengeance; but I did not like the notion of his coming suddenly from the position of a small shopkeeper to that of a man with an income of between three and four thousand a year. Too sudden a jump from bad fortune to good is just as dangerous as one from good to bad; besides, poverty is very wearing; it is a quasi-embryonic condition, through which a man had better pass if he is to hold his later developments securely, but like measles or scarlet fever, he had better have it mildly and get it over early.

No man is safe from losing every penny he has in the world, unless he has had his facer. How often do I not hear middle-aged women and quiet family men say that they have no speculative tendency; *they* never had touched, and never would touch, any but the *very* soundest, best reputed investments, and as for unlimited liability, oh dear! dear! and they throw up their hands and eyes.

Whenever a person is heard to talk thus he may be recognised as the easy prey of the first adventurer who comes across him; he will commonly, indeed, wind up his discourse by saying that in spite of all his natural caution, and his well knowing how foolish speculation is, yet there are some investments which are called speculative but in reality are not so, and he will pull out of his pocket the prospectus of a Cornish gold mine. It is only on having actually lost money that one realises what an awful thing the loss of it is, and finds out how easily it is lost by those who venture out of the middle of the most beaten path. Ernest had had his facer, as he had had his attack of poverty, young, and sufficiently badly for a sensible man to be little likely to forget it. I can fancy few pieces of good fortune greater than this as happening to any man, provided, of course, that he is not damaged irretrievably.

So strongly do I feel on this subject that if I had my way I would have a speculation master attached to every school. The boys would be encouraged to read the *Money Market Review*, the *Railway News*, and all the best financial papers, and should establish a stock exchange amongst themselves in which pence should stand as pounds. Then let them see how this making haste to get rich moneys out in actual practice. There might be a prize awarded by the headmaster to the most prudent dealer, and the boys who lost their money time after time should be dismissed. Of course if any boy proved to have genius for speculation and made money – well and good, let him speculate by all means.

If Universities were not the worst teachers in the world I should like to see professorships of speculation established at Oxford and Cambridge. When I reflect, however, that the only things worth doing which Oxford and Cambridge can do well are cooking, cricket, rowing, and games, of which there is no professorship, I fear that the establishment of a professorial chair would end in teaching young men neither how to speculate, nor how not to speculate, but would simply turn them out as bad speculators.

I heard of one case in which a father actually carried my idea into practice. He wanted his son to learn how little confidence was to be placed in glowing prospectuses and flaming articles, and found him five hundred pounds which he was to invest according to his lights. The father expected he would lose the money; but it did not turn out so in practice, for the boy took so much pains and played so cautiously that the money kept growing and growing till the father took it away again, increment and all – as he was pleased to say, in self-defence.

I had made my own mistakes with money about the year 1846,

when everyone else was making them. For a few years I had been so scared and had suffered so severely, that when (owing to the good advice of the broker who had advised my father and grandfather before me) I came out in the end a winner and not a loser, I played no more pranks, but kept henceforward as nearly in the middle of the middle rut as I could. I tried in fact to keep my money rather than to make more of it. I had done with Ernest's money as with my own – that is to say I had let it alone after investing it in Midland ordinary stock according to Miss Pontifex's instructions. No amount of trouble would have been likely to have increased my godson's estate one half so much as it had increased without my taking any trouble at all.

Midland stock at the end of August, 1850, when I sold out Miss Pontifex's debentures, stood at £32 per £100. I invested the whole of Ernest's £15,000 at this price, and did not change the investment till a few months before the time of which I have been writing lately – that is to say until September, 1861. I then sold at £129 per share and invested in London and North-Western ordinary stock, which I was advised was more likely to rise than Midlands now were. I bought the London and North-Western stock at £93 per £100, and my godson now in 1882 still holds it.

The original £15,000 had increased in eleven years to over £60,000; the accumulated interest which, of course, I had reinvested, had come to about £10,000 more, so that Ernest was then worth over £70,000. At present he is worth nearly double that sum, and all as the result of leaving well alone.

Large as his property now was, it ought to be increased still further during the year and a half that remained of its minority, so that on coming of age he ought to have an income of at least £3,500 a year.

I wished him to understand book-keeping by double entry. I had myself as a young man been compelled to master this not very difficult art; having acquired it, I have become enamoured of it, and consider it the most necessary branch of any young man's education after reading and writing. I was determined, therefore, that Ernest should master it, and proposed that he should become my steward, book-keeper, and the manager of my hoardings, for so I called the sum which my ledger showed to have accumulated from £15,000 to £70,000. I told him I was going to spend the income as soon as it had amounted up to £80,000.

A few days after Ernest's discovery that he was still a bachelor, while he was still at the very beginning of the honeymoon, as it were, of his renewed unmarried life, I broached my scheme, desired him to give up his shop, and offered him £300 a year for managing (so far indeed as it required any managing) his own property. This £300 a year, I need hardly say, I made him charge to the estate.

If anything had been wanting to complete his happiness it was this. Here, within three or four days he found himself freed from one of the most hideous, hopeless *liaisons* imaginable, and at the same time raised from a life of almost squalor to the enjoyment of what would to him be a handsome income.

'A pound a week,' he thought, 'for Ellen, and the rest for myself.'

'No,' said I, 'we will charge Ellen's pound a week to the estate also. You must have a clear £300 for yourself.'

I fixed upon this sum because it was the one which Mr Disraeli gave Coningsby when Coningsby was at the lowest ebb of his fortunes. Mr Disraeli evidently thought £300 a year the smallest sum on which Coningsby could be expected to live, and make the two ends meet; with this, however, he thought his hero could manage to get along for a year or two. In 1862, of which I am now writing, prices had risen, though not so much as they have since done; on the other hand, Ernest had had less expensive antecedents than Coningsby, so on the whole I thought £300 a year would be about the right thing for him.

Chapter Seventy-Nine

The question now arose what was to be done with the children. I explained to Ernest that their expenses must be charged to the estate, and showed him how small a hole all the various items I proposed to charge would make in the income at my disposal. He was beginning to make difficulties, when I quieted him by pointing out that the money had all come to me from his aunt, over his own head, and reminded him there had been an understanding between her and me that I should do much as I was doing, if occasion should arise.

He wanted his children to be brought up in the fresh pure air, and among other children who were happy and contented; but being still ignorant of the fortune that awaited him, he insisted that they should pass their earlier years among the poor rather than the rich. I remonstrated, but he was very decided about it; and when I reflected that they were illegitimate, I was not sure but that what Ernest proposed might be as well for everyone in the end. They were still so young that it did not much matter where they were, so long as they were with kindly decent people, and in a healthy neighbourhood.

'I shall be just as unkind to my children,' he said, 'as my grandfather was to my father, or my father to me. If they did not succeed in making their children love them, neither shall I. I say to myself that I should like to do so, but so did they. I can make sure that they shall not know how much they would have hated me if they had had much to do with me, but this is all I can do. If I must ruin their prospects, let me do so at a reasonable time before they are old enough to feel it.'

He mused a little and added with a laugh:

'A man first quarrels with his father about three-quarters of a year before he is born. It is then he insists on setting up a separate establishment; when this has been once agreed to, the more complete the separation for ever after the better for both.' Then he said more seriously; 'I want to put the children where they will be well and happy, and where they will not be betrayed into the misery of false expectations.'

In the end he remembered that on his Sunday walks he had more than once seen a couple who lived on the waterside a few miles below Gravesend, just where the sea was beginning, and who he thought would do. They had a family of their own fast coming on and the children seemed to thrive; both father and mother indeed were comfortable well-grown folks, in whose hands young people would be likely to have as fair a chance of coming to a good development as in those of any whom he knew.

We went down to see this couple, and as I thought no less well of them than Ernest did, we offered them a pound a week to take the children and bring them up as though they were their own. They jumped at the offer, and in another day or two we brought the children down and left them, feeling that we had done as well as we could by them, at any rate for the present. Then Ernest sent his small stock of goods to Debenham's, gave up the house he had taken two and a half years previously, and returned to civilisation.

I had expected that he would now rapidly recover, and was disappointed to see him get as I thought decidedly worse. Indeed, before long I thought him looking so ill that I insisted on his going with me to consult one of the most eminent doctors in London. This gentleman said there was no acute disease but that my young friend was suffering from nervous prostration, the result of long and severe mental suffering, from which there was no remedy except time, prosperity and rest.

He said that Ernest must have broken down later on, but that he might have gone on for some months yet. It was the suddenness of the relief from tension which had knocked him over now.

'Cross him,' said the doctor, 'at once. Crossing is the great medical discovery of the age. Shake him out of himself by shaking something else into him.'

I had not told him that money was no object to us and I think he had reckoned me up as not over rich. He continued: 'Seeing is a mode of touching, touching is a mode of feeding, feeding is a mode of assimilation, assimilation is a mode of re-creation and reproduction, and this is crossing – shaking yourself into something else and something else into you.'

He spoke laughingly, but it was plain he was serious. He continued:

'People are always coming to me who want crossing, or change, if you prefer it, and who I know have not money enough to let them get away from London. This has set me thinking how I can best cross them even if they cannot leave home, and I have made a list of cheap London amusements which I recommend to my patients; none of them cost more than a few shillings or take more than half a day or a day.'

I explained that there was no occasion to consider money in this case.

'I am glad of it,' he said, still laughing. 'The homoeopathists use *aurum* as a medicine, but they do not give it in large doses enough; if you can dose your young friend with this pretty freely you will soon bring him round. However, Mr Pontifex is not well enough to stand so great a change as going abroad yet; from what you tell me I should think he had had as much change lately as is good for him. If he were to go abroad now he would probably be taken seriously ill within a week. We must wait till he has recovered tone a little more. I will begin by ringing my London changes on him.'

He thought a little and then said:

'I have found the Zoological Gardens of service to many of my patients. I should prescribe for Mr Pontifex a course of the larger mammals. Don't let him think he is taking them medicinally, but let him go to their house twice a week for a fortnight, and stay with the hippopotamus, the rhinoceros, and the elephants, till they begin to bore him. I find these beasts do my patients more good than any others. The monkeys are not a wide enough cross; they do not stimulate sufficiently. The larger carnivora are unsympathetic. The reptiles are worse than useless, and the marsupials are not much better. Birds, again, except parrots, are not very beneficial; he may look at them now and again, but with the elephants and the pig tribe generally he should mix just now as freely as possible.

'Then, you know, to prevent monotony I should send him, say, to morning service at the Abbey before he goes. He need not stay longer than the *Te Deum*. I don't know why, but *Jubilates* are seldom satisfactory. Just let him look in at the Abbey, and sit quietly in Poets' Corner till the main part of the music is over. Let him do this two or three times, not more, before he goes to the Zoo.

'Then next day send him down to Gravesend by boat. By all means let him go to the theatres in the evenings – and then let him come to me again in a fortnight.'

Had the doctor been less eminent in his profession I should have doubted whether he was in earnest, but I knew him to be a man of business who would neither waste his own time nor that of his patients. As soon as we were out of the house we took a cab to Regent's Park, and spent a couple of hours in sauntering round the different houses. Perhaps it was on account of what the doctor had told me, but I certainly became aware of a feeling I had never experienced before. I mean that I was receiving an influx of new life, or deriving new ways of looking at life – which is the same thing – by the process. I found the doctor quite right in his estimate of the larger mammals as the ones which on the whole were most beneficial, and observed that Ernest, who had heard nothing of what the doctor had said to me, lingered instinctively in front of them. As for the elephants, especially the baby elephant, he seemed to be drinking in large draughts of their lives to the re-creation and regeneration of his own.

We dined in the gardens, and I noticed with pleasure that Ernest's appetite was already improved. Since this time, whenever I have been a little out of sorts myself I have at once gone up to Regent's Park, and have invariably been benefited. I mention this here in the hope that some one or other of my readers may find the hint a useful one.

At the end of his fortnight my hero was much better, more so even than our friend the doctor had expected. 'Now,' he said, 'Mr Pontifex may go abroad, and the sooner the better. Let him stay a couple of months.'

This was the first Ernest had heard about his going abroad, and he talked about my not being able to spare him for so long. I soon made this all right.

'It is now the beginning of April,' said I, 'go down to Marseilles at once, and take steamer to Nice. Then saunter down the Riviera to Genoa – from Genoa go to Florence, Rome and Naples, and come home by way of Venice and the Italian lakes.'

'And won't you come too?' said he eagerly.

I said I did not mind if I did, so we began to make our arrangements next morning, and completed them within a very few days.

Chapter Eighty

We left by the night mail, crossing from Dover. The night was soft, and there was a bright moon upon the sea. 'Don't you love the smell of grease about the engine of a Channel steamer? Isn't there a lot of hope in it?' said Ernest to me, for he had been to Normandy one summer as a boy with his father and mother, and the smell carried him back to days before those in which he had begun to bruise himself against the great outside world. 'I always think one of the best parts of going abroad is the first thud of the piston, and the first gurgling of the water when the paddle begins to strike it.'

It was very dreamy getting out at Calais, and trudging about with luggage in a foreign town at an hour when we were generally both of us in bed and fast asleep, but we settled down to sleep as soon as we got into the railway carriage, and dozed till we had passed Amiens. Then waking when the first signs of morning crispness were beginning to show themselves, I saw that Ernest was already devouring every object we passed with quick sympathetic curiousness. There was not a peasant in a blouse driving his cart betimes along the road to market, not a signalman's wife in her husband's hat and coat waving a green flag, not a shepherd taking out his sheep to the dewy pastures, not a bank of opening cowslips as we passed through the railway cuttings, but he was drinking it all in with an enjoyment too deep for words. The name of the engine that drew us was Mozart, and Ernest liked this too.

We reached Paris by six, and had just time to get across the town and take a morning express train to Marseilles, but before noon my young friend was tired out and had resigned himself to a series of sleeps which were seldom intermitted for more than an hour or so together. He fought against this for a time, but in the end consoled himself by saying it was so nice to have so much pleasure that he could afford to throw a lot of it away. Having found a theory on which to justify himself, he slept in peace.

At Marseilles we rested, and there the excitement of the change proved, as I had half-feared it would, too much for my godson's still enfeebled state. For a few days he was really ill, but after this he righted. For my own part I reckon being ill as one of the great pleasures of life, provided one is not too ill and is not obliged to work till one is better. I remember being ill once in a foreign hotel myself and how much I enjoyed it. To lie there careless of everything, quiet and warm, and with no weight upon the mind, to hear the clinking of the plates in the far-off kitchen as the scullion rinsed them and put them by; to watch the soft shadows come and go upon the ceiling as the sun came out or went behind a cloud; to listen to the pleasant murmuring of the fountain in the court below, and the shaking of the bells on the horses' collars and the clink of their hoofs upon the ground as the flies plagued them; not only to be a lotus-eater but to know that it was one's duty to be a lotus-eater. 'Oh,' I thought to myself, 'if I could only now, having so forgotten care, drop off to sleep for ever, would not this be a better piece of fortune than any I can ever hope for?'

Of course it would, but we would not take it though it were offered us. No matter what evil may befall us, we will mostly abide by it and see it out.

I could see that Ernest felt much as I had felt myself. He said little, but noted everything. Only once did he frighten me. He called me to his bedside just as it was getting dusk and said in a grave, quiet manner that he should like to speak to me.

'I have been thinking,' he said, 'that I may perhaps never recover from this illness, and in case I do not I should like you to know that there is only one thing which weighs upon me. I refer,'

415

he continued after a slight pause, 'to my conduct towards my father and mother. I have been much too good to them. I treated them much too considerately,' on which he broke into a smile which assured me that there was nothing seriously amiss with him.

On the walk of his bedroom were a series of French Revolution prints representing events in the life of Lycurgus. There was 'Grandeur d'âme de Lycurgue,' and 'Lycurgue consulte l'oracle,' and then there was 'Calciope à la Cour.' Under this was written in French and Spanish: 'Modèle de grâce et de beauté, la jeune Calciope son moins sage que belle avait mérité l'estime et l'attachement du vertueux Lycurgue. Vivement épris de tant de charmes, l'illustre philosophe la conduisait dans le temple de Junon, où ils s'unirent par un serment sacré. Après cette auguste cérémonie, Lycurgue s'empressa de conduire sa jeune épouse au palais de son frère Polydecte, Roi de Lacédémon. Seigneur, lui ditil, la vertueuse Calciope vient de recevoir mes vœux aux pieds des autels, j'ose vous prier d'approuver cette union. Le Roi témoigna d'abord quelque surprise, mais l'estime qu'il avait pour son frère lui inspira une réponse pleine de bienveillance. Il s'approcha aussitôt de Calciope qu'il embrassa tendrement, combla ensuite Lycurgue de prévenances et parut très satisfait.'

He called my attention to this and then said somewhat timidly that he would rather have married Ellen than Calciope. I saw he was hardening and made no hesitation about proposing that in another day or two we should proceed upon our journey.

I will not weary the reader by taking him with us over beaten ground. We stopped at Siena, Cortona, Orvieto, Perugia and many other cities, and then after a fortnight passed between Rome and Naples went to the Venetian provinces and visited all those wondrous towns that lie between the southern slopes of the Alps and the northern ones of the Apennines, coming back at last by the S. Gothard. I doubt whether he had enjoyed the trip more than I did myself, but it was not till we were on the point of returning that Ernest had recovered strength enough to be called fairly well, and it was not for many months that he so completely lost all sense of the wounds which the last four years had inflicted on him as to feel as though there were a scar and a scar only remaining.

They say that when people have lost an arm or a foot they feel pains in it now and again for a long while after they have lost it. One pain which he had almost forgotten came upon him on his return to England, I mean the sting of his having been imprisoned. As long as he was only a small shopkeeper his imprisonment mattered nothing; nobody knew of it, and if they had known they would not have cared; now, however, though he was returning to his old position he was returning to it disgraced, and the pain from which he had been saved in the first instance by surroundings so new that he had hardly recognised his own identity in the middle of them, came on him as from a wound inflicted yesterday.

He thought of the high resolves which he had made in prison about using his disgrace as a vantage ground of strength rather than trying to make people forget it. 'That was all very well then,' he thought to himself, 'when the grapes were beyond my reach, but now it is different.' Besides, who but a prig would set himself high aims, or make high resolves at all?

Some of his old friends, on learning that he had got rid of his supposed wife and was now comfortably off again, wanted to renew their acquaintance; he was grateful to them and sometimes tried to meet their advances half-way, but it did not do, and ere long he shrank back into himself, pretending not to know them. An infernal demon of honesty haunted him which made him say to himself: 'These men know a great deal, but do not know all – if they did they would cut me – and therefore I have no right to their acquaintance.'

He thought that everyone except himself was *sans peur et sans reproche.* Of course they must be, for if they had not been, would they not have been bound to warn all who had anything to do with them of their deficiences? Well, he could not do this, and he would not have people's acquaintance under false pretences, so he gave up even hankering after rehabilitation and fell back upon his old tastes for music and literature.

Of course he has long since found out how silly all this was, how silly, I mean, in theory, for in practice it worked better than it ought to have done, by keeping him free from *liaisons* which would have tied his tongue and made him see success elsewhere than where he came in time to see it. He did what he did instinctively and for no other reason than because it was most natural to him. So far as he thought at all, he thought wrong, but what he did was right. I said something of this kind to him once not so very long ago, and told him he had always aimed high. 'I never aimed at all,' he replied a little indignantly, 'and you may be sure I should have aimed low enough if I had thought I had got the chance.'

I suppose after all that no one whose mind was not, to put it mildly, abnormal, ever yet aimed very high out of pure malice aforethought. I once saw a fly alight on a cup of hot coffee on which the milk had formed a thin skin; he perceived his extreme danger, and I noted with what ample strides and almost super-muscan effort he struck across the treacherous surface and made for the edge of the cup – for the ground was not solid enough to let him raise himself from it by his wings. As I watched him I fancied that so supreme a moment of difficulty and danger might leave him with an increase of moral and physical power which might even descend in some measure to his offspring. But surely he would not have got the increased moral power if he could have helped it, and he will not knowingly alight upon another cup of hot coffee. The more I see the more sure I am that it does not matter why people do the right thing so long only as they do it, nor why they may have done the wrong if they have done it. The result depends upon the thing done and the motive goes for nothing. I have read somewhere, but cannot remember where, that in some country district there was once a great scarcity of food, during which the poor suffered acutely; many indeed actually died of starvation, and all were hard put to it. In one village, however, there was a poor widow with a family of young children, who, though she had small visible means of subsistence, still looked well-fed and comfortable, as also did all her little ones. 'How,' everyone asked, 'did they manage to live?' It was plain they had a secret, and it was equally plain that it could be no good one; for there came a hurried, hunted look over the poor woman's face if anyone alluded to the way in which she and hers throve when others starved; the family, moreover, were sometimes seen out at unusual hours of the night, and evidently brought things home, which could hardly have been honestly come by. They knew they were under suspicion, and, being hitherto of excellent name, it made them very unhappy, for it must be confessed that they believed what they did to be uncanny if not absolutely wicked; nevertheless, in spite of this they throve, and kept their strength when all their neighbours were pinched.

At length matters came to a head and the clergyman of the parish cross-questioned the poor woman so closely that with many tears and a bitter sense of degradation she confessed the truth; she and her children went into the hedges and gathered snails, which they made into broth and ate – could she ever be forgiven? Was there any hope of salvation for her either in this world or the next after such unnatural conduct?

So again I have heard of an old dowager countess whose money was all in Consols; she had had many sons, and in her anxiety to give the younger ones a good start, wanted a larger income than Consols would give her. She consulted her solicitor and was advised to sell her Consols and invest in the London and North-Western Railway, then at about 85. This was to her what eating snails was to the poor widow whose story I have told above. With shame and grief, as of one doing an unclean thing – but her boys must have their start – she did as she was advised. Then for a long while she could not sleep at night and was haunted by a presage of disaster. Yet what happened? She started her boys, and in a few years found her capital doubled into the bargain, on which she sold out and went back again to Consols and died in the full blessedness of fund-holding.

She thought, indeed, that she was doing a wrong and dangerous thing, but this had absolutely nothing to do with it. Suppose she had invested in the full confidence of a recommendation by some eminent London banker whose advice was bad, and so had lost all her money, and suppose she had done this with a light heart and with no conviction of sin – would her innocence of evil purpose and the excellence of her motive have stood her in any stead? Not they.

But to return to my story. Towneley gave my hero most trouble. Towneley, as I have said, knew that Ernest would have money soon, but Ernest did not of course know that he knew it. Towneley was rich himself, and was married now; Ernest would be rich soon, had *bona fide* intended to be married already, and would doubtless marry a lawful wife later on. Such a man was worth taking pains with, and when Towneley one day met Ernest in the street, and Ernest tried to avoid him, Towneley would not have it, but with his usual quick good nature read his thoughts, caught him, morally speaking, by the scruff of his neck, and turned him laughingly inside out, telling him he would have no such nonsense.

Towneley was just as much Ernest's idol now as he had ever been, and Ernest, who was very easily touched, felt more gratefully and warmly than ever towards him, but there was an unconscious something which was stronger than Towneley, and made my hero determine to break with him more determinedly perhaps than with any other living person; he thanked him in low hurried voice and pressed, his hand, while tears came into his eyes in spite of all his efforts to repress them. 'If we meet again,' he said, 'do not look at me, but if hereafter you hear of me writing things you do not like, think of me as charitably as you can,' and so they parted.

'Towneley is a good fellow,' said I, gravely, 'and you should not have cut him.'

'Towneley,' he answered, 'is not only a good fellow, but he is without exception the very best man I ever saw in my life – except,' he paid me the compliment of saying, 'yourself; Towneley is my notion of everything which I should most like to be – but there is no real solidarity between us. I should be in perpetual fear of losing his good opinion if I said things he did not like, and I mean to say a great many things,' he continued more merrily, 'which Towneley will not like.'

A man, as I have said already, can give up father and mother for Christ's sake tolerably easily for the most part, but it is not so easy to give up people like Towneley.

Chapter Eighty-One

So he fell away from all old friends except myself and three or four old intimates of my own, who were as sure to take to him as he to them, and who like myself enjoyed getting hold of a young fresh mind. Ernest attended to the keeping of my account books whenever there was anything which could possibly be attended to, which there seldom was, and spent the greater part of the rest of his time in adding to the many notes and tentative essays which had already accumulated in his portfolios. Anyone who was used to writing could see at a glance that literature was his natural development, and I was pleased to see him settle down to it so spontaneously. I was less pleased, however, to observe that he would still occupy himself with none but the most serious, I had almost said solemn, subjects, just as he never cared about any but the most serious kind of music.

I said to him one day that the very slender reward which God had attached to the pursuit of serious inquiry was a sufficient proof that He disapproved of it, or at any rate that He did not set much store by it nor wish to encourage it.

He said: 'Oh, don't talk about rewards. Look at Milton, who only got £5 for "Paradise Lost."'

'And a great deal too much,' I rejoined promptly. 'I would have given him twice as much myself not to have written it at all.'

Ernest was a little shocked. 'At any rate,' he said laughingly, 'I don't write poetry.'

This was a cut at me, for my burlesques were, of course, written in rhyme. So I dropped the matter.

After a time he took it into his head to reopen the question of his getting £300 a year for doing, as he said, absolutely nothing, and said he would try to find some employment which should bring him in enough to live upon.

I laughed at this but let him alone. He tried and tried very hard for a long while, but I need hardly say was unsuccessful. The older I grow the more convinced I become of the folly and credulity of the public; but at the same time the harder do I see it is to impose oneself upon that folly and incredulity.

He tried editor after editor with article after article. Sometimes an editor listened to him and told him to leave his articles; he almost invariably, however, had them returned to him in the end with a polite note saying that they were not suited for the particular paper to which he had sent them. And yet many of these very articles appeared in his later works, and no one complained of them, not at least on the score of bad literary workmanship. 'I see,' he said to me one day, 'that demand is very imperious, and supply must be very suppliant.'

Once, indeed, the editor of an important monthly magazine accepted an article from him, and he thought he had now got a footing in the literary world. The article was to appear in the next issue but one, and he was to receive proof from the printers in about ten days or a fortnight; but week after week passed and there was no proof; month after month went by and there was still no room for Ernest's article; at length after about six months the editor one morning told him that he had filled every number of his review for the next ten months, but that his article should definitely appear. On this he insisted on having his MS. returned to him.

Sometimes his articles were actually published, and he found the editor had edited them according to his own fancy, putting in jokes which he thought were funny or cutting out the very passage which Ernest had considered the point of the whole thing, and then, though the articles appeared, when it came to paying for them it was another matter, and he never saw his money. 'Editors,' he said to me one day about this time, 'are like the people who bought and sold in the book of Revelation; there is not one but has the mark of the beast upon him.'

At last after months of disappointment and many a tedious hour wasted in dingy ante-rooms (and of all ante-rooms those of editors appear to me to be the dreariest), he got a *bona fide* offer of employment from one of the first-class weekly papers through an introduction I was able to get for him from one who had powerful influence with the paper in question. The editor sent him a dozen long books upon varied and difficult subjects, and told him to review them in a single article within a week. In one book there was an editorial note to the effect that the writer was to be condemned. Ernest particularly admired the book he was desired to condemn, and feeling how hopeless it was for him to do anything like justice to the books submitted to him, returned them to the editor.

At last one paper did actually take a dozen or so of articles from him, and gave him cash down a couple of guineas apiece for them, but having done this it expired within a fortnight after the last of Ernest's articles had appeared. It certainly looked very much as if the other editors knew their business in declining to have anything to do with my unlucky godson.

I was not sorry that he failed with periodical literature, for writing for reviews or newspapers is bad training for one who may aspire to write works of more permanent interest. A young writer should have more time for reflection than he can get as a contributor to the daily or even weekly press. Ernest himself, however, was chagrined at finding how unmarketable he was. 'Why,' he said to me, 'if I was a well-bred horse, or sheep, or a pure-bred pigeon or lop-eared rabbit I should be more saleable. If I was even a cathedral in a colonial town people would give me something, but as it is they do not want me'; and now that he was well and rested he wanted to set up a shop again, but this, of course, I would not hear of.

'What care I,' said he to me one day, 'about being what they call a gentleman?' And his manner was almost fierce.

'What has being a gentleman ever done for me except make me less able to prey and more easy to be preyed upon? It has changed the manner of my being swindled, that is all. But for your kindness to me I should be penniless. Thank heaven I have placed my children where I have.'

I begged him to keep quiet a little longer and not talk about taking a shop.

'Will being a gentleman,' he said, 'bring me money at the last, and will anything bring me as much peace at the last as money will? They say that those who have riches enter hardly into the kingdom of Heaven. By Jove, they do; they are like Struldbrugs; they live and live and live and are happy for many a long year after they would have entered into the kingdom of Heaven if they had been poor. I want to live long and to raise my children, if I see they would be happier for the raising; that is what I want and it is not what I am doing now that will help me. Being a gentleman is a luxury which I cannot afford, therefore I do not want it. Let me go back to my shop again, and do things for people which they want done and will pay me for doing for them. They know what they want and what is good for them better than I can tell them.'

It was hard to deny the soundness of this, and if he had been dependent only on the £300 a year which he was getting from me I should have advised him to open his shop again next morning. As it was, I temporised and raised obstacles, and quieted him from time to time as best I could.

Of course he read Mr Darwin's books as fast as they came out and adopted evolution as an article of faith. 'It seems to me,' he said once, 'that I am like one of those caterpillars which, if they have been interrupted in making their hammock, must begin again from the beginning. So long as I went back a long way down in the social scale I got on all right, and should have made money but for Ellen; when I try to take up the work at a higher stage I fail completely.' I do not know whether the analogy holds good or not, but I am sure Ernest's instinct was right in telling him that after a heavy fall he had better begin life again at a very low stage, and as I have just said, I would have let him go back to his shop if I had not known what I did.

As the time fixed upon by his aunt drew nearer I prepared him more and more for what was coming, and at last, on his twenty-eighth birthday, I was able to tell him all and to show him the letter signed by his aunt upon her death-bed to the effect that I was to hold the money in trust for him. His birthday happened that year (1863) to be on a Sunday, but on the following day I transferred his shares into his own name, and presented him with the account books which he had been keeping for the last year and a half.

In spite of all that I had done to prepare him, it was a long time before I could get him actually to believe that the money was his own. He did not say much – no more did I, for I am not sure that I did not feel as much moved at having brought my long trustee-ship to a satisfactory conclusion as Ernest did at finding himself owner of more than £70,000. When he did speak it was to jerk out a sentence or two of reflection at a time. 'If I were rendering this moment in music,' he said, 'I should allow myself free use of the augmented sixth.' A little later I remember his saying with a laugh that had something of a family likeness to his aunt's: 'It is not the pleasure it causes me which I enjoy so, it is the pain it will cause to all my friends except yourself and Towneley.'

I said: 'You cannot tell your father and mother – it would drive them mad.'

'No, no, no,' said he, 'it would be too cruel; it would be like Isaac offering up Abraham and no thicket with a ram in it near at hand. Besides, why should I? We have cut each other these four years.'

Chapter Eighty-Two

It almost seemed as though our casual mention of Theobald and Christina had in some way excited them from a dormant to an active state. During the years that had elapsed since they last appeared upon the scene they had remained at Battersby, and had concentrated their affection upon their other children.

It had been a bitter pill to Theobald to lose his power of plaguing his first-born; if the truth were known I believe he had felt this more acutely than any disgrace which might have been shed upon him by Ernest's imprisonment. He had made one or two attempts to reopen negotiations through me, but I never said anything about them to Ernest, for I knew it would upset him. I wrote, however, to Theobald that I had found his son inexorable, and recommended him for the present, at any rate, to desist from returning to the subject. This I thought would be at once what Ernest would like best and Theobald least.

A few days, however, after Ernest had come into his property, I received a letter from Theobald enclosing one for Ernest which I could not withhold.

The letter ran thus:

'To My Son Ernest, – Although you have more than once rejected my overtures I appeal yet again to your better nature. Your mother, who has long been ailing, is, I believe, near her end; she is unable to keep anything on her stomach, and Dr Martin holds out but little hopes of her recovery. She has expressed a wish to see you, and says she knows you will not refuse to come to her, which, considering her condition, I am unwilling to suppose you will.

'I remit you a Post Office order for your fare, and will pay your return journey.

'If you want clothes to come in, order what you consider suitable, and desire that the bill be sent to me; I will pay it immediately, to an amount not exceeding eight or nine pounds, and if you will let me know what train you will come by, I will send the carriage to meet you. Believe me, Your affectionate father,

'T. Pontifex.'

Of course there could be no hesitation on Ernest's part. He could afford to smile now at his father's offering to pay for his clothes, and his sending him a Post Office order for the exact price of a second-class ticket, and he was of course shocked at learning the state his mother was said to be in, and touched at her desire to see him. He telegraphed that he would come down at once. I saw him a little before he started, and was pleased to see how well his tailor had done by him. Towneley himself could not have been appointed more becomingly. His portmanteau, his railway wrapper, everything he had about him, was in keeping. I thought he had grown much better looking than he had been at two or three and twenty. His year and a half of peace had effaced all the ill effects of his previous suffering, and now that he had become actually rich there was an air of *insouciance* and good humour upon his face, as of a man with whom everything was going perfectly right, which would have made a much plainer man good-looking. I was proud of him and delighted with him. 'I am sure,' I said to myself, 'that whatever else he may do, he will never marry again.'

The journey was a painful one. As he drew near to the station and caught sight of each familiar feature, so strong was the force of association that he felt as though his coming into his aunt's money had been a dream, and he were again returning to his father's house as he had returned to it from Cambridge for the vacations. Do what he would, the old dull weight of *home-sickness* began to oppress him, his heart beat fast as he thought of his approaching meeting with his father and mother, 'And I shall have,' he said to himself, 'to kiss Charlotte.'

Would his father meet him at the station? Would he greet him as though nothing had happened, or would he be cold and distant? How, again, would he take the news of his son's good fortune? As the train drew up to the platform, Ernest's eye ran hurriedly over the few people who were in the station. His father's well-known form was not among them, but on the other side of the palings which divided the station yard from the platform, he saw the pony carriage, looking, as he thought, rather shabby, and recognised his father's coachman. In a few minutes more he was in the carriage driving towards Battersby. He could not help smiling as he saw the coachman give a look of surprise at finding him so much changed in personal appearance. The coachman was the more surprised because when Ernest had last been at home he had been dressed as a clergyman, and now he was not only a layman, but a layman who was got up regardless of expense. The change was so great that it was not till Ernest actually spoke to him that the coachman knew him.

'How are my father and mother?' he asked hurriedly, as he got into the carriage. 'The Master's well, sir,' was the answer, 'but the Missis is very sadly.' The horse knew that he was going home and pulled hard at the reins. The weather was cold and raw – the very ideal of a November day; in one part of the road the floods were out, and near here they had to pass through a number of horsemen and dogs, for the hounds had met that morning at a place near Battersby. Ernest saw several people whom he knew, but they either, as is most likely, did not recognise him, or did not know of his good luck. When Battersby church tower drew near, and he saw the Rectory on the top of the hill, its chimneys just showing above the leafless trees with which it was surrounded, he threw himself back in the carriage and covered his face with his hands.

It came to an end, as even the worst quarters of an hour do, and in a few minutes more he was on the steps in front of his father's house. His father, hearing the carriage arrive, came a little way down the steps to meet him. Like the coachman, he saw at a glance that Ernest was appointed as though money were abundant with him, and that he was looking robust and full of health and vigour.

This was not what he had bargained for. He wanted Ernest to return, but he was to return as any respectable, well-regulated prodigal ought to return – abject, broken-hearted, asking forgiveness from the tenderest and most long-suffering father in the whole world. If he should have shoes and stockings and whole clothes at all, it should be only because absolute rags and tatters had been graciously dispensed with, whereas here he was swaggering in a grey ulster and a blue and white neck-tie, and looking better than Theobald had ever seen him in his life. It was unprincipled. Was it for this that he had been generous enough to offer to provide Ernest with decent clothes in which to come and visit his mother's death-bed? Could any advantage be meaner than the one which Ernest had taken? Well, he would not go a penny beyond the eight or nine pounds which he had promised. It was fortunate he had given a limit. Why he, Theobald, had never been able to afford such a portmanteau in his life. He was still using an old one which his father had turned over to him when he went up to Cambridge. Besides, he had said clothes, not a portmanteau.

Ernest saw what was passing through his father's mind, and felt that he ought to have prepared him in some way for what he now saw; but he had sent his telegram so immediately on receiving his father's letter, and had followed it so promptly that it would not have been easy to do so even if he had thought of it. He put out his hand and said laughingly, 'Oh, it's all paid for – I am afraid you do not know that Mr Overton has handed over to me Aunt Alethea's money.'

Theobald flushed scarlet. 'But why,' he said, and these were the first words that actually crossed his lips – 'if the money was not his to keep, did he not hand it over to my brother John and me?' He stammered a good deal and looked sheepish, but he got the words out.

'Because, my dear father,' said Ernest still laughing, 'my aunt left it to him in trust for me, not in trust either for you or for my Uncle John – and it has accumulated till it is now over £70,000. But tell me how is my mother?'

'No, Ernest,' said Theobald excitedly, 'the matter cannot rest here, I must know that this is all open and above board.'

This had the true Theobald ring and instantly brought the whole train of ideas which in Ernest's mind were connected with his father. The surroundings were the old familiar ones, but the surrounded were changed almost beyond power of recognition. He turned sharply on Theobald in a moment. I will not repeat the words he used, for they came out before he had time to consider them, and they might strike some of my readers as disrespectful; there were not many of them, but they were effectual. Theobald said nothing, but turned almost of an ashen colour; he never again spoke to his son in such a way as to make it necessary for him to repeat what he had said on this occasion. Ernest quickly recovered his temper and again asked after his mother. Theobald was glad enough to take this opening now, and replied at once in the tone he would have assumed towards one he most particularly desired to conciliate, that she was getting rapidly worse in spite of all he had been able to do for her, and concluded by saying she had been the comfort and mainstay of his life for more than thirty years, but that he could not wish it prolonged.

The pair then went upstairs to Christina's room, the one in which Ernest had been born. His father went before him and prepared her for her son's approach. The poor woman raised herself in bed as he came towards her, and weeping as she flung her arms around him, cried: 'Oh, I knew he would come, I knew, I knew he would come.'

Ernest broke down and wept as he had not done for years.

'Oh, my boy, my boy,' she said as soon as she could recover her voice. 'Have you never really been near us for all these years? Ah, you do not know how we have loved you and mourned over you, papa just as much as I have. You know he shows his feelings less, but I can never tell you how very, very deeply he has felt for you. Sometimes at night I have thought I have heard footsteps in the garden, and have got quietly out of bed lest I should wake him, and gone to the window to look out, but there has been only dark or the greyness of the morning, and I have gone crying back to bed again. Still I think you have been near us though you were too proud to let us know – and now at last I have you in my arms once more, my dearest, dearest boy.'

How cruel, how infamously unfeeling Ernest thought he had been.

'Mother,' he said, 'forgive me – the fault is mine, I ought not to have been so hard; I was wrong, very wrong'; the poor blubbering fellow meant what he said, and his heart yearned to his mother as he had never thought that it could yearn again. 'But have you never,' she continued, 'come although it was in the dark and we did not know it – oh, let me think that you have not been so cruel as we have thought you. Tell me that you came if only to comfort me and make me happier.'

Ernest was ready. 'I had no money to come with, mother, till just lately.'

This was an excuse Christina could understand and make allowance for; 'Oh, then you would have come, and I will take the will for the deed – and now that I have you safe again, say that you will never, never leave me – not till – not till – oh, my boy, have they told you I am dying?' She wept bitterly, and buried her head in her pillow.

Chapter Eighty-Three

Joey and Charlotte were in the room. Joey was now ordained, and was curate to Theobald. He and Ernest had never been sympathetic, and Ernest saw at a glance that there was no chance of a *rapprochement* between them. He was a little startled at seeing Joey dressed as a clergyman, and looking so like what he had looked himself a few years earlier, for there was a good deal of family likeness between the pair; but Joey's face was cold and was illumined with no spark of Bohemianism; he was a clergyman and was going to do as other clergymen did, neither better nor worse. He greeted Ernest rather *de haut en bas*, that is to say he began by trying to do so, but the affair tailed of unsatisfactorily.

His sister presented her cheek to him to be kissed. How he hated it; he had been dreading it for the last three hours. She, too, was distant and reproachful in her manner, as such a superior person was sure to be. She had a grievance against him inasmuch as she was still unmarried. She laid the blame of this at Ernest's door; it was his misconduct, she maintained in secret, which had prevented young men from making offers to her, and she ran him up a heavy bill for consequential damages. She and Joey had from the first developed an instinct for hunting with the hounds, and now these two had fairly identified themselves with the older generation – that is to say as against Ernest. On this head there was an offensive and defensive alliance between them, but between themselves there was subdued but internecine warfare.

This at least was what Ernest gathered, partly from his recollections of the parties concerned, and partly from his observation of their little ways during the first half-hour after his arrival, while they were all together in his mother's bedroom – for as yet, of course, they did not know that he had money. He could see that they eyed him from time to time with a surprise not unmixed with indignation, and knew very well what they were thinking.

Christina saw the change which had come over him – how much firmer and more vigorous both in mind and body he seemed than when she had last seen him. She saw too how well he was dressed, and, like the others, in spite of the return of all her affection for her first-born, was a little alarmed about Theobald's pocket, which she supposed would have to be mulcted for all this magnificence. Perceiving this, Ernest relieved her mind and told her all about his aunt's bequest, and how I had husbanded it, in the presence of his brother and sister – who, however, ever, pretended not to notice, or at any rate to notice as a matter in which they could hardly be expected to take an interest.

His mother kicked a little at first against the money's having gone to him as she said 'over his papa's head.' 'Why, my dear,' she said in a deprecating tone, 'this is more than ever your papa has had'; but Ernest calmed her by suggesting that if Miss Pontifex had known how large the sum would become she would have left the greater part of it to Theobald. This compromise was accepted by Christina, who forthwith, ill as she was, entered with ardour into the new position, and taking it as a fresh point of departure, began spending Ernest's money for him.

I may say in passing that Christina was right in saying that Theobald had never had so much money as his son was now possessed of. In the first place he had not had a fourteen years' minority with no outgoings to prevent the accumulation of the money, and in the second he, like myself and almost everyone else, had suffered somewhat in the 1846 times – not enough to cripple him or even seriously to hurt him, but enough to give him a scare and make him stick to debentures for the rest of his life. It was the fact of his son's being the richer man of the two, and of his being rich so young, which rankled with Theobald even more than the fact of his having money at all. If he had had to wait till he was sixty or sixty-five, and become broken down from long failure in the meantime, why then perhaps he might have been allowed to have whatever sum should suffice to keep him out of the workhouse and pay his death-bed expenses; but that he should come into £70,000 at eight and twenty, and have no wife and only two children – it was intolerable. Christina was too ill and in too great a hurry to spend the money to care much about such details as the foregoing, and she was naturally much more good-natured than Theobald.

'This piece of good fortune' – she saw it at a glance – 'quite wiped out the disgrace of his having been imprisoned. There should be no more nonsense about that. The whole thing was a mistake, an unfortunate mistake, true, but the less said about it now the better. Of course Ernest would come back and live at Battersby until he was married, and he would pay his father handsomely for board and lodging. In fact, it would be only right that Theobald should make a profit, nor would Ernest himself wish it to be other than a handsome one; this was far the best and simplest arrangement; and he could take his sister out more than Theobald or Joey cared to do, and would also doubtless entertain very handsomely at Battersby.

'Of course he would buy Joey a living, and make large presents yearly to his sister – was there anything else? Oh! yes – he would become a county magnate now; a man with nearly £4,000 a year should certainly become a county magnate. He might even go into Parliament. He had very fair abilities, nothing indeed approaching such genius as Dr Skinner's, nor even as Theobald's, still he was not deficient and if he got into Parliament – so young too – there was nothing to hinder his being Prime Minister before he died, and if so, of course, he would become a peer. Oh! why did he not set about it all at once, so that she might live to hear people call her son 'my lord' – Lord Battersby she thought would do very nicely, and if she was well enough to sit he must certainly have her portrait painted at full length for one end of his large dining-hall. It should be exhibited at the Royal Academy: 'Portrait of Lord Battersby's mother,' she said to herself, and her heart fluttered with all its wonted vivacity. If she could not sit, happily, she had been photographed not so very long ago, and the portrait had been as successful as any photograph could be of a face which depended so entirely upon its expression as her own. Perhaps the painter could take the portrait sufficiently from this. It was better after all that Ernest had given up the Church – how far more wisely God arranges matters for us than ever we can do for ourselves! She saw it all now – it was Joey who would become Archbishop of Canterbury and Ernest would remain a layman and become Prime Minister' . . . and so on till her daughter told her it was time to take her medicine.

I suppose this reverie, which is a mere fragment of what actually ran through Christina's brain, occupied about a minute and a half, but it, or the presence of her son, seemed to revive her spirits wonderfully. Ill, dying indeed, and suffering as she was, she brightened up so as to laugh once or twice quite merrily during the course of the afternoon. Next day Dr Martin said she was so much better that he almost began to have hopes of her recovery again. Theobald, whenever this was touched upon as possible, would shake his head and say: 'We can't wish it prolonged,' and then Charlotte caught Ernest unawares and said: 'You know, dear Ernest, that these ups and downs of talk are terribly agitating to papa; he could stand whatever comes, but it is quite too wearing to him to think half a dozen different things backwards and forwards, and up and down in the same twenty-four hours, and it would be kinder of you not to do it – I mean not to say anything to him even though Dr Martin does hold out hopes.'

Charlotte had meant to imply that it was Ernest who was at the bottom of all the inconvenience felt by Theobald, herself, Joey and everyone else, and she had actually got words out which should convey this; true, she had not dared to stick to them and had turned them off, but she had made them hers at any rate for one brief moment, and this was better than nothing. Ernest noticed throughout his mother's illness that Charlotte found immediate occasion to make herself disagreeable to him whenever either doctor or nurse pronounced her mother to be a little better. When she wrote to Crampsford to desire the prayers of the congregation (she was sure her mother would wish it, and that the Crampsford people would be pleased at her remembrance of them), she was sending another letter on some quite different subject at the same time, and put the two letters into the wrong envelopes. Ernest was asked to take these letters to the village post-office, and imprudently did so; when the error came to be discovered Christina happened to have rallied a little. Charlotte flew at Ernest immediately, and laid all the blame of the blunder upon his shoulders.

Except that Joey and Charlotte were more fully developed, the house and its inmates, organic and inorganic, were little changed since Ernest had last seen them. The furniture and the ornaments on the chimney-piece were just as they had been ever since he could remember anything at all. In the drawing-room, on either side of the fireplace there hung the Carlo Dolci and the Sassoferrato as in old times; there was the water colour of a scene on the Lago Maggiore, copied by Charlotte from an original lent her by her drawing master, and finished under his direction. This was the picture of which one of the servants had said it must be good, for Mr Pontifex had given ten shillings for the frame. The paper on the walls was unchanged; the roses were still waiting for the bees; and the whole family still prayed night and morning to be made 'truly honest and conscientious.'

One picture only was removed – a photograph of himself which had hung under one of his father and between those of his brother and sister. Ernest noticed this at prayer time, while his father was reading about Noah's ark and how they daubed it with slime, which, as it happened, had been Ernest's favourite text when he was a boy. Next morning, however, the photograph had found its way back again, a little dusty and with a bit of the gilding chipped off from one corner of the frame, but there sure enough it was. I suppose they put it back when they found how rich he had become.

In the dining-room the ravens were still trying to feed Elijah over the fireplace; what a crowd of reminiscences did not this picture bring back! Looking out of the window, there were the flower beds in the front garden exactly as they had been, and Ernest found himself looking hard against the blue door at the bottom of the garden to see if there was rain falling, as he had been used to look when he was a child doing lessons with his father.

After their early dinner, when Joey and Ernest and their father were left alone, Theobald rose and stood in the middle of the hearthrug under the Elijah picture, and began to whistle in his old absent way. He had two tunes only, one was 'In my Cottage near a Wood,' and the other was the Easter Hymn; he had been trying to whistle them all his life, but had never succeeded; he whistled them as a clever bullfinch might whistle them – he had got them, but he had not got them right; he would be a semitone out in every third note as though reverting to some remote musical progenitor, who had known none but the Lydian or the Phrygian mode, or whatever would enable him to go most wrong while still keeping the tune near enough to be recognised. Theobald stood before the middle of the fire and whistled his two tunes softly in his own old way till Ernest left the room; the unchangedness of the external and changedness of the internal he felt were likely to throw him completely off his balance.

He strolled out of doors into the sodden spinney behind the house, and solaced himself with a pipe. Ere long he found himself at the door of the cottage of his father's coachman, who had married an old lady's maid of his mother's, to whom Ernest had been always much attached as she also to him, for she had known him ever since he had been five or six years old. Her name was

Susan. He sat down in the rocking-chair before her fire, and Susan went on ironing at the table in front of the window, and a smell of hot flannel pervaded the kitchen.

Susan had been retained too securely by Christina to be likely to side with Ernest all in a moment. He knew this very well, and did not call on her for the sake of support, moral or otherwise. He had called because he liked her, and also because he knew that he should gather much in a chat with her that he should not be able to arrive at in any other way.

'Oh, Master Ernest,' said Susan, 'why did you not come back when your poor papa and mamma wanted you? I'm sure your ma has said to me a hundred times over if she has said it once that all should be exactly as it had been before.'

Ernest smiled to himself. It was no use explaining to Susan why he smiled, so he said nothing.

'For the first day or two I thought she never would get over it; she said it was a judgement upon her, and went on about things as she had said and done many years ago, before your pa knew her, and I don't know what she didn't say or wouldn't have said only I stopped her; she seemed out of her mind like, and said that none of the neighbours would ever speak to her again, but the next day Mrs Bushby (her that was Miss Cowey), you know, called, and your ma always was so fond of her, and it seemed to do her a power o' good, for the next day she went through all her dresses and we settled how she should have them altered; and then all the neighbours called for miles and miles round, and your ma came in here and said she had been going through the waters of misery, and the Lord had turned them to a well.

'"Oh yes, Susan," said she, "be sure it is so. Whom the Lord loveth he chasteneth, Susan," and here she began to cry again. "As for him," she went on, "he has made his bed, and he must lie on it; when he comes out of prison his pa will know what is best to be done, and Master Ernest may be thankful that he has a pa so good and so long-suffering."

'Then when you would not see them, that was a cruel blow to your ma. Your pa did not say anything; you know your pa never does say very much unless he's downright waxy for the time; but your ma took on dreadful for a few days, and I never saw the master look so black; but bless you, it all went off in a few days, and I don't know that there's been much difference in either of them since then, not till your ma was took ill.'

On the night of his arrival he had behaved well at family prayers, as also on the following morning; his father read about David's dying injunctions to Solomon in the matter of Shimei, but he did not mind it. In the course of the day, however, his corns had been trodden on so many times that he was in a misbehaving humour, on this the second night after his arrival. He knelt next to Charlotte and said the responses perfunctorily, not so perfunctorily that she should know for certain that he was doing it maliciously, but so perfunctorily as to make her uncertain whether he might be malicious or not, and when he had to pray to be made truly honest and conscientious he emphasised the 'truly.' I do not know whether Charlotte noticed anything, but she knelt at some distance from him during the rest of his stay. He assures me that this was the only spiteful thing he did during the whole time he was at Battersby.

When he went up to his bedroom, in which, to do them justice, they had given him a fire, he noticed what indeed he had noticed as soon as he was shown into it on his arrival, that there was an illuminated card framed and glazed over his bed with the words, 'Be the day weary or be the day long, at last it ringeth to evensong.' He wondered to himself how such people could leave such a card in a room in which their visitors would have to spend the last hours of their evening, but he let it alone. 'There's not enough difference between "weary" and "long" to warrant an "or",' he said, 'but I suppose it is all right.' I believe Christina had bought the card at a bazaar in aid of the restoration of a neighbouring church, and having been bought it had got to be used – besides, the sentiment was so touching and the illumination was really lovely. Anyhow, no irony could be more complete than leaving it in my hero's bedroom, though assuredly no irony had been intended.

On the third day after Ernest's arrival Christina relapsed again. For the last two days she had been in no pain and had slept a good deal; her son's presence still seemed to cheer her, and she often said how thankful she was to be surrounded on her death-bed by a family so happy, so God-fearing, so united, but now she began to wander, and, being more sensible of the approach of death, seemed also more alarmed at the thought of the Day of Judgment.

She ventured more than once or twice to return to the subject of her sins, and implored Theobald to make quite sure that they were forgiven her. She hinted that she considered his professional reputation was at stake; it would never do for his own wife to fail in securing at any rate a pass. This was touching Theobald on a tender spot; he winced and rejoined with an impatient toss of the head, 'But Christina, they *are* forgiven you'; and then he entrenched himself in a firm but dignified manner behind the Lord's prayer. When he rose he left the room, but called Ernest out to say that he could not wish it prolonged.

Joey was no more use in quieting his mother's anxiety than Theobald had been – indeed he was only Theobald and water; at last Ernest, who had not liked interfering, took the matter in hand, and, sitting beside her, let her pour out her grief to him without let or hindrance.

She said she knew she had not given up *all* for Christ's sake; it was this that weighed upon her. She had given up much, and had always tried to give up more year by year, still she knew very well that she had not been so spiritually minded as she ought to have been. If she had, she should probably have been favoured with some direct vision or communication; whereas, though God had vouchsafed such direct and visible angelic visits to one of her dear children, yet she had had none such herself – nor even had Theobald.

She was talking rather to herself than to Ernest as she said these words, but they made him open his ears. He wanted to know whether the angel had appeared to Joey or to Charlotte. He asked his mother, but she seemed surprised, as though she expected him to know all about it, then, as if she remembered, she checked herself and said, 'Ah! yes – you know nothing of all this, and perhaps it is as well.' Ernest could not of course press the subject, so he never found out which of his near relations it was who had had direct communication with an immortal. The others never said anything to him about it, though whether this was because they were ashamed, or because they feared he would not believe the story and thus increase his own damnation, he could not determine.

Ernest had often thought about this since. He tried to get the facts out of Susan, who he was sure would know, but Charlotte had been beforehand with him. 'No, Master Ernest,' said Susan, when he began to question her, 'your ma has sent a message to me by Miss Charlotte as I am not to say nothing at all about it, and I never will.' Of course no further questioning was possible. It had more than once occurred to Ernest that Charlotte did not in reality believe more than he did himself, and this incident went far to strengthen his surmises, but he wavered when he remembered how she had misdirected the letter asking for the prayers of the congregation. 'I suppose,' he said to himself gloomily, 'she does believe in it after all.'

Then Christina returned to the subject of her own want of spiritual mindedness, she even harped upon the old grievance of her having eaten black puddings – true, she had given them up years ago, but for how many years had she not persevered in eating them after she had had misgivings about their having been forbidden! Then there was something that weighed on her mind that had taken place before her marriage, and she should like –

Ernest interrupted: 'My dear mother,' he said, 'you are ill and your mind is unstrung; others can now judge better about you than you can; I assure you that to me you seem to have been the most devotedly unselfish wife and mother that ever lived. Even if you have not literally given up all for Christ's sake, you have done so practically as far as it was in your power, and more than this is not required of anyone. I believe you will not only be a saint, but a very distinguished one.'

At these words Christina brightened. 'You give me hope, you give me hope,' she cried, and dried her eyes. She made him assure her over and over again that this was his solemn conviction; she did not care about being a distinguished saint now; she would be quite content to be among the meanest who actually got into heaven, provided she could make sure of escaping that awful Hell. The fear of this evidently was omnipresent with her, and in spite of all Ernest could say he did not quite dispel it. She was rather ungrateful, I must confess, for after more than an hour's consolation from Ernest she prayed for him that he might have every blessing in this world, inasmuch as she always feared that he was the only one of her children whom she should never meet in heaven; but she was then wandering, and was hardly aware of his presence; her mind in fact was reverting to states in which it had been before her illness.

On Sunday Ernest went to church as a matter of course, and noted that the ever receding tide of Evangelicalism had ebbed many a stage lower, even during the few years of his absence. His father used to walk to the church through the Rectory garden, and across a small intervening field. He had been used to walk in a tall hat, his Master's gown, and wearing a pair of Geneva bands. Ernest noticed that the bands were worn no longer, and lo! greater marvel still, Theobald did not preach in his Master's gown, but in a surplice. The whole character of the service was changed; you could not say it was high even now, for high-church Theobald could never under any circumstances become, but the old easy-going slovenliness, if I may say so, was gone for ever. The orchestral accompaniments to the hymns had disappeared while my hero was yet a boy, but there had been no chanting for some years after the harmonium had been introduced. While Ernest was at Cambridge, Charlotte and Christina had prevailed on Theobald to allow the canticles to be sung; and sung they were to old-fashioned double chants by Lord Mornington and Dr Dupuis and others. Theobald did not like it, but he did it, or allowed it to be done.

Then Christina said: 'My dear, do you know, I really think' (Christina always 'really' thought) 'that the people like the chanting very much, and that it will be a means of bringing many to church who have stayed away hitherto. I was talking about it to Mrs Goodhew and to old Miss Wright only yesterday, and they *quite* agreed with me, but they all said that we ought to chant the "Glory be to the Father" at the end of each of the psalms instead of saying it.'

Theobald looked black – he felt the waters of chanting rising higher and higher upon him inch by inch; but he felt also, he knew not why, that he had better yield than fight. So he ordered the 'Glory be to the Father' to be chanted in future, but he did not like it.

'Really, mamma dear,' said Charlotte, when the battle was won, 'you should not call it the "Glory be to the Father," you should say "Gloria." '

'Of course, my dear,' said Christina, and she said 'Gloria' for ever after. Then she thought what a wonderfully clever girl Charlotte was, and how she ought to marry no one lower than a bishop. By and by when Theobald went away for an unusually long holiday one summer, he could find no one but a rather high-church clergyman to take his duty. This gentleman was a man of weight in the neighbourhood, having considerable private means, but without preferment. In the summer he would often help his brother clergymen, and it was through his being willing to take the duty at Battersby for a few Sundays that Theobald had been able to get away for so long. On his return, however, he found that the whole psalms were being chanted as well as the Glorias. The influential clergyman, Christina, and Charlotte took the bull by the horns as soon as Theobald returned, and laughed it all off; and the clergyman laughed and bounced, and Christina laughed and coaxed, and Charlotte uttered unexceptionable sentiments, and the thing was done now, and could not be undone, and it was no use grieving over spilt milk; so henceforth the psalms were to be chanted, but Theobald grisled over it in his heart, and he did not like it.

During the same absence what had Mrs Goodhew and old Miss Wright taken to doing but turning towards the east while repeating the Belief? Theobald disliked this even worse than chanting. When he said something about it in a timid way at dinner after service, Charlotte said, 'Really, papa dear, you *must* take to calling it the "Creed" and not the "Belief" '; and Theobald winced impatiently and snorted meek defiance, but the spirit of her aunts Jane and Eliza was strong in Charlotte, and the thing was too small to fight about, and he turned it off with a laugh. 'As for Charlotte,' thought Christina, 'I believe she knows *everything.*' So Mrs Goodhew and old Miss Wright continued to turn to the east during the time the Creed was said, and by and by others followed their example, and ere long the few who had stood out yielded and turned eastward too; and then Theobald made as though he had thought it all very right and proper from the first, but like it he did not. By and by Charlotte tried to make him say 'Alleluia' instead of 'Hallelujah,' but this was going too far, and Theobald turned, and she got frightened and ran away.

And they changed the double chants for single ones, and altered them psalm by psalm, and in the middle of psalms, just where a cursory reader would see no reason why they should do so, they changed from major to minor and from minor back to major; and then they got 'Hymns Ancient and Modern,' and, as I have said, they robbed him of his beloved bands, and they made him preach in a surplice, and he must have celebration of the Holy Communion once a month instead of only five times in the year as heretofore, and he struggled in vain against the unseen influence which he felt to be working in and out of season against all that he had been accustomed to consider most distinctive of his party. Where it was, or what it was, he knew not, nor exactly what it would do next, but he knew exceedingly well that go where he would it was undermining him; that it was too persistent for him; that Christina and Charlotte liked it a great deal better than he did, and that it could end in nothing but Rome. Easter decorations indeed! Christmas decorations – in reason – were proper enough, but Easter decorations! well, it might last his time.

This was the course things had taken in the Church of England during the last forty years. The set had been steadily in one direction. A few men who knew what they wanted made cats' paws of the Christinas and the Charlottes, and the Christinas and the Charlottes made cats' paws of the Mrs Goodhews and the old Miss Wrights, and the Mrs Goodhews and the old Miss Wrights told the Mr Goodhews and young Miss Wrights what they should do, and when the Mr Goodhews and the young Miss Wrights did it the little Goodhews and the rest of the spiritual flock did as they did, and the Theobalds went for nothing; step by step, day by day, year by year, parish by parish, diocese by diocese this was how it was done. And yet the Church of England looks with no friendly eyes upon the theory of Evolution or Descent with Modification.

My hero thought over these things, and remembered many a *ruse* on the part of Christina and Charlotte, and many a detail of the struggle which I cannot further interrupt my story to refer to, and he remembered his father's favourite retort that it could only end in Rome. When he was a boy he had firmly believed this, but he smiled now as he thought of another alternative clear enough to himself, but so horrible that it had not even occurred to Theobald – I mean the toppling over of the whole system. At that time he welcomed the hope that the absurdities and unrealities of the Church would end in her downfall. Since then he has come to think very differently, not as believing in the cow jumping over the moon more than he used to, or more, probably, than nine-tenths of the clergy themselves – who know as well as he does that their outward and visible symbols are out of date – but because he knows the baffling complexity of the problem when it comes to deciding what is actually to be done. Also, now that he has seen them more closely, he knows better the nature of those wolves in sheep's clothing, who are thirsting for the blood of their victim, and exulting so clamorously over its anticipated early fall into their clutches. The spirit behind the Church is true, though her letter – true once – is now true no longer. The spirit behind the High Priests of Science is as lying as its letter. The Theobalds, who do what they do because it seems to be the correct thing, but who in their hearts neither like it nor believe in it, are in reality the least dangerous of all classes to the peace and liberties of mankind. The man to fear is he who goes at things with the cocksureness of pushing vulgarity and self-conceit. These are not vices which can be justly laid to the charge of the English clergy.

Many of the farmers came up to Ernest when service was over, and shook hands with him. He found every one knew of his having come into a fortune. The fact was that Theobald had immediately told two or three of the greatest gossips in the village, and the story was not long in spreading. 'It simplified matters,' he had said to himself, 'a good deal.' Ernest was civil to Mrs Goodhew for her husband's sake, but he gave Miss Wright the cut direct, for he knew that she was only Charlotte in disguise.

A week passed slowly away. Two or three times the family took the sacrament together round Christina's death-bed. Theobald's impatience became more and more transparent daily, but fortunately Christina (who even if she had been well would have been ready to shut her eyes to it) became weaker and less coherent in mind also, so that she hardly, if at all, perceived it. After Ernest had been in the house about a week his mother fell into a comatose state which lasted a couple of days, and in the end went away so peacefully that it was like the blending of sea and sky in mid-ocean upon a soft hazy day when none can say where the earth ends and the heavens begin. Indeed she died to the realities of life with less pain than she had waked from many of its illusions.

'She has been the comfort and mainstay of my life for more than thirty years,' said Theobald as soon as all was over, 'but one could not wish it prolonged,' and he buried his face in his handkerchief to conceal his want of emotion.

Ernest came back to town the day after his mother's death, and returned to the funeral accompanied by myself. He wanted me to see his father in order to prevent any possible misapprehension about Miss Pontifex's intentions, and I was such an old friend of the family's that my presence at Christina's funeral would surprise no one. With all her faults I had always rather liked Christina. She would have chopped Ernest or any one else into little pieces of mincemeat to gratify the slightest wish of her husband, but she would not have chopped him up for any one else, and so long as he did not cross her she was very fond of him. By nature she was of an even temper, more willing to be pleased than ruffled, very ready to do a good-natured action, provided it did not cost her much exertion, nor involve expense to Theobald. Her own little purse did not matter; any one might have as much of that as he or she could get after she had reserved what was absolutely necessary for her dress. I could not hear of her end as Ernest described it to me without feeling very compassionate towards her, indeed her own son could hardly have felt more so; I at once, therefore, consented to go down to the funeral; perhaps I was also influenced by a desire to see Charlotte and Joey, in whom I felt interested on hearing what my godson had told me.

I found Theobald looking remarkably well. Every one said he was bearing it so beautifully. He did indeed once or twice shake his head and say that his wife had been the comfort and mainstay of his life for over thirty years, but there the matter ended. I stayed over the next day, which was Sunday, and took my departure on the following morning after having told Theobald all that his son wished me to tell him. Theobald asked me to help him with Christina's epitaph.

'I would say,' said he, 'as little as possible; eulogies of the departed are in most cases both unnecessary and untrue. Christina's epitaph shall contain nothing which shall be either the one or the other. I should give her name, the dates of her birth and death, and of course say she was my wife, and then I think I should wind up with a simple text – her favourite one for example, none indeed could be more appropriate, "Blessed are the pure in heart for they shall see God."'

I said I thought this would be very nice, and it was settled. So Ernest was sent to give the order to Mr Prosser, the stonemason in the nearest town, who said it came from 'the Beetitudes.'

Chapter Eighty-Four

Of our way to town Ernest broached his plans for spending the next year or two. I wanted him to try and get more into society again, but he brushed this aside at once as the very last thing he had a fancy for. For society indeed of all sorts, except of course that of a few intimate friends, he had an unconquerable aversion. 'I always did hate those people,' he said, 'and they always have hated and always will hate me. I am an Ishmael by instinct as much as by accident of circumstances, but if I keep out of society I shall be less vulnerable than Ishmaels generally are. The moment a man goes into society, he becomes vulnerable all round.'

I was very sorry to hear him talk in this way; for whatever strength a man may have he should surely be able to make more of it if he act in concert than alone. I said this.

'I don't care,' he answered, 'whether I make the most of my strength or not; I don't know whether I have any strength, but if I have I dare say it will find some way of exerting itself. I will live as I like living, not as other people would like me to live; thanks to my aunt and you I can afford the luxury of a quiet unobtrusive life of self-indulgence,' said he laughing, 'and I mean to have it. You know I like writing,' he added after a pause of some minutes, 'I have been a scribbler for years. If I am to come to the fore at all it must be by writing.'

I had already long since come to that conclusion myself.

'Well,' he continued, 'there are a lot of things that want saying which no one dares to say, a lot of shams which want attacking, and yet no one attacks them. It seems to me that I can say things which not another man in England except myself will venture to say, and yet which are crying to be said.'

I said: 'But who will listen? If you say things which nobody else would dare to say is not this much the same as saying what everyone except yourself knows to be better left unsaid just now?'

'Perhaps,' said he, 'but I don't know it; I am bursting with these things, and it is my fate to say them.'

I knew there would be no stopping him, so I gave in and asked what question he felt a special desire to burn his fingers with in the first instance.

'Marriage,' he rejoined promptly, 'and the power of disposing of his property after a man is dead. The question of Christianity is virtually settled, or if not settled there is no lack of those engaged in settling it. The question of the day now is marriage and the family system.'

'That,' said I dryly, 'is a hornet's nest indeed.'

'Yes,' he said no less dryly, 'but hornet's nests are exactly what I happen to like. Before, however, I begin to stir up this particular one I propose to travel for a few years, with the especial object of finding out what nations now existing are the best, comeliest and most lovable, and also what nations have been so in times past. I want to find out how these people live, and have lived, and what their customs are.

'I have very vague notions upon the subject as yet, but the general impression I have formed is that, putting ourselves on one side, the most vigorous and amiable of known nations are the modern Italians, the old Greeks and Romans, and the South Sea Islanders. I believe that these nice peoples have not as a general rule been purists, but I want to see those of them who can yet be seen; they are the practical authorities on the question – What is best for man? and I should like to see them and find out what they do. Let us settle the fact first and fight about the moral tendencies afterwards.'

'In fact,' said I laughingly, 'you mean to have high old times.'

'Neither higher nor lower,' was the answer, 'than those people whom I can find to have been the best in all ages. But let us change the subject.' He put his hand into his pocket and brought out a letter. 'My father,' he said, 'gave me this letter this morning with the seal already broken.' He passed it over to me, and I found it to be the one which Christina had written before the birth of her last child, and which I have given in an earlier chapter.

'And you do not find this letter,' said I, 'affect the conclusion which you have just told me you have come to concerning your present plans?'

He smiled, and answered: 'No. But if you do what you have sometimes talked about and turn the adventures of my unworthy self into a novel, mind you print this letter.'

'Why so?' said I, feeling as though such a letter as this should have been held sacred from the public gaze.

'Because my mother would have wished it published; if she had known you were writing about me and had this letter in your possession, she would above all things have desired that you should publish it. Therefore publish it if you write at all.'

This is why I have done so.

Within a month Ernest carried his intention into effect, and having made all the arrangements necessary for his children's welfare left England before Christmas.

I heard from him now and again and learnt that he was visiting almost all parts of the world, but only staying in those places where he found the inhabitants unusually good-looking and agreeable. He said he had filled an immense quantity of notebooks, and I have no doubt he had. At last in the spring of 1867 he returned, his luggage stained with the variation of each hotel advertisement 'twixt here and Japan. He looked very brown and strong, and so well favoured that it almost seemed as if he must have caught some good looks from the people among whom he had been living. He came back to his old rooms in the Temple, and settled down as easily as if he had never been away a day.

One of the first things we did was to go and see the children;

we took the train to Gravesend, and walked thence for a few miles along the riverside till we came to the solitary house where the good people lived with whom Ernest had placed them. It was a lovely April morning, but with a fresh air blowing from off the sea; the tide was high, and the river was alive with shipping coming up with wind and tide. Seagulls wheeled around us overhead, seaweed clung everywhere to the banks which the advancing tide had not yet covered, everything was of the sea sea-ey, and the fine bracing air which blew over the water made me feel more hungry than I had done for many a day; I did not see how children could live in a better physical atmosphere than this, and applauded the selection which Ernest had made on behalf of his youngsters.

While we were still a quarter of a mile off we heard shouts and children's laughter, and could see a lot of boys and girls romping together and running after one another. We could not distinguish our own two, but when we got near they were soon made out, for the other children were blue-eyed, flaxen-pated little folks, whereas ours were dark and straight-haired.

We had written to say that we were coming, but had desired that nothing should be said to the children, so these paid no more attention to us than they would have done to any other stranger, who happened to visit a spot so unfrequented except by seafaring folk, which we plainly were not. The interest, however, in us was much quickened when it was discovered that we had got our pockets full of oranges and sweeties, to an extent greater than it had entered into their small imaginations to conceive as possible. At first we had great difficulty in making them come near us. They were like a lot of wild colts, very inquisitive, but very coy and not to be cajoled easily. The children were nine in all – five boys and two girls belonging to Mr and Mrs Rollings, and two to Ernest. I never saw a finer lot of children than the young Rollings, the boys were hardy, robust, fearless little fellows with eyes as clear as hawks; the elder girl was exquisitely pretty, but the younger one was a mere baby. I felt as I looked at them that if I had had children of my own I could have wished no better home for them, nor better companions.

Georgie and Alice, Ernest's two children, were evidently quite as one family with the others, and called Mr and Mrs Rollings uncle and aunt. They had been so young when they were first brought to the house that they had been looked upon in the light of new babies who had been born into the family. They knew nothing about Mr and Mrs Rollings being paid so much a week to look after them. Ernest asked them all what they wanted to be. They had only one idea; one and all, Georgie among the rest, wanted to be bargemen. Young ducks could hardly have a more evident hankering after the water.

'And what do you want, Alice?' said Ernest.

'Oh,' she said, 'I'm going to marry Jack here, and be a barge-man's wife.'

Jack was the eldest boy, now nearly twelve, a sturdy little fellow, the image of what Mr Rollings must have been at his age. As we looked at him, so straight and well grown and well done all round, I could see it was in Ernest's mind as much as in mine that she could hardly do much better.

'Come here, Jack, my boy,' said Ernest, 'here's a shilling for you.' The boy blushed and could hardly be got to come in spite of our previous blandishments; he had had pennies given him before, but shillings never. His father caught him good-naturedly by the ear and lugged him to us.

'He's a good boy, Jack is,' said Ernest to Mr Rollings, 'I'm sure of that.'

'Yes,' said Mr Rollings, 'he's a werry good boy, only that I can't get him to learn his reading and writing. He don't like going to school, that's the only complaint I have against him. I don't know what's the matter with all my children, and yours, Mr Pontifex, is just as bad, but they none of 'em likes book learning, though they learn anything else fast enough. Why, as for Jack here, he's almost

as good a bargeman as I am.' And he looked fondly and patronis-
ingly towards his offspring.

'I think,' said Ernest to Mr Rollings, 'if he wants to marry Alice
when he gets older he had better do so, and he shall have as many
barges as he likes. In the meantime, Mr Rollings, say in what way
money can be of use to you, and whatever you can make useful
is at your disposal.'

I need hardly say that Ernest made matters easy for this good
couple; one stipulation, however, he insisted on, namely, there
was to be no more smuggling, and that the young people were to
be kept out of this; for a little bird had told Ernest that smuggling
in a quiet way was one of the resources of the Rollings family. Mr
Rollings was not sorry to assent to this, and I believe it is now
many years since the coastguard people have suspected any of
the Rollings family as offenders against the revenue law.

'Why should I take them from where they are,' said Ernest to
me in the train as we went home, 'to send them to schools where
they will not be one half so happy, and where their illegitimacy
will very likely be a worry to them? Georgie wants to be a barge-
man, let him begin as one, the sooner the better; he may as well
begin with this as with anything else; then if he shows developments I can be on the lookout to encourage them and make
things easy for him; while if he shows no desire to go ahead, what
on earth is the good of trying to shove him forward?'

Ernest, I believe, went on with a homily upon education generally, and upon the way in which young people should go
through the embryonic stages with their money as much as with
their limbs, beginning life in a much lower social position than
that in which their parents were, and a lot more, which he has
since published; but I was getting on in years, and the walk and
the bracing air had made me sleepy, so ere we had got past Green-
hithe Station on our return journey I had sunk into a refreshing
sleep.

Chapter Eighty-Five

Ernest being about two and thirty years old and having had his fling for the last three or four years, now settled down in London, and began to write steadily. Up to this time he had given abundant promise, but had produced nothing, nor indeed did he come before the public for another three or four years yet.

He lived as I have said very quietly, seeing hardly anyone but myself, and the three or four old friends with whom I had been intimate for years. Ernest and we formed our little set, and outside of this our godson was hardly known at all.

His main expense was travelling, which he indulged in at frequent intervals, but for short times only. Do what he would he could not get through more than about fifteen hundred a year; the rest of his income he gave away if he happened to find a case where he thought money would be well bestowed, or put by until some opportunity arose of getting rid of it with advantage.

I knew he was writing, but we had had so many little differences of opinion upon this head that by a tacit understanding the subject was seldom referred to between us, and I did not know that he was actually publishing till one day he brought me a book and told me that it was his own. I opened it and found it to be a series of semi-theological, semi-social essays, purporting to have been written by six or seven different people, and viewing the same class of subjects from different standpoints.

People had not yet forgotten the famous *Essays and Reviews*, and Ernest had wickedly given a few touches to at least two of the essays which suggested vaguely that they had been written by a bishop. The essays were all of them in support of the Church of England, and appeared both by implied internal suggestion, and their *prima facie* purport to be the work of some half-dozen men of experience and high position who had determined to face the difficult questions of the day no less boldly from within the bosom of the Church than the Church's enemies had faced them from without her pale.

There was an essay on the external evidences of the Resurrection; another on the marriage laws of the most eminent nations of the world in times past and present; another was devoted to a consideration of the many questions which must be reopened and reconsidered on their merits if the teaching of the Church of England were not to cease to carry moral authority with it; another dealt with the more purely social subject of middle-class destitution; another with the authenticity or rather the un-authenticity of the fourth gospel; another was headed 'Irrational Rationalism,' and there were two or three more.

They were all written vigorously and fearlessly as though by people used to authority; all granted that the Church professed to enjoin belief in much which no one could accept who had been accustomed to weigh evidence; but it was contended that so much valuable truth had got so closely mixed up with these mistakes, that the mistakes had better not be meddled with. To lay great stress on these was like cavilling at the Queen's right to reign, on the ground that William the Conqueror was illegitimate.

One article maintained that though it would be inconvenient to change the words of our prayer book and articles, it would not be inconvenient to change in a quiet way the meanings which we put upon those words. This, it was argued, was what was actually done in the case of law; this had been the law's mode of growth and adaptation, and had in all ages been found a righteous and convenient method of effecting change. It was suggested that the Church should adopt it.

In another essay it was boldly denied that the Church rested upon reason. It was proved incontestably that its ultimate foundation was and ought to be faith, there being indeed no other ultimate foundation than this for any of man's beliefs. If so, the writer claimed that the Church could not be upset by reason. It was founded, like everything else, on initial assumptions, that is to say, on faith, and if it was to be upset it was to be upset by faith, by the faith of those who in their lives appeared more graceful, more lovable, better bred, in fact, and better able to overcome difficulties. Any sect which showed its superiority in these respects might carry all before it, but none other would make much headway for long together. Christianity was true in so far as it had fostered beauty, and it had fostered much beauty. It was false in so far as it fostered ugliness, and it had fostered much ugliness. It was therefore not a little true and not a little false; on the whole one might go farther and fare worse; the wisest course would be to live with it, and make the best and not the worst of it. The writer urged that we become persecutors as a matter of course as soon as we begin to feel very strongly upon any subject; we ought not therefore to do this; we ought not to feel very strongly even upon that institution which was dearer to the writer than any other – the Church of England. We should be churchmen, but somewhat lukewarm churchmen, inasmuch as those who care very much about either religion or irreligion are seldom observed to be very well bred or agreeable people. The Church herself should approach as nearly to that of Laodicea as was compatible with her continuing to be a Church at all, and each individual member should only be hot in striving to be as lukewarm as possible.

The book rang with the courage alike of conviction and of an entire absence of conviction; it appeared to be the work of men who had a rule-of-thumb way of steering between iconoclasm on the one hand and credulity on the other; who cut Gordian knots as a matter of course when it suited their convenience; who shrank from no conclusion in theory, nor from any want of logic in practice so long as they were illogical of malice prepense, and for what they held to be sufficient reason. The conclusions were conservative, quietistic, comforting. The arguments by which they were reached were taken from the most advanced writers of the day. All that these people contended for was granted them, but the fruits of victory were for the most part handed over to those already in possession.

Perhaps the passage which attracted most attention in the book was one from the essay on the various marriage systems of the world. It ran:

'If people require us to construct,' exclaimed the writer, 'we set good breeding as the corner-stone of our edifice. We would have it ever present consciously or unconsciously in the minds of ail as the central faith in which they should live and move and have their being, as the touchstone of all things whereby they may be known as good or evil according as they make for good breeding or against it.'

'That a man should have been bred well and breed others well; that his figure, head, hands, feet, voice, manner and clothes should carry conviction upon this point, so that no one can look at him without seeing that he has come of good stock and is likely to throw good stock himself, this is the *desiderandum*. And the same with a woman. The greater number of these well-bred men and women, and the greatest happiness of these well-bred men and women, this is the highest good; towards this all government, all social conventions, all art, literature and science should directly or indirectly tend. Holy men and holy women are those who keep this unconsciously in view at all times whether of work or pastime.'

If Ernest had published this work in his own name I should think it would have fallen still-born from the press, but the form he had chosen was calculated at that time to arouse curiosity, and as I have said he had wickedly dropped a few hints which the reviewers did not think anyone would have been impudent enough to do if he were not a bishop, or at any rate someone in authority. A well-known judge was spoken of as being another of the writers, and the idea spread ere long that six or seven of the leading bishops and judges had laid their heads together to produce a volume, which should at once outbid *Essays and Reviews* and counteract the influence of that then still famous work.

Reviewers are men of like passions with ourselves, and with them as with everyone else *omne ignotum pro magnifico*. The book was really an able one and abounded with humour, just satire, and good sense. It struck a new note and the speculation which for some time was rife concerning its authorship made many turn to it who would never have looked at it otherwise. One of the most gushing weeklies had a fit over it, and declared it to be the finest thing that had been done since the *Provincial Letters* of Pascal. Once a month or so that weekly always found some picture which was the finest that had been done since the old masters, or some satire that was the finest that had appeared since Swift or some something which was incomparably the finest that had appeared since something else. If Ernest had put his name to the book, and the writer had known that it was a nobody, he would doubtless have written in a very different strain. Reviewers like to think that for aught they know they are patting a Duke or even a Prince of the blood upon the back, and lay it on thick till they find they have been only praising Brown, Jones or Robinson. Then they are disappointed, and as a general rule will pay Brown, Jones or Robinson out.

Ernest was not so much up to the ropes of the literary world as I was, and I am afraid his head was a little turned when he woke up one morning to find himself famous. He was Christina's son, and perhaps would not have been able to do what he had done if he was not capable of occasional undue elation. Ere long, however, he found out all about it, and settled quietly down to write a series of books, in which he insisted on saying things which no one else would say even if they could, or could even if they would.

He has got himself a bad literary character. I said to him laughingly one day that he was like the man in the last century of whom it was said that nothing but such a character could keep down such parts.

He laughed and said he would rather be like that than like a modern writer or two whom he could name, whose parts were so poor that they could be kept up by nothing but by such a character.

I remember soon after one of these books was published I happened to meet Mrs Jupp to whom, by the way, Ernest made a small weekly allowance. It was at Ernest's chambers, and for some reason we were left alone for a few minutes. I said to her 'Mr Pontifex has written another book, Mrs Jupp.'

'Lor' now,' said she, 'has he really? Dear gentleman! Is it about love?' And the old sinner threw up a wicked sheep's eye glance at me from under her aged eyelids. I forget what there was in my reply which provoked it – probably nothing – but she went rattling on at full speed to the effect that Bell had given her a ticket for the opera, 'So, of course,' she said, 'I went. I didn't understand one word of it, for it was all French, but I saw their legs. Oh dear, oh dear! I'm afraid I shan't be here much longer, and when dear Mr Pontifex sees me in my coffin he'll say, "Poor old Jupp, she'll never talk broad any more"; but bless you I'm not so old as all that, and I'm taking lessons in dancing.'

At this moment Ernest came in and the conversation was changed. Mrs Jupp asked if he was still going on writing more books now that this one was done. 'Of course I am,' he answered, 'I'm always writing books; here is the manuscript of my next;' and he showed her a heap of paper.

'Well, now,' she exclaimed, 'dear, dear me, and is that manuscript? I've often heard talk about manuscripts, but I never thought I should live to see some myself. Well! well! So that is really manuscript?'

There were a few geraniums in the window and they did not look well. Ernest asked Mrs Jupp if she understood flowers. 'I understand the language of flowers,' she said, with one of her most bewitching leers, and on this we sent her off till she should choose to honour us with another visit, which she knows she is privileged from time to time to do, for Ernest likes her.

Chapter Eighty-Six

And now I must bring my story to a close. The preceding chapter was written soon after the events it records – that is to say in the spring of 1867. By that time my story had been written up to this point; but it has been altered here and there from time to time occasionally. It is now the autumn of 1882, and if I am to say more I should do so quickly, for I am eighty years old and though well in health cannot conceal from myself that I am no longer young. Ernest himself is forty-seven, though he hardly looks it.

He is richer than ever, for he has never married and his London and North-Western shares have nearly doubled themselves. Through sheer inability to spend his income he has been obliged to hoard in self-defence. He still lives in the Temple in the same rooms I took for him when he gave up his shop, for no one has been able to induce him to take a house. His house, he says, is wherever there is a good hotel. When he is in town he likes to work and be quiet. When out of town he feels that he has left little behind him that can go wrong, and he would not like to be tied to a single locality. 'I know no exception,' he says, 'to the rule that it is cheaper to buy milk than to keep a cow.'

As I have mentioned Mrs Jupp, I may as well say here the little that remains to be said about her. She is a very old woman now, but no one now living, as she says triumphantly, can say how old, for the woman in the Old Kent Road is dead, and presumably has carried her secret to the grave. Old, however, though she is, she lives in the same house, and finds it hard work to make the two ends meet, but I do not know that she minds this very much, and it has prevented her from getting more to drink than would be good for her. It is no use trying to do anything for her beyond paying her allowance weekly, and absolutely refusing to let her anticipate it. She pawns her flat iron every Saturday for 4d., and takes it out every Monday morning for 4½d. when she gets her allowance, and has done this for the last ten years as regularly as the week comes round. As long as she does not let the flat iron actually go we know that she can still worry out her financial problems in her own hugger-mugger way and had better be left to do so. If the flat iron were to go beyond redemption, we should know that it was time to interfere. I do not know why, but there is something about her which always reminds me of a woman who was as unlike her as one person can be to another – I mean Ernest's mother.

The last time I had a long gossip with her was about two years ago when she came to me instead of to Ernest. She said she had seen a cab drive up just as she was going to enter the staircase, and had seen Mr Pontifex's pa put his Beelzebub old head out of the window, so she had come on to me, for she hadn't greased her sides for no curtsey, not for the likes of him. She professed to be very much down on her luck. Her lodgers did use her so dreadful, going away without paying and leaving not so much as a stick behind, but to-day she was as pleased as a penny carrot. She had had such a lovely dinner – a cushion of ham and green peas. She had had a good cry over it, but then she was so silly, she was.

'And there's that Bell,' she continued, though I could not detect any appearance of connection, 'it's enough to give anyone the hump to see him now that he's taken to chapel-going, and his mother's prepared to meet Jesus and all that to me, and now she ain't a-going to die, and drinks half a bottle of champagne a day, and then Grigg, him as preaches, you know, asked Bell if I really was too gay, not but when I was young I'd snap my fingers at any "fly by night" in Holborn, and if I was togged out and had my teeth I'd do it now. I lost my poor dear Watkins, but of course that couldn't be helped, and then I lost my dear Rose. Silly faggot to go and ride on a cart and catch the bronchitics. I never thought when I kissed my dear Rose in Pullen's Passage and she gave me the chop, that I should never see her again, and her gentleman friend was fond of her too, though he was a married man. I dare say she's gone to bits by now. If she could rise and see me with my bad finger, she would cry, and I should say, "Never mind, ducky, I'm all right." Oh! dear, it's coming on to rain. I do hate a wet Saturday night – poor women with their nice white stockings and their living to get,' etc., etc.

And yet age does not wither this godless old sinner, as people would say it ought to do. Whatever life she has led, it has agreed with her very sufficiently. At times she gives us to understand that she is still much solicited; at others she takes quite a different tone. She has not allowed even Joe King so much as to put his lips to hers this ten years. She would rather have mutton chop any day. 'But ah! you should have seen me when I was sweet seventeen. I was the very moral of my poor dear mother, and she was a pretty woman, though I say it that shouldn't. She had such a splendid mouth of teeth. It was a sin to bury her in her teeth.'

I only knew of one thing at which she professes to be shocked. It is that her son Tom and his wife Topsy are teaching the baby to swear. 'Oh! it's too dreadful awful,' she exclaimed, 'I don't know the meaning of the words, but I tell him he's a drunken sot.' I believe the old woman in reality rather likes it.

'But surely, Mrs Jupp,' said I, 'Tom's wife used not to be Topsy. You used to speak of her as Pheeb.'

'Ah! yes,' she answered, 'but Pheeb behaved bad, and it's Topsy now.'

Ernest's daughter Alice married the boy who had been her playmate more than a year ago. Ernest gave them all they said they wanted and a good deal more. They have already presented him with a grandson, and I doubt not, will do so with many more. Georgie though only twenty-one is owner of a fine steamer which his father has bought for him. He began when about thirteen going with old Rollings and Jack in the barge from Rochester to the upper Thames with bricks; then his father bought him and Jack barges of their own, and then he bought them both ships, and then steamers. I do not exactly know how people make money by having a steamer, but he does whatever is usual, and from all I can gather makes it pay extremely well. He is a good deal like his father in the face, but without a spark – so far as I have been able to observe – of any literary ability; he has a fair sense of humour and abundance of common sense, but his instinct is clearly a practical one. I am not sure that he does not put me in mind almost more of what Theobald would have been if he had been a sailor, than of Ernest. Ernest used to go down to Battersby and stay with his father for a few days twice a year until Theobald's death, and the pair continued on excellent terms, in spite of what the neighbouring clergy call 'the atrocious books which Mr Ernest Pontifex' has written. Perhaps the harmony, or rather the absence of discord which subsisted between the pair was due to the fact that Theobald had never looked into the inside of one of his son's works, and Ernest of course, never alluded to them in his father's presence. The pair, as I have said, got on excellently, but it was doubtless as well that Ernest's visits were short and not too frequent. Once Theobald wanted Ernest to bring his children, but Ernest knew they would not like it, so this was not done.

Sometimes Theobald came up to town on small business matters and paid a visit to Ernest's chambers; he generally brought with him a couple of lettuces, or a cabbage, or half-a-dozen turnips done up in a piece of brown paper, and told Ernest that he knew fresh vegetables were rather hard to get in London, and he had brought him some. Ernest had often explained to him that the vegetables were of no use to him, and that he had rather he would not bring them; but Theobald persisted, I believe through sheer love of doing something which his son did not like, but which was too small to take notice of.

He lived until about twelve months ago, when he was found

dead in his bed on the morning after having written the following letter to his son:

'Dear Ernest, – I've nothing particular to write about, but your letter has been lying for some days in the limbo of unanswered letters, to wit my pocket, and it's time it was answered.

'I keep wonderfully well and am able to walk my five or six miles with comfort, but at my age there's no knowing how long it will last, and time flies quickly. I have been busy potting plants all the morning, but this afternoon is wet.

'What is this horrid Government going to do with Ireland? I don't exactly wish they'd blow up Mr Gladstone, but if a mad bull would chivvy him there, and he would never come back any more, I should not be sorry. Lord Hartington is not exactly the man I should like to set in his place, but he would be immeasurably better than Gladstone.

'I miss your sister Charlotte more than I can express. She kept my household accounts, and I could pour out to her all my little worries, and now that Joey is married too, I don't know what I should do if one or other of them did not come sometimes and take care of me. My only comfort is that Charlotte will make her husband happy, and that he is as nearly worthy of her as a husband can well be. – Believe me, Your affectionate father,

'Theobald Pontifex.'

I may say in passing that though Theobald speaks of Charlotte's marriage as though it were recent, it had really taken place some six years previously, she being then about thirty-eight years old, and her husband about seven years younger.

There was no doubt that Theobald passed peacefully away during his sleep. Can a man who died thus be said to have died at all? He has presented the phenomena of death to other people, but in respect of himself he has not only not died, but has not even thought that he was going to die. This is not more than half-dying, but then neither was his life more than half-living. He presented so many of the phenomena of living that I suppose on the whole it would be less trouble to think of him as having been alive than as never having been born at all, but this is only possible because association does not stick to the strict letter of its bond.

This, however, was not the general verdict concerning him, and the general verdict is often the truest.

Ernest was overwhelmed with expressions of condolence and respect for his father's memory. 'He never,' said Dr Martin, the old doctor who brought Ernest into the world, 'spoke an ill word against anyone. He was not only liked, he was beloved by all who had anything to do with him.'

'A more perfectly just and righteously dealing man,' said the family solicitor, 'I have never had anything to do with – nor one more punctual in the discharge of every business obligation.'

'We shall miss him sadly,' the bishop wrote to Joey in the very warmest terms. The poor were in consternation. 'The well's never missed,' said one old woman, 'till it's dry,' and she only said what everyone else felt. Ernest knew that the general regret was unaffected as for a loss which could not be easily repaired. He felt that there were only three people in the world who joined insincerely in the tribute of applause, and these were the very three who could least show their want of sympathy. I mean Joey, Charlotte, and himself. He felt bitter against himself for being of a mind with either Joey or Charlotte upon any subject, and thankful that he must conceal his being so as far as possible, not because of anything his father had done to him – these grievances were too old to be remembered now – but because he would never allow him to feel towards him as he was always trying to feel. As long as communication was confined to the merest commonplace all went well, but if these were departed from ever such a little he invariably felt that his father's instincts showed themselves in immediate opposition to his own. When he was attacked his father laid whatever stress was possible on everything which his opponents said. If he met with any check his father was clearly pleased. What the old doctor had said about Theobald's speaking ill of no man was perfectly true as regards others than himself, but he knew very well that no one had injured his reputation in a quiet way, so far as he dared to do, more than his own father. This is a very common case and a very natural one. It often happens that if the son is right, the father is wrong, and the father is not going to have this if he can help it.

It was very hard, however, to say what was the true root of the mischief in the present case. It was not Ernest's having been imprisoned. Theobald forgot all about that much sooner than nine fathers out of ten would have done. Partly, no doubt, it was due to incompatibility of temperament, but I believe the main ground of complaint lay in the fact that he had been so independent and so rich while still very young, and that thus the old gentleman had been robbed of his power to tease and scratch in the way which he felt he was entitled to do. The love of teasing in a small way when he felt safe in doing so had remained part of his nature from the days when he told his nurse that he would keep her on purpose to torment her. I suppose it is so with all of us. At any rate I am sure that most fathers, especially if they are clergymen, are like Theobald.

He did not in reality, I am convinced, like Joey or Charlotte one whit better than he liked Ernest. He did not like anyone or anything, or if he liked anyone at all it was his butler, who looked after him when he was not well, and took great care of him and believed him to be the best and ablest man in the whole world. Whether this faithful and attached servant continued to think this after Theobald's will was opened and it was found what kind of legacy had been left him I know not. Of his children, the baby who had died at a day old was the only one whom he held to have treated him quite filially. As for Christina he hardly ever pretended to miss her and never mentioned her name; but this was taken as a proof that he felt her loss too keenly to be able ever to speak of her. It may have been so, but I do not think so.

Theobald's effects were sold by auction, and among them the Harmony of the Old and New Testaments which he had compiled during many years with such exquisite neatness and a huge collection of MS. sermons – being all in fact that he had ever written. These and the Harmony fetched ninepence a barrow load. I was surprised to hear that Joey had not given the three or four shillings which would have bought the whole lot, but Ernest tells me that Joey was far fiercer in his dislike of his father than ever he had been himself, and wished to get rid of everything that reminded him of him.

It has already appeared that both Joey and Charlotte are married. Joey has a family, but he and Ernest very rarely have any intercourse. Of course, Ernest took nothing under his father's will; this had long been understood, so that the other two are both well provided for.

Charlotte is as clever as ever, and sometimes asks Ernest to come and stay with her husband near Dover, I suppose because she knows that the invitation will not be agreeable to him. There is a *de haut en bas* tone in all her letters; it is rather hard to lay one's finger upon it but Ernest never gets a letter from her without feeling that he is being written to by one who has had direct communication with an angel. 'What an awful creature,' he once said to me, 'that angel must have been if it had anything to do with making Charlotte what she is.'

'Could you like,' she wrote to him not long ago, 'the thoughts of a little sea change here? The top of the cliffs will soon be bright with heather: the gorse must be out already, and the heather I should think begun, to judge by the state of the hill at Ewell, and heather or no heather the cliffs are always beautiful, and if you come your room shall be cosy so that you may have a resting corner to yourself. Nineteen and sixpence is the price of a return ticket which covers a month. Would you decide just as you would yourself like, only if you come we would hope to try and make it bright for you; but you must not feel it a burden on your mind if you feel disinclined to come in this direction.'

'When I have a bad nightmare,' said Ernest to me, laughing as he showed me this letter, 'I dream that I have got to stay with Charlotte.'

Her letters are supposed to be unusually well written, and I believe it is said among the family that Charlotte has far more real literary power than Ernest has. Sometimes we think that she is writing at him as much as to say. 'There now – don't you think you are the only one of us who can write; read this! And if you want a telling bit of descriptive writing for your next book, you can make what use of it you like.' I dare say she writes very well, but she has fallen under the dominion of the words 'hope,' 'think,' 'feel,' 'try,' 'bright,' and 'little,' and can hardly write a page without introducing all these words and some of them more than once. All this has the effect of making her style monotonous.

Ernest is as fond of music as ever, perhaps more so, and of late years has added musical composition to the other irons in his fire. He finds it still a little difficult, and is in constant trouble through getting into the key of C sharp after beginning in the key of C and being unable to get back again.

'Getting into the key of C sharp,' he said, 'is like an unprotected female travelling on the Metropolitan Railway, and finding herself at Shepherd's Bush, without quite knowing where she wants to go to. How is she ever to get safe back to Clapham Junction? And Clapham Junction won't quite do either, for Clapham Junction is like the diminished seventh – susceptible of such enharmonic change, that you can resolve it into all the possible termini of music.'

Talking of music reminds me of a little passage that took place between Ernest and Miss Skinner, Dr Skinner's eldest daughter, not so very long ago. Dr Skinner had long left Roughborough, and had become Dean of a Cathedral in one of our Midland counties – a position which exactly suited him. Finding himself once in the neighbourhood, Ernest called, for old acquaintance sake, and was hospitably entertained at lunch.

Thirty years had whitened the Doctor's bushy eyebrows – his hair they could not whiten. I believe that but for that wig he would have been made a bishop.

His voice and manner were unchanged, and when Ernest remarking upon a plan of Rome which hung in the hall, spoke inadvertently of the Quirĭnal, he replied with all his wonted pomp: 'Yes, the Quirĭnal – or as I myself prefer to call it, the Quirīnal.' After this triumph he inhaled a long breath through the corners of his mouth, and flung it back again into the face of Heaven, as in his finest form during his head-mastership. At lunch he did indeed once say, 'next to impossible to think of anything else,' but he immediately corrected himself and substituted the words, 'next to impossible to entertain irrelevant ideas,' after which he seemed to feel a good deal more comfortable. Ernest saw the familiar volumes of Dr Skinner's works upon the book-shelves in the Deanery dining-room, but he saw no copy of *Rome or the Bible – Which*?

'And are you still as fond of music as ever, Mr Pontifex?' said Miss Skinner to Ernest during the course of lunch.

'Of some kinds of music, yes, Miss Skinner, but you know I never did like modern music.'

'Isn't that rather dreadful? – Don't you think you rather' – she was going to have added, 'ought to?' but she left it unsaid, feeling doubtless that she had sufficiently conveyed her meaning.

'I would like modern music, if I could; I have been trying all my life to like it, but I succeed less and less the older I grow.'

'And pray, where do you consider modern music to begin?'

'With Sebastian Bach.'

'And don't you like Beethoven?'

'No, I used to think I did, when I was younger, but I know now that I never really liked him.'

'Ah! how can you say so? You cannot understand him, you never could say this if you understood him. For me a simple chord of Beethoven is enough. This is happiness.'

Ernest was amused at her strong family likeness to her father – a likeness which had grown upon her as she had become older, and which extended even to voice and manner of speaking. He remembered how he had heard me describe the game of chess I had played with the doctor in days gone by, and with his mind's ear seemed to hear Miss Skinner saying, as though it were an epitaph:

'Stay:
I may presently take
A simple chord of Beethoven,
Or a small semiquaver
From one of Mendelssohn's Songs without Words.'

After luncheon when Ernest was left alone for half an hour or so with the Dean he plied him so well with compliments that the old gentleman was pleased and flattered beyond his wont. He rose and bowed. 'These expressions,' he said, *voce suâ*, 'are very valuable to me.' 'They are but a small part, sir,' rejoined Ernest, 'of what any one of your old pupils must feel towards you,' and the pair danced as it were a minuet at the end of the dining-room table in front of the old bay window that looked upon the smooth shaven lawn. On this Ernest departed; but a few days afterwards, the Doctor wrote him a letter and told him that his critics were $\sigma\varkappa\lambda\eta\rho oi\,\varkappa\alpha i$ $\dot{\alpha}\nu\tau i\tau\upsilon\pi oi$, and at the same time $\dot{\alpha}\nu\dot{\varepsilon}\varkappa\pi\lambda\eta\varkappa\tau oi$. Ernest remembered $\sigma\varkappa\lambda\eta\rho oi$, and knew that the other words were something of like nature, so it was all right. A month or two afterwards, Dr Skinner was gathered to his fathers.

'He was an old fool, Ernest,' said I, 'and you should not relent towards him.'

'I could not help it.' he replied, 'he was so old that it was almost like playing with a child.'

Sometimes, like all whose minds are active, Ernest overworks himself, and then occasionally he has fierce and reproachful encounters with Dr Skinner or Theobald in his sleep – but beyond this neither of these two worthies can now molest him further.

To myself he has been a son and more than a son; at times I am half afraid – as for example when I talk to him about his books – that I may have been to him more like a father than I ought; if I have, I trust he has forgiven me. His books are the only bone of contention between us. I want him to write like other people, and not to offend so many of his readers; he says he can no more change his manner of writing than the colour of his hair, and that he must write as he does or not at all.

With the public generally he is not a favourite. He is admitted to have talent, but it is considered generally to be of a queer unpractical kind, and no matter how serious he is, he is always accused of being in jest. His first book was a success for reasons which I have already explained, but none of his others have been more than creditable failures. He is one of those unfortunate men, each one of whose books is sneered at by literary critics as soon as it comes out, but becomes 'excellent reading' as soon as it has been followed by a later work which may in its turn be condemned.

He never asked a reviewer to dinner in his life. I have told him over and over again that this is madness, and find that this is the only thing I can say to him which makes him angry with me.

'What can it matter to *me*,' he says, 'whether people read my books or not? It may matter to *them* – but I have too much money to want more, and if the books have any stuff in them it will work by and by. I do not know nor greatly care whether they are good or not. What opinion can any sane man form about his own work? Some people must write stupid books just as there must be junior ops and third-class poll men. Why should I complain of being among the mediocrities? If a man is not absolutely below mediocrity let him be thankful – besides, the books will have to stand by themselves some day, so the sooner they begin the better.'

I spoke to his publisher about him not long since. 'Mr Pontifex,' he said, 'is a *homo unius libri*, but it doesn't do to tell him so.'

I could see the publisher, who ought to know, had lost all faith in Ernest's literary position, and looked upon him as a man whose failure was all the more hopeless for the fact of his having once made a *coup*. 'He is in a very solitary position, Mr Overton,' continued the publisher. 'He has formed no alliances, and has made enemies not only of the religious world but of the literary and scientific brotherhood as well. This will not do nowadays. If a man wishes to get on he must belong to a set, and Mr Pontifex belongs to no set – not even to a club.'

I replied, 'Mr Pontifex is the exact likeness of Othello, but with a difference – he hates not wisely but too well. He would dislike the literary and scientific swells if he were to come to know them and they him; there is no natural solidarity between him and them, and if he were brought into contact with them his last state would be worse than his first. His instinct tells him this, so he keeps clear of them, and attacks them whenever he thinks they deserve it – in the hope, perhaps, that a younger generation will listen to him more willingly than the present.'

'Can anything,' said the publisher, 'be conceived more impracticable and imprudent?'

To all this Ernest replies with one word only – 'Wait.'

Such is my friend's latest development. He would not, it is true, run much chance at present of trying to found a College of Spiritual Pathology, but I must leave the reader to determine whether there is not a strong family likeness between the Ernest of the College of Spiritual Pathology and the Ernest who will insist on addressing the next generation rather than his own. He says he trusts that there is not, and takes the sacrament duly once a year as a sop to Nemesis lest he should again feel strongly upon any subject. It rather fatigues him, but 'no man's opinions,' he sometimes says, 'can be worth holding unless he knows how to deny them easily and gracefully upon occasion in the cause of charity.' In politics he is a Conservative so far as his vote and interest are concerned. In all other respects he is an advanced Radical. His father and grandfather could probably no more understand his state of mind than they could understand Chinese, but those who know him intimately do not know that they wish him greatly different from what he actually is.

A Victorian Son

by V. S. Pritchett

The Way of All Flesh is one of the time-bombs of literature. One thinks of it lying in Butler's desk at Clifford's Inn for thirty years, waiting to blow up the Victorian family and with it the whole great pillared and balustraded edifice of the Victorian novel. The book Thackeray failed to write in *Pendennis* had at last been written. After Butler we look back upon a scene of devastation. A spiritual slum has been cleared, yet one is not entirely heartened. Was that the drawing-room where mamma daydreamed about marrying off her daughters to the school-friends of her sons? Was that the fireplace where papa warmed the seat of his trousers and worked up the power politics of godly inertia? Did guilty sons go up those stairs? Did catty sisters hiss from those landings and aunts conduct their warfare of headaches and slammed drawers in those upper rooms? Yes, says Samuel Butler, this was Heartbreak House. Yet not all of his very few admirers agreed with him. Butler writes to Miss Savage in 1883 when the book was circulating in manuscript:

> 'Mr. Heatherley said I had taken all the tenderest feelings of our nature and, having spread them carefully on the floor, stamped upon them till I had reduced them to an indistinguishable mass of filth, and then handed them round for inspection.'

I think it must be agreed that at least Butler spread them on the floor. Now that the floor has collapsed twice in a generation we begin to wonder whether it is still the best place for them; whether Norman Douglas was not right when he said, in *South*

Wind, that Butler lacked the male attributes of humility, reverence and sense of proportion?

As Irish life runs to secret societies, so English life seems to run naturally to parricide movements. We are a nation of father-haters. *The Way of All Flesh* assuaged a thirst which, one supposes, began with the law of primogeniture and the disinheritance of younger sons. In the working class which sets little material start in life from its parents and which has to support them and house them in their old age, the obsession is noticeably rare. The normal human desire seems to be to bite the hand that feeds us, and not the hand we feed. But one has only to compare the quarrels of fathers and sons in, say, the eighteenth-century theatre, with Butler's development of the theme, to see a private struggle turning into a national disease. The thunder of the eighteenth-century father as he is helped out of the coach towards the trembling figure of a young scapegrace who has rejected one heiress in order to abduct another and prettier one, comes from a Jupiter engorged (by the generosity of nature) with biological authority and the gout. The eighteenth-century father is a pagan bursting a blood vessel in the ripeness of time; the nineteenth-century father is a Jehovah dictating an inexhaustible Deuteronomy. Money, as Butler saw, makes the difference; and money, in the nineteenth century, is very different from money in the eighteenth century. Fortune, the speculator's goddess – not money – pours out its plenty from the South Sea bubbles and the slave trade in the eighteenth century. Sacks of gold descend from heaven by fantastic parachute, and are stored in the gloating caves, and trade is still spacious and piratical. How different is the nineteenth century, when Economics appears as a regulated science. With the rise of industrialism, Fortune has given place to cash, cash has become Consols and debentures. Investment does not float down from on high. It seeps in, it is secreted, it accumulates. Its accumulation gives birth to new laws of property and these become moral laws and obtain divine sanction. Investment is a token of energy and a huge will to power, and the fathers who exerted this will expected their families to run like the machines that were making their money.

The Way of All Flesh struck this system at its most vulnerable points: its sentiment, its priesthood and their myth. Butler ignored questions of justice and went for the enfeeblement of religious life and the paralysis which crept upon the emotions. The Musical Banks of *Erewhon* pour out a useless coinage; and when Ernest Pontifex kneels in prayer he fails to save either the souls of the poor, who have no time for him, or his own investments. He is useless to God and Mammon, and to offend Mammon is as serious, for Butler, as to offend God, for Mammon is so much richer in vitality and meaning than the stuffed Anglican God. But what Butler really opposed to Victorianism was not the sort of responsibility we would oppose to it; Butler opposed a system and its myth not with another system but with the claims of human personality. Against Victorianism he placed himself; himself with both feet on the ground, telescope to blind eye and in perverse self-possession, against people whose dreary will to power – and whose hold on spiritual and material property as well – had dried the sap of sense and life.

We cannot think of Butler without the Butleriana. We always come back to Butler as a man. We come back to the undigested slice of rebel egotism. Full of theories himself, he is constantly leaving the ranks of the specialists and joining the amateur ranks of the human beings. George Eliot may be all very fine, but he has bought a dictionary in order to read *Daniel Deronda* in the original! Now this is not nineteenth century at all. To start with, there is no ambition in it; and the more one thinks of him and his failure to fit in, the more one feels he is not a prophet, or at any rate not the prophet of Mr Shaw's invention. On the contrary, he is a sport or throwback. He looks more and more like a throwback to the eighteenth century. His science – with its affection for Buffoon – smacks of it. That science, one suspects, is a rather literary science. His literary antecedents suggest the eighteenth century, too. *The Way of All Flesh* by its egocentricity, its very flatness and discursiveness, calls to mind the autobiographies of the eighteenth century, things like the *Autobiography* of Gibbon.

The genius of that age was to display a man to the full and yet to contain him within some intellectual assumption. The worldliness, the curiosity, the plainness, the tolerance, the irony, the comeliness of the eighteenth century are qualities which *The Way of All Flesh* revives. Not wholly so, for he was kicking irritably against the pricks; but he leapfrogs over the backs of the Victorians to alight beside the author of *Jonathan Wild* and *Amelia* – those novels in which Fielding was especially concerned with the moral and financial illusions of the virtuous. Butler would be at home in the cudgelling matches of Johnson or in Swift's dry and incinerating indignations. *Erewhon* is a straight descendant of *Gulliver* – a poorer book because it lacks savagery and the sublime, plain figure of Gulliver himself – it is no fellow to a mild book like *New from Nowhere*. Where, but in Swift of Fielding, shall we find the suave parallel to this passage from *The Way of All Flesh*:

'It seems to me' he continued, 'that the family is a survival of the principle which is more logically embodied in the compound animal – and the compound animal is a form of life which has been found incompatible with high development. I would do with the family among mankind what nature has done with the compound animal, and confine it to the lower and less progressive races. Certainly there is no inherent love for the family system on the part of nature herself. Poll the forms of life and you will find it in a ridiculously small minority. The fishes know it not and they get along quite nicely. The ants and the bees, who far outnumber man, sting their fathers to death as a matter of course, and are given to the atrocious mutilation of nine-tenths of the offspring committed to their care, yet where shall we find communities more universally respected? Take the cuckoo again – is there any bird which we like better?'

Shooting out his hatred and his contradictions, taking back his hatred with laughter, begging us, like Montaigne, to get our dying done as we go along, Butler is certainly an attempt at a rotund man, even though we know that the common-sense view of life is so often a refuge of the injured and the timid, and is neighbour to the conventional.

One's criticism is that the priggishness of Butler, rather than the roundness, gets into the characters of *The Way of All Flesh*. We must except Butler's working-class characters, those collector's pieces, like Mrs Jupp, the landladies, charladies and servants. A novelist picks those up as he goes along. It is the great weakness of *The Way of All Flesh* that the characters are dwarfed and burned dry by Butler's argument. They are often very tedious. He chose them for their mediocrity and then cursed them for it. They can't stand up to his tweakings. Here Miss Savage was a sound critic when she pointed out the dangers of his special pleading; and although one can feel the years ripening the book, one ends with the feeling that Ernest Pontifex does not amount to much. Why should he come into his fortune? Merely that the unrighteous should have their reward? One does not feel that Ernest has very deeply developed because of suffering or fortune. He has escaped only. And he seems rather lost without his enemy. The weakness is that Butler is doing all the talking. There is no contradictory principle. Ultimately the defence of orthodoxy, even an orthodoxy as dim as Theobald's, is the knowledge of human passions. The strange thing is that Ernest does not give us the impression of a man who enjoys himself; he sounds like a man whose hedonism is a prig's hygiene. He looks like becoming the average bachelor of the room marked Residents Only.

One would give anything to have met Butler. For Ernest, Butler's shadow, one cares very little. Unlike Butler he does not act;

because of the necessities of the book he is acted upon. His indiscretions are passive. He has no sins; he has merely follies. Still, Butler made more of a hand of self-portraiture in this reminiscence than Thackeray made of Arthur Pendennis and Butler seems to have learned from Thackeray's disquisitional method. These two misfit novelists, born a hundred years too late, have many things in common. Christina is another Amelia from the latter pages of *Vanity Fair*, but filled out with richer comic truth. Her ruthless daydreams are wonderful, her play-acting diplomacy is observed with wicked affection. She is one of those mothers whose right breast never lets on what the left breast is feeling. We are given the great Jekyll and Hyde masquerade of the female bosom:

> As regards Ernest, the suspicions which had already crossed her mind were deepened, but she thought it better to leave the matter where it was. At present she was in a very strong position. Ernest's official purity was firmly established, but at the same time he had shown himself so susceptible that she was able to fuse two contradictory impressions concerning him into a single idea and consider him as a kind of Joseph and Don Juan in one. This was what she had wanted all along, but her vanity being gratified by the possession of such a son, there was an end of it; the son himself was naught.

'The matter' she was 'leaving', as the reader will remember, was a maternal plot to make him betray his friends. The paragraph goes on just as penetratingly into the male version of this kind of humbug:

> No doubt if John had not interfered Ernest would have had to expiate his offence with ache, penury and imprisonment. As it was the boy was 'to consider himself' as undergoing these punishments . . .

One is made to feel the pathos of human jealousies, hatreds and humbug. One is tricked into forgetting that they are inevitable. Butler believed that living, like money, should be in the foreground of human life and not an anxiety in its background. He hated the efficient mechanic doctrine, the mechanistic science and (as one sees in *Erewhon*) the machine with its stereotyped response. He pitied the conscious Ernest who toes the line and tried to inflame in Ernest the healthy sabotage of the unconscious. What, strangely enough, Butler failed to find, in this early introduction of the unconscious into English fiction, was the passion. It was odd going to the unconscious and finding there – what? That chronic perversity: common sense.

PENGUIN ENGLISH
LIBRARY

OTHER TITLES IN THIS SERIES

Humphry Clinker
TOBIAS SMOLLETT

"What is the society of London, that I should be tempted, for its sake, to mortify my senses, and compound with such uncleanness as my soul abhors?"

Smollett's savage, boisterously funny lambasting of eighteenth-century British society charts the unfortunate journey of the gout-ridden and irascible squire Matthew Bramble across Britain, who finds himself everywhere surrounded by decadents, pimps, con-men, raucousness and degeneracy – until the arrival of the trusty manservant Humphry Clinker promises to improve his fortunes.

Populated with unforgettable grotesques and written with a relish for earthy humour and wordplay, and a ferocious pessimism, *Humphry Clinker* is Smollett's masterpiece.

PENGUIN ENGLISH
LIBRARY

OTHER TITLES IN THIS SERIES

Melmoth the Wanderer
CHARLES MATURIN

**"My hour is come ... the clock of eternity is about to strike,
but its knell must be unheard by mortal ears!"**

This violent, profound, baroque and blackly humorous novel is the story of
Melmoth, who has sold his soul in exchange for immortality in a satanic bargain, and now preys on the helpless in their darkest moments, offering to ease
their suffering if they will take his place and release him from his centuries of
tortured wanderings.

Melmoth the Wanderer (1820) blended Gothic fiction and psychological realism
to create a work of hallucinatory power.

PENGUIN ENGLISH
LIBRARY

OTHER TITLES IN THIS SERIES

Barchester Towers
ANTHONY TROLLOPE

> **"What! to come here a stranger, a young, unknown, and un-friended stranger, and tell us, in the name of the bishop his master, that we are ignorant of our duties, old-fashioned and useless!"**

Trollope's comic masterpiece of plotting and backstabbing opens as the Bishop of Barchester lies on his deathbed. Soon a pitched battle breaks out over who will take power, involving, among others, the zealous reformer Dr Proudie, his fiendish wife and the unctuous schemer Obadiah Slope.

Barchester Towers is one of the best-loved novels in Trollope's *Chronicles of Barsetshire* series, which captured ninenteenth-century provincial England with wit, worldly wisdom and an unparalleled gift for characterization.

PENGUIN ENGLISH
LIBRARY

OTHER TITLES IN THIS SERIES

David Copperfield
CHARLES DICKENS

> '**Whether I shall turn out to be the hero of my own life, or whether that station will be held by anybody else, these pages must show**'

Dickens's epic, exuberant novel is one of the greatest coming-of-age stories in literature. It chronicles David Copperfield's extraordinary journey through life, as he encounters villains, saviours, eccentrics and grotesques, including the wicked Mr Murdstone, stout-hearted Peggotty, formidable Betsey Trotwood, impecunious Micawber and odious Uriah Heep.

Dickens's great *Bildungsroman* (based, in part, on his own boyhood, and which he described as a 'favourite child') is a work filled with life, both comic and tragic.

PENGUIN ENGLISH
LIBRARY

OTHER TITLES IN THIS SERIES

Where Angels Fear to Tread
E. M. FORSTER

> "I had got an idea that everyone here spent their lives in making little sacrifices for objects they didn't care for, to please people they didn't love; that they never learned to be sincere — and, what's as bad, never learned how to enjoy themselves"

E. M. Forster's first novel is a witty comedy of manners that is tinged with tragedy. It tells the story of Lilia Herriton, who proves to be an embarrassment to her late husband's family as, in the small Tuscan town of Monteriano, she begins a relationship with a much younger Italian man – classless, uncouth and highly unsuitable.

A subtle attack on decorous Edwardian values and a humanely sympathetic portrayal of the clash of two cultures, *Where Angels Fear to Tread* is also a profound exploration of character and virtue.